Perfectly
Reflected

S.C. Ransom

'Small Blue Thing'

Today I am
A small blue thing
Like a marble
Or an eye

With my knees against my mouth
I am perfectly round
I am watching you

I am cold against your skin
You are perfectly reflected
I am lost inside your pocket
I am lost against
Your fingers
I am falling down the stairs
I am skipping on the sidewalk
I am thrown against the sky
I am raining down in pieces

· · · · · · · · · · ·

For Mum and Dad

PERFECTLY REFLECTED

Published in the UK in 2011 by Nosy Crow Ltd
Crow's Nest, 11 The Chandlery
50 Westminster Bridge Road
London, SE1 7QY, UK

Nosy Crow and associated logos are trademarks and or registered trademarks of
Nosy Crow Ltd

Printed and bound in the UK by Clays Ltd, St. Ives Plc
Typeset by Tiger Media Ltd, Bishops Stortford, Hertfordshire

Papers used by Nosy Crow are made from wood grown in sustainable forests.

1 3 5 7 9 10 8 6 4 2

ISBN: 978 0 85763 012 4

www.nosycrow.com

Caution ⌾

Breaking glass exploded into my bedroom. The cold, early morning air rushed in as I leapt up and pushed my feet into my flip-flops, not sure for a moment if I had been dreaming. The crunch of glass under my soles proved I was awake. Switching on the light, I quickly scanned the room, but it didn't look as if anything had been thrown in. I raced over to the window. The drawn curtains had held back a large part of the debris, but piles of lethal-looking shards of glass on the floor meant that I didn't want to get much closer without proper shoes on. Leaning over, I pulled back the curtain. The early dawn light showed that the road was completely empty.

At that moment my dad burst through the door, closely followed by Mum. "Alex! What on earth was that? Are you OK?" He surveyed the damage as he spoke, and then carefully picked his way over to join me by the window. "Did you see anyone?" he asked, peering out in both directions.

I realised that my heart was racing, and had to take a deep breath before I could answer. "No. By the time I got there, whoever did it was gone."

"Now, let's not get all overdramatic," interrupted Mum, obviously trying to calm everything down. "It could have been a bird flying into the window. Don't assume that a person was responsible."

Dad and I exchanged a quick glance of perfect understanding. We both knew that what she had said was nonsense. Still shaking slightly, I looked through the window down to the ground below. "I can't see a bird from here. Maybe you should go and look. If there is one, it might need putting out of its misery."

"OK," Mum nodded and backed out of the room.

"Is there anything in here?" asked Dad as soon as she was out of earshot. "I mean, what was it? A brick?"

"I can't see anything," I said. "But there has to be something somewhere. Whatever it was that hit the glass was either very big or very fast; the window's completely disintegrated."

He grunted in agreement, taking another look down the road. "We need to get this cleared up," he said, giving me a quick hug. "I'll go and get my trainers on and I suggest you do the same. I'll be back in a second with the dustpan and a sack." Dad's voice changed as he went through the door. "Oh, hello. I didn't think you were actually alive at this time of day."

My brother tried to give him a withering look but at five in the morning he was too sleepy. "Thought maybe we were under attack. Coming to see if you needed help," he mumbled in my general direction as Dad disappeared.

"You play too many computer games. What were you planning to do – throw your console at them?"

"Ha ha. Very funny. What's happened then?"

"We don't know yet. My window's been broken, Mum thinks it was a bird strike, and Dad and I think someone threw something, but I can't see a stone or anything." I tried hard to keep my voice light, not show him how shaken I was.

"Oh, freaky." He looked mildly interested for a moment. "Jealous boyfriend? Irate mate? Anything like that?"

"Huh," I grunted, giving him my best scathing look. "Hardly. When did I last upset anyone?"

He considered the room again briefly. "There you go then. Maybe it *was* a bird." And it was true. I couldn't think of anyone who would do such a thing to me. Perhaps Mum was right.

"Well, if you don't need me I'll be nipping back to bed before Dad gets me up a ladder to fix that hole," he mumbled as he turned round and headed back towards his room.

I picked my way over to my desk and sat down to change my shoes. Despite the flip-flops, my right foot was already studded with tiny shards, one of which had drawn blood. I pulled a tissue from the box and wiped it clean. The wound was hardly more than a scratch, not worth getting a plaster for. I pressed the tissue against it until it stopped bleeding, and then fished around under the desk for my Converse. I was about to put them on when I realised that there was something in one of them, so I turned it upside down. A small, heavy, white ball dropped on to the carpet.

I looked at it for a second, then hesitantly reached down for it. The ball was covered in paper, which was secured by sticky tape. I carefully peeled back the corner of the tape and the paper unravelled. The golf ball inside dropped on to my desk while I turned over the crumpled sheet, holding my breath. I didn't recognise the handwriting on the sheet, but my blood ran cold as I read the words:

I know your secret, Alex.

My heart pounding, I shoved the piece of paper under my maths textbook as I heard Dad come back up the stairs. I had no idea what it was about, but I was pretty sure I didn't want to involve my parents.

My day didn't improve much. The clearing up and waiting for the guy to come and board up the window meant that I was late for the school coach, but then that was late too, so I spent half an hour standing at the bus stop listening to the inane chatter of the junior kids. I longed to be able to drive myself to school, but that was a pretty distant dream; I was due to visit the police station that afternoon to answer to various driving offences, and fully expected to lose my provisional licence.

None of my friends was on the coach either, not even my best friend Grace, so when I finally got to school I walked over to the sixth form on my own. As I rounded the corner my way was blocked by a familiar figure. I began to smile but her face was stony. Without warning, she suddenly slapped me across the cheek. My head flew back with the force of it and a stinging feeling crept outwards from my cheekbone towards my ear.

I tried not to stagger backwards as I turned back to face her again, tears pricking at my eyes. The thin veneer of friendship between us had gone; she looked ready to kill me. She was standing facing me, balanced on the balls of her feet, preparing to swing again. As the ringing in my ears subsided I became conscious of the absence of other noises around us. In this corner of the school there was little activity; everyone else was already inside the building, and it wasn't yet time for the younger girls to be out on the pitches. No one was around to step in.

I could feel my cheek starting to redden. The stinging was slowly being replaced by a hot burning, and I could feel the welts rising where her long fingernails had scratched my skin.

"What on earth was that for?" I demanded, trying to stop my voice trembling.

"Don't play any of your stupid games with me!" she hissed. "I thought we were supposed to be friends."

It wasn't exactly the way I would have described our relationship, but this wasn't the time to disagree with her. "So did I, but friends don't usually go around hitting each other." I took a step towards her, rubbing my sore cheek. "Come on, tell me. What am I supposed to have done?"

"All right then, if you want me to spell it out. I want to know what you're doing with my boyfriend. Why is he so interested in you? You're nothing special."

A short snort of laughter escaped me before I could stop it. "What! I'm not doing anything with him, and I really can't imagine why you'd think I was."

"You're bound to say that, aren't you?" she spat, and there was real venom in her voice.

"What do you mean?"

"You two have got some secret little thing going on. I know it."

"That's such rubbish. What on earth gives you that idea?"

"Why else would he have a whole bunch of stuff on his computer about you?" Her voice was sneering now.

"About me? What sort of stuff?"

"I don't know. Lots of files."

"Why would he want files about me? What's in them?"

"I don't know yet, but I will, just as soon as I break the passwords. In the meantime you keep well away from him, do you understand me? Rob's mine!"

"Ashley, I know he is! And after all, it's you who's going to Cornwall with him, isn't it?" I gazed at her steadily.

"How do you know about Cornwall?" Her voice had turned

low and ominous. That had touched a nerve. I cursed myself silently and tried to think of a suitable response.

"Oh, you know, gossip in the common room. A few of the others were quite keen to share the news with me."

The thought that some of our friends saw her holiday with Rob as evidence that she'd beaten me in some competition between us obviously pleased her, and the look in her eyes reminded me of one I'd seen before, in a face that, thankfully, I would never see again; Ashley wore the same look of triumph that Catherine had worn weeks ago when she had me completely in her power in Kew Gardens. The memory chilled me so much that I took a step backwards and looked away. Ashley knew she had won.

She turned and started to walk away, but before she had gone more than a few paces she wheeled around and shouted, "You keep away from him, you hear me? You go anywhere near him and there'll be trouble!"

Curious eyes from some passing kids swivelled in my direction, but I kept mine firmly on Ashley as she walked away, still battling with my tears and a growing sense of injustice. I wondered briefly if she could have thrown that ball, but why would she then slap me? Two enemies before nine o'clock. Fear clutched at my stomach, and for a moment I seriously considered going home to hide in bed. The sharp pain in my cheek was turning to a dull ache, and I knew I should get something cold on it. With a groan I realised that I really had to sort it out quickly; my appointment with the police was in only a few hours, and I didn't want to look like I'd been in a fight. Cursing Ashley under my breath I made for the nearest toilet block.

* * *

The police officer looked over the top of her glasses at me, shook her head a little and returned to considering the papers in her hand.

"Well, Alexandra? What do you have to say for yourself?" she asked eventually.

I swallowed hard, wishing that there was a tumbler of water on my side of the desk. "I'm truly sorry for everything. I just can't remember any more. All I know is that I *had* to get to my friend Grace quickly. The rest is blank."

My eyes dipped to my lap, and I fiddled with the bracelet on my wrist. I couldn't hold her gaze any more, not when I was lying so comprehensively. "The doctor's report – does that help?" I added lamely.

Luckily my dad jumped in at that point. "We have provided all the relevant medical reports, Officer. You should have them there."

The police officer started turning over the sheets of paper in her file, pursing her thin lips as she started to read. It was getting uncomfortably warm in the featureless room in Twickenham Police Station that doubled as the Restorative Justice Centre. The open windows did little to help move the stale air around as the protective mesh stopped them opening more than a chink. I tried very hard not to fidget as she turned the last page, and kept my eyes down.

"Well, it's certainly very curious," she said, tapping the file with one long skinny finger, then picking up the medical report again.

"We've submitted a reference from Alex's headmistress," Dad added, pointing at a letter that could just be seen sticking out of the back of the file. "As you can see from that, Miss Harvey felt that the most appropriate response to the incident was to strip Alex of her prefect's privileges."

I think I had been a prefect for the shortest time in the history of the school. They had added my name to the list for the following year when I was in a coma following the incident in Kew Gardens, then promptly stripped me of it when I regained consciousness and got hauled up for driving on my own with a provisional driving licence. I never even got to see a badge.

The policewoman, who had been looking as if she was going to tell Dad off for talking out of turn, fished the letter from the back of the file and scanned it.

"Keep calm; you're doing really well," said the soothing voice in my head. "Don't overdo the grovelling though."

I sighed in relief; Callum was back. It had been a long, stressful morning and I hadn't had a minute to call him to me, but he was finally here, making my wrist tingle as usual, as he moved his arm so that the identical bracelets we wore overlapped, his in his world, and mine in my own. I glanced up briefly at my reflection in the reinforced glass door and caught a glimpse of Callum's blindingly handsome face behind my shoulder. All my worries faded away as my love for him swamped every other emotion. He saw me looking and winked, then looked stern.

It had been a fortnight since I got out of hospital, and his voice in my head was a source of love and comfort, commentating on my world.

"Concentrate! Don't mess it up now!" He was right. The end was in sight. I looked briefly at the policewoman but made sure that my face didn't reflect my sudden contentment.

There was a knock and a young PC appeared nervously

at the door. "I'm sorry to disturb you, Inspector Kellie, but you wanted to know when that forensic report was in."

I looked quickly back at the policewoman; her stony exterior was now belied by the yellow light that was suddenly bouncing around above her head. I knew what it meant: she was either very happy about getting the report, or was very happy about seeing the fit-looking policeman. I hoped for her sake it was the policeman.

I was still astounded by the difference it made to me, to be able to tell when people were thinking happy or miserable thoughts. It seemed to be an unexpected side effect of the miraculous recovery I had made from my vegetative coma. Only two of us knew what had really happened to me: me and Callum, whose mysterious reflection only I could see.

Callum was waiting patiently, as he always did. I tried hard to not look at him in the shiny surface of the glass and instead concentrate on the police officer as he advised. But it was so hard to ignore him. My love for him felt so profound, and I knew, given what he'd risked for me, that he loved me too. Knowing that we were separated by – I swallowed and forced myself to remember – the fact that he had drowned, made no difference to the intensity of my feeling for him. Ever since we'd seen one another under the dome of St Paul's Cathedral I had loved him completely. I shook myself mentally, then refocused on Inspector Kellie; as I watched closely I could see a slight softening of her gaze as she looked at the young policeman. "Thank you, Constable," she said formally. "I'll be with you shortly and you can take me through the main points."

I looked swiftly at the PC; he too had a bouncing yellow flicker just above his head. I wondered if the two of them would ever admit anything to the other. Whatever happened next though, it was enough for me that the inspector was in a good mood; maybe I was going to get away with it.

She looked back at me, and pushed the file away.

"Well, Alexandra, I see that you have clearly already been punished by your school. And I think that, under the circumstances," and she waved her hand at the medical report, "there is little to be gained by prosecuting you for these offences."

I felt my heart lift at her words but tried to continue to look contrite.

"However," she continued, and my heart sank again, "I shall have to issue you with a formal reprimand. You have expressed regret, and as your driving didn't cause any accidents we won't take it any further. We will keep the reprimand on file though, and if there is any repeat offence, there will be no leniency shown."

Dad wasn't quite so happy when we finally got outside. "I have no idea what a reprimand will do to the insurance policy," he grumbled. "It may be best for you to give up driving for a while until the dust settles."

"I'm sure I'll manage, Dad." I grinned at him briefly, unable to contain my joy. "I'll enjoy having you both ferry me around, especially once Josh is off in the autumn."

He groaned again as he realised I was right. If he didn't insure me to finish my lessons he was definitely going to get stuck with a lot more driving as soon as my brother Josh went off to university. He was in a no-win situation and he knew it, so I was surprised when he suddenly smiled back.

"I'll talk to the insurers today," he said, "and get an update on the increase. Then you can give me a cheque for the difference."

I had no quick answer to that. He had won after all. He knew that I had quite a lot of money saved up to buy my own car when the time came, as I had been putting away all the babysitting money I made. I felt my arm tingle and could hear Callum chuckle as he caught up with the last part of the conversation.

"He's right, you know. It's your own fault you're in all this trouble. If you hadn't believed Catherine's lies about me in the first place, none of this would have happened."

I made a non-committal noise that would convey my feelings to Callum without alarming Dad. As we got into the car I considered the changes in my life. Less than a month ago I had been a perfectly happy, normal teenager, out celebrating the end of my exams. Now I was lying to the police and finding every opportunity I could to be alone with a strange and gorgeous apparition who was summoned by a bracelet I'd found in the Thames. I glanced down at the amulet on my wrist, its fiery stone glinting in the light, and felt overwhelmingly grateful to have found it and discovered its extraordinary power.

I settled back into the passenger seat and couldn't help smiling as I thought of him. He was tall, dark blond and extremely athletic. I could see him beside me in the mirror or in other reflective surfaces, and hear him when the amulets on our wrists were in the same space, but most of the time I could only feel the faintest of touches as he sat behind my shoulder when we talked. He was a Dirge, a soul caught in a terrible half-life of misery after falling into the River Fleet and drowning. These days the Fleet was mostly covered over, and very few Londoners even realised it was there, but centuries before it had been a busy river running from Hampstead in north London, and something about its water, still flowing into the Thames, had a mysterious power to transform those who drowned in it, though none of the Dirges understood what it was. All they knew was that day after day they were compelled to feed on the happy thoughts and memories that they stole from unsuspecting people and stored in the amulets they all wore. And every night another fierce compulsion drove them back to St Paul's Cathedral, the place they now called home.

They knew of only one way to end their misery, but it carried a huge price for the living human who trusted them. Callum's sister Catherine had made me believe that he didn't really love me. In my despair, she had very nearly succeeded in tricking me into sacrificing myself. She had sucked away every memory I had ever had and left me for dead. I was only alive because Callum had been prepared to risk himself to save me, emptying his own amulet of stolen happiness so he could capture a copy of all my memories as Catherine spooled them out of me. And after she had finally escaped their life of purgatory in an explosion of sparks and died, he gave them back to me, leaving himself with nothing. Every time I thought about it, I felt breathless with love and gratitude. Most of the time, at least around me, he seemed to be able to tolerate the desperate wretchedness that he must be feeling without a good store of the thing that was so essential to him. And he wouldn't tell me what he was having to resort to in order to refill his amulet. I didn't want to ask. Whatever he was doing, though, he was as loving towards me as he had been when we had first met.

There was no one else in when we got back to the house, so I didn't have to spend hours telling Mum all about the police caution. As soon as I could, I ran up to my bedroom to see if he was already there. The bedroom was gloomy from the boarded-up window, but as I slipped on to the chair by my desk, the tingle was back in my arm and a sense of peaceful contentment washed through me.

Callum's face behind my shoulder was perfectly clear in the mirror, his blue eyes sparkling with amusement.

"I like what you've done with the place," he said, surveying the carnage of my bedroom.

"Well, you know, windows are so last year." I couldn't bring myself to burden him by recounting my horrible morning. I hated to do anything that might add to the weight of his misery; it could wait until we had more time.

"I can't believe you sat there and lied so convincingly to that poor policewoman. You obviously have a hidden talent."

I tried to look ashamed, but failed miserably. I was too happy to see him again. "It was all perfectly true," I objected. "I did have to get there to save Grace, and I really didn't know why because I didn't have any clear idea about what Catherine was going to do. I mean, I guess I could have gone into a little more detail, but she would never have believed it anyway."

"No, it's probably not the sort of thing she hears every day."

"And with Catherine dead and gone we don't exactly have anyone to pin the blame on." I paused, wondering if now was the right time to ask a question that had been bothering me. "Did she *really* hate life over there that much?"

It was Callum's turn to pause. "She was always really depressed, and I guess she must have been as bad when she was alive. On top of that, existence over here is, as you know, bleak. I guess she was desperate."

"Given the option, would you all choose to die?"

"Oh yes." He smiled ruefully. "With a notable exception, there isn't one of us who wouldn't take the chance to be released."

"I can't believe that you have to live like that. It's all so, so unfair!"

Callum sighed. "I still can't help wishing that I had told you everything from the beginning. . ."

"I know, I know. Then none of this would ever have happened. I believe you might have mentioned that before," I teased him, trying to lighten the mood. "But at least now we have our regular trips to St Paul's, and that wouldn't have happened without Catherine."

When Callum had saved my life, he had unexpectedly given me the ability to see him – and touch him – as a proper flesh-and-blood human. But only at the very top of the dome of St Paul's Cathedral. Before the accident the amulet allowed me to see him face to face only under the very centre of the famous dome, and even then I hadn't been able to touch him. In my opinion it was worth a near-death experience to be able to caress his face, hold his hand, kiss those firm lips . . . my thoughts wandered off into dangerous territory.

"That is very true," he agreed, his lips brushing the back of my neck in the reflection. "Although this is great for me, it's so much better to be able to hold you properly. When can you next make it into town?"

"I'm not sure. Maybe at the weekend. Term will be finishing next week too, so after that it should be easier. I still don't think Mum and Dad will be keen, though. They've been so worried about me since I came out of hospital. I'm going to have to come up with a really good excuse."

"Hmm. Can you get Grace to help?"

"I'd love to, but I can't tell her about you. She'll think I'm mad."

"I suppose so. I wish you didn't have to keep things secret from your best friend, though."

"It's not so bad. Now she just thinks you're some sort of cyber-boyfriend."

I hated lying about Callum to Grace. She and I had shared so much over the years that it was almost impossible to deal with the practicalities of life with Callum without talking to her about it. I had got round the problem by telling her I had met someone I really loved over the Internet, and for now she was happy with that. At last I was able to indulge in a bit of mutual boyfriend-comparing with her. She was getting increasingly impatient to see a photo though, and I was planning to scour the Internet that night for something that would keep her happy.

"I'd like to meet Grace sometime," Callum said reflectively. "She seems so happy and lively."

"Steady!" I laughed. "Her happy thoughts and memories might be too much for you to resist!"

"Well, I *am* an uncontrollable monster, as you know." He pretended to bite my neck.

"I'm not sure that I want you to meet her anyway," I said in my best prim voice. "Everyone always loves her and you might end up preferring her to me. After all, it could just as easily have been her who found the amulet."

"Ah, but it wasn't though, was it? You were the one prepared to go digging for it." He fell silent for a moment, remembering. "I still can't believe that you did find it . . . and that it found me," he murmured eventually. "What are the chances of that happening? It could all have been so different."

I looked into his eyes, which were soft with emotion, and tried not to think of the scenario where I had not pulled the wire out of the Thames mud to find the amulet tied to the end of it. My

15

life would be calm, uncomplicated and, well, *dull* really. My mouth started to twitch into a smile.

"You could have got some really sad beachcomber bloke with a metal detector, so think yourself lucky. Besides, there aren't many people who wouldn't have run screaming into the sunset once you started talking to them." I thought back to those uncertain days not so many weeks ago when I really thought that I was losing my mind.

All too soon it was time for Callum to go and start his usual evening task at the local multiplex. His preference for the happy thoughts generated by people watching cheesy comedies meant that he could do quite a bit of gathering pretty quickly in a full cinema. He said that the other Dirges all thought he was crazy. They said that the quality of this superficial happiness wasn't as good as real happy memories, but it made Callum feel better about what he was doing. And right now he had a lot of gathering to do. He was still trying to get back to a reasonable state of equilibrium by refilling his amulet, but it was obviously difficult; although he tried to hide it from me, there were times when I caught a look of melancholy creeping over his features. Gathering occupied his every moment when he wasn't with me, whereas I spent every spare moment trying to devise plans that would bring him over to me. How could I change things? I wondered yet again. What new surprises could I get the amulet to reveal that would allow Callum to hold me in his arms somewhere other than the top of the dome? There had to be a way and I was determined to find it.

I knew he needed to go so I smiled broadly at him. There was no point in making him feel any worse than he already did. With a promise to return as soon as possible the next morning he was gone, and my evening stretched ahead of me.

There were only a few days of term left now, and the teachers had mostly given up on setting us homework. They wanted to mark it about as much as we wanted to do it. I had some catching up to do though, as I had spent a lot of time in hospital, so my time was not yet my own.

I stretched and reached for my schoolbag to see if I could remember what I was supposed to be doing. I had been given the afternoon off to go to the police station earlier, but the long list of work I was supposed to cover was waiting for me.

I was just opening up my laptop when my mobile phone rang. I smiled as I shut the lid of the laptop back down again and pressed the answer button on the phone; it was Abbi, so we were bound to chat for ages.

"Hi, Abbi," I said. "Hey, guess what? The police didn't prosecute me!"

There was a strange, slightly muffled silence on the other end of the phone.

"Abbi? Are you there?"

"I don't know how you can talk to me like that, like nothing's happened!" bit the voice at the other end of the line. "After what you've done!"

"I'm sorry . . . Abbi? Is that you?" The voice was familiar but almost unrecognisable.

"I never want to speak to you again, and once I've told the others what you've done, I shouldn't think many of them will want to, either. How could you be so cruel? I thought you were my friend." Her voice cracked with emotion.

I couldn't believe this was happening again, and this time with someone I cared about so much.

"Abbi, I have no idea what you're talking about! What's the

matter? What's wrong?"

There was a strangled-sounding sob. "How could you do it? How could you?"

"Abbi," I said gently. "Please, I have absolutely no idea what you mean. Take a deep breath and tell me what I'm supposed to have done."

There was a short grunt on the other end of the line. "As if you don't know! Check your e-mail and see if you've had a reply from Miss Harvey yet."

From the headmistress? This was getting more and more bizarre.

"Why would I get an e-mail from Miss Harvey? What on earth would she be replying to?"

"Well, check your sent box and remind yourself, then. I can't wait to hear what she has to say."

"OK, OK. Give me a minute. I'm not logged on at the moment." I wedged the mobile to my ear with my shoulder and opened up the laptop again. I quickly switched it on and opened my e-mail account. It was terribly slow as usual, and I could hear Abbi sniffing in the background. "Right, I'm in. What exactly am I looking for?" I was trying to navigate to the sent folder as I spoke, wondering what I was going to find. Then I saw it, partway down the list, a message with the subject line *Abbi Hancock*. I quickly opened it and scanned the contents, feeling more and more horrified as I went down the page.

"What on earth. . .? Abbi, what's all this about? How did this happen?"

"Oh, stop pretending!" she snapped. "Why would you do this to me? You'll get me expelled!"

"I . . . I haven't done anything, Abbi. I promise!" I needed some time to work this out. "Look, give me a minute will you? Let me read it properly at least."

The e-mail was long. It was addressed to Miss Harvey, and was a comprehensive list of all Abbi's school misdemeanours over the years, none of which she had been punished for as she was brilliant at appearing innocent. They ranged from breaking windows, putting green food dye in the swimming pool on St Patrick's Day, skipping school and, most recently, burning the toast in the common room, which had brought the fire brigade out again. Sending an e-mail like that was the kind of thing no friend would do, and I could feel a creeping horror as I realised why she was so upset. It had come from my e-mail account, addressed to Miss Harvey, and whoever had sent it had copied Abbi in for good measure. It was vicious. "Abbi, what can I say? It really wasn't me. You must know I'd never do anything like this. Someone must have hacked into my account."

"Really?" she sneered. "So explain the bit about the swimming pool? You're the only person I *ever* told about that – the only one. Explain that! And don't think you can talk me round. Miss Harvey is going to annihilate me tomorrow. She's been waiting to pounce on someone for weeks about the toast and you've just handed me to her on a plate. But before she gets to me I'm going to let absolutely everyone know just what sort of a friend you really are!"

My mind was racing as she spoke, and then I noticed something: I checked the e-mail addresses at the top, and looked again a bit more closely. The address was wrong, with an "n" instead of an "m" in the middle of it. Abbi obviously hadn't spotted it. I quickly opened my inbox and there, part way down was a message saying that the e-mail had been returned undelivered.

"Abbi!" I shouted over her. "The e-mail didn't get to Miss Harvey — it bounced back. She won't know anything about it."

I could hear tapping as Abbi scanned through her inbox, and an audible sigh of relief; she had seen the mistake in the address. Her secrets were still safe. But the sigh was followed by a prolonged silence.

"Abbi, are you still there?"

Nothing.

"Abbi, speak to me."

"If this is your idea of a joke," she hissed, "you've got a really sick sense of humour. Have you any idea what I've been going through since I read that e-mail? I didn't have you down as cruel, but now I know better. Don't speak to me tomorrow, or ever again for that matter." The phone went dead.

I sat back, appalled, staring at the handset. Fear clutched at my stomach again. What was going on?

Visitor

The next morning at school Abbi blanked me completely, but she didn't seem to have told the others about the e-mail. I tried to talk to her a couple of times but she kept turning her back and eventually I gave up. At lunchtime I found a quiet part of our corner of the common room to sit, and kept my head down. The thought of that e-mail kept coming back to me, and every time it made my stomach flip. I couldn't imagine the trouble Abbi would have been in if it had actually arrived. After she had called I had scoured through my e-mail account to see if I could find any clue to what had happened, but the only thing that was unusual was the deleted items folder. It was completely empty, and I wasn't able to recover any items either; someone must have wiped everything when they'd hacked into it. I changed the password to something obscure and hoped that it would be enough, wishing that I could talk through the whole thing with Callum.

He didn't usually arrive unannounced at school any more. The amount of gathering he had to do kept him pretty busy, and I was keen that he did as much as possible during the day to keep his late afternoons and early evenings free. But I missed having him around; that excitement of when he might appear, the welcome tingle in my arm before he spoke. I let my thoughts drift to the weekend, when I was sure I could find an excuse to get up to London and see him face to face again. We had only been able to meet twice so far, and the logistics were really difficult, but it was worth it to hold him and feel his strong arms around me.

As I relived the memories of our last encounter Grace arrived and squeezed on to the beanbag next to me.

"Hiya," she said. "You're very quiet today. What's up?"

I smiled briefly. "Oh, I'm all right, I suppose. I seem to have upset Abbi though, so now she's not talking to me."

"Oh, no! What have you gone and done now?" Grace laughed.

"It's not funny, and I haven't done anything!" I told her indignantly. "Can I tell you about it later? I don't really want everyone earwigging."

"OK, course. You can fill me in at Eloïse's party tonight. Now, that'll cheer you up, anyway. Want a lift?"

Grace had just passed her driving test and her parents had given her the use of a little car, so we were now able to whizz around without involving her dad quite so much. I wasn't really sure I felt up to a party, not with Abbi going, but I had agreed it with Grace after we had both got out of hospital and we had been looking forward to it.

"I guess. I'm not sure how long I'll stay though."

"Are the parents still giving you grief?"

"No, it's not that, they're fine about the whole thing. I'm just not sure I want to spend the evening with. . ." I nodded my head towards Abbi. "Or, more to the point, if she'll want to spend the evening with me."

"Look, whatever it is you two have fallen out over, you can't let it ruin Eloïse's party – that's not fair," Grace whispered. "After all, it's not her fault."

"I know. I just don't feel very party-ish. . ."

"Don't tell me you'd rather spend the evening on the Internet again!" Grace looked at me accusingly. "Callum'll understand that you have a life, surely; you can't be online all the time."

Once again, I really wished I could tell Grace the truth about Callum. She was always asking awkward questions about how we'd first got in touch, and why he didn't have a Facebook page, and did he have any plans to come over from Venezuela? I was really regretting giving her that particular detail. Sooner or later she was going to stop buying the Internet story anyway, even though I'd finally given her a picture, which seemed to have satisfied her curiosity about what he looked like.

I sighed audibly. "I know, he does understand really, he's delighted when I go out. But it's not about him, it's all the other stuff."

"Well, the best way to deal with Abbi is to ignore her. She'll come round eventually, you know she will."

"OK, you win. I'd love a lift, thanks, but are you sure I won't be in the way? I don't want to play gooseberry with you and Jack."

"Oh, don't worry, he's not coming with us. His mum's dragging him to some sort of work party first, poor boy."

Grace smiled contentedly, thinking of Jack. He was a great friend of mine and I was delighted that the two of them were getting on so well. Grace's recent hospital scare had made him even more attentive so he was always keen to make the extra effort to see her.

"OK, you had better give me my orders then. What time will you pick me up and what should I be wearing?" I said, resigned to being organised by her as usual.

"Well." She looked me up and down, pursing her lips. "I know you've got Callum so you won't want to attract *too* many other blokes this evening. But . . . on the other hand he won't be there, and you don't want Rob to think that you are going to pieces, so I think we're going to go with the full-on beautiful babe look."

"Rob'll be there? Really? Right, that's it, I'm definitely not going." I had been doing my best to avoid Rob, my ex-almost-boyfriend. As far as I could tell he was still being insufferably smug about the whole Kew Gardens affair, dropping hints and letting everyone know that he had saved the day. I knew that he had been responsible for some unsubtle comments at the time, and although I didn't think he was still making the accusation, he was failing to squash the rumours that it had been a suicide attempt on my part. He had even tried to give the impression that I was upset over him and the fact that we were no longer going out together. I wasn't sure that I would be able to resist giving him a piece of my mind if I saw him.

"Oh come on, you can't let him get away with all that rubbish. And what better way of sticking it to him than turning up looking gorgeous and completely unavailable?"

I turned that thought over, and it did have a certain appeal. "All right, you're on. What are my wardrobe instructions?"

Grace sat up, suddenly excited. "Can I really choose everything? Excellent! Now, let me think. . ."

My heart sank as I realised she was really going to go for it, but I had to let her have her fun. After all, I had been responsible for her recent near-death experience. Every time I thought about it my blood ran cold, and that made me feel even meaner for deceiving her. I hated keeping secrets from her but I couldn't see a sensible way out of the problem; she was never going to believe me if I told her the truth about how Callum's sister had tried to kill us both before successfully killing herself. That was the only good thing about it; Catherine was gone from my life and Callum's, and neither of us was going to miss her.

In the end, Grace decided to come to my house to make sure that I did things properly. Mum had organised for someone to fix the window, so I had daylight again, and the room had been left unnaturally tidy after all the vacuuming to clear up the glass. My old hair straighteners had been unearthed, and Grace leapt on them with enthusiasm, spending nearly an hour trying to get out the little kinks in my almost-straight hair before insisting on supervising my make-up. When I finally got to look in the mirror I nearly didn't recognise myself. My long tangle of blonde hair had been tamed into sleek lines, and the outfit she had put together from the dregs in my wardrobe made me look tall and elegant.

Grace stood back to review her work, smirking gently as I gaped at my reflection. "Rob is going to be *sooo* cross with himself tonight. You look stunning."

I nodded mutely and the stranger in the mirror mimicked my movements.

"Now," she continued, suddenly businesslike, "we need to go in about ten minutes and I don't seem to be ready yet. Give me two minutes to use your bathroom and then I'll just touch up my make-up. Don't fiddle with anything!"

As she said it my hand, which had been twitching up towards my hair, dropped back down to my side. "OK, I promise," I said meekly.

"Good. I'll be back in a sec. Just sit still." The door swung shut behind her and I heard her fighting with the temperamental bathroom lock.

I turned back to look in the mirror. I knew that Callum

would have been watching, so I waited for the tingle in my arm. Within seconds he was at my side, his unruly dark-blond hair looking even more appealing than usual next to my carefully coiffed look. "I'm sorry," I whispered. "I don't have long; she'll be back in a second."

"I know, but I just wanted to say goodnight before you went off to the party, as I'm not sure I'll be able to be here when you get back."

I pouted at him. "I'd much rather be spending the evening here with you, you do know that, don't you?"

He gave me one of his most devastating smiles. "I know, but you can't stay in for ever. You have to go out with your friends sometimes."

"I'm just not looking forward to it very much. I don't want to spend the evening gossiping with the girls, and watching the boys try their luck before seeing who can drink the most without being sick. I want to be with you, and we've had so little time over the last few days. There's loads of stuff I wanted to talk to you about." I still hadn't found the right moment to tell him about the note and Ashley's unprovoked attack.

A strange look crossed his face. "You do look spectacularly gorgeous tonight." His free hand, the one not lined up with my amulet, reached up to stroke my hair, then hesitated. "I almost don't dare touch you, I'm frightened of messing things up."

"Don't worry about that," I objected. "It's not for anyone's benefit."

"I wish it were for mine," he said in a voice so quiet I almost didn't hear it.

I could practically feel my heart twisting. "It *is* for you, always. You know that."

This time the smile was rueful. "You know how much I wish that were possible. But you do have a life, and I don't want to get in the way."

"You'll never be in the way!" I reached up and tried to stroke his face, feeling as usual just the merest hint of resistance in the air. He looked glum. "Was the gathering not so good today?"

"No, it was fine, really. I . . . I just. . ." he hesitated and looked away.

"Callum, what is it? Tell me quickly before Grace comes back or I'll be worrying all night."

"You look different, so . . . sophisticated. And stunning, of course. You just don't look much like my Alex. And this is how it should be, you getting ready with your mates to go out partying. This is what you deserve." He finally looked into my eyes and I could see the sorrow there.

"Don't you dare think like that!" I flashed back at him as loudly as I could. "I really don't care what the others think, and all of this is just nonsense." I gestured towards the clothes and my fancy hair. "It's you, Callum, only you." My voice softened. "I wouldn't swap any of them for you. I love you."

He seemed to relax a little. "I know you do, truly. I guess I'm just a little . . . well, jealous, I suppose."

"Well, why don't you come? You could get to meet – or at least *see* – a few of my friends, even if they don't get to meet you. Then you can be absolutely sure that you have no competition whatsoever."

He gave the smallest of smiles. "Thanks for the offer, but I'm not sure that would be a good idea. I've never minded being just an observer before, watching concerts or people at parties, but it's much harder when you know some of the real participants, now

I know you and your friends. It makes me even more aware of what I'm missing, and it gets a bit . . . difficult."

It was my turn to look glum. "I'm so sorry. I wish things were different." I heard the lock turn on the bathroom door. "Quick, Grace is coming back. Can I see you in St Paul's tomorrow? I can probably find an excuse to be getting out on a Saturday."

"I'd love that. I'll see you in the morning, then. Have a good night." His hand moved to touch my hair but fell away before he reached it. The rueful smile was back.

"I love you, Callum."

The smile finally reached his eyes. "I love you too. See you." His face disappeared as the bedroom door opened and Grace walked in.

"Hmm, you've not ruined anything, well done. I thought you'd have started rearranging everything the minute I turned my back."

I turned quickly so that she couldn't see the tears. However much I loved Callum this life was hugely difficult, and I could see no way to make it any easier. I took a deep breath to steady myself. There was no point in getting emotional, especially not now.

"Right, let's go before I smudge my mascara or something." I handed Grace her bag, scooped mine from the floor and switched off the light, glancing in the mirror as I did so. For a second I thought I saw him there, watching, but when I looked closer he was gone.

Eloïse's seventeenth birthday party was being held in a hall near her home, as too many people had been invited to make it either comfortable or sensible to have it in the house. This way she could relax too. There were a small number of adults lurking unobtrusively early on, but they soon disappeared behind the bar to keep some control over the potent mixture of teenagers and alcohol. One of the school bands was playing, and we spent a lot of the evening dancing wildly in front of the stage, encouraging them as much as possible, and trying to ignore the terrible acoustics in the institutional-looking room. Eloïse had done what she could to liven it up with balloons and streamers, and it *did* look much less like an old village hall than usual.

I had done my best to ignore Rob, who was leaning nonchalantly on the end of the bar. Grace had made sure he'd seen me as soon as we walked in, and I could feel his eyes following me around the room. His girlfriend Ashley was conspicuous by her absence.

"Where's Ashley?" I whispered to Grace fairly early on, when it became apparent that Rob wasn't waiting for her.

"Ah, well, funny you should ask. . . I was just in the loo with Mia and she told me that Ashley and Rob have had a bit of a row."

"Really? What about?"

"Well, it seems that Ashley still thinks Rob's got a thing about you, and she's given him an ultimatum." Grace dropped her voice and looked around. "She told him that she didn't want him hanging around at parties where you'd be and refused to come, assuming he'd stay at home with her. Of course, he just came anyway."

"Well, how dim can you get? Did she really think he'd let her boss him around like that?"

"I know, you think she'd have picked up something from all the problem pages she's read over the years. But actually, it looks like she was right about one thing: he can't take his eyes off you."

"Huh, well, he can look all he likes; I'm not going to fall

for any of his drivel again," I snorted, trying not to look in Rob's direction. I could see that he was watching us both over the rim of his glass, so I turned my back in what I hoped was a subtle manoeuvre.

Grace smiled at me; I was obviously not being quite as casual as I'd thought. But at least I could no longer see Rob; I didn't want him ruining my evening.

Abbi was there, keeping her distance, but didn't seem quite as wound up as she had been earlier. I took Grace's advice and left her alone, hoping that in time she'd come round. About halfway through the evening Jack turned up, and Grace became welded to his side.

It made me smile to watch the pair of them. They were very well suited and I hoped that the relationship would last the summer. They were both pretty loyal, so I thought it was likely, especially as Grace ending up in hospital had obviously proved to Jack how much he cared about her, and they had become inseparable. I watched while the two of them danced together, so comfortable and at ease with each other. He was always looking out for her, checking that she had what she needed, if she wanted to dance or not, or needed air. I could happily watch them all night. I knew that if Callum were here, that is how he would have been behaving towards me. The idea made me smile, but as I watched I became aware of another, unfamiliar, feeling too. I was jealous; jealous of their ability to be together, to hold each other, to do the mundane things in life. I couldn't do any of that with Callum, and there was no chance that I *would* be able to do them either, however long I waited.

I was lost in my thoughts and realised too late that Rob was heading in my direction. I was standing at the side of the hall, and when he got to me he leaned towards me to talk, bracing himself against the wall with his arm above my shoulder. It was an odd stance, as if he were trying to box me in.

I crossed my arms and glared at him, then raised my voice to be heard over the pounding music. "What do you want?" I asked in my best dismissive tone. We hadn't actually spoken since he'd abandoned me in a restaurant. I wondered if he was going to mention that.

"You," he shouted back, looking me deliberately up and down. I quickly looked away before his eyes made it back to mine, which threw him rather. "So how are you? Fully recovered?" he continued quickly.

I shrugged, and wondered briefly if I should ask him about the computer files. I really wanted to know what he was up to, but didn't fancy explaining that it was Ashley who had told me; I bet he didn't know she had been snooping on his computer. In the end I said nothing, and waited to see what he was going to do next.

He was obviously keen to talk. "I'm glad to see you're feeling better. You gave us all a bit of a scare." He smiled his most melting smile, which just a short month ago would have made me weak at the knees, but I had become immune to his charms.

"I'm feeling perfectly OK, thank you," I replied icily. "The only thing that's still upsetting me is the fact that someone – *someone*," I emphasised, "is spreading a rumour that it was a suicide attempt." I glared at him again. "Aside from being a complete lie, it'll really upset my parents if they hear it."

"Really? Has someone being doing that?" He shook his head in mock disgust. "Some people just don't think."

I had to admire his attempt to brazen the whole thing out. He was almost completely convincing. But I didn't reply, just continued to glower at him. I wasn't going to blink first. It took all my self-control not to smile when he finally dropped his gaze to the floor.

"It must be tough for you, watching him, though, eh?" He nodded in Jack's direction. When I had dumped Rob he had quickly made the assumption that I was carrying a torch for Jack, as he knew the two of us were friends, and Jack had just started seeing Grace. What Rob had never noticed, because he wasn't really interested in anyone but himself, was that Jack and I were more like brother and sister, and fancying him was the last thing on my mind.

I looked at him, trying to decide what value there was in putting him straight. In the end I gave him what I hoped was a disgusted look, then turned back to watch the dance floor again. Grace and Jack were giving their all to the current number one, oblivious to everyone else around them, their yellow auras as bright and vibrant as the pulsing disco lights.

Rob tried again, determined not to be put off, raising his voice as the music ramped up. "It's good to see you, and looking so gorgeous too. . ."

I looked up at him; the disco lights were flashing on his face now, giving him an eerie green look and dead-looking eyes. I couldn't help thinking that it rather suited him. I leaned in towards him and shouted in his ear. "Where's Ashley? Had enough of you already, has she?"

"Ah, well, you know. I think she had other plans. . ." He was squirming a bit now, and I was enjoying myself.

"Oh, really? I heard that she dumped you. Bit mean of her, don't you think? I know you were so looking forward to your little Cornish holiday." I stood up straight and put my hands on my hips, daring him to deny that he'd found a substitute for me on his little jaunt.

"Actually, Ashley hasn't dumped me, as you so poetically put it. But, well, you know, sometimes plans need to be a little ... flexible. In fact, I was hoping to talk to you about that again." His hand, which was still bracing his weight against the wall as he leaned in, slid a little further down so that his arm was resting on my shoulder.

I couldn't believe it. After all that had happened, he was trying to chat me up again! I really didn't have the stomach for all that. "Rob, don't flatter yourself. You know perfectly well that I refused you before, and I'm not about to change my mind now!"

"Alex, I think you're still a bit confused. Maybe when you came round from the coma you forgot a few things. But I've not forgotten how much we fancy each other. How about letting me give you a refresher course?" He ran the fingers of his free hand through his beautifully cut blond hair, giving me the full benefit of his smouldering eyes: eyes that flashed with confidence.

I quickly stepped to one side as he tried to lean in towards me and he fell slightly forwards, a look of surprise on his face. "What do you think you're playing at?" I raised my voice even further. "I told you before, I have no intention of going out with you. Not now, not ever. Understand? I'm amazed that Ashley hasn't seen through you yet. It can only be a matter of time." Luckily the music was still loud, so although I was shouting at him, no one else seemed to have noticed.

Rob stood there smiling at me, in an almost creepy way. "Hey, don't panic. It's cool. All I'm saying is that we can still be friends." As he said it his eyes dropped to my hands and then to the amulet. His eyes flicked back to my face for a second, and then his tone changed. "Is that the bracelet that Grace gave back to you in the hospital? The one you found in the river?"

I automatically folded my arms again so that the amulet was protected. "Who told you that?"

"Someone mentioned it when you were recovering. It's very unusual. . . Can I see it?"

I felt my eyes narrow. Something felt very wrong about this conversation. "Actually, Rob, no you can't. And we are not going to be friends either. Do you really think this is the best way to treat Ashley?"

"Oh, she'll get over it," he said in his more usual swaggering way, then swiftly became conciliatory again. "Honestly, Alex, I know we had a bit of a false start, but we could put that all behind us and start again." He reached towards me as he spoke. As his hand reached my arm I saw his eyes flick down to the amulet and a little yellow light popped on above his head. I snatched my hands back behind me. I couldn't put my finger on why, but I knew that I didn't want Rob anywhere near my only link with Callum.

"Come on," he wheedled, pulling my arm out in front of me. He was too strong to resist without making a scene, and was soon holding my wrist firmly, examining the amulet from all angles. The yellow light over his head was getting brighter, but I couldn't work out why.

I tried to jerk my hand back. "Leave it, Rob. I asked you not to do that!" I looked wildly around for some way to escape, but just as suddenly he let me go, a strange smile on his face.

"Touchy! I only wanted to have a look. Grace told me it was a bit unusual, that's all."

The whole thing stank, but I couldn't understand why he'd

be so interested. "Whatever," I grunted, as I crossed my arms firmly, making sure the amulet was safely out of sight.

Suddenly the music changed; it was coming towards the end of the evening and the DJ who had taken over from the band was winding things down with a ballad. I didn't want to be anywhere near Rob when the slow dancing started. I stood up as straight as I could. "Are we done? Good, go back to Ashley, Rob, and stop spreading your sick lies about me." Before he could respond I turned quickly on my ridiculous heels and moved as purposefully as possible towards the Ladies.

A number of my friends were in there, moaning about how rubbish the boys were being. As usual all the best-laid plans about who was supposed to be dancing with whom at this point had fallen down, largely due to the lack of involvement of the boys in the planning process. The ones who were dancing had picked the wrong girls, and the vast majority were still clustered around the room, watching what was going on.

"Oh, hi Alex," said Lydia when I appeared. "No one to dance with then? I thought you and Rob might be. . .?" She left the question dangling.

"Not a chance. After what he did to me I don't even want to talk to him. He was just a bit difficult to shake off. How about you? I thought that you were going to have a go at Marcus?"

Lydia looked forlorn for a moment. "He's taken no notice of me all evening. He's never going to ask me to dance."

"Well, he's going to have a hard job when you're in here," I pointed out. "When I came in he seemed to be scanning the room. Maybe he was looking for you? You could always surprise him by asking him to dance, you know."

"Do you think I should? Really?"

"What have you got to lose? He's a bloke. They never refuse to dance, not when it's the slow ones."

"Maybe I will!" she announced with surprising vigour, and marched out of the room. I smiled to myself, and then couldn't help looking in the mirror, just in case. But Callum wasn't there. I suppose it was late, so I wasn't expecting him, but his absence always left me feeling just a little empty.

After washing my hands and checking my make-up as slowly as possible I wandered back to the hall. The last dance was just finishing. Grace and Jack were entwined, as I expected, so I looked around to see what other gossip was going to be doing the rounds on Monday morning. Through the flickering cloud of little yellow lights, which only I could see, I could make out Lydia and Marcus in a limpet-like embrace, so that strategy had clearly worked. As the lights came up and the music faded others emerged blinking from the arms of their partners. As ever, some looked smug and didn't let go, but some, if not actually leaping away from each other, looked vaguely embarrassed.

Grace and Jack sauntered towards me. "Hi, Alex, had fun?" Jack asked, ruffling my hair, which made Grace shriek in horror. "You girls wait here for a minute and I'll walk you to the car." He wandered off in the direction of the Gents. Grace and I started on the usual hunt for the bags and various bits and pieces we had distributed round the room during the evening. We ended up behind the bar, looking through a pile of jumpers that had been dumped in a corner.

"What were you and the gorgeous Rob talking about earlier?" asked Grace, her eyes twinkling mischievously. "Are you guys friends again now?"

"You must be kidding; he's such a loser. I can't believe he's treating Ashley so badly. And anyway, after what he did, trying to come between us over Jack and letting people think I was suicidal because of him, I don't want to be anywhere near the creep!"

"He couldn't tempt you away from Callum then?"

"Absolutely not! Callum is a decent guy with morals, unlike slimeball Rob Underwood."

"It's *such* a shame Callum's not here. I'd really like to meet him."

"Callum, eh? I'd like to meet him too." The unexpected voice made us both jump. Rob was standing in the doorway, looking very smug. "Secret boyfriend, is he?"

"He's hardly a secret, just none of your business," I retorted. "We were actually having a private conversation, if you don't mind."

"It wasn't that private. I was just standing here, keeping myself to myself. You mentioned Callum!"

"But not to you." I turned my back on him. "Grace, have you got everything? I can see Jack waiting for us," I added pointedly.

Rob whipped around to look for Jack, clearly still nervous about what he might do. Grace and I exchanged a conspiratorial glance. "Oh, good," said Grace, winking at me. "I think he wanted a word with you, Rob."

"Yeah, well, some other time. Got to go now," he mumbled, heading off quickly in the other direction. I hoped he could hear us laughing.

It took a while to get home as Grace drove very slowly, anxious not to make any mistakes. She pulled up outside my house but couldn't park in her usual spot; an unfamiliar car was already there, and we could see someone sitting inside it.

"Hmm, I'll watch until you're in the house, I think. Shame

we didn't bring Jack with us," she said, peering over her steering wheel at the back of the stranger's head.

"I'm sure I'll be fine, but thanks for waiting." I gave her a swift hug, then got out of the car, calling back to her. "I'll talk to you tomorrow. Night."

"Goodni—" She broke off suddenly. "I don't believe it! It's Geeky Graham!"

I spun around and looked at the figure getting out of the car parked just in front of us. It was a boy who had been in the same class as Jack and the others at school, but who had left a year before to go to the local sixth-form college. He was known as Geeky Graham as he only seemed able to relate to a computer screen. He had spent his entire childhood, as far as any of us knew, plugged into the Internet, hacking into other people's networks, playing online war games and never getting involved with anything in the real world. A year or so back, and much to my surprise, he had plucked up the courage to ask me out. I had turned him down as gently as I knew how, but he had got pretty upset about it. Shortly after that there had been a scandal at the boys' school when he had hacked into their systems and been discovered after a random audit with the entire set of forthcoming exam papers in his account. He had been promptly expelled. I'd been really relieved when he had left and there was no chance of bumping into him any more.

He had gained a brief notoriety as a result of the expulsion, as most of us thought it was over the top, but he had few actual supporters as he no real friends. He had found out too late that being world champion at MegaDeath 4 wasn't the same as having some mates.

And now he was standing outside my house with a nervous

smile on his face, which looked even more pallid than usual in the orange glow of the streetlight.

"Umm, hi . . . Graham." I remembered just in time to drop the Geeky bit. "What on earth are you doing here?"

"Waiting for you, course." He gave a nervous laugh. "Though I was beginning to think you weren't going to show."

"Oh, really?" I asked hesitantly, completely confused. Something odd was going on. Again.

"Everything OK, Alex?" Grace's voice came from inside the car.

"Yes, don't worry. I'll talk to you tomorrow." I leaned into the car window to give her a hug. "I'll text you when I get in, let you know what happens." She nodded almost imperceptibly.

"OK, night, Alex," she said loudly. "See you, Graham." With that she drove off and both Graham and I watched as her tail lights disappeared.

"So, umm," I started, unsure of what to do. "Long time, no see."

"Yeah, it's been a while."

"You OK then? New school working out?" I cast desperately around for something to say.

"Yeah, yeah, that's all fine," he muttered, looking at the floor, kicking small stones off the pavement. He seemed to have been struck dumb.

"Well, er. . ." Inspiration deserted me and I looked at the floor too, wondering where this bizarre conversation was going. There was a long pause as both of us considered our feet.

Graham's next words came out in a rush. "I was kind of surprised when you got in contact." He hesitated but before I could say anything, he continued, "Pleased, but surprised. After last time, I guess I didn't expect that you would, well, you know. . ." His voiced faded out as he continued looking at the floor. "And I was even more surprised to realise that we had so much in common."

I was too stunned to speak. What on earth was he talking about?

"Graham, it's, er, great to see you, but I'm really confused. Why are you waiting for me?"

"Oh, come on! You can't possibly have forgotten; it was your idea!" He took one look at my face and carried on, but less certainly. "You said you wanted to come with me to the convention in Birmingham this weekend, the MegaDeath one. You said. . ." He tailed off, and even in the strange streetlight I could see the colour rising in his face.

This was getting worse and worse. I had to stop it as painlessly as I could. "Graham," I said gently. "I've not spoken to you for ages. . ." Actually, I couldn't remember speaking to him at all since he'd asked me out, but now probably wasn't the time to mention that. "Not since before you left the school. When did we fix all this up?"

"You've been talking to me all week on Facebook. I didn't believe you were serious at first but you convinced me." He paused for a second but then looked me straight in the eye. "Is this some sort of joke?"

Yet again I felt a shiver of horror up my neck. "Someone has been messing us both about. I'm sure you're a great guy, but I didn't agree to go to Birmingham with you." I watched as his face crumpled, and felt awful; he stood there looking like a kicked puppy. I rushed to explain, words tumbling out as I tried, unsuccessfully, to make it better. "Someone has a vendetta against me, you see. They've sabotaged my e-mail, broken my window and now this. I'm really sorry; you don't deserve to be involved."

"So it wasn't you on Facebook?"

I shook my head slowly, and I saw his shoulders slump even further as he turned away. Who would be this vindictive? "I'm so sorry." I risked a quick glance at him but he was struggling to stay in control. "I don't know what to say."

"Don't say anything!" he spat as he turned back towards me. "You've had your fun, now leave me alone!"

"Honestly, it wasn't me! And I've no idea who would do such an awful thing." But I was talking to thin air. Graham had jumped back in his car and was trying to make an exit. The car fired but died and I could see him sitting rigid in the driving seat. I'm not sure which of us was wishing harder that the car would work. He tried again and this time the old engine spluttered into life, and with a spin of tyres he was gone. I stood alone at the edge of the road, almost shaking with fear. Who could possibly be that mean, and what were they going to do next?

Olivia

I had a terrible night, thinking of poor Graham. Every time I remembered the look on his face I could feel myself going all clammy. My mind kept circling around the questions of who and why, but nothing came to me. And Grace had been clueless too, when I'd told her about it. "Poor old Geeky Graham," was all she'd managed.

In the morning I stretched as I lay in bed, remembering at last with a smile that I was due to go to St Paul's again to see Callum. I put everything else out of my mind as I thought about standing in his arms and kissing him properly. I just had to negotiate my release from household duties for the day. Downstairs I could smell the home-baked loaf that Mum made every Saturday, and jumped out of bed to put my plan into action.

But it wasn't to be quite that simple. Mum had obviously had a conversation with Graham the night before, and was keen to get to the bottom of things. As we sat in the kitchen with our coffees and the warm cinnamon loaf I knew she had me trapped.

"So what did that poor boy want, Alex? I've never seen anyone look quite so gutted when he heard you weren't in."

"What time did he turn up?"

"Oh, it wasn't late. About half-past eight? I told him that you were at Eloïse's party. I take it he didn't try and find you there?"

I felt my stomach churn, and surreptitiously pushed my

plate away from me. He had been waiting outside for over three hours. "What exactly did he say?" I asked, wondering how much I was going to have to tell Mum.

"Well, he said he was here to pick you up, but as soon as I told him that you were out, he got very flustered, and barely said another word."

I heaved a silent sigh of relief. If Graham hadn't mentioned going away for the weekend, I certainly didn't have to. "It was all a bit of a misunderstanding, Mum. He got the wrong end of the stick from something that someone had told him, that's all." I tried to leave it at that, but her eyebrow was up.

"And. . .?"

"And nothing. Really. He's just a guy I used to know, that's all. Seems he's been carrying a bit of a torch. I let him down gently," I added quickly as I saw her draw breath to interrupt. "It's all fine now, I promise."

"Hmm, well. I know you won't have been leading him on, Alex, you're too nice. But I'll not forget the look on his face for a long time." She shook her head as she cut herself another slab of the loaf. "So what are your plans for today? What do you and Grace have cooked up?"

"I think Grace is seeing Jack today, he's playing in a match so she's off to support him."

"Are you going to watch too?"

"I don't really fancy going again; I always feel a bit in the way these days."

Mum reached over and squeezed my hand. "Never mind. It's always tough when your best friend gets their first serious boyfriend. You'll have plenty of time for that, when you find someone you like."

"It's fine Mum, I'm really happy for them. But I don't want to be trailing around after them. It's just. . ." I felt really mean manipulating her, but the chance was too good to miss. "It's just difficult finding other things to do. I thought I might pop up to London, have a look at some of the shops on Oxford Street, maybe go to the Tate Modern. What do you think?"

"That sounds like a great idea. Why don't you call Abbi or Mia and see if they want to go with you?"

"Yeah, I might just do that. I'd better get in the shower then, otherwise I'll miss the train."

"I'll run you down to the station, if you like. When you go upstairs will you wake up your brother? He's supposed to be helping Dad with the garden this morning."

"OK, I'll go and get him now."

I ran up the stairs and along the corridor to Josh's room. It was always like entering a dark cave; he never opened the curtains and great towers of used deodorant spray cans threatened to topple off the chest of drawers every time I went in there. I tapped gently on the door and there was an answering grunt.

I put my head round the door and could see his face illuminated in the gloom by his laptop screen.

"Hiya. Mum wants me to wake you up. She thinks you have forgotten about the digging."

"Yeah, right. Why do you think I've been hiding up here? I don't even like vegetables."

"Well, she'll be up herself soon, so you might not want to be caught on that." I gestured towards the computer as I edged gingerly into the room.

"True. So has she done interrogating you now? What on earth was Geeky Graham doing here last night?"

"Did you see him too? The poor bloke!" It was my turn to shake my head. "Someone hijacked my Facebook account and set up a date with him. He thought I was going to go to a MegaDeath convention with him."

"No! Really?" Josh started laughing. "How dumb can he be? No girls *ever* go to those things. Why the hell did he think you'd be up for that?"

"Whoever was impersonating me was very persuasive. And stop laughing, Josh, it's not funny." Josh tried to smother his amusement but he wasn't very successful.

I was about to ask him if he had any thoughts about who might've been so cruel when we were interrupted by the sound of the old school bell clanging at the bottom of the stairs. Josh sighed and shut down his laptop. He was being summoned.

"Looks like my lie-in is over."

"Have fun!" I smiled at him as I picked my way back across his bedroom floor, through the piles of discarded clothes. I quickly went to my bedroom, shutting the door carefully so that no one would hear me, and checked my watch. It was nearly half-past nine, so hopefully not too early for Callum. I sat at my desk with the mirror positioned in front of me and called to him softly.

He was there in an instant, the tingle in my arm starting almost before I had finished saying his name. He was sitting just behind me with his left arm superimposed across my right wrist as usual. His other hand was already busy stroking my hair.

"Hi. Looks like you've been having a busy morning."

"Hello. I wondered if you'd been watching. So you know what's been going on?"

"I think so. Some poor kid thought he was in with a chance." Callum gave me one of his most gorgeous smiles.

45

"You don't know the half of it." I quickly gave him the full details of the hideous event, finding myself blushing furiously yet again at the horror of it. Callum's brow furrowed in confusion.

"Who can possibly have a grudge against you? I mean, none of your friends would do that, would they?

"No, absolutely not! And anyway, some of them might be able to make a lucky guess at my password, but none of them would hack into my e-mail as well as my Facebook account. Someone who knew every school secret I have ever had broke into my account and e-mailed the headmistress on Thursday. Luckily for me they got the address wrong so it never got delivered. I've obviously upset somebody who knows me really, really well, but I can't even think who would know that stuff."

In the mirror I could see Callum's strong arm enfolding me, holding me close and safe. "That's so weird. It's almost as if someone was in your head, but how could that be?"

"I know. I keep trying to figure out who can have all that information and why they would be doing this to me. What have I done to them?"

"I'm sure you haven't done anything. It's someone else with the problem, not you."

I knew he was trying to make me feel better, but I wasn't sure I believed him. "It can't be a coincidence though, not all of it."

"Well, maybe it's someone from school. What about Ashley?"

"That's another thing! She gave me a slap the other morning – I didn't even tell you about it. It can't be her doing the rest of it, though. Slapping is about as sophisticated as she gets."

"So that's at least two different people with grudges. Why did she slap you?"

"Oh, it was just nonsense. She thinks I still like Rob. As if!" Callum's lips pressed together in a thin line as he considered that fact. "Come on, don't you get all grumpy on me too! You know that he's no competition for you." To prove my point I reached up and in the mirror saw my fingers gently stroking his face from the cheekbone to his jaw. He leaned towards my hand, shutting his eyes briefly, and the lightest of tickles traced across my palm. My heart melted again as I looked at him. Whatever the pain and the problems, I loved him and wanted to be with him. "Hey, enough bad news; I need to be getting a shift on. Mum has offered to take me to the station as she thinks I'm going to Tate Modern. Meet me at the dome?"

A gentle smile appeared slowly on his face but his eyes stayed sad. "My favourite place. I'm not sure that the Golden Gallery will be shut though. I didn't have time to check this morning."

"Come on! Don't look so gloomy! After all this nonsense I could do with cheering up, and the best way to do that is to have a proper cuddle from you."

"Even with everyone watching?"

"I won't notice them for a second, not when I have you." In the mirror I could see his free arm tighten around me, then he dropped a kiss on the top of my head.

"See you there then. Give me a call when you get to the Tube station."

I looked quickly at my watch. "Two hours, that's all. See you soon." He gave me another quick squeeze and was gone.

I spent the time on the train trying hard not to think about all the bad things that were going on, but it was difficult not to keep coming back to it. I had somehow accumulated a lot of enemies in a very short space of time. As I turned them over in my mind yet again I started to fidget with the amulet on my wrist. It was such a beautiful piece of jewellery, with the mysterious stone that was exactly the same colour as Callum's eyes, held in the cage of finely twisted silver ropes. I still couldn't believe my luck in finding it, whatever the other problems. I sat and traced its outline with my finger as I thought about the matching one on Callum's arm. Soon we would be together, his strong, smooth fingers laced together with mine as we watched the London skyline. Whatever was causing my other problems, I could deal with them all if I had Callum.

The suburbs of London streamed past my window, slowly turning into the industrial parks and markets, and finally the snake-like structure of the old Waterloo International came into view. At the station I found that the Tube link directly to Bank was shut, and the woman at the information desk directed me to a bus. Sitting on the top deck as we drove over Waterloo Bridge I could see St Paul's in the distance, the late morning sun glinting off the Golden Gallery, which encircled the very top of the dome. That was my special place, where the amulet and my new talents allowed Callum to appear to be real, where I could touch him and hold him. And kiss him. The thought made me smile again. Whatever else was going on at least there was the chance that I might get to kiss him again.

But it was a Saturday, so I wasn't sure how practical it was going to be. Even from the bridge I could just glimpse people up there, enjoying the view from one of the best vantage points in London. Previously Callum had been able to ensure that there was maintenance going on, which kept the tourists away. I had no idea how he managed it, but it meant that our visits had been reasonably private, apart from all the other

Dirges. Kissing an invisible man in a crowd of people would be interesting.

The bus slowly worked its way down Fleet Street, but came to a standstill at the bottom of Ludgate Hill. I could see the queue of traffic snaking up towards the cathedral. I checked that my headphones were secure and was about to pretend to make a call to speak to Callum when the phone rang, making me jump. It was Rob. I debated ignoring it, but curiosity got the better of me.

"What do you want?" I said, abruptly.

"And good morning to you, you gorgeous creature! What are you doing today?"

"I'm going out, actually. Not that it's any of your business."

"Well, how about I join you? Keep you company while that boyfriend of yours is away?"

"Are you mad? Why would I want to spend the day with you?"

"Now, don't be like that, Alex. We had one little misunderstanding, that's all. Can't a guy get a second chance? Let me show you what it's like to have a boyfriend who isn't away all the time." His voice was smooth and oozed confidence, which irritated me even more.

"I'm not going to listen to this, Rob. Don't call me again!" As I angrily snapped my phone shut I became horribly aware of how loud I had become. The people around me on the bus were all obviously listening. Ignoring them I stabbed quickly at the keys on the phone.

"Callum, hi. I'm stuck on a bus." I tried to keep my voice low and unemotional. "The Tube was shut. Do you want to meet me on the steps? I'll call you back in a minute to check and see if you got the message."

I waited for a few seconds, knowing that it would take him almost no time to run from the Tube station to where I was on the bus. Very quickly I felt the tingle in my arm, and automatically started to relax. I picked up the phone again.

"Hi. I seem to be stuck. I'm going to see if the driver will let me off."

"OK. There's a massive queue all round St Paul's so if you can get off, you should."

No one took any notice of me at all as I made my way down the stairs and joined the group of people pleading with the bus driver to open the doors. He kept protesting that we weren't at a stop, but eventually gave in and we all piled out.

As I approached the building I looked at the two long queues of people waiting to get inside the cathedral. "This could take a while," I murmured as I headed towards the back of one of the lines, digging my season ticket out of my bag. "Which of these will go faster, can you see?"

"Oh, you don't have to wait there, not if you have your ticket. Nip down to the café and go into the entrance in the crypt."

"Really? OK, let me know if I'm heading in the wrong direction."

The café was noisy and packed, and a strong smell of toast wafted across the long, low space. It seemed odd that such a busy café should be nestled right underneath the main part of the cathedral, and not at all in keeping with the hushed silence just above. I worked my way round the tables and chairs towards the far end of the vast room where there was a fancy iron grille. At the far side was a bored-looking attendant. I quickly flashed my ticket at him and was soon through to the rest of the crypt.

Callum and I walked towards Nelson's monument on our way to the stairs. As we passed I stole a quick glance at him. Ever since he'd restored my memories, I could always see him inside the building – properly see him, not just a reflection in a mirror – and he got more solid the higher up we went. I wondered what he would be like down here. The glimpse I got stopped me in my tracks.

"Callum!" I called after him, remembering just in time to talk into my phone mouthpiece. We were right by the big black casket that sat under the middle of the dome, as close as we could possibly get to being directly underneath the centre of it.

"Hey, what's up?" He wheeled around and stepped back towards me, smiling. His beautiful face was worn and tired, looking as if a million cares and worries were heaped on him.

"Are . . . are you OK?" I asked hesitantly. He had looked just fine in the mirror earlier. I couldn't imagine what it was that had affected him so drastically.

"I'm fine." He smiled at me but the lines etched in his face didn't match his words. He saw my frown and instantly looked even worse. "What's the matter? Has something else happened?" He stood in front of me, his amulet within mine, the shimmer of his translucent figure strangely clear in the dim lighting of the crypt.

"It's not me. You look . . . so tired. I've never seen you look anything other than perfect before. Has something terrible happened since this morning?"

He blushed briefly at the compliment, but the worry was still evident on his face. "No, nothing. In fact I'm really excited about getting up to the top of the dome with you."

"I don't understand then. Why do you look so awful?"

His puzzled frown was suddenly replaced by one of comprehension. "Of course, you can see it too!"

"See what?"

"We don't tend to come down here too much because this far down under the dome it shows our general state of mind. I guess I look pretty miserable to you?"

I nodded mutely as a couple of tourists stopped to peer at the tomb, then moved on.

"I . . . I thought you were excited. You just said you were, but you look, well, devastated."

"Huh, believe me, this isn't close to devastated. As you know I'm about the happiest Dirge there is, and I still look suicidal down here. It's why we hide in our hoods. Catherine only came the once. I never want to see anything like that again." He shuddered at the memory.

"So this is how miserable you *ought* to look? Is that right?"

"That's what I reckon. Some people, especially those that have been here for a long time, they don't look much different at all when they come down here, but I guess that's because they've long since given up on trying to keep a balanced view. I'm a bit luckier than that."

I looked at him with open curiosity. He was solid enough for me to see the lines in his face, the shadows under the eyes, the gaunt cheeks. "Honestly, Callum, you look middle-aged down here. Let's get up to the top where you are your usual gorgeous self."

"Suits me," he smiled, momentarily lighting up his gloomy face. "Next time we take this short-cut I'll keep my hood up so I don't frighten you."

I smiled back, but a small shiver ran down my spine. The

amulet and St Paul's were doing their best to make my life truly weird as usual.

As we walked across the big mosaic star in the main part of the cathedral I stole another glance at him, and was relieved to see that at ground level he was looking more his usual self. Before we got to the bottom of the main staircase he stopped me.

"Can I ask a favour?"

"Of course."

"Do you mind making a short stop at the Whispering Gallery? There's someone there who would really like to talk to you."

I hesitated a fraction too long. I didn't really want to talk to Matthew again. It was a strangely intimate thing to do, letting someone else into your head with the amulet. It didn't feel right with anyone but Callum, but I realised I probably shouldn't let him know that. "Sure, whatever. Do you know what he wants to talk about?"

"It's not Matthew, it's Olivia."

"Oh. What does she want to talk to me for?"

"She feels really bad about what happened with Catherine, and she's worried that you think some of it was her fault."

I felt a brief twinge of guilt. I *had* taken an automatic dislike to Olivia, never having even seen her, just because Catherine had told me that Callum preferred her to me. I knew that it was mean and petty, and I absolutely believed it when Callum told me that it was all nonsense, but I still didn't really want to chat with her. But if Callum wanted me to talk with her, then I would.

"That's fine. Will you take me to her?"

"Great. I'll go and let her know while you make your way

up. Go round to your left when you get up there and I'll tell you when to stop."

"OK. See you there." I felt the waft of air as he stooped to kiss my cheek, then waved my ticket at the woman sitting behind the desk. Joining the long queue of people edging up the long spiral staircase I tried not to think about my natural dislike for Olivia. I visualised her as tall, dark and hauntingly beautiful, someone who was able to be comforted by Callum in his own dimension. My fists clenched automatically and I forced myself to relax. She couldn't be that bad, I reasoned, not if she wanted to talk to me. And Callum seemed to really like her. I tried unsuccessfully to put her out of my mind as I trailed up the endless stairs. When I reached the top I stopped for a moment to catch my breath before I worked my way through the little maze of tiny corridors that led to the gallery itself. I couldn't resist the temptation to have a quick peek in the mirror. If I was going to meet my rival, I wanted to make sure I didn't have something stuck in my teeth. But the image that peered back at me was red-faced and breathless. Sighing in resignation, I made for the corridor.

I was walking up the last few narrow steps when I saw the translucent figure coming towards me. I smiled at Callum and felt the familiar tingle in my wrist as he put his amulet in the same space as mine. "Hi," he said. "Are you OK? I saw you hesitating at the top of the main stairs."

"Just a bit nervous, that's all," I admitted.

"You — nervous? That doesn't seem likely!"

"Much you know about women then," I muttered under my breath, forgetting for a moment that he could hear every word.

"You're serious? You really are nervous of meeting Olivia?" He hooted with laughter. "That's brilliant. She's been beside herself

54

with worry all morning, ever since I said you were coming. Both of you are scared of the other!"

"I'm not scared," I huffed. "Just, well, *nervous*, like I said." I didn't want to use the word jealous, even though I knew that's what it was.

"Come on then, better get the introductions done. She's waiting in the gallery." I could hear the smile in his voice; for some reason he was really amused by my discomfort. I pulled open the door and as always was taken aback by the sheer volume of space in front of me. The Whispering Gallery gave a spectacular view of the floor of the cathedral as well as revealing the full scale of the dome itself. As usual there were a large number of tourists sitting on the long seat that hugged the wall of the gallery, whispering with their mouths up against the wall in the hope that someone further along was going to hear them. Most didn't seem to realise that just sitting normally and talking quietly would have the same effect, and no one but me knew just exactly who was responsible for the strange acoustic phenomenon. The Dirges were sitting and standing around the gallery, unseen by everyone else, and it was their presence that somehow reflected the sound.

I took a deep breath. "To the left, did you say?"

Callum smiled at me, and I was momentarily distracted by seeing him next to me. "Yes, left. She's right along here. I promise it'll be OK."

"If you say so," I muttered, fiddling unnecessarily with my phone mouthpiece.

"Ah, there you are. Come and meet Alex."

His tone was annoyingly affectionate so I watched the approaching figure closely. She was more transparent than Callum, and I couldn't see her as clearly as I could him, but I could tell that she was completely swathed in her cloak, with her hood hanging low over her face. I sat down on a part of the seat unoccupied by human or Dirge, and got out my mirror. Olivia came into full focus in the little piece of glass. As I watched, small, delicate hands appeared from the heavy folds of cloth and moved hesitantly to the hood. "It's OK, really," Callum encouraged.

The head dipped as the hands grasped the hood and threw it back. I couldn't help but gasp at the figure in front of me: she was delicate and pretty, with chin-length chestnut hair and brown eyes that sparkled gently in the dull light. She was also very, very young, no more than about twelve or thirteen, I guessed. I felt myself choke up at the thought that this child was stuck in the unrelenting world of misery of the Dirges. She looked terrified, but was clearly trying to be brave.

"Hi, you must be Olivia."

I felt Callum whisper in my ear. "She feels awful that you thought she was my girlfriend after what Catherine said. She's worried that you will hate her."

I looked up into the troubled eyes of the child standing by me, and I realised just how wrong I had been. "I'll get out of the way so that you two can talk," he continued, and yet again the tingle went from my wrist. I watched in the mirror as Callum gave Olivia a brief hug, then propelled her towards me. She sat gingerly on the seat next to me and held out her arm, blushing furiously. Her amulet looked big and heavy on such a tiny frame. I moved my arm so that the two amulets were together. The tingle I got from Olivia was different, lighter somehow, than from Callum.

"Hello," I said again. "It's good to meet you."

Olivia looked almost paralysed with fear, and I could see in the very bottom of the mirror that her hands were in constant motion: she had made two interlocking circles with her thumbs and forefingers, like a chain, and was pulling one against the other. It reminded me of the sad, repetitive movements of caged animals.

"You don't have to say that if you don't mean it," she mumbled, so low I almost didn't catch it.

"Look, none of that stuff with Catherine was your fault, you do know that, don't you? She lied about everything. You're not to blame for anything. In fact, I should be thanking you."

Her head shot up in surprise and her hands stopped still for a moment. "Why?"

"Helping you every day has clearly given Callum a sense of purpose, has kept back some of the grief. He's really very fond of you." I leaned in towards her and lowered my voice. "He would much rather have had you as a sister than Catherine, I think." I smiled towards him as I said it.

Olivia turned an even prettier shade of pink. "Really? You don't hate me?"

"Of course not. I couldn't possibly hate you." I resisted the urge to try and give her a hug. It wouldn't have worked and might well have frightened her. "I'd really like the chance to get to know you a bit better. How about we try and organise some girl time, have a proper chat?"

The smile that appeared was hesitant at first, but became stronger as I smiled back at her. "Are you sure? I don't want to be a pain. . ."

"Absolutely sure! It'd be great to hang out a bit."

Olivia turned quickly to look at Callum as if to check whether I was joking or not. Callum's smile widened and I could see him say something. Olivia practically bounced with excitement. "He says," she started breathlessly, "he says that when you go home

57

I can go with you! I don't think I've ever been that far before. I can't wait! Do you have a little sister I could meet too? Is it a big house? Do you have any pets?" I could barely keep up with her, she had started talking so quickly. It was as if a dam had burst, releasing her from the constraints that had bound her for however long she had been there.

"We'll have plenty of time for all of that, I promise. I'll give you a full tour and show you my family. No little sister, I'm afraid, but I do have a big brother. He's not too bad as big brothers go, just a bit of a pain sometimes." Olivia was still beaming as I talked, and she would clearly have been happy to sit and listen all day, but I had other plans. When her questions slowed down a little I grabbed my chance. "So, you think of what gossip you can tell me while Callum and I run up to the top of the dome. I don't think we'll be that long, and then you can come back to my house. Deal?"

Olivia nodded, a beautiful smile lighting up her young face. "OK, it's a deal. You won't be too long, will you?"

"I'm sure we won't be – I don't think the Golden Gallery is shut today." I tried to squeeze her hand but I couldn't feel her at all. "Wait here, and we'll be back soon."

I got up from the seat and glanced across the void towards the door up to the next gallery. As I scanned along the various figures I was going to have to manoeuvre past, my eye was caught by woman in a cassock. She was staring at me intently, and I wondered if I was about to get told off for appearing to use my mobile inside the cathedral. But suddenly, as soon as she saw that I had seen her, she looked away. Even from that distance she seemed pretty old, and in the cassock she looked weirdly like one of the Dirges.

I knew that I didn't want to have to squeeze past her to get to the doorway, even if she had stopped looking at me, so I quickly turned and went around the other way. I heaved a quick sigh of relief as I made it through the door and tackled the tight spiral staircase up to the Stone Gallery. Callum joined me as I made it out into the light.

"Hey, we're in luck! It looks like the top gallery will be shut after all. The maintenance signs went up about twenty minutes ago." He beamed at me.

"Really? That's excellent. Do you want to let Olivia know she'll have to wait a bit longer for us?"

"OK. You go ahead. Bet I still beat you, though!"

"That's hardly a fair bet," I said, smiling. Time alone with Callum on the Golden Gallery – my absolutely favourite thing! I practically skipped over the maintenance barrier and into the dark recesses of the inner dome. The old iron staircase creaked and groaned in the silence as I worked my way up, and I was concentrating hard on my breathing when I became aware of a misty cloaked figure on the landing above me. It was only about twenty steps down from the little room with the viewing panel, so I was expecting Callum to be rather more solid.

"Hi," I gasped, catching my breath. "That's cheating. You're supposed to let me compose myself before I get to the top, not ambush me here. Now you can see how unfit I really am."

He stepped towards me with his arm outstretched, amulet glinting in the dim light. His face was obscured by his heavy hood. "Is everything OK, Callum?" I asked, extending my wrist. It wasn't like him to wear his hood up around me.

The tingle in my wrist was accompanied by a sudden hideous roaring noise and, as I jumped in surprise, the figure in front of me pushed back his hood with his free hand. I realised with shock that *he* was making the noise; he was bellowing at me without seeming to take any sort of breath. My head was beginning to pound. With his mouth open wide, he leaned even closer to me, his shoulder-length, greasy-looking black hair brushing my face. The volume went up yet another notch.

"Who on earth are you?" I cried, but my voice was drowned out by the shouting in my head. I tried to move my amulet away but he was too quick; every time I moved he seemed to be able to anticipate it and keep his amulet with mine. How could one person make such a noise? I couldn't think straight, I just kept trying to back away. All too soon I realised that I was at the edge of the top step. Below me the dizzying drop disappeared into the gloom. I couldn't go backwards, and he was blocking my way forwards. I could feel a strange blackness creeping into the edges of my mind as the relentless noise continued, and my knees buckled. As I fell I managed to throw my weight forwards on to the landing and for the briefest of seconds the noise let up and I could hear a distant voice.

"Take it off, Alex; it's your only chance. Take off the amulet and you won't be able to hear him. . ."

I reached for the band on my wrist as the onslaught resumed. The voice was right; without it on I wouldn't be able to hear any of them. I had my finger under the silver and was starting to pull, desperate to make it stop, when I realised what I was doing. I couldn't – *mustn't* – take off the amulet!

"Callum!" I shouted as loudly as I could manage. "Help me! I'm being attacked!"

There was a blur of movement, and almost as if a switch had been thrown in my head, the noise stopped. The silence was shocking and I fell sideways towards the iron railings. The dark-haired Dirge was backing along the landing with Callum advancing towards him. Then, faster than I could see, they were fighting, cloaks whirling. I pressed myself as far as I could into the corner, unable to keep a track of who had the upper hand. For a brief second they were still; I saw Callum's blond hair and the face of the other Dirge, a face showing naked fury. I couldn't help tightening my grip on the ironwork and my stomach churned at the thought of what he might be capable of doing. Suddenly Callum caught his arm, wrenched it up behind his back and threw him over the railings. Before I could react he had jumped after him into the void. Horrified, I leapt up and ran to the edge. Below me I could see them wrestling on the curved surface of the dome, rolling over and over and heading towards the shadows.

I jumped when another strange tingle suddenly appeared in my arm. Looking round I saw Olivia, her face a picture of horror, watching the fight below.

"Who is he?" I gasped as the fighting got more and more intense. But before Olivia could answer, a crowd of misty cloaked figures swarmed in from all directions and joined the fray. It was eerie, watching such a vicious fight in complete silence, and with everyone wearing an identical cloak it was impossible to tell what was going on. Suddenly everything became still, and the crowd parted. I could see the greasy-haired Dirge was being dragged away.

All I could hear was the pounding of my own heart. I released my vice-like grip on the railings and slumped back towards the steps, sitting down before my legs gave way. Olivia stayed with me.

"That was Lucas. He's, well, he's really scary. I try to keep out of his way," she finally answered.

"I think he was trying to kill me."

"He's one of the most desperate people here. He'd do *anything* to be gone."

I watched as the dark shapes below became more distinct. Callum and Matthew were deep in a heated discussion, punctuated by gestures towards me. I gulped; it didn't look like my day was about to improve.

"What will they do to him?" I whispered to Olivia as we both watched.

"I'm not really sure. I don't remember anyone needing to be punished before. None of us have anything to take, so there don't tend to be any fights."

I was considering that fact as Matthew and Callum finally stopped talking, and Callum started to make his way up the stairs towards me.

Olivia murmured, "I think I'd better get out of the way," and before I could respond she was gone and Callum was back in her place.

"What was all that about?" I asked.

He sighed, running his free hand through his hair. "Olivia's right, Lucas is desperate. He decided to take a chance, see if he could get you to remove the amulet."

"I nearly did. The noise he made was awful."

He grabbed my free hand with his, and this far up the dome I could feel it quite clearly. "You mustn't, Alex! If you take it off, even for a second, with someone like Lucas around . . . you'll be dead." The pain was etched across his face.

"I know. That's why I called for you. I knew that you wouldn't let that happen." I squeezed his hand and gave him as much of a smile as I could muster.

"The trouble is, what if I don't get there in time? I could try and copy everything like before, but how would we get the amulet back to you so I could download it all again? I mean, seriously, this is bad news." He was shaking his head as he considered the floor.

I didn't know what to say, what to do, to comfort him, so I opted for being generally upbeat. "Well, at least I now know what he might do. It's only noise; he can't actually hurt me. If he tries again I'll just ignore it until you can get there."

"And what if you're driving? Or crossing a road? He could get you killed that way too!"

"Well, that would be pointless, wouldn't it? If he got me killed he could hardly steal my memories, could he? Calm down, Callum, I'm sure it will be OK."

"Matthew doesn't think so."

That stopped me in my tracks. Callum thought the world of Matthew, the Dirges' leader. "Oh, I see. So what does he reckon?"

"He thinks that we need to leave the cathedral now, and think very carefully about whether or not I bring you back. We hadn't realised quite how . . . unpleasant some of our companions could be when they know you're around."

He raised his head and his stunning blue eyes held mine. "I *will* look after you, I promise. No one from here is going to hurt you while I'm around to stop it." His voice was low, urgent, and I couldn't doubt that he meant every word. "I think, though, that we ought to do as he says, and leave now."

I felt disappointment mingle with fear; I had been really looking forward to another opportunity to hold Callum, to touch him and kiss him. I bit back a sigh. His face was strained, the jaw muscles tight, his body still held tense and ready to fight, but he was slightly transparent, and touching him was like touching candyfloss. I realised just how much I wanted to be able to stroke his arm properly, kiss the hollow of his neck, pull his head down towards mine . . . I shook myself to concentrate on the problem in hand. If someone killed me first I'd never be able to work out how to get Callum into my dimension.

"OK, you're the boss," I agreed reluctantly, with a last forlorn glance back at the stairs up to the top. I tried to keep it light-hearted, but I could tell he was still tense. "I guess we should start heading back then. You can protect me while I'm walking to Waterloo station, and I can't get into too much trouble when I'm actually on the train."

Callum nodded glumly, obviously still lost in his thoughts about Lucas. "I suppose not," he said eventually. "I need to talk to Matthew but I daren't leave you alone, not in here. I'll wait till you're safely on the train."

I glanced around the galleries as we made our way down to see if any of the other Dirges were still about, but no one was in sight. Matthew must have been keeping them away, I assumed. I wondered how you threatened someone whose existence was already appalling, who didn't need to eat or drink, who was already trapped for an eternity. What punishment would stop Lucas attacking me again? I shivered as I remembered his face, so full of hate. Callum was right; it was time to go.

We started the long walk back to the station. I had a little pocket map of the area so could see exactly where we needed to go. We walked in silence for a bit, Callum lost in thought again.

"Come on," I said eventually. "Talk to me, Callum."

He grunted non-committally. As we were walking I couldn't see the expression on his face, but I could imagine it only too well. I tried again.

"Tell me what you are thinking. What are we going to do?"

"You've got to stay away from every other Dirge. I'll have to make sure that none of them follow you home, that no one else decides to try to use you as a way out of this existence."

"What about Olivia? Surely she can be trusted? And Matthew?"

"I suppose," he agreed grudgingly. "But I can't see how I can keep you completely safe when I have to spend so much time gathering."

He was right. He couldn't be with me all the time. I felt my shoulders slump as we walked along, then straightened up, not wanting to be defeated. "But, Callum, we can't be scared by how dangerous all this is." I gestured to the amulet on my wrist. "We can't spend our time worrying about the next attack."

"There's always Matthew's idea," he said in a quiet voice as we negotiated the pedestrian-crossing at Ludgate Circus. I was distracted by a stray cyclist who seemed intent on ignoring all the signals, so it wasn't until we reached the other side and started walking up Fleet Street that I processed what he was saying.

"What do you mean? What idea?"

"Throw the amulet away. Hurl it back into the river where it can never hurt you again. If it's off your wrist and far away you're at no more risk from us than anyone else. It's only being close to it that makes it dangerous." His voice had got louder, more vehement.

We had reached a little side road so I walked down it, off the main pavement, which was full of tourists, and into a little oasis of calm. "Listen," I hissed, holding up the phone microphone to my mouth for the benefit of some nosy passers-by. "I've told you before. That's not an option. I'm not going to give you up, whatever the risk!" I turned towards the wall and fished the mirror out of my pocket. He was at my shoulder, looking particularly stubborn. "If you were in my position, would you? Would *you* choose never to see me again, just to keep yourself safe?"

"It's not the same!"

"Of course it is! It's not going to happen, all right? Now can we think of something else?"

"I just want you to be safe. More than anything. I couldn't bear it if you – well, if anything happened to you. Not again . . ." His voice tailed off and I could see his eyes were focused in the distance, remembering. I reached up and tried to stroke his cheek.

"Then help me find a way to make this work! None of you can hurt me physically. I just need to learn to resist if someone like Lucas tries again."

I could see his strong arms folding around me, trying to protect me. I wished it were that simple, but I smiled back as encouragingly as I could. Finally he smiled, but it didn't reach his eyes. His reflection held me tighter and kissed the top of my head. I felt the lightest of touches, then he rested his cheek against my hair, sighing. "You're too stubborn for your own good," he murmured, defeated for now.

I relaxed a little, trying to feel the whisper of his arms, and wishing that we had had the opportunity to meet at the top of the dome where he could really hold me tightly. I took another quick peep at his face and was surprised to see him scanning around as if he was looking for something.

"What's up?" I asked, concerned that maybe the others from St Paul's had been following us.

"This place – I don't like it here. It doesn't feel right."

I turned away from the wall to consider the little side road. At one end was bustling Fleet Street, at the other an old stone gateway. Beyond was a ramp up to an old wooden door, open to show the cool interior of a church. Above was a huge spire. The sun made the white stonework glisten, and it was almost painful to look at after the dark gloom of the narrow pavement. It was beautiful. "I can't see anything wrong." I said. "In fact, it's rather peaceful."

"I don't like it. Come on, let's go."

There was clearly going to be no argument. I put the mirror back in my pocket and turned to walk back up towards the bustle and the noise. Callum was beside me, his fingers lightly brushing mine as we walked along with our amulets together. We went along Fleet Street towards the huge gothic building that held the High Court. Opposite was a long line of banks.

"Oh, Callum, hang on for a moment; I need to take some cash out." One bank had a row of ATMs outside. I got into the shortest queue and was quickly at the front of the line. I put my card in the slot and punched in my PIN and my request for cash. Nothing happened, and then the machine flashed an error message at me. I frowned. It seemed unlikely that there was a problem; they must have made a mistake. I tried again. The same message popped up: *You have insufficient funds for this transaction.* I knew it was wrong; the account held all my money, all the savings for buying my car, all my babysitting takings, everything. I quickly pressed the button to ask for a mini-statement. The machine finally spat out a small piece of paper, then returned my card.

I looked at the statement with a sinking feeling in my stomach. My bank account had been wiped clean.

Bank Robber

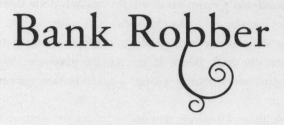

Not a penny was left. I became aware of the queue of people behind me pressing to get to the machine, and at the same time Callum's voice, getting more urgent.

"Alex, what's wrong? What's happened?"

I mumbled an apology to the guy behind me then stumbled to the side of the pavement, out of the way. "It's all gone," I whispered, holding up the mouthpiece. "All my money, everything. Look!" I lifted up the statement as if I was reading it, giving Callum the chance to scan it over my shoulder before I buried my head in my hands. I couldn't believe that my mystery tormentor had found another way to get to me.

From what seemed to be a great distance I could hear a voice in my head, calling me anxiously. "Alex! Can you hear me? We have to keep calm, work this out."

I opened my eyes and found that I was slumped on the steps outside the door to the bank, with my fists pressed against my forehead. "Alex?" The voice was now gentle, with a hint of relief. "Come on, you need to move. You're attracting attention." I lifted my head and looked around. Several people were staring at me, and across the road a women standing next to a policeman was pointing in my direction. I levered myself upright, muttering to the little crowd, "I'm all right, just felt a little dizzy." I took a deep breath and started to walk down the Strand. Callum quickly caught up.

"Are you OK? For a second there you went a bit weird."

"I'm fine. Well, not fine, I guess. This is so unfair!" I couldn't stop the outburst any more than I could stop the tears that suddenly appeared. I walked as quickly as I could, brushing past the dawdling tourists who cluttered the pavements. I dived into the courtyard of Somerset House trying to find somewhere private, but it was full of families enjoying the fountains. I knew that if I went through the building at the end I could get to the river terrace. I couldn't trust myself to speak, and Callum was obviously waiting until I stopped moving. He kept up with me though; I could feel the comforting tingle in my arm. I practically ran through the cool marble entrance hall and out of the door back into the bright sunshine. The river terrace was busy, with most of the tables taken up with people eating sandwiches and poring over maps and guidebooks. But the east end was practically empty. It had no tables and was occupied only by a few kids running around. I walked quickly to the far end, where I could see St Paul's in the distance, towering over the local office blocks.

By then the tears were well on their way, streaming down my face. I reached the stone balustrade and sank down in the corner, pulling my knees in tight, overwhelmed by the problems I was facing. Callum was there, stroking my hair in as soothing a way as he could manage, trying to make me feel better as usual.

I realised I was being unfair. He lived in a world of misery and grief, yet *he* was trying to comfort *me*. I sniffed loudly and tried unsuccessfully to find a tissue in my jeans pocket. "I'm sorry, Callum. I didn't mean to lose it like that." My hand found the mirror so I propped it up on my knee where I could see his face.

His usually sparkling blue eyes were shadowed with concern, a frown creasing his forehead as the gentle breeze ruffled his thick hair. I smiled weakly. "We're a right pair, aren't we?"

"Alex, don't joke. Someone over there really does have it in for you. What if they're dangerous as well as criminal?"

"It's OK," I sniffed. "Come on, we both need to keep a sense of perspective. I'm sorry, I didn't mean to cry. It was just the shock." I tried to keep my voice even as the panic and fear crawled through my stomach again. My breathing was ragged, uneven; I had to calm down.

I fixed my eyes on his, and as I watched the concern on his face I felt my resolve strengthen. I could see that he knew what I was thinking, and I watched as he rested his cheek against mine.

"Are you sure you're OK, Alex?"

I could feel the echo of a touch where his face had pressed mine, and love made me strong. I wiped away the tears.

"Absolutely. We need to find out who is doing this and stop them. I promise not to fall apart if you promise to help me. Deal?"

His tone was dubious, but I felt him gather himself together. "OK then, deal. We fight. I guess we need a bit of a plan." It was his turn to take a deep breath. "So, what do we know? Let's look at what's happened so far and see if we can guess what they might do next."

I nodded. That seemed reasonable. I lifted up my free hand and started to tick things off. "First was the golf ball, then the e-mail with all the personal information about Abbi, and then the stuff with Graham. And now – now they've stolen all the money from my account."

"Right. The broken window has been the most straightforward attack so far, it didn't need any specific knowledge like a password or anything, but, even so, your name was on the note so it wasn't a random thing." He paused for a moment, frowning. "How easy is it to empty a whole bank account? How much money was in there?"

"Nearly two thousand pounds. I've been saving to get a car when I finally pass my test."

"So how was it taken out? Was it transferred into another account, or was it taken out as cash? Can you tell from the statement?"

"Just a sec, I'll check." I rummaged in my pockets until I found the crumpled piece of paper. I smoothed it out over my knee, then held it down so that the gentle breeze blowing along the terrace didn't whisk it away. I looked at the faint lettering. The last transaction had been in Richmond, in the main branch there, but although it gave the date, it didn't say what time or how the money had been taken out.

"Well, it was stolen on Thursday, so not that long ago," Callum said, reading over my shoulder. "Once you talk to the bank you should be able to get some more details. Let's go back in there now, see what we can find out."

"Brilliant!" I said, leaping to my feet and disturbing a small flock of pigeons that had settled on the wall next to us. "Hang on though, it's Saturday afternoon. They won't be open. I'll have to check online when we get home."

I saw Callum peer across my shoulder and down at my watch. "Come on then. If we hurry you can get the next train, otherwise it's a long wait."

I checked my watch. His idea of how quickly I could get to Waterloo and mine were entirely different. "You might be able to go that fast, but my legs don't work like that. I could probably get the bus though." I pulled myself upright and adjusted my earpiece. "See you at the station," I called as I started to run to the bus stop. The tingle went from my wrist and I concentrated on getting to the train on time.

I made it to the platform with just a minute to spare, and grabbed a seat at the back of the train. It was so frustrating to have to sit and do nothing. I scanned through a discarded newspaper, but that didn't take long. In the end I pulled out my phone and scrolled down to the little-used notes function. I might as well spend the time trying to work out who disliked me so much and who also knew all my personal details. But after twenty minutes I shut it down with a sigh. I had a shortlist of girls from school who didn't like me for various reasons, but no one with a particularly vicious grudge. I had no idea who it could be.

When the train finally arrived at my station I practically jogged home. I wished yet again that I was fitter and that I had Callum's speed. Back at the house everyone was out, so I quickly ran up to my bedroom and switched on the computer. The silence in the house was interrupted only by the noise of the odd passing car and the impatient drumming of my fingers on the desk. I was conscious of Callum next to me, but he didn't speak, letting me concentrate on getting logged on. Finally I got to enter the bank details and the screen I wanted opened.

"Are you looking at this, Callum?" I asked as I scanned down the list of transactions to get to the most recent.

"Uh-huh. I'm right here. So what do you—" He stopped abruptly. I got there a fraction after him. The transaction was very clear: at 15.37pm on Thursday, when I was sitting in the police station, the entire balance of my account had been withdrawn as cash.

"So someone walked in there, bold as brass, and took every last penny. How dare they?" I was incensed. Did they know where I was at the time, that there was no chance of them being caught in the act, or was it all a coincidence? How much more about my life were they going to try and ruin? I could feel my eyes prick with tears again, tears of frustration because it felt that there was nothing I could do.

"Alex, I'm so sorry. What can I do to help?"

I pinched the bridge of my nose in an effort to stop the tears, and breathed in sharply. It was pointless getting upset; that would be what they wanted. I had to focus, to think. I looked up at Callum's concerned face. "Talk to me. We need to see if we can thrash this out, find a common thread, *something*! You don't get this level of abuse from your average stalker. There has to be something tying this all together."

As I spoke I could feel his gentle embrace around me, as if he were trying to keep me safe. For a second I longed to be up at the dome, to be feeling the full strength of his arms as he protected me. I wanted to let someone else take charge for a moment, to let someone else make the decisions and face the consequences, and I wanted that person to be Callum. This was just getting too hard for me to bear.

But there *was* no one else who could help; I was going to have to keep going alone, relying only on Callum's support to see me through. "Help me, Callum," I whispered. "Help me to figure this out."

I could see him frown as he stared unseeingly at the mess strewn across my desk. "Well," he said eventually, "this seems to be a straightforward theft, and they *will* have left clues. You need to report it, and quickly. They are bound to have some record, some proof of who took the money out, and we can then see who it is who is doing all this. You might also get the money back given that you do have a cast-iron alibi."

For the first time in hours I felt myself smile; he was absolutely right. I quickly scanned the website for a phone number to call out of hours, then had a lengthy and really frustrating conversation with the bank. They initially refused to believe that it had been nothing to do with me. Apparently the person taking out the money had all the right passwords and security numbers for the account, so there had been no problems in handing all the money over. I wasn't getting anywhere so I told the woman on the phone that I would be calling the police. That didn't worry her as much as I had hoped, so I realised I was going to have to follow through with my threat.

By then I had finally managed to get myself immensely angry about the whole mess, so I demanded a number from her and promised her I would be ringing back. Callum had stayed quiet throughout the conversation, as I couldn't follow two of them at the same time. As I angrily cut her off he was back by my side doing his best to calm me down.

"I think you should talk to your parents about this. I'm sure they'll be able to help – if nothing else they'll be able to shout at the bank for you."

I lifted my head from where I had buried it in my arm on the desk in frustration. "I suppose," I agreed reluctantly. I really hadn't wanted to involve them in any of this, but the situation had gone way beyond my ability to control it.

"They're downstairs now," he added gently. "They got home about five minutes ago."

I knew he was right. I sighed loudly, then quickly took a

printout of the transactions so that I could show them. "You won't go anywhere, will you? You'll stay with me?"

He smiled one of his most devastating smiles. "Of course. I'll be right here."

Downstairs my parents were unloading the shopping.

"Hi, sweetheart. You're back early," said Mum from the depths of one of the kitchen cupboards. "What's wrong?" she added when she stood up and looked at my face. "Has something happened?"

Dad was quickly at my side as I told them about the theft. They fired questions at me and pored over the printout.

"This is getting beyond a joke, Alex," Dad said darkly. "Someone really doesn't like you very much."

"Honestly Dad, I haven't a clue who it could be."

"Well, I'm calling the bank, and then I guess it's probably back to the police station."

I was pleased to have handed some responsibility over to him. He had several really long calls to various people at the bank, and then the police. It was pretty clear that it couldn't have been me, not with the alibi I had, but the bank were very keen to make a formal identification of the person making the transaction, and obviously believed that it would be someone I knew and that I would be able to help.

It all took an incredible amount of time. I finally managed to slip away to the bathroom and talk with Callum. "It looks like this could take the rest of the night, so you might as well go and do your gathering and get back to St Paul's. We can start working on our plan tomorrow."

"Well, if you're sure," he agreed dubiously. "I don't like leaving you but I can't see any way around it."

"I'm sure I'll be fine. It would just be good to know that you'll be here as soon as you can in the morning."

"OK. I know where there's an all-night cinema event tonight anyway, so I can be waiting there first thing, as they all come out." He looked at me apologetically.

"You go ahead and gather wherever you need to, just as long as you are back here with me as soon as you can after I wake up. You have to do what you have to do." I tried to look philosophical about it, and really, I didn't care. I just had to be practical. "I'm going to have to go now – Dad wanted me to be there when he called the police again."

The strong arms in the perfect white shirt tightened around me in the mirror, and I felt the gentle brush of his lips against my hair. "If you're sure? Be careful though. I hate leaving you . . . unprotected."

"Don't worry, I've got Dad on the case at the moment. I'm sure I'll be fine." I tried to smile as reassuringly as I could, but honestly I had no idea what might happen next. From the distance I could hear my mum's voice, calling. "I really have to go now. I'll see you in the morning." I stared into his mesmerising blue eyes. "I love you."

"Good." A tiny smile appeared on his soft lips. "I love you too. Keep yourself safe." With a final kiss he was gone. I splashed some cold water on my face and went back to join my parents.

It was getting late on Saturday evening, and I was fairly sure that my theft wasn't that far up the priority list for the local police. We had a lengthy conversation with the CID officer who had come to the house, taken my statement and then pored over the details of my bank account. He seemed reasonably interested in the case, but

I didn't mention the e-mail; I couldn't see how to do that without landing Abbi in trouble, and it wasn't her fault. He finally left, promising to get back to us as soon as he had spoken with the bank.

We had just sat down to a late dinner when the phone rang. Dad swore gently and went to see who it was. The conversation from his end was mostly "I see," "Yes," and grunts, but little else, then he said in a resigned voice, "Give us half an hour, we'll be there." Mum and I exchanged puzzled glances as he put the phone down and came back to the table.

"That was the police again. Apparently the bank has been testing some new real-time image-capture system from the Richmond branch, which gets streamed directly to head office. There's no need to wait until Monday to look at the CCTV video. They have the pictures right there."

I felt myself go cold. What if I knew whoever it was? What had I done to make them so angry with me? I was suddenly very scared and wished I hadn't suggested to Callum that he leave. But I couldn't let Dad see that. I forced a smile. "Great – so we can see the pictures tonight, can we?"

He looked glumly at the glass of wine that was sitting untouched next to his dinner. "Yup, half an hour. That should give us time to eat this quickly and get down there." He pushed the glass to one side and reached for the jug of water. "I guess that'll have to wait until later too."

My mouth was so dry I struggled to eat the food in front of me, but luckily Mum didn't seem to think that was strange and as soon as it was polite Josh reached over and slid my plate over to his side of the table. Dad sat back, looking at the badly disguised fear on my face.

"Are you OK to do this, sweetheart? We can call them back and say we'll come tomorrow if you would rather."

I tried hard to control myself. "No, Dad, it's fine. I'd much rather know now, and not spend the rest of the weekend worrying about it." I quickly left the table to go and get my bag and paperwork; that way I wouldn't have to look at any of the concerned faces around the table.

The trip to Twickenham Police Station was very quick at that time of the evening, and all too soon we were walking up the familiar steps. After a brief stop in the shabby waiting area our names were called and we were ushered into a small, windowless room with a desk, chairs and a television. The TV was old and grubby, with tape holding on the front panel that hid the buttons. After a few minutes the door opened again and two figures came in. One was the slightly cynical CID officer who had taken my statement earlier; the other was a much younger and more excited-looking guy. He was also in plain clothes, and he was introduced as being from "Technical Liaison". A little yellow light bounced around his head.

"Hi," he said, shaking my hand vigorously. "I'm Oliver. I'm responsible for all the IT round here." He waved his hand about as if he were including the prehistoric TV in his proud domain. I smiled weakly as I tried to surreptitiously wipe my hand down the leg of my jeans. He was very sweaty. "Now," he continued, "this is very exciting. The software is all very new and it's the first time we have been able to use it."

His partner cleared his throat and mumbled, "Get on with it," to him. Oliver flushed slightly but wasn't about to be put off. The yellow aura, which had flickered briefly, returned brighter than before.

"All the images from the bank branch get automatically streamed to the head office in real time, then compressed for storage. So when we have a case like this, all we have to do is give their data centre the details of the branch, the date and time, and bingo! They can find it all. It's so much clearer than the old *Crimewatch*-style footage. No mistaking anyone with this baby!"

All the time he was talking he was fiddling with the remote control, flicking though the channels on the TV. He hesitated briefly over a football match, and both Dad and the officer suddenly sat up and took a bit more notice, but then that too was gone. Finally he stopped at a blank screen. Within a few seconds it flickered and there was a picture of a man standing in front of a bank cashier. The picture was taken from above the cashier, looking straight at the face of the customer. Oliver was right, the picture was crystal clear; I could see every button on his shirt, the details of the comb-over hairstyle and the pattern on his jumper. And I had absolutely no idea who he was.

"I'm afraid I've never seen him before in my life, Officer," I said to the policeman, trying not to sound too relieved that it wasn't someone I knew.

"Oh, that's not them; look at the time stamp," cut in Oliver. "He was a few minutes ahead of the one we want. We just need to wait a moment. . ."

I couldn't help holding my breath. Who was it that hated me so much and knew every detail of my life?

"Fifteen thirty-seven, that's what we are waiting for, that's when the transaction completed," announced Oliver to no one in particular. We were all staring intently at the screen, and as the numbers ticked over the half hour we all unconsciously leaned a little closer. The angle of the camera was quite steep, so until the person actually stepped into position in front of the cashier there was nothing to see except their feet. But the feet behind the unknown man were clearly female. I could feel my heart pounding in my chest and my hands gripped the seat of the chair I was perched on. Finally the man finished his transaction and moved away, and the feet moved forwards.

The girl looked at the cashier and then, slowly and confidently, directly at the camera lens, directly at me. With a level of self-control I had no idea I possessed, I stayed in my seat, not giving anything away while the policemen waited for my reaction. And up on the screen, as if she knew I would be watching, a brief, smug smile flashed across Catherine's face.

Realisation

I didn't get much sleep that night; my mind was racing and I desperately wanted to talk to Callum. Catherine was alive! The implications and the possibilities kept going round in my head, and I could feel a great surge of hope within me. Catherine had made it over to my side, which meant that Callum could too!

But before I could give any time to thinking about that, I had to convince the police and my dad that I didn't know Catherine, that she wasn't some friend I'd fallen out with and that I couldn't just give them a name. It was really hard to hide the excitement that was surging through me. There was a solution! After all we had been through there was an answer. I was questioned for a long time, but it wasn't difficult to keep to my story as I really didn't know anything about her or where she might be.

In the early hours of Sunday morning Dad and I finally got home, and I had some time to myself to try and make sense of it all. But by that point my brain felt really fried; it had been a long and eventful day, with the near-death experience in St Paul's, then losing the money and ending with another trip to the police station. And woven through all of my thoughts was Catherine.

I was woken early the next morning by the strange sensation of the tingle coming and going from my wrist. As soon as I lurched into consciousness, Callum was in my head.

"Are you OK? What happened?" His voice was loud and urgent.

"Umm, I'm fine really, there's nothing wrong. Just give me a second," I mumbled, trying to make my brain work.

"I got here as early as I could," he went on, "and I overheard your parents talking about being at the police station again, and that you were behaving a bit oddly. What was it? What's happened now?"

"I'm fine, honestly, and I do have some news, but I think it would be better if we could talk properly rather than having to whisper all the time. Let me get dressed and we can walk somewhere."

"Sure, if you would rather do that. As long as you're OK – I've been worrying all night, and then when I heard your parents, well, I guess I panicked a bit. Sorry."

I had managed to open the mirror and hold it up so that I could see his face, the rueful smile smoothing out the frown lines. The hope that had been swirling around in my head the night before grew and intensified, and I couldn't help beaming at him. He sat back, shocked.

"Are you sure you're OK?"

"Yes, I'm really all right, and I'm delighted to see you! Now go and loiter somewhere else while I get changed." I couldn't wait to get him outside to talk to him properly.

It was still pretty early so my parents were sitting in bed with their morning coffee. They looked surprised to see me up and dressed quite so soon after such a late night, but seemed to accept the explanation that I couldn't sleep. I offered to walk to the shops to get the papers as that gave me a great excuse to be getting out. I put my earpiece in as I went down the stairs and practically ran out of the house. Callum was with me instantly.

"Well?" he asked as I hurried along the road. "What is it? Why were you at the police station again? Did they find who took your money?"

"Hang on a minute. I really, really want to be sitting down having a proper conversation with you. Let's get to the swings first."

Just round the corner from the house was a small playground with swings and roundabouts. It wasn't used very much and Grace and I often came here as a quiet place to sit and gossip away from interfering brothers and parents. A woman was just strapping a toddler into a pushchair as I arrived, but otherwise it was deserted. As I waited for her to get out of earshot I sat on the top of the roundabout and set up the mirror in front of me so I could see as much of Callum as possible. The wait was obviously getting to him.

"Come on! Tell me! This is doing my head in!"

"Well, I went to the police station last night with Dad because they had a video of the person who stole my money. And now I've seen her, I know she's the same person who has been doing all the other things too."

Callum sat up straighter. "Her? So who was it? Do I know her?"

"Oh, you know her, all right, but I'm not sure you're going to believe me."

"So come on, who was it?"

I took a deep breath. "Catherine."

He looked at me blankly for a moment. "Catherine?"

"Your sister, Catherine. Human, real, in the flesh. Living and breathing and stealing all my money. Smiling as she did it, too."

I watched the shock cross his face, then he shook his head. "You must've been mistaken. Catherine's dead. I saw her explode in a shower of sparks and die."

"I'm *not* mistaken. It was her, and they have her on the video. She looked directly at the camera and smiled, as if she knew that we would see it. She's alive! Don't you see what this means?" I wanted to shake him, to stop him worrying and think about how exciting this all was.

"Catherine's alive?" His voice was barely above a whisper.

"Alive," I agreed, "and obviously out to cause trouble." I could see him frowning again, a shadow crossing his deep-blue eyes as he stared into the distance. A couple of times he looked like he was about to speak, but then stopped himself. I waited for him to come to terms with what I had told him, and eventually he straightened his shoulders and looked at me.

"Catherine is alive." This time it was a statement, not a question.

"Yes, alive and kicking."

"And she's the one who's been making your life miserable." Another statement.

"I guess so," I agreed. "But more importantly, she's escaped being a Dirge and come back to life."

The faraway look was back on Callum's face. "That's what happens when we empty a mind – we get our lives back." His voice was low but excited. "We don't die, as everyone thinks, but we get our lives back!"

"I know – isn't that brilliant! There is a way out of there for you after all – you don't have to spend eternity reliving the misery of death. You can come over here and join me!"

He was glowing, as if the excitement had lit him up from

within. "We can be together after all," he breathed, holding me close in the mirror and kissing my ear. "So Catherine must still have your memories and that's why she knows all the stuff about you."

"I know. I've been trying not to think too much about that bit. I don't like the idea of her knowing all the private details about my life," I admitted.

His mesmerising eyes scanned the horizon again, and the early morning sunshine picked out the gold in his hair. "She'll know everything. Every fact about your life so far."

I gulped as I thought about that. It wasn't just the stuff about my friends, or my bank details, that she knew. Every thought I had ever had about Callum, all my desires and fantasies, all could be in her grasp. I hadn't worked through the implications of that before. "Do you think that's really likely?" I asked, trying not to sound too horrified.

"Well, she took everything from you, so I guess she still has it all."

"That is *so* embarrassing. My every thought – not something I really wanted to share with someone else, especially not Catherine." I paused for a moment. "Mind you, I bet she'll find some of it pretty nauseating – she doesn't feel the same way about you as I do!"

"I'm sure." There was the ghost of a smile on his lips as he considered that and then his face suddenly fell.

"What is it?"

"We're not going to be able to get me over to you any time soon. There's a pretty huge problem to solve first."

"What's another problem? We've solved plenty already."

"I might be able to escape, but I need someone's memories to do it. I'd have to kill someone."

How had I not figured that out? I felt winded; all my excitement suddenly evaporated. Catherine had only succeeded because she had been willing to leave me for dead, and I knew Callum wouldn't want to do that to anyone.

"But, can't we take a copy, like we did before? Is there any way that would work?"

"Not without involving another Dirge, and I can't see too many who would be willing to make the sacrifice of their own memory store to keep you safe, can you?"

I knew the pain he was still in every day from what he had done for me, to keep me alive. And I was pretty sure I only knew about a fraction of it. He loved me too much to let me know the truth. There was no one else who would do that for us. We both sat silently for a moment, him staring into the distance, me considering the scuffed surface of the playground equipment. My mind whirred.

"Callum, I don't know what to say. You know that I'll help in any way I can. Can I give you some of my memories? Can't we make that work?"

He looked at me as if I were mad. "What? Don't be ridiculous!"

"I'm not being ridiculous. I'm just trying to explore all the options."

He pressed the fingers of his free hand into the bridge of his nose and shut his eyes briefly. "Look, I know what you're doing, and I love you for it, but there are no *options*. Don't you understand? Either I kill someone or I stay here!"

I was stunned into silence. What on earth was the matter with him? He was concentrating on the floor, periodically shaking his head. Eventually I gave in. "Callum, are you OK? You don't seem yourself this morning."

"Of course I'm—" he snapped, then bit off his words. "Morning – that's the problem. I've not done enough gathering this morning. I came straight here to make sure you were safe. I can't think straight."

I inwardly heaved a sigh of relief. He had told me before that the amulet needed filling first thing because the memories start to fade away overnight, and I had never seen him this early before. He didn't usually need to gather too much in the morning because he wasn't as miserable as the others, but his preference only to take unimportant memories and happy thoughts made this process much slower. I knew that most mornings he went to stations and found people on stationary trains reading their books, which kept him going until the cinemas opened. "Well, as we now know who is causing all this, I'll be able to watch out while you go and get your breakfast." I gave him the perkiest smile that I could manage.

He shot me a grateful look. "Maybe I will. But in the meantime, we have to be very careful who we tell about this."

"Good point," I agreed, thinking of the potential problems I would face if all the Dirges knew that there was a way to get their lives back. "But can we tell Matthew? Shouldn't he know?"

"Let me think about it. In some ways it might be even crueller to know that there is a way to become real again and that they don't have it."

"But don't you all deserve hope?" I asked, looking down at the amulet with the twisted silver that held the strange blue stone safe in its cage, trying to understand its bizarre but exciting power. "I mean, it just seems wrong to keep it from everyone, that's all."

"I have to keep you safe," he whispered. "I can't allow

anything to happen to you. You saw what happened yesterday, and if they knew that it wasn't oblivion that you offered them, but the chance to live again, well, the temptation may be too much. . ."

I swallowed hard, looking deep into his eyes. They were darker than usual, the gold flecks less obvious despite the early morning sunshine. They were filled with pain. .

"Let's not talk any more about this now; you have more important things to do. Go and get your breakfast and I'll get mine, and then we can talk later. If one of the others happens to find me I'll be safe with the amulet on and I won't say a word."

"If you're sure," he agreed grudgingly. "I won't be long." He kissed the top of my head and was suddenly gone. Sighing, I picked up the mirror and slowly made my way out of the deserted playground.

Back home I divided up the huge Sunday newspaper and took most of it up to Mum and Dad, then settled down in the kitchen with the review section and a large mug of coffee. I flicked idly through the pages, not really expecting anything to distract me from our impossible situation. There was the usual selection of political exposés, celebrity gossip and human interest stories. I skimmed them all briefly until one small story at the bottom of the page caught my eye.

Mystery Amnesia Victim Missing
Police and social services were yesterday winding down the search for the mystery woman pulled from the Thames earlier this month. Able to identify herself only as Catherine, the woman has been under observation in Guy's Hospital since her lucky rescue from the river two weeks ago. She disappeared on Wednesday and could

still be suffering from mental trauma. The authorities are urging the woman to get back in touch and complete her treatment.

I reread the article quickly before sitting back and exhaling gently. The bits of the jigsaw were slotting into place. Catherine and Callum had drowned in the waters of the River Fleet, just where it joined the Thames. It looked like the amulet took the Dirges back to the places where their bodies disappeared, and that would make any rescue attempt even more dangerous. Yet another problem to solve then, before we could even think about trying to get him over.

I could worry about that later though. As I munched on my cereal I considered my immediate problem: I needed to find Catherine, and find out why she was making my life quite so miserable, and that was going to be tricky.

I wished for the thousandth time that Grace knew everything. It felt so wrong to be bottling everything up inside. I hadn't realised how much I relied on her help when I had a problem to solve. I couldn't remember a time when I hadn't asked her advice about something important, but since Callum, well I had been forced to keep everything to myself. Thankfully it had coincided with her starting to go out with Jack and I didn't think that she had noticed anything was wrong. But right then though, some advice would have been really welcome.

I read the article again, then crept silently upstairs to my laptop. There was bound to be some more stuff online about a story like that. The murmuring of voices and the rustle of papers were still evident in my parents' room, so I sneaked past avoiding all the creaky floorboards, and carefully shut my bedroom door behind me. My search of the Internet quickly paid off, and in a few minutes I had a selection of articles about the mystery woman. All seemed to contain the same basic facts, although some had elaborated more than others.

On the day she had taken my memories, Catherine had been spotted in the water of the Thames. She had been extremely lucky; the tide was out and there had been very little rain for the previous week, so the water levels were very low. It was still dangerous though, and it sounded like the lifeboat had only just got there in time. I was skimming another report when the tingle was back in my arm.

"Hi there, gorgeous! I'm sorry about earlier. I really didn't mean to snap at you. Am I forgiven?" Callum's gossamer touch was on my neck and I could see in the mirror that he was looking up at me from under his long lashes as he nuzzled my shoulder.

"Hi," I whispered. "Definitely forgiven. But Mum and Dad are still in their room so I need to be quiet. You should read this." I angled the laptop screen back so that he could see it more easily, and I watched as his frown deepened. Eventually he sat up straight and looked at me.

"Interesting. . . She clearly has some of her own memories too or she wouldn't know her own name, just yours. I wonder how we can use this?"

"Well, I know there's the small detail of getting the memories in the first place, but once we work out a way to do that, as least we know what the amulet does to you. Sounds like it could be a bit dangerous too."

"Yes, that would be ironic wouldn't it? Go to all the trouble to come back to life and promptly drown before anyone can save you." He sighed, then smiled. "I'm just relieved that it's only Catherine and not a random stalker doing all this."

"I know – me too! I'm almost pleased to see her again." I smiled at him as I tucked a stray piece of hair behind my ear.

"I'm not sure I would go quite that far," he murmured as his lips found my hand. "She's still a nasty piece of work."

I found it increasingly difficult to concentrate as he kissed each of my fingers in turn. I could see his soft lips in the mirror and I yearned to be able to touch them again properly. "Is it safe to go back to St Paul's today?" I asked hopefully. I had been really disappointed that the trip the day before had been cut short and longed to feel his arms around me.

Callum pursed his lips as he considered his answer, and I could see the gold flecks flashing deep in his eyes. "I don't think that's such a good idea, not after all the aggro yesterday."

I sighed, but I knew he was right. I never wanted to meet Lucas again. Just thinking about how close I came to taking off the amulet made me shiver. "Lucas seems particularly vicious."

"He's the only one here who knows anything at all about his past life, and I think it's made everything even worse for him."

"Really?" I asked, intrigued. "What does he know?"

"He has a tattoo on his arm that says *Emily*, so he knows that somewhere, someone meant something to him."

"Oh, that must be tough."

"Well, we might be more sympathetic if he was a nicer character, but honestly, he's a really nasty piece of work."

"How long has he been over there with you?"

"Since before Catherine and I appeared. He spends his entire time winding people up, as if it's his mission to make everything even more miserable than it is already. I mean, we don't exactly have friends over here, life's not like that for us, but no one ever, ever chooses to spend time with Lucas." He paused for a second. "But he's the only one who knows anything at all. . ."

"You know about Catherine, that she's your sister; doesn't that count?"

"I don't think it does, because we're both here together. We died in the river at the same time but don't remember anyone else. What Lucas has is proof that someone else existed for him, that he had a wife or girlfriend who he cared about. Maybe knowing what he's lost is why he's so twisted."

I hesitated, thinking of those cruel eyes. "Maybe. Or perhaps he's just a horrible person." I forced myself to smile, and reached for his face. "Good job I have you, eh?" I breathed, letting my fingers wander gently down his jawline. "How long can you stay?"

He peered over my shoulder at my watch. "Not long, unfortunately. I have to go and help Olivia with her gathering. You know I help her most days, but I left too early this morning to do anything useful."

"I really liked Olivia. It's awful that such a young girl is stuck with your terrible life. What can she possibly have done to deserve that?"

"She was very excited about meeting you too, once she got over her nerves. I guess I could still bring her back with me later, if you want me to."

"It would be nice to talk to her." I looked at him as innocently as possible. "She could tell me a little bit more about you!"

"Umm, not so sure that's a good idea. You might go off me once you know all about my bad habits."

"Bad habits?" I raised an eyebrow at him. "What can you possibly have been doing that would count as bad?"

"I guess I'll let Olivia tell you. She'd enjoy that."

"OK, that's a deal then. You go and sort out your gathering, and I'll give some thought to where we can start searching for Catherine. I'll see you with Olivia later. When do you think you'll be back?"

He frowned slightly and his arm snaked back around me. "It could be a while; this afternoon OK?"

"Sure. Can't wait..."

As I watched in the mirror I could see him hesitate, his mouth opening and shutting a couple of times as if he was trying to work out how to say something. The gentle touch on my arm became fractionally stronger. I smiled and raised an eyebrow in a question, and he looked at me almost shyly.

"What is it?" I asked eventually.

"I – I just wanted to apologise. . . again." He was starting to look extremely embarrassed.

"Apologise? What for?"

"For this morning. I'm really sorry; I shouldn't have come here so early. I'm not good at that time of day."

"Oh, that doesn't matter. Don't worry." I couldn't work out why he was getting so wound up about it.

"But I was really horrible. You deserve better than that." His fingers were tracing lines down the length of my hair, from my shoulder to my waist. It was hugely distracting.

"Oh, well . . . that." It was my turn to be embarrassed. "It's not your fault, really."

"Thank you for trying to help anyway. It makes me love you even more."

"I would do anything for you, you know that."

"It's not going to come to that. We'll find some other way of

93

making it work, trust me." He hesitated a moment as he started to gently move my hair to one side, and I could see him stroking my shoulder next to the spaghetti strap of my top. "Now, I probably don't have to leave for another five or ten minutes," he muttered as his head bent down and I felt the briefest of touches as he started kissing my neck.

"Or even quarter of an hour. . ." I whispered, feeling myself melt at his touch.

The morning dragged on after he left, and I even volunteered to help with the gardening to occupy some time. I wasn't used to getting up quite so early at the weekend. I hoped that by making myself useful all morning, I would avoid being called on to help with the dinner. My grandparents were coming over, and that meant the full roast, whatever the weather, and I had other plans for my afternoon.

I was taking a well-deserved break at lunchtime when there was a knock at the door. Outside was our neighbour with her new puppy. The little brown Labrador was leaping all around her, enthusiastically chewing on his lead and planting his big front paws on her knees. "Hi, Lynda," I smiled at her. "Hi, Beesley," I added, stroking the dog's head. He turned to leap up at me, licking my fingers.

"Oh, Alex, I'm glad you're in. I was hoping you could do me a favour."

"Sure, how can I help?"

"Well, there's a bit of a problem at work, and I have to go into the office. I was hoping I could leave Beesley on his own, but he's already chewed through two cushions and a shoe this morning. You know you offered to take him for a few hours...?" She lurched sideways as Beesley saw a bird land on the garage roof and tried to make a break for it. Hauling him back in on his lead she looked up at me apologetically. "It would really help me out. He's still a bit of a handful as he hasn't had many of his obedience classes yet."

I dropped into a crouch and called softly to the puppy. He bounded towards me, his chocolate-brown eyes full of mischief and his tongue lolling out of the side of his mouth. He was gorgeous!

"I'd love to look after him for a while. How long do you need?" As I looked at her Beesley leapt up and started trying to lick my face. "Down, boy, that's enough," I murmured.

"Could you hang on to him until six?"

"No probs. Do I need any of his stuff?"

"I'll run home and get everything now. It's not too much, just his dinner and a couple of toys. And his basket of course." As she was speaking Lynda was already walking down the drive, keen to get away. "I'll be right back."

Mum looked somewhat surprised when I appeared in the garden with Beesley on his lead, and even more surprised when she saw the huge pile of stuff that Lynda had brought back with her. "How long's he staying?" she asked, surveying the basket, which was heaving with toys and blankets and rolls of little plastic bags.

"Well, she said until six," I said dubiously. "But it looks like he's moving in."

"It's more stuff than you need for a baby," Mum added, sorting through the pile. Beesley shot towards her, spotting his bag of treats in her hand. She ruffled his head.

"Hmm, you're not so dumb, are you? After your treats when you've done nothing to deserve them." The little dog gave her a playful nudge. "What are you going to do with him all afternoon? He shouldn't really be left on his own for too long."

"He'll need a walk after lunch; that should take a while." *And give me plenty of time alone*, I added to myself. I wondered what Beesley would make of the Dirges.

In fact, both Beesley and the Dirges took a while getting used to each other. When Callum arrived I was out in the garden, and Beesley was sniffing in the bushes on the end of a very long lead as our fences weren't good enough to let him loose. Beesley went berserk, barking and jumping up towards Callum.

"I see," he said as he reached me. "I've been replaced in your affections already, have I?" Although I couldn't see him I just knew that he was raising his eyebrow at me.

"Well, I wanted someone reliable, you know, someone who would come when I called, that sort of thing," I teased back.

"I think I've been very reliable," he murmured as he started to stroke my neck. "And I'm sure I have some other benefits too. . ."

"Maybe," I agreed grudgingly, hiding a smile and trying not to wriggle too much in full view of the kitchen. "Some, anyway."

"Well, if you can control that mutt for a moment, Olivia's here. She's waiting just outside – I said I'd come and check what you were doing before we both appeared. Shall I go and get her now?"

"It might be easier if we all take the dog for a walk. Then he should be used to both of you by the time we get back." I had to shout the last bit over the noise of barking as Beesley, who had momentarily lost interest in Callum, noticed him again.

I gathered up some toys and plastic bags, then grabbed my phone, pocket mirror and keys as I went through the kitchen and headed out of the front door. "I really must remember to have my phone on me when I'm pretending to talk to you with the earphones," I mumbled, mostly to myself. Luckily Mum hadn't noticed.

Once I was on the driveway I quickly scanned around with the mirror. Olivia was sitting on the bonnet of Dad's car, her hands still in constant motion as she made the links of a chain with her forefingers and thumbs. The repetitive movement gave away her nervousness, and as soon as she saw me she jumped up guiltily. Then she saw Beesley and her face was transformed.

Beesley loped over to her and started to jump up and lick at where her hands would be, barking a greeting. I could see Olivia looking at Callum, presumably asking what she should do. "Stand up straight, put your hand out towards him palm down and slowly lower it. It seems to do the trick for me." I couldn't resist watching although I knew I looked a bit peculiar, standing there holding the mirror. Beesley looked up at Olivia and stood still for a moment, his eyes fixed on her hand. As she lowered it he gave one last bark and was silent.

"Good dog!" I said, quickly walking towards him with a treat and shortening the lead. He wolfed it down, dribbling slightly, and turned to look at me with a happy expression on his face. "Hi, Olivia, let's get to the park and then we can talk a bit more easily. Is that OK?" I caught a quick nod and a smile before I stashed the mirror back in my pocket and we started walking.

It was a strange procession, me talking to the dog and to Callum, Callum talking to me and to Olivia, and Olivia playing with the dog. It was bizarre how quickly I had accepted such weird events in my life. I led them to the field near the playground, which was bordered by a large stream and had a small ford. As kids we had come here regularly to wade in our wellies and try and catch the fish, and I was sure Beesley would love it.

We quickly discovered that Beesley really enjoyed having the Dirges to play with. After a little gentle persuasion, Olivia was more than happy to play with the puppy, running in and out of the ford and letting the dog follow her.

While they were busy Callum and I had the chance to talk briefly. "Have you had any ideas yet? How we can use what we know about Catherine to help you get away from there?" I asked when Olivia was out of earshot.

"I've thought about nothing else," he replied quietly. "You realise that you are in the most terrible danger? If someone like Lucas had any idea, any idea at all, that draining someone of all their memories would bring him back to life, he'd stop at nothing to kill you."

"Look, I know about the danger, and I'm prepared for it. What we need to do is find Catherine and get her to tell us what she knows and why she hates me so much. Maybe that way we'll get some clues to help us get you over."

Callum was silent for a moment. "And we need to stop her hounding you."

"I wonder if she's living round here somewhere."

"I wonder what she remembers," Callum said quietly.

"How do you mean?"

"Well, she obviously has all your memories, and she knows her own name, but did she get back all of her past as well? That's what I'd like to know. If she did, she would know who we both were. . ." His voice tailed off.

"Oh Callum, I'm so sorry, I hadn't thought about that." I reached across and gently stroked his arm, trying to smooth away the pain I could see in his eyes. He looked so downcast, almost defeated and yet again I yearned to be able to comfort him properly. "But don't you think that this is good news? I mean, if she knows who you are, you could find out a bit about yourself and, well, I don't know, maybe that would also give us some clues about what we can do."

He shook his head. "I don't think I could bear knowing anything about my past. It's one thing living this life of endless misery when that's all you know, it would be quite different if you could remember everything you had lost. That would a nightmare. Look at Lucas."

I thought about my own life, my family and friends and how I would feel if I could see them and hear them, but know that they thought I was dead. That would be unbearable. "I'm so sorry," I said again. "What do you think we should do? I mean, we can forget all about Catherine if you want. I'm sure she's not going to be persecuting me for ever."

Callum sighed. "I don't understand why she would be bothering in the first place. I mean, what's she got to gain?"

"I know. You would've thought that she'd have had enough of me by now, given that she has to live with all my memories. In fact," I added, my brain leaping forward a few steps, "if she had any of her own memories why would she bother with me at all? What would be the point? I bet that means that she doesn't have any of her own, or maybe just the ones from life as a Dirge."

Despite my efforts Callum still looked pretty glum. "You could be right," he agreed grudgingly, "but she may just be vindictive. We really can't know until we talk to her."

"Would that be a good idea? Think about it – she really hates me, and you can't talk to her unless I hand over my amulet, and *that's* not going to happen." I couldn't imagine having the cosy three-way communication we had just had with Olivia with

Catherine, and there was absolutely no way I would give her the amulet. I shuddered at the thought.

"We – well, *you* – are going to have to talk to her at some point. If we know more about what happened when she came over it will really help us work out what we can do."

"So that's what we've got to do – track her down and get some answers."

"I guess so, and we need a bit of a plan to do that. How about— Oops, time to change the subject; Olivia is coming back over."

I turned to watch the puppy coming towards us from the stream. He was soaking wet and stopped every few metres to give himself a good shake. The water sprayed out in an arc around him, catching the sunlight. Between each shake he jumped up, wagging his tail and giving a playful bark. Even without looking in the mirror I could imagine Olivia there, jumping up and down in excitement with him. I turned back and looked over my shoulder in the mirror. It was exactly as I had pictured it: Olivia was bounding along with Beesley, her cloak thrown back over her shoulders, her young face flushed and excited. Even though he couldn't hear her, Beesley seemed to be able to see her as well as Callum could. He was jumping up and licking her outstretched palm, making her giggle. The two of them arrived next to us in a flurry of spray.

"I think he likes you," Callum said drily, looking at Olivia. She answered him, and I could see the colour in her cheeks and her shoulders rising as she caught her breath. "I'm sure that won't be a problem. Do you want me to ask?" She nodded and turned towards me, looking a bit embarrassed. I smiled at her as Callum turned his attention back to me. "Olivia would really like it if she could come and play with Beesley again some time. She thinks they get on pretty well."

"Of course. I think that my neighbour would be more than happy for me to volunteer for walking duties any time. We could make it a regular fixture if you like."

Olivia looked like she was about to expire with excitement, bouncing up and down on the spot and linking her thumbs again as if she were trying to keep her hands under control. She nodded violently, then seemed to burst; words I couldn't hear were tumbling out of her, her hands fluttering about and punctuating the speech. I didn't need to hear her talking to know that she was almost overwhelmed with happiness. She positively glowed.

"I think I better let her speak to you," murmured Callum. I saw him move away and guide Olivia to the seat next to me. The unfamiliar tingle in my arm arrived at the same time as the barrage of noise. I could see Callum was smirking behind me as I tried hard not to flinch under the onslaught. Her high-pitched, excited voice was relentless, but her enthusiasm was infectious. Beesley was clearly a high point in her day, and I couldn't help smiling at her. She finally wound herself down and stopped for long enough for me to get a word in.

"I think he likes you too, you know." I gestured towards the dog, who was sitting patiently in front of me, staring intently just to my right. "I've never seen him this well behaved."

"Really? Do you think so? I mean, he was kind of jumpy, but I think I've sorted him out now." The pride was evident in her voice.

"Absolutely. He's not even finished his obedience lessons, so you've done really well."

"Honestly?" She beamed with pride. "Perhaps I had dogs of my own before . . . well, before. You know."

"I know." I tried to squeeze her hand, but didn't seem able to feel her the way I could feel Callum. "It's clear you are a natural, and you'll have to come with me every time I take him for a walk. I'm sure he won't behave as well just with me."

"I can't wait! Will it be tomorrow? What do you think? Will your neighbour let you take him again so soon? Will you call me straightaway? Now that I know the way I won't have to wait for Callum the next time. . ." Her voice carried on, asking more and more questions but not really expecting any answers. It was fabulous to see. Her eyes, which were a chestnut brown, shone with excitement, the gold flecks in them catching the sunlight as she periodically turned to stroke the top of Beesley's head. He clearly liked it, even if he couldn't feel that much.

We stayed in the park for an hour until the puppy was almost too tired to walk back, then Callum suggested that he take Olivia home. She wasn't keen, but I could hear him reminding her that she would need to do some more gathering that evening. Eventually the two of them agreed it was time to leave, and I promised Olivia that I would call her the next time I had the opportunity to take Beesley for a walk.

"Thank you so much!" she enthused as she said goodbye. "It's been the best – the very best – day of my life!"

I smiled at her. "It's been great to meet you properly, and I can't wait until we can do it again. I promise I'll call you."

She beamed back at me, and I could see Callum leaning in to speak to her. She pouted, and with a last "Bye!" her tingle went from my wrist to be replaced by Callum's. I felt myself relax.

"I'll be back in an hour or so, if that's OK. I just need to make sure that she can find her way and that she does enough gathering this evening." His voice fell to a whisper and he glanced quickly at Olivia, but she was bending over Beesley, totally absorbed in trying to scratch his ears. "She's going to have to do a lot more than usual."

"Poor kid. Why is that?"

"If you have a fun day the amulet demands payback, as I found out to my cost when we first met. I have to gather a lot more happy thoughts and memories than I would usually collect. I don't think any of the others have ever really had to worry about that, so she has no idea. I did try explaining it to her this morning but I don't think she was listening."

"I understand. Do what you have to do, and if you have to stay out, well, I'll just see you tomorrow."

"I'm sure I'll be able to make it back. We have to start making our plans to find Catherine."

My face fell. I had been able to forget about her for a while. "Exactly, and before she does something else really horrible to me. I just wish we had a bit of a clue where to start; right now we have no idea where she is or where to find her."

"I know," he agreed, "but we'll talk about it later, OK?" I felt a tickle on my forehead as his lips fluttered against my skin, and they were both gone. Beesley suddenly looked around as if he had just woken up, jumping to his feet and peering around behind me. He barked in a slightly forlorn manner, then sank into an exhausted heap on the grass. I sat and watched him for a while as he panted gently with his long pink tongue hanging out of the side of his mouth. The sunlight was making longer shadows, picking out the clouds of tiny insects hovering above the water, and the bushes rustled with the sound of birds jumping from branch to branch. It was an idyllic scene and I wanted to stay exactly where

I was and not have to worry about Catherine or banks or the police. I just needed Callum here to make it perfect. Making sure I had Beesley's lead tightly wrapped around my wrist I let my eyelids droop and felt myself drift off, finding a world where Callum and I were free to walk hand-in-hand through the fields, throwing sticks for dogs, stopping by the babbling brook where we could lie on the soft grass and...

Within what seemed like seconds I was jolted out of my pleasant doze by a vast rumbling roar that almost made the ground shake. Looking up I saw the outline of one of the huge new double-decker planes lumber overhead, its engines straining as it slowly arced away from nearby Heathrow. "It's a sign, Beesley," I told the curious dog with a sigh. "Time to stop daydreaming and go home."

Murder

Callum reappeared very briefly that evening; Olivia had needed much more help with her gathering, exactly as he had predicted. Our short conversation inevitably revolved around Catherine.

"I think I'm going to have to talk to Matthew," he admitted. "He's really good at thinking through stuff that you or I would never even consider, and he might know something useful. I'll just need to make sure that no one overhears us this time." He smiled ruefully and I remembered the last time he spoke to Matthew about our strange situation, when Catherine overheard and started devising her terrible plan.

"Is that possible? Can you really get away from the others?"

"It *is* possible," he said slowly, thinking about it. "But I'll have to be very careful – and very subtle. Not my strong point, I'm afraid. And it's doubly difficult now that the others know all about you. Every time I do something unusual they assume it's to do with you."

"I'm sure you'll be fine. Perhaps you can get Olivia to help you?"

"It's not really fair to involve her, I think. If the others put pressure on her she'd crumble pretty quickly."

"I guess you're right. Well, you'll work it out – you always do." I gave him an encouraging smile, then sighed contentedly as he wrapped his long, strong arm around my reflection. His face in the mirror looked worried though; the lines on his forehead seemed deeper than before. Yet again my heart ached over the harm I was doing to him. It seemed so unfair that I was inflicting so much pain.

All too soon he had to go, leaving me to fill the rest of my Sunday evening. It was too late to join Grace and Jack and the others down the pub. The two of them seemed to have slipped quite naturally into coupledom, and without Callum to keep me diverted I was sure I would have been just a little jealous of their obvious happiness in each other. Grace's hospitalisation after the Kew Gardens mystery had propelled their relationship forward much more quickly than it might otherwise have done, and that helped to take away some of the guilt I still felt about putting her in such terrible danger. Our friends assumed there would be trouble looming, as none of them believed that I really didn't fancy Jack. Grace was the only one who understood and, as ever, I was grateful that I had her as my best friend.

A dull evening of watching TV with my parents stretched unappetisingly ahead of me. There were some interesting noises coming from Josh's room though, so I went to investigate what he was doing.

"Oh, it's you," he grunted as I peeped around the door after knocking; he was clearly about to shut things down on his laptop. As usual he was sitting on his bed surrounded by a mountain of discarded clothes, the laptop propped up on his knee and his mobile within easy reach. I cleared a small space next to him and threw myself down.

"Hi, don't mind me. Who are you chatting to?"

"Oh, no one important." He was trying to sound casual, but

he was given away by the bright yellow aura dancing above his head. I made a grab for the computer.

"You lying hound! You're chatting someone up! Come on, show me who it is!" We wrestled with the machine for a minute, then he gave in.

"You tell Mum anything you see on there and you're dead meat, OK?"

"Yeah, yeah, I know that. When do I ever tell her your secrets? You know too many of mine."

"I suppose that's true," Josh said grudgingly.

"So who is it? Who's the girl?" I asked impatiently, scanning through all his open browser tabs.

"Cliona," he said sheepishly.

"Cliona! How is she? We've not spoken for – well, years! Is she OK? What's she doing in London?"

Cliona was the daughter of a family friend. She had spent her childhood in Italy and Hong Kong, and when we were little we had been regular pen-friends. But we had got out of the habit and would have lost touch but for the Christmas cards our parents exchanged.

"She's here for some sort of sixth-form exchange, and she has a free evening. We're going for a drink in Richmond tomorrow."

"Cool, I'll be in town too. I'm going to the cinema with Grace, but I can rearrange that. I'd love to see her."

I realised just too late that Josh was going rather pink. "Umm, well. You don't have to, you know. She'll be here a while . . ." he mumbled, avoiding my eyes.

"Josh Walker! Do you have a date with her? Is that why you're being quite so obstructive?"

"Maybe." He still wouldn't look at me.

"You do! You sly thing, you! How long has this been going on?"

"Oh, a little while. We've been e-mailing. She got in touch as soon as she knew that she was going to be in town."

"Great, I'll send her a message then."

There was no response. Under his thick curly hair Josh was clearly about to start sulking. "What?" I demanded. "Can't I even e-mail her? She's my friend too!"

"Gimme a break, won't you?" he said suddenly. "Can't you let me have her to myself for a few hours?"

I sat back, surprised by his outburst. "Of course. I'm sorry, I didn't realise you two had a thing going on."

"Well, we don't, not yet. And we never will if you're there too."

"OK, OK. I won't come near the pub, I promise."

"OK then," he agreed grudgingly. "And promise that you won't e-mail her just yet either?"

"Whatever you want. I'll catch up with her later." I hesitated, but couldn't resist. "Poor girl, she's clearly not been well, looks like the balance of her mind has been terribly affected. . ." I leapt up from the bed and bolted for the door. I managed to get behind it just as the old slipper bounced off it, precisely at head height. Josh was always a good shot.

I slipped back into my room, smiling to myself. I was pleased for Josh, despite my teasing, and I hoped for his sake that the evening went well. I sat back at my desk for a moment, but that just made me miss Callum. And thinking about Callum made me worry about Catherine and whatever she might be planning to do next. Sighing, I went downstairs to make a cup of coffee.

I still didn't want to watch TV with my parents, so I opted

to get some fresh air. I took my drink out into the back garden, where it was still just light enough to see my way. There was a surprising chill in the air for late June, and I hugged my arms around myself as I wandered down to the seat by the vegetable patch. I realised as I got there that the shiver was now a tingle in my arm, and heaved a great sigh of relief; Callum was back after all.

"Hi, I'm so glad you're here. I can't stop thinking about Catherine and her malicious tricks. How did it go with Matthew? What did he say about her being alive?"

There was a strange silence, with just a few muffled noises. As I sat there I realised that the tingle in my arm wasn't quite right. "Who's there?" I called, horrified at what I'd just said. "Which of you is it?"

"I'm sorry, I didn't mean to be nosy, it was just — I so wanted to come back! I had such a good time this afternoon and I didn't want it to stop." Olivia's voice had risen to a squeak.

My heart sank. What had she heard, and what would she make of it? "That's OK, I was just surprised to find that it wasn't Callum." I kept my tone as light as possible. "Did you both have a good gathering session this evening?"

Olivia's voice was still strained. "It was fine. Callum took me to a cinema where they were showing a romantic comedy, you know, the one with the hairdresser."

"Oh, yes, I've heard of it, but I've not seen it. Is it any good?"

"I can't say that I really noticed. The audience seemed to be enjoying it, and that's all I was really interested in."

"Yes, I guess it would be. . ." I tailed off, wondering what I should do next. Carry on, and assume she hadn't heard enough to put two and two together? Or explain in some form or another, despite Callum's reluctance to do so? I was wavering between the alternatives when she spoke again, her voice stronger than before.

"I'm not a child, you know. I mean, yes I was when I came over, but really, with what I have had to put up with for all this time, there's not much child left. You can tell me – I promise I'll keep it secret."

"I'm not sure I quite follow you." I played for time, hoping for inspiration.

"You were talking about Catherine, just now when you thought I was Callum. She's over there, isn't she?"

I hesitated, wondering which option Callum would prefer: to lie or to reveal the truth.

"Please. I deserve to know." The voice was imploring and I was grateful that I didn't have my mirror with me so I couldn't see the pain in those big brown eyes.

"You have to promise me," I said slowly, "to keep this absolutely secret. Tell no one at all what I've told you, not even Callum – let me do that. He thought it would be too painful for you. Are you sure you want to hear?"

There was another muffled sound, then a big sniff. "Cross my heart and hope to – well, die again, I suppose. *Was* it Catherine?"

"Yes. Taking all my memories allowed her to escape and come back alive to the real world. She's been causing me a lot of trouble. She knows everything about me."

There was a brief silence. "So . . . there is a way out of here after all. Maybe I don't have to be stuck in this life for ever." There was more than a hint of wonder in her tone.

"It's true, but it's still really difficult. You need someone over here to be wearing the amulet," I gestured to my wrist, "you need to make sure it's low tide, and you have to be willing to kill."

"Yes, I see. Not to be undertaken lightly then." There was a brief pause. I stared out across the vegetable beds, my eyes slowly adjusting to the dark, and I became aware of the usual arrival of the small animals who liked to be close to any Dirges. Olivia's voice suddenly cut through the silence. "Who is Callum going to kill?"

"He isn't going to kill anyone! It's all so frustrating – we know how we *could* do it, but we need a way to do it without hurting anyone else. That's why we need to talk to Catherine; there might be something else that will work and she might know what that is. We can't just kill someone so we can be together!"

Olivia made a dismissive snorting noise. "Of course you can. Isn't that what you both want?"

"It's a bit more complicated than that, really." I was beginning to appreciate why Callum had been keen to keep our news to ourselves. She was very persistent, and I quickly realised that she didn't miss much.

"What was that about low tide? What does that have to do with anything?"

I sighed inwardly. "After she stole all my memories, Catherine ended up in the river. In the Thames, near to where she went missing. If it hadn't been low tide then she probably would have drowned. As it was, she was lucky that someone saw her floating unconscious in the water and called out the lifeboat. She has spent the last couple of weeks in hospital."

"And why is she tormenting you?" asked Olivia. "What have you done to her?"

"Good question. I don't know, but I've obviously really upset her somehow. She's been playing havoc with my life, pretending to be me, e-mailing my friends, all sorts. She even took all my money out of my bank account."

"She must really hate you," Olivia said with a hint of awe. "She's such a cow, too. You'd better be careful. I . . . I . . ." She suddenly fell silent.

"What is it?" There was no answer and I checked my pockets just in case I had brought the mirror. "Olivia? What is it – what's wrong?"

"I . . . I'm going to have to go. It's getting late and I can't stay here. I've got to get back to St Paul's."

"You won't mention this to anyone, will you?" I asked urgently. "I mean, I'm sure Callum was going to tell you at some point, but he doesn't want everyone knowing just yet. He thinks it might be dangerous."

"Don't worry. Your secret is safe." Her voice seemed suddenly strained. "I'm sorry, it's time. I've got to go."

"I'll see you tomorrow," I called as the tingle abruptly left my arm. I sat back, blinking into the dark garden. "Crap!" I couldn't help exclaiming. How was I going to tell Callum what I had done? There was a brief rustling noise as I spoke, and my eyes locked with a small pair of dark, beady eyes that had emerged from behind the blackcurrants. The hedgehog blinked once, then returned to snuffling about in the dead leaves.

I thought long and hard about trying to avoid telling Callum, but in the end I knew I had to confess. There was no way that I was going to be able to keep something like that from him. I was right too. He had spotted my guilty face immediately. I had called for him in the school field at lunchtime, as I didn't want him to be in the dark for too long. He was going to have to keep an eye on Olivia and make sure she really understood that she couldn't tell anyone.

It had been quite hard to get away from my friends; the common room was constantly full. We were in the last few days of term, so very little actual work was being done. There were also end-of-year activities for most of the clubs, some of which required us to be there as supervisors. Grace and Eloïse had been made prefects, so they were in charge of the library, while Abbi and Alia were busy bossing about the junior art club. I had had a very quick lunch with Mia, who was keen to find out if there was any truth in the rumour that Ashley and Rob had split up over the weekend because of me.

"Honestly," I repeated for about the tenth time, "I know nothing about it, and I care even less. I really don't want to go out with Rob!"

"Well, he tells it differently," replied Mia, biting reflectively into her cheese baguette. Great chunks of tomato slid out of the other end and landed in her lap. "Damn!" she muttered under her breath, picking up the bits and putting them on her plate. She finally looked up from wiping the mayonnaise off her jeans. "He says you two have kissed and made up – he talks about the kissing part quite a lot – and that it's all back on."

"Well, he's a complete lunatic, and you can tell him I said so. I can't stand the guy!" I couldn't work out why Rob kept going on about it. I had made myself perfectly clear at the party.

"Ashley's taken it really badly. I'm not sure she'll be in for the rest of the term."

"That's a bit of an overreaction; she was only going out with him for about a fortnight."

Mia's voice dropped and she leaned in towards me. "Actually, I agree with you, but she won't hear differently. She's determined to be miserable."

"Not my problem," I shrugged as I finished my rather dull salad. "Listen, would you mind covering for me at choir practice? I have to go and call the bank."

"Rather you than me – it sounds like a nightmare. See you at break." Mia gave me a quick smile then started trying to rebuild her sandwich.

"Thanks, I'll catch you in the common room later."

The fields were hot and dusty after a long term of frenetic activity. Great patches of bare earth showed through the grass and in several places the white lines of the running track had been painted directly on to the mud. It was too hot for most of the girls to be outside unless they were sunbathing, so my favourite spot under the big horse-chestnut tree was deserted. When I called Callum he arrived very quickly, and my guilty conscience made me immediately worried that something had already gone wrong.

"Everything OK?" I asked as innocently as I could, trying to gauge from his reflection in the tiny mirror what he knew.

"I *think* so," he replied with a frown. "But there's something weird about Olivia this morning."

"How so? What's she been doing?"

"Well, nothing I can put my finger on, to be honest. She's just acting a bit strangely." He looked down for a moment, shaking his head. "It's almost as if, well, something was really worrying her but she was frightened to say. I wish she would let me help; I hate to see her like this."

He looked up and immediately saw the look on my face. "You know what this is all about, don't you?"

"I do," I confessed, grimacing. "I'm sorry, I had no idea she would be quite so transparent."

"What? What have the two of you done?"

"It was a mistake, honestly. I was sat in the garden last night and I felt a tingle in my arm so I thought you were there and I mentioned something about Catherine. . ." Finally I had to stop to take another breath. "It didn't take Olivia long to put two and two together," I added apologetically.

He sighed. "Damn it! How am I going to keep her quiet? This puts you in even more danger; what if Lucas finds out?" His expression was exasperated, but at least he didn't look furious.

"I'll be fine," I said as soothingly as I could. "I'm in no more danger now than I was before we started worrying about Catherine and her antics. This is staying firmly on my wrist." I nodded towards the amulet, which was glinting in the dappled sunlight, the rich colours flashing as I moved. I couldn't think of any situation that would compel me to take it off.

"I told Matthew, like we agreed," Callum said after a pause. "We were able to go somewhere on our own and I told him everything."

"What did he say?"

"He thought that it would be better to keep quiet about it for now. It'll be the safest thing to do. But he did make an interesting suggestion," Callum said reflectively. "I'm fairly sure that you aren't going to like it though." As I watched he started stroking his chin, looking at me with narrowed eyes.

"Well, you'd better tell me then. It's the only way to find out!"

Callum drew himself up, suddenly serious. "OK, but hear me out before you throw a fit, right?"

"OK, OK, just tell me!"

"Catherine managed to get over there with you by stealing your memories. She left you for dead and she nearly killed Grace as well. Since she's been there, she's done nothing but make your life a misery and she shows no sign of stopping."

"Yes, I know all that. So what?"

"To get me over to you, we need a mind we can wipe clean, but we don't want to hurt anyone, obviously. But what if there was someone who hadn't been so scrupulous herself, who kind of deserved it..."

"You mean, Catherine? Kill Catherine and use her – my – memories to bring you back here?"

Callum nodded. "That's what Matthew suggested. Two birds, one stone."

It was horrific, but the more I thought about it, it did have an appealing symmetry. She tried to kill me to get my memories, so Callum could kill her to get those memories back. An eye for an eye...

A sharp breeze suddenly swept across the sports field, whisking the dust into mini tornadoes as I watched. I shivered, realising that I had, if only for a second, contemplated murdering someone.

I clenched my fists tight. I was appalled with myself for even thinking about it. "We can't do that, Callum. We just can't. It would make us as bad as her." He had been watching me closely, and as I spoke I saw him exhale.

"I know. And I'm glad you feel the same way." He gave me one of his rueful smiles. "Tempting though, isn't it?"

"Hugely." I smiled back, nodding. "But definitely not the right choice for us."

"That wasn't Matthew's only idea. He didn't think either of us would go for that, but he did have another thought."

"OK, I'm listening, as long as this one isn't immoral."

"Don't worry." He was smiling again. "This one could stop Catherine pretty effectively. I quite like it."

I nestled back against him, straining to feel the tiny resistance against my shoulders. "Go on."

"Catherine is human again, has all your memories, and she's using them to make trouble, but – and this is the interesting bit – she doesn't have an amulet. I could stalk her and start picking off those memories as she thinks of them, then she's sunk! She won't be able to make any more plans. What do you think?"

He was grinning at me, eyebrows raised. I took a deep breath. "Callum, that will only wind her up even faster. Can you imagine just how mad she's going to get if she realises what's going on? We would only make things worse." In fact, the more I thought about it, the more I was against the idea. Callum could take the memories only as they actually crossed her mind, so it could take weeks or months, and she was bound to notice the gaps. Actively provoking someone that angry and vicious would be madness.

I could see the truth of what I was saying sinking into him. "No, you're right. Bad plan, especially as I can't actually see the memories when I gather like that. It's an all-or-nothing choice with Catherine. No half measures."

I reached for where his hand was. "I'm sorry," I whispered. "I didn't mean to dismiss all your good ideas, especially when it's so hard. I just can't bring myself to behave like her. I hope you understand."

"Of course I understand, and I didn't really expect you to go for either idea. I thought it was worth mentioning anyway. Am I forgiven?" His feather-light touch was soft on my hair.

"Always. All the ideas are worth discussing, even the terrible ones. If she's so miserable that having all my happy memories doesn't even cheer her up, she's a lost cause. Let's hope she gets bored and finds someone else to persecute."

"Very true." He paused for a moment to stroke my arm just above the heavy silver band. The touch made me sigh. "Gone off me, have you?" he asked in a lighter tone, stroking further up my arm and brushing his lips against my temple.

"Not at all. We just don't seem to have had much time for this sort of thing over the last few days. Far too much drama. . ."

"And there was me thinking that you just didn't care any more."

"Ha! As if. I just wish we were somewhere a bit more private, or even better, at the top of the dome. There are too many prying eyes around here." I was aware of a group of junior schoolgirls heading my way, so I couldn't even try to kiss him back.

"I'm sure I can arrange another bout of maintenance at the dome soon. When did you say term finishes?"

"End of this week. How do you do that anyway – make them shut the dome?"

He nuzzled deeper into my neck. "Trade secret. Couldn't possibly tell you." His voice was muffled.

"Well, it's very impressive, however you manage it. I can't wait!"

"It's one of my many talents," he said drily, raising his head to look at me. I could see my desire mirrored there.

"*Very* many," I murmured, sitting up a bit straighter as the younger girls arrived in the shade. "Hang on a sec." I put on my best sixth-form voice and waved my phone mouthpiece at them. "Hey, private conversation going on here. Find your own tree." They quickly turned and headed off, and I could see them muttering and glancing back in my direction.

"Now, *that's* what I call impressive! Such command."

"It's not so hard when they're only nine," I confessed. "I can't see that working on any of my year."

"I'm sure that you would find some way of getting what you wanted," he said, smiling at me lazily. "You usually seem to manage."

I glanced at my watch. "Damn. One thing I can't change is the timetable – I've got to go back inside. Will you be able to come to the house after school?"

"Sure. Do you want me to bring Olivia?"

"I don't think so. I'm not going to be able to walk the dog as Grace and I are going to the cinema later. You've not managed to put me off seeing films completely just yet."

"That's fine. I'll take her somewhere quiet and I can make sure she knows how important it is to keep her news to herself. What are you going to see?"

I smiled. "We thought that new one about the hairdresser."

Callum's face was a picture. "Really? It's terrible, you know. That actor spends the entire time taking his shirt off."

"We know," I smirked.

He laughed. "You have appalling taste!" Before I could agree he was gone.

Blame

I was really looking forward to my night out with Grace. Over the last few weeks we had both become absorbed in our boyfriends, and had spent rather less time together than usual. Things were going so well between her and Jack that they were planning a trip together during the holidays. She gave me some of the details when she came round to pick me up.

"We're going to drive down to the Gower a couple of weeks after the end of term," she told me when we were in the privacy of my bedroom. She was lounging on the futon chair, her long legs practically touching the door. I stepped over her to get my shoes out of the wardrobe. Thankfully she was too preoccupied to worry about what I was wearing.

"Mmm, lovely. Have you been there before?"

"The Gower? No, all I know about it is what you've told me and the videos from those geography lessons. It's at the bottom of Wales, isn't it?"

"Yes, with one of the largest beaches in Europe. Where are you staying?"

"Jack's godfather has a caravan down there at one of the big campsites by the beach. The picture looks lovely." Her aura danced and glowed a vibrant gold.

"Are you talking about the beach or the caravan?"

I murmured under my breath, smiling. She obviously heard me as one of my soft toys thudded against my shoulder.

"Behave! Jack's godfather will be there too, you know, or Mum would have refused to let me go. It will be so romantic to go walking on the beach. I'm really looking forward to it." She sat back, eyes focused on the distance. I closed the wardrobe door and waited. It took a couple of seconds but she finally looked at me, and then did a double take. "I'm not going out with you wearing that! Not even to the cinema. Get changed immediately."

"I thought you'd never notice," I laughed, taking off the pink hoodie. "You were away with the fairies!"

"I can't help it," she said in a dreamy voice, the yellow light dancing just above her hair. "Jack is so – well, Jack. I can't believe my luck." She paused for a moment and the light suddenly flicked out. "You are OK about all of this, aren't you? I mean, you've been friends for Jack far longer than I have."

"Of course I am," I reassured her, "because that's exactly what he is to me – a friend. Really, gorgeous as he is, I've known him for so long I sort of think him as another brother. I could *never* go out with him."

"Are you sure? Because he is, as you say, quite gorgeous."

"No really, he's absolutely not for me, and he'd tell you the same thing. We've seen each other on camping trips, and we're both a *lot* less gorgeous there, that's for sure. Anyway, you certainly seem to be happy, Grace. Not like Ashley – did you hear the latest?"

"I heard that they'd split up, but no big surprise there. Is there something more exciting?" She sat up straight and started considering me again.

"Apparently Rob's been saying. . ." It got a bit muffled then as Grace started pulling off the T-shirt I was wearing too.

"Have I taught you nothing about clothes?" I heard her mutter as she dived into my wardrobe.

". . . that he's going out with me instead!"

Grace stopped in her tracks. "No! Not after all that garbage a few weeks ago, surely?"

"That's what Mia says, and she should know."

Grace abandoned trying to find anything exotic and uncreased in my wardrobe and handed me a non-contentious top. "Well, what are you going to do about it?"

"I put Mia straight, and hopefully she'll tell Ashley. He's been so cruel to her."

"You're going to have to talk to him."

"I know. I'm just not looking forward to it."

"Tell you what, how about we go to the pub after the film?" Grace had a scheming look in her eye. "I think a bunch of them are due to be there tonight, and if Rob's with them you can tell him how it is in front of all his mates."

"Hmm, I'm not supposed to go to the pub tonight, I promised Josh. He's got a date with an old friend of ours and thinks his baby sister will cramp his style."

"Oh well, it'll wait then. Come on, you look a bit better now. If we don't get a shift on we'll be late and I don't want to miss the opening scene – you know, you've seen the trailers. It's when he gets his shirt ripped off him for the first time, remember?"

Callum was right; the film was terrible, but it was so bad it was funny, and Grace and I roared with laughter at all the wrong places. We were still laughing about it as we made our way out and I checked my mobile. There was a text from Josh: *Interesting development. Come to pub after cinema if you can.*

"Do you mind a quick detour to the pub after all?" I asked Grace.

"Course not. Perhaps we'll see Rob and you can tell him what you think!"

As we arrived at the pub we could see Rob and some of the others sitting near the open terrace windows. Next to him was Ashley.

"Oh no, I'm not going anywhere near them," I hissed at Grace, pulling her arm to stop her marching across the room. "If they've made up again and Ashley sees me here there'll be all sorts of trouble. I could do without another slap."

"It would put a stop to it for good if they can both see that you mean what you say."

"I know, but I really don't want to ruin our night out by getting involved in a slanging match. Because that's what'll happen, you know it will."

Grace pursed her lips as she thought about it. "Fair enough, but you do have to do something about Rob Underwood. And soon." She looked around the bar. "Where's Josh got to, then? Are you sure he's in here?"

"Yes, look, he's over there." In the far corner of the bar was a more secluded area. Josh was sitting there alone, finishing the last of his pint. "Let's go and see what's up."

As we weaved our way through the bar towards him I could see him looking at his watch and then around towards the Ladies; on the table there was another glass, which was half full. "Oops," I said smiling as we reached him. "Are we interrupting? You did say to come over."

"It's all been really weird, actually. You might as well sit down; I think she's gone anyway."

"Cliona? Without saying goodbye?"

Josh took a deep breath and tried to take another swig of his drink before he remembered it was empty. He put the glass carefully down on the table and looked at me. "Yeah, well, here's the thing. It wasn't Cliona. Do you want to tell me what's going on?"

I could feel the hairs on the back of my neck rise. "What do you mean? What's it got to do with me?"

"You tell me. She said it was a joke that you would get. Did you set me up with one of your mates for a laugh?"

"What! Of course not! I'd never do that, not even to you. Who was it, if it wasn't Cliona?"

"I've no idea, but she was a real oddball. Probably too oddball to be one of your friends, actually. You know, it was flattering to start with. She's absolutely gorgeous and she'd gone to a lot of trouble to set this all up, but after a while it got a bit too creepy. I mean, even a gorgeous stalker is still a stalker, right?"

I tried again, forcing myself to stay calm. "So come on, description? What does she look like?"

"Mid-height, long, dark-blonde hair, stunning green eyes. Actually I've never seen eyes like it. She must have had some weird contacts in. Fit as well."

I could feel the blood draining out of my face. "Where is she now? When did she leave?"

"About five minutes ago – just after you came in, now I think about it – she went off to the loo. Either there's a very long queue or she saw you and legged it."

I had been looking around the bar as he spoke, but there was no sign of anyone matching his description. "You two wait here for a second. I'm just going to check the loos." I stood up a bit too quickly and my chair clattered noisily to the floor, making me flinch and momentarily silencing our part of the bar. I picked it up and hurried to the Ladies. What would I say if it *was* Catherine? What on earth was all this about?

As I got to the door to the toilets a large gaggle of girls burst through it, laughing. Catherine wasn't with them. I took a deep breath and walked in, my heart fluttering. The room was deserted. I checked each cubicle, but no one was hiding. Almost disappointed, I headed back to the corridor to return to the bar and felt an unexpected breeze. Down at the end of the passage the fire exit was open. I silently crept up to it and cautiously put my head round the door to look outside, but it was very dark in the alleyway. I stepped through to get a better look but there was no sign of anyone. If it had been her she had disappeared into the night. Sighing gently I turned around to make my way back to the others. The sudden voice cut through the darkness like a knife.

"So," she sneered, "this is your life, is it? Quite pathetic really."

I spun round. Catherine was emerging from the shadows with a smile on her face that didn't reach her eyes. She was even more stunning in the flesh than she had been in the mirror, with her long blonde hair lying in thick folds on her shoulders and her hands resting on her tiny hips. But what was even more stunning was that she was *actually there*, as alive as it was possible to be. I felt my mouth drop in wonder before the anger kicked in. I couldn't decide what to tackle first – the fact that she was a resurrected Dirge or the fact that she was clearly determined to make my life hell. My excitement quickly gave way to fury when I remembered that her most recent act of spite was toying with my unsuspecting brother.

"What do you think you've been playing at?" I demanded, squaring up to her.

Her green eyes were flashing in anger as she folded her arms and regarded me with contempt. "As I said, pathetic. Utterly pathetic."

"Look, whatever I've done to upset you, don't you go dragging my brother into it, or any more of my friends."

Her lip curled. "Those friends are almost even more pathetic than you. Poor Geeky Graham! Do you think he had a nice drive to the convention the other night? And did Abbi have an enjoyable conversation with Miss Harvey?"

"What *is* your problem? What have any of these people done to you?"

"Nothing." She shrugged. "I'm just doing it to get back at you." She looked me up and down. "It seems to be working."

My fingers were clenched into tight fists but I forced them to relax. "Really? If you think that, then you haven't seen me really angry." I smiled as genuine a smile as I could manage.

"Excellent. I was hoping that was the case, because once your friend Grace finds out about all the breathless little love notes that you're about to start sending the lovely Jack, well, then there should be some real fireworks."

I was momentarily speechless with anger, so she took the opportunity to carry on. "And on the subject of Jack, what were you thinking? He's the hottest boy in the year, and you let your best friend have him? I've decided that, once I've finished with the adorable Josh, I'll have a little crack at him." She gestured towards herself. "Am I irresistible or what?"

"Do you seriously think that either of them will fall for your shallow charms?"

"Shallow is what they like, sweetie, don't you know?"

I shut my eyes for a second to try and calm down. "Look,

Catherine, the police know that it was you who stole all my money. I won't tell them where to find you if you leave my friends alone."

"That would be such a generous offer if you actually *knew* where to find me, but you don't, so I don't care."

"Why? Why do you hate me so? You wanted to escape being a Dirge, and now you're here. I made that happen, so why are you doing all this?"

Catherine continued to look at me as if I were something nasty she had trodden in, but I tried again. "Please, Catherine, tell me! What happened when you took my mind? Did you get all your own memories back too? Do you know who you and Callum are?"

"Oh, that's rich, coming from you," she sneered. "Do you know who you and Callum are?" She mimicked my voice.

"What do you mean? I don't understand."

She took a couple of steps towards me, her lips drawing back in a snarl. "Really? Well, perhaps you should! It's been fascinating, this whole regeneration business. The things I've learned! And all your memories for me to consider too; pity they're such rubbish. I'm so very glad I didn't get your personality too. I don't think I could bear to be that . . . perky." She spat out the final word with considerable venom.

"Well, that's hardly my fault. It was you who stole my memories, so it's your tough luck if you don't like them."

"Really? It's time to make you suffer, you unbearable little troublemaker!"

Her cool, casual façade suddenly crumbled and I realised too late that I wasn't safe, that she was utterly, utterly mad. She was standing directly in front of me, fists clenched and naked hatred on her face. I started weighing up my options: fight or run? Or scream for help? I could hear the occasional blast of noise from the pub as people went to and from the toilets, but no one had come to see why the fire door was standing ajar. I swallowed hard, trying to control my breathing. She looked pretty fit, so I wasn't convinced that I would win a fight. In desperation I shouted for the only person she might be wary of. "Callum! Quickly – I need help!" I stared at her defiantly as I could manage. "It'll only take him a few minutes to get here."

She suddenly stepped back, the mask of hatred gone. "I won't need that long. This makes it much more fun; I'm going to tell you something, something that concerns your *boyfriend.*" Catherine suddenly looked maliciously happy. "I might even hang around to watch his lovely little world fall apart."

I was torn. I wanted to get away, to protect myself, but I was also curious. What was she talking about? And what had it got to do with Callum? I knew he would be racing towards us, even though it was getting late and difficult for him to leave St Paul's. But it seemed that Catherine wasn't going to wait until he arrived. "Which secret to tell you? That's the question," she said, as if to herself. "How it is that Dirges can escape, or why I hate you so very, very much?" She pursed her lips while she deliberated. "No, you deserve to know your little part in all this."

The smile remained on her face, and for the first time a small yellow light flicked on above her head. "It's all down to you, all of this is *your* fault," she started, thrusting a pointed finger at me. "You were the one—" Then she abruptly stopped. The yellow light flicked out again at the same instant. "The one who. . ." she began again, but less certainly. Her beautifully manicured fingers pressed hard on her forehead for a moment, then her hands dropped to her sides. There was a moment of silence as she looked at the floor. The face that finally lifted to look at me was filled with pure loathing.

"How dare you do that to me? How *dare* you!" she hissed. "One day you'll come begging to me, begging for knowledge, and I'll remember this. If you think I've been bad so far, just you wait. You have no idea how appalling your life is about to become. And if you shop me to the police, if you tell them *one word*, I'll tell them that you were in on it all." She paused briefly, looking me up and down. "You are going to wish you were dead!" She turned and was gone, leaving me standing alone in the alley.

"What?" I called after her. "What have I done? I don't understand . . ." I felt the darkness suddenly envelop me. This was very, very bad, whatever it was about. I felt completely alone, staring down the alley towards the corner where she had disappeared.

As I finally turned to go there was a quick tingle in my wrist, and Callum's voice was urgent in my head.

"What is it? What's wrong? And what was Olivia doing here?"

"Olivia? I didn't know she was around. She wasn't with me. I've been having a little chat with Catherine."

"Are you OK? She didn't try to hurt you, did she?"

"No, not physically. She was going to tell me why she hated me – and, boy, does she hate me – when she suddenly stopped. She seemed to be delighted to be giving me some sort of bad news; she even had a yellow aura for a moment, but then she went a bit strange."

"By strange, do you mean that she went a bit blank, perhaps?" His voice was controlled, but I could feel the anger.

"Yes," I said hesitantly. "As if she had suddenly forgotten what she was about to say. . ." Finally I put it all together.

"Exactly," Callum agreed grimly. "As if she had forgotten. I bet Olivia sneaked up and took her memory away, whatever it was."

"Oh, no!"

"And Catherine thinks that we did it; that we put her up to it!"

"No wonder she was livid! This is exactly what I didn't want to happen!"

"Look, it's late. I can't be here for much longer. Stay with your friends and I'll go and talk to Olivia, see if she got any clues from the memory about what's going on. I'll come and find you tomorrow, as soon as I can."

"OK, that's fine, but don't be too hard on her, will you? I guess she was trying to save me from whatever Catherine planned to do to me. She won't have meant any harm to us."

"No, I know." His voice sounded strained, exhausted. "I have to go. I'm sorry, but I really can't stay. We'll talk tomorrow."

"I love you. Be careful."

He sighed, exasperated. "It's not me who needs to be careful, it's you. I love you too. See you in the morning." There was a brief waft across my face and I knew he had gone.

"Sorry I was so long," I announced as I sat back down on my chair in the noisy bar. "I had to wait to check she wasn't in one of the cubicles. There was no sign of her, although the back door was open to the alley, so she may well have legged it." Josh and Grace looked equally puzzled.

"It was her, wasn't it? The same woman who's been pretending to be you," asked Grace. I nodded unhappily.

"What!" exploded Josh. "I've been sitting talking to the

woman who stole all your money? You're joking!"

"So what did she want, Josh? What have you been chatting about all evening?" I was grateful to Grace for getting to the point and asking the question I most wanted answered. I felt too stunned to speak.

My brother ran his hands thorough his bushy hair and frowned. "She didn't seem to want anything very much. Clearly the whole conversation was a bit difficult to start with as she had got me here under false pretences. When I asked her why she pretended to be Cliona, she said it was for a joke and that you would understand. She said that the two of you had been to primary school together. I have to say that after a while it began to sound plausible. She knew *all* about you. Everything. And lots about me too. And then she asked *loads* of questions." He shook his head, muttering to himself. "I can't believe that I got taken in by her."

"This is really important – did you tell her anything? Was there anything significant?"

Josh shifted a little in his seat. "Hey, calm down, I can't think of anything that would have counted as *significant*. Most of it was mundane, everyday type of stuff. That's what made it so odd. I mean, who wants to know about how often we get the coach to school or where we walk the neighbour's dog or who puts out the recycling? It's just not interesting. I mean, most of it was almost like she was checking what she already knew, y'know?" He paused to fiddle with his glass. "She did drop in a question about your boyfriend though. I told her you didn't have one, which seemed to make her smile. Is there something I should know?"

Grace and I exchanged quick glances. "No, nothing relevant," I said quickly.

He hadn't missed the look. "Not sure I believe that, but I guess you'll only tell me what you want to anyway."

"It's all a bit complicated, that's all."

"So who is this girl?" he asked. "What's her problem?"

I put my head in my hands as I tried to come up with the best answer. There was no easy way out of it; I didn't want to lie but I couldn't explain. "I honestly don't know. Somehow I've really, really annoyed her, and she's making it her mission to make my life as miserable as possible. She's the person who has been causing all the trouble, hacking into my e-mail, upsetting my friends and stealing all my money. I'm pretty sure it's about to get worse. She told me just now that she's about to start sending Jack love notes from me." I looked unhappily at Grace. "I think she might be completely unhinged..."

The two of them looked at me, open-mouthed. Grace was the first to recover. "We should get the police. I mean, she's a criminal; we should get her arrested."

"I know. I just don't have any idea about who she is and where to find her, so what can I tell the police?"

"It's really weird," said Grace, absently eyeing the glass on the table. "Did she give you any other personal info in the e-mails, Josh? Anything that would help to find her?"

"No, nothing. All I have is an e-mail address."

"Well, she's gone for today; perhaps that will be it. Maybe she's had her fun," I suggested, desperate to get away somewhere where I could sit and think about what Catherine had said. "Come on, it's getting late. We aren't going to learn anything else here. Josh, do you want a lift home? That's OK, isn't it, Grace?"

"Yes, of course." She seemed distracted, but stood up and followed us out on to the street. It wasn't until we were halfway over the bridge towards where we had left the car that she suddenly stopped dead.

"What's the matter?" I asked quickly, paranoid that Catherine was somehow up to her tricks again.

"The glass!" exclaimed Grace, turning back towards the pub. "The glass will have her fingerprints on it!"

I sighed inwardly. How was I going to get out of that one? The last thing I wanted was to spend another three hours in the police station getting questioned; I would never be able to keep my story straight and as soon as they realised I knew her there was going to be all sorts of trouble. "Excellent idea! Let's go back and get it." I tried to put as much enthusiasm in my voice as possible, while hoping that the staff had actually done some table clearing. We raced back towards the pub, Josh running on ahead. By the time Grace and I got there he was having a heated conversation with the barman. I peered over at the table where we had been sitting and was hugely relieved to see that it had been wiped clean.

"It looks like we're too late," I said in what I hoped was a disappointed voice, just as Josh joined us.

"He's a miserable git. He wouldn't even let me look through the empties. I'm sure I could have recognised it."

"Josh, be sensible. It's a half-empty glass in a bar – there will be hundreds of them. I'm afraid we've missed our chance."

"I'm really sorry, Alex, I should have thought of it sooner," said Grace, looking contrite. "I knew there was something that was bugging me, it just didn't come to me quickly enough. We could have solved the whole thing."

"Really, both of you, thanks, but it was a long shot anyway. Let's get home."

"Look! There's a tray of empties on the counter down there," exclaimed Josh. "The barman didn't see those! Just give me a sec." He quickly worked his way through the crowds of people to the far end of the bar and started peering at the large tray of glasses. While we waited, Grace carried on apologising for being too slow and I tried to keep calm, hoping that Josh wasn't going to suddenly appear with a lipstick-stained glass. Suddenly I felt a hand on the small of my back. Glancing over my shoulder I saw Rob, and stepped sideways in shock at how close he was.

"Couldn't leave without saying goodbye, eh?" he said smarmily. "I'm not surprised. You know, you really should reconsider your position. We would make a great team."

I looked over his shoulder. Ashley was still sitting at the table, her back to us. "Nice touch, Rob, trying to chat me up while your girlfriend sits and waits for you. Shall we go over there and continue this conversation? I'm sure she'd love to hear what you are really like."

He shrugged. "She's not important, you know that. It's you I'm interested in." He turned on his most devastating smile and ran his fingers down my cheek, waiting for me to melt.

"Leave me alone!" I hissed, batting his hand away.

"Oh, come on! You didn't complain that time in the car."

"I've just about had it with you, Rob. You deserve a smack in the mouth."

"I know *exactly* where I want to put my mouth," he said in an oily voice, taking another step forward. "Isn't it time you realised that you really did want to kiss me again?"

"You need to learn some manners, Underwood." Josh's deep voice came from behind, and Rob's face fell as he spun round. Rob was tall, but Josh was taller. "She said no."

Rob began to bluster and mutter something, but Josh had had a bad evening. "Oh, what the hell – he deserves it," he said, and punched him hard.

Rob hit the ground like a sack of potatoes.

Club

Mum appeared in the kitchen as I was rummaging in the freezer for ice to put on Josh's hand. "What on earth . . .?" she said. "Have you been fighting?"

"He was defending my honour, actually, Mum. Someone didn't seem to understand the meaning of 'No'."

"Good for you then!" She planted a quick kiss on Josh's mop of curly hair. "Anything broken?" She took his hand and examined it quickly but gently.

"No, just bruised, I think. I was aiming for his stomach but I think I must have caught a rib. He'll certainly know about it, anyway."

"Your dad will want hear all the details when he gets back from Rome. He's not had to defend my honour for decades!" She was remarkably cheerful, and Josh and I stared at her in bewilderment.

"Dad – in a fight?" I couldn't bring that picture to mind.

"Well, not a fight exactly, but it was close, and it was years and years ago now, though. He's very protective, your dad."

Josh and I exchanged glances. "Come on then, spill the beans! What happened?"

Mum smiled enigmatically. "Ask your father. But I can tell you this, if anyone else ever refuses to take no for an answer, your dad would be more than happy to put them straight, just like your brother." She ruffled his hair. "Keep that compress on for half an hour or so. That should sort it out."

"Thanks, Mum," mumbled Josh, clearly still having trouble processing the new information.

"Now, is this fighting going to become a habit? I was about to ask the two of you a favour."

"No, Mum, just a one-off," I said as I sat down next to her at the kitchen table. "What favour?"

"Well, I need to go to Milan for a meeting tomorrow, and as your dad is in Rome, I thought I'd join him afterwards for a few days instead of coming straight back. But frankly I'm a bit worried about leaving you, Alex. I mean, someone impersonating you to steal all your money? It's not your usual mugging, is it? I don't want to go if there's any possibility things might get worse."

Josh and I exchanged a quick glance, and I could tell we'd both had the same thought: the benefit of having the house to ourselves for the rest of the week far outweighed any problems we might have. And luckily Mum didn't know that Catherine had been stalking Josh too.

We both started at once, talking over each other. "No, we'll be fine, don't you worry. . ."

"And it also depends on whether I think you two can look after yourselves for a few days without killing each other, or anybody else." She looked pointedly at Josh.

"Honestly, Mum, I'm not going to punch anyone for a long while – this hurts like hell."

"OK, well, if you're sure. And no parties, either! Remember what happened over the road."

"Yes, Mum," we groaned in unison. Years before, the kids opposite had held a party when their parents were away, and the house had been completely trashed before Dad had realised and called the police. We had been too young to go and had been watching from our bedroom windows when the riot squad arrived. The family moved away not long afterwards. "No parties, we promise."

"Great. Well. I'm off to bed as my flight is first thing. Don't make too much noise coming to bed, will you? I'll see you in the morning before I go."

We sat silently as we listened to her climbing the stairs. "Yesss!" exclaimed Josh in a loud whisper, putting up his hand for a high five, then wincing in pain. "Argh! Wrong hand – I forgot."

We both got up to see Mum off in the morning, having had to convince her all over again that we would be all right, then Josh ambled back to bed. "Have a good day at school," he called from the landing. "I'll probably be up by the time you get home. Probably. . ."

School was not too challenging; the end of term was fast approaching so most of the lessons weren't covering anything new. I was relaxing in the common room during yet another free period when Ashley appeared.

"I thought I told you to keep away from Rob?"

"Now what are you talking about?"

"Last night. You came to the pub."

"I popped in after the cinema to meet my brother, not that it's any of your business. I'm allowed to go to the pub, I think." I couldn't help snapping at her, despite trying to keep calm.

"The same brother who then, completely unprovoked, viciously attacked Rob?"

"Oh, grow up, Ashley. It was just one punch and Rob thoroughly deserved it."

"Really? Well, he will be pressing charges for assault. I thought you'd like to know. No one does that to *my* boyfriend!"

"Boyfriend? I thought you two had split up."

Ashley bristled, but carried on. "I mean it. I'll get the police!"

"If I were you I wouldn't go down that route. You might not like what you find out."

"What do you mean?"

"I mean, there are plenty of witnesses who heard what *your boyfriend* said before Josh floored him, and I don't think that you want to know what it was." Ashley stood there open-mouthed, so I took my chance to throw my books in my bag and get up. "Honestly, Ashley, he's so not worth it." I stalked out of the room before she had time to answer.

I managed a quick conversation with Callum at lunchtime, but as all the upper-sixth girls had finished their exams and left, my year was needed to supervise more and more activities and I didn't have a lot of time. Olivia had been distraught about what had happened, so he didn't want to press her for too much in the way of detail, but it had been clear that Catherine's warped mind was dangerous to touch.

"Olivia had been trying to keep you safe," Callum told me, "and had tried to remove whatever it was from Catherine's mind that had made her angry. But whatever she took, it seems to have scarred the poor kid. I'll keep trying to get the details out of her, but I'm not hopeful."

"I thought you couldn't really tell what is in the memories that you take."

"We can't. It really is just more of a flavour, nothing specific. The only time I've been able to see more detail," he paused and gave me an apologetic half-smile, "is when I was copying all your memories as Catherine drained them out of you. Downloading is completely different to our normal sort of gathering, which really is just a hint of the happy thoughts and memories we are stealing. I'm not sure we'll ever know what was in Catherine's mind at the time."

"It's so frustrating! What on earth can be bugging her that much? What can I have possibly done?"

"I don't know. It beats me too."

"That's not the only thing she said that you need to hear. Just before Olivia turned up, she said something about knowing how to free all the Dirges." I could see the surprise on his face in the tiny mirror. "I've no idea if she was just messing with me. She told me she couldn't decide between letting me know how you could all escape or why she hates me so. Just after that her memory was taken."

"So whatever that was, it's all gone now anyway?"

"I suppose. That's when she went really crazy."

"No wonder Olivia's so devastated; not only has she got Catherine's warped thoughts to deal with, but she knows that what she did, even with the best of intentions, has just made things worse for us. I'm not surprised that she's feeling so bad."

"Poor Olivia, it's really not fair on her." I sighed. "Let's talk more tonight," I said as we walked towards the sports hall. "We need to work out how to find Catherine and at least try to talk to her, maybe get some information out of her? But first, why don't you bring Olivia over and I'll see if I can borrow Beesley. That should cheer her up a bit. I won't be able to be with you all evening though; Grace is coming over."

"OK," he promised, kissing me briefly. "See you later."

Grace was coming round after dinner. She had seemed

a little distracted at school and I hoped everything was all right between her and Jack, because whatever it was she wanted to talk to me about, she clearly didn't want to do it with an audience. I mulled over the possibilities on the way home then headed next door to borrow the puppy.

Beesley was as enthusiastic as ever. He nearly pulled Lynda off her feet as he made a break for the open front door, but I caught him by the collar. His tail was wagging so hard that he knocked over a pot plant on the doorstep. I quickly found myself being dragged down the pavement. It usually only took about five minutes to walk to the golf course, but I tried to get Beesley to stop and sit at every road we crossed, and that took a while. I wanted to get him used to being with me on the path before I called Callum and Olivia. The little stream with the ford that went through the meadow also went through the golf course, but there it was a bit more manicured and controlled. There were still plenty of ducks though, and some rather fat ducklings, looking all punky with their new big feathers sticking up at random intervals.

I kept Beesley on a short lead, otherwise he would have been in the water and chasing every duck he could see. He grumbled a bit at first, but his sunny nature soon won out and within minutes he was gambolling about, jumping at flies and sniffing every tuft of grass he came across. I knew that there was a bench further down the path, so I decided to call the others from there.

It was a beautiful afternoon, and still early enough that the golf course wasn't too busy with the after-work players. It was easy to forget my problems as I wandered along with the puppy. He stopped suddenly at one point and when I looked at him I realised I was going to need one of the little plastic bags that Lynda had given me. I was scooping up the mess, making sure that

I didn't actually touch it, when I was suddenly aware of a strange whooshing noise behind me. I felt a huge, sudden force on my shoulder and above my ear and I realised I was falling sideways. Sparks seemed to explode across the inside of my head and then everything went black.

The pain in my head was staggering, and I couldn't work out why someone was rubbing warm, wet sandpaper over my cheek. The other side of my face was pressed into something sharp. I gingerly opened one eye, but the light was blinding. I carefully moved my hand up to my face, and finally worked out that I was being licked. I tried to get up but slumped back down on the gravel path in defeat. "Beesley? Good boy, stay here," I slurred at him. It was easier to stay where I was.

The ground started to thud rhythmically and I was slowly aware of voices. They were getting louder, like the thudding.

"Alan! Alan – quick, is she breathing?"

"Give me a second to have a look at her. All right, love, don't move. Let's see what the problem is." The voices were kind and I could feel someone deftly checking me out.

"What's the matter with her? Has she fainted?"

"Argh, what happened?" I ventured when I thought I had regained control over my mouth.

"It's OK, just stay still. I'm a doctor. Let me finish examining you," the voice soothed. "Can you tell me your name?"

"Uh, Alex. Alex Walker. Owww! What happened to me?" The pain above my ear was excruciating.

"I'm not sure. We just came over the ridge there and saw you lying on the ground. Do you feel faint now?"

I knew I hadn't fainted. Someone had attacked me from

behind, and I had a pretty good idea of who might have been responsible. My head and arm felt as if they had been whacked with something really, really hard.

"Now, let's see if we can sit you up. Turn over slowly, please." I straightened out my neck and turned my face up towards the sky. I could feel the bits of gravel falling off my cheek, and I was aware of the metallic taste of blood in my mouth. "OK, now let's sit up." The hands were on my neck, checking my spine. I opened my eyes again, and blinked at the bright sunshine. The two golfers had abandoned their clubs on the far fairway, and I could see other people hurrying towards us.

"You must have gone down with a spectacular thump. That's a really nasty graze on your cheek," the guy continued.

"What . . . what happened?" I tried again. "Please, tell me!"

"OK, OK. Here, have this." He pulled the bottle of water from my pocket, uncapped it and handed it to me. The water tasted sweet and cool. I sat up gingerly and poured some in my hands and splashed it over my face, wincing a little as I moved my head. "We were playing over on the next fairway, behind that hill. We were just walking up it to get to the balls when we saw you lying on the ground, the dog licking your face. I've no idea how long you've been unconscious. We really ought to get you properly checked out. You shouldn't just collapse like that."

Two more golfers arrived. Both were very red in the face and looked in more need of the doctor than I did.

"Is everything OK? Has she been mugged?" the older one gasped.

"We're not sure yet. I don't *think* so. What makes you say that?"

"A woman just sprinted past us, looking really suspicious,

and then we saw you all over here. Thought she might have had something to do with it."

"Where did she go?"

"Through the gate back there that heads towards town. She'll be long gone by now."

I tried to keep up with the conversation as it continued, but my concentration was elsewhere. Catherine hadn't waited long before making good on her promise to make my life hell. My head was absolutely pounding and my arm felt really stiff. I knew that I had to convince the doctor that I was OK though. I couldn't afford to involve the police or the hospital again.

"I think the dog pulled me over and I banged my head a little when I hit the ground. I don't think I was unconscious at all, just a bit stunned," I said quickly, hoping to deflect them from all this talk of muggers.

"What else hurts?" the second man asked. "You must have jarred everything when you went down."

I raised my arm carefully, gritting my teeth to stop from crying out, but everything seemed to be moving. I gently tested my elbow and wrist, but they were fine. Beesley was still sitting patiently by my side, tail swishing the gravel. I reached over with my good arm and ruffled his ears. "You're a hopeless guard dog, aren't you? At least you stayed put though, I suppose." He woofed happily in agreement. I turned my attention to the group of men.

The first two were both in their early thirties, I guessed, and dressed quite well for golfers. The other pair were much older. One of them was shaking his mobile phone.

"Can't get a signal down here. I'll just run up to the top of the rise and call the ambulance."

"No! Please, no ambulance, I'll be fine, nothing's broken."

"Look, love, you can't take a bump to the head and not get it looked at. You might have concussion."

I looked up pleadingly at the one who had examined me. "Didn't you say you were a doctor? You can see I'm all right, then."

"Well, yes, I am, but I don't specialise in this sort of injury, not now. You really do need to go to A&E and get an X-ray." He sounded pretty firm, but I wasn't about to spend another day in the hospital.

"I live just over there." I waved vaguely in the direction of the house. "And my family are in. If there is a problem later one of them will be able to take me to the hospital, I promise." As I spoke I searched for a tissue in my pocket to stem the bleeding from my lip where I had bitten it as I fell into the gravel.

"I'm really not sure about that," he said uncertainly.

"Honestly, I'll be OK. I'm pretty robust."

"Well, at least sit still for a moment, and we'll see."

Sighing in relief, I relaxed and pulled Beesley closer. The little dog was bouncing around with excitement, keen to continue with the fun game. I petted him absently, rubbing his ears and trying to stop him jumping up to lick my face again. The doctor continued to regard me with a worried expression. I needed to show them that I was OK, that they didn't need to call the ambulance, so I got gingerly to my feet. I made sure that I used my good arm to lever myself up, biting my lip to stop myself gasping with the pain. As soon as I was back upright I smiled at them all.

"Really, I'm OK, honestly. Please just carry on with your game, there's no need to disrupt your afternoon."

The doctor looked at me dubiously. "I'm still not sure. If you hit your head when you fell you ought to be checked out."

"Truly, I'm fine. As I said, it was the dog. He – umm – he

pulled me over when we were running along and I got all tangled up in the lead, that's all. Hardly any bump to the head. I'll be fine once I get some antiseptic on these cuts." I felt a tiny pang of guilt about blaming Beesley, but he was jumping up so much it seemed like a credible story.

They exchanged glances and the first one shrugged. "Well, you seem all right now. But, please, if you start to feel dizzy at all, call someone and go to the hospital, OK?"

"I will, and thank you for all your help, but I'm feeling much better," I lied with a small smile.

I finally managed to get away, clutching Beesley's lead tightly. I walked as carefully as I could, not letting him run ahead at all. He seemed to know that I wasn't going to take any nonsense, and walked sedately by my side. I left the golf course and went across the road to the little park where the men wouldn't be able to see me, and sank on to the nearest bench. My cheek was really smarting and it was difficult to move my upper arm, but all of that paled into comparison with the throbbing in my head. I was going to have to go home pretty soon to get some painkillers. First though, I needed to call Callum. I wanted to feel his soothing touch and to know that he was around to warn me of any further attacks. "Callum, can you hear me? I'm in the playground."

I sat trying to catch my breath as I waited for him to arrive, not daring to shut my eyes. I had no idea where Catherine had gone, so I couldn't be sure that she wouldn't come back for another go. I just knew it was her, and I realised I should have gone straight home where I would be safe. But I consoled myself with the knowledge that Callum would be able to warn me if she came close again.

"You keep a better eye out next time, you daft dog,"

I scolded Beesley, jiggling his soft ears. Callum was taking his time, I thought, but maybe Olivia slowed him down. I reached into my back pocket for my little mirror, but had to stop. "Oww, that hurts!" I exclaimed out loud, gingerly putting my right arm back down into my lap. I managed to ease the mirror out with my left arm, and finally set it up on my knee. There was no sign of either Callum or Olivia behind me.

"That's a bit strange, don't you think, Beesley?" He looked up hopefully at his name, but then realised I wasn't about to move, so he flopped down with his wet nose on his paws. It had never taken Callum so long to reach me before. I reached for the amulet as I called again. "Callu. . ." My voice failed me as I realised that I couldn't feel the amulet in its usual place.

With a gasp of panic I finally put together what had happened. I wrenched back my sleeve and couldn't help crying out in horror. My amulet was gone, just a tan line and scratches on my skin showing where it used to be. Catherine had stolen my only link to Callum.

Desperation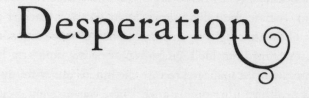

Barely holding myself together, I staggered home. Catherine hadn't been trying to kill me, she had just wanted me unconscious for long enough to be able to steal my amulet. She had taken it and I had no idea of where she might go or how I was ever going to get it back.

I had to stay calm, at least for a little while. I knew that I needed to tidy myself up a bit before I could take Beesley back to his house. Overwhelmed with the excitement of the afternoon he had gone to sleep almost immediately, and I left him snoring gently on the rug in front of the sofa. Up in the bathroom I surveyed the damage. My lip was swollen where my teeth had bitten it as I fell, and there was a huge graze across my cheekbone from the gravel. A lump the size of a small egg was rising just behind my ear, and I was glad I'd kept back some of the ice from treating Josh's hand the night before. I carefully peeled off my shirt and gasped when I saw the bruise that was blooming across my upper arm and shoulder. Bright red, it showed the imprint of a golf-club head where it first hit and then scraped up and off the edge of my shoulder towards my head. If I hadn't been in the process of standing up, her swing would have caught me fully just by my ear, and I was pretty sure I wouldn't have got up again after that. It was excruciating, and I wasn't entirely sure that I believed what I had told the golfers. Something didn't feel quite right, but I was able to move my arm in most directions. I ran a couple of flannels under the cold tap then laid them across it, letting the damp cloth cool the inflamed skin.

All the time I was sorting out the practical details of making myself presentable I forced back the screaming panic that was desperate to escape. I washed my face and changed out of my bloodstained shirt into a soft top with long sleeves and a collar. It was far too warm to wear on a hot summer's day, but it covered up all the bruises. The lump was hidden by my hair. I checked myself in the mirror again. I looked white and strained, and there was no escaping the fact that I had hurt my face. I was just going to have to lie my way out of it.

Downstairs Beesley had moved from the rug to the sofa and was pretending to be asleep. But his furiously wagging tail gave him away and I couldn't bring myself to tell him off. I gathered everything together and clipped on his lead to take him home. I obviously looked worse than I had hoped; Lynda visibly recoiled when she opened the front door.

"My goodness, Alex, whatever's happened? Are you OK?"

"Oh, I'll be fine," I said, trying to look as sheepish as possible. "I was just running with Beesley and he pulled me over. I got my hands all tangled up in the lead so I ended up falling face down. I feel like a complete lemon." I kept my face averted as if I was embarrassed, hoping that she wouldn't ask too much more about it.

"Oh, you poor thing! Have you got some antiseptic to put on those scratches? I'm sure I have some upstairs somewhere."

"No, honestly, don't worry. Mum has an entire cupboard full of first-aid supplies. I swear she could deal with a major incident with all the stuff she insists we need." I smiled at her, trying really hard not to wince as I did so.

"Well, I'm really sorry that your good deed ended so badly." She took Beesley's lead and looked at him sternly. "You mustn't pull people over, Beesley. You nearly did that to me the other day." Luckily he didn't seem to understand that he was getting told off, and jumped up at her, licking her hands and barking happily.

"It absolutely wasn't Beesley's fault, truly. I'd love to come and take him out again if you don't mind."

"If you're sure," she said hesitantly. "Come round whenever you want to."

I smiled again briefly, then bent down to pat the dog's head. Reaching out with my arm was getting more painful, but I managed to bite back a gasp just in time. "See you, Beesley. Bye, Lynda." I turned quickly and walked as carefully as I could down her drive and round to our house. Josh's car was still missing, so I knew that I had the place to myself. I shut the door carefully behind me, and the anger and grief that had been building for the last half an hour finally overwhelmed me. Sinking to my knees I banged my fists on the hall floor, howling. The tears came thick and fast, mingling with the blood that had started to drip from my lip again. Catherine had promised to make my life a misery and she had succeeded. I sat back, holding my knees tight to my chest and let the grief take me.

I lifted my head when I heard the sound of tyres on the gravel outside, and was able to rouse myself just in time to be sitting at the kitchen table when Josh bounced through the door. He was in a good mood, humming a tune as he slammed the front door.

"Anyone in?" he bellowed as he made his way into the kitchen, then stopped dead as he saw me. He was at my side in an instant.

"Alex? What on earth have you done?" He gently moved my hair behind my ear, and I heard the sharp intake of breath as he saw the state of my face. I was torn about what to tell him. He had met Catherine and so knew how malignant she could be, but on the other hand I could just expand on the falling-over story. It would be much quicker and less messy than trying to explain the truth. I had spent the previous hour trying to come to a decision, but now, looking at him, I knew what I had to do: I needed help.

"I was mugged. Out on the golf course when I was walking Beesley."

"But who would do that? And what did they mug you for? What did they take?"

I hesitated for a second, but then went for it. "I think it was the woman from last night – Catherine." As I told him I could see the shock cross his face.

"Your mystery stalker?" I nodded mutely. "But why?" he pressed again.

"She stole my bracelet," I said bleakly, lifting my arm to show him the scratches where she had ripped the amulet from my wrist.

"Are you sure it was her? Did you see her?"

"No. She knocked me out from behind with a golf club and when I came round, the bracelet was gone. Some guys saw a woman running away from the scene, and I can't think of anyone else who would want to hurt me. It has to be her."

"*Are* you hurt?"

"I think I'm OK. I was really lucky that one of the men who found me was a doctor, and he checked me out there and then."

"Don't you think you should get an X-ray? Something could be broken."

"Really, no. I'll be fine. I just need to take some paracetamol and stay quiet for a bit."

"OK, you have a bit of a rest and then we can call the police. This woman has got to be stopped!" He slapped his palm down on the table and the noise made me jump.

"No," I said quietly. "No police. I need to sort this out with her on my own."

He snorted dismissively. "That's ridiculous. This girl is seriously dangerous. She's making your life a misery, she's stolen from you – twice – and now she's nearly killed you. You can't possibly sort it out yourself!"

"No police," I repeated quietly, shaking my head carefully, then wincing as pain shot across my head just behind my eyes.

Josh sat back in his chair and looked at me shrewdly. "Alex, what the hell is going on? What does she know?"

"She knows a lot of stuff about me. A *lot* of stuff. I can't risk her going to the police."

"But—"

"Please," I interrupted. "Believe me. She has information, and lots of it, that would make the police believe that I knew all about the loss of my money. I'll get done for perverting the cause of justice or something."

"*Did* you have anything to do with it?" He peered at me intently.

"No, nothing! Everything is just – just too difficult to explain at the moment. Please believe me," I whispered, trying hard not to cry.

Josh was suddenly out of his chair and pacing up and down the kitchen, the creaky old floorboards protesting as he stomped across them. "She's got a nerve, that woman, coming here and making you so miserable." I turned to watch him but the movement caught me off guard and I cried out in pain before I could stop myself. He was back at the table in an instant, leaning across and looking at me intently. "I think you're wrong; you should be going to the hospital for an X-ray," he said gently. "But I'm not going to make you do that, or go to the police. I wish you'd tell me the truth, though."

"I'm sorry, I would if I could, but it's all a bit too . . . weird. Please just trust me," I pleaded.

"OK, if that's what you want. But I'm going to get on the Web and see what it says about concussion, then at least I can keep an eye on you."

After that he disappeared for a while to do his research and I made myself comfortable on the sofa with some terrible children's TV programme. He reappeared briefly with some ultra-strong painkillers I'd been prescribed when I'd crashed and wrecked my bicycle. Before long I was sound asleep.

I was woken by the smell of burning and some very loud swearing; Josh was trying to cook dinner. I levered myself into an upright position and moved my head from side to side experimentally. It all seemed to work, and the painkillers were still doing their stuff. I could even move my arm without wincing too much. But without the pain of my injuries to distract me, the pain in my heart became much, much harder to bear.

I clenched my fists and took a deep breath. It was not the time to let it go; I had to keep everything under control. Wincing slightly, I made my way to the kitchen where I met a wall of smoke. I looked around and saw half the contents of the fridge spread across the work surface. From the wreckage it looked as if Josh had been attempting bacon and eggs. He glanced up from where he was standing in front of the hob. "Umm, yes, sorry about the mess. I thought I'd do dinner for us both but it's not gone well."

I tried to smile. "Thanks for the thought, Josh, but really, I'm not hungry."

"You have to eat."

"You sound like Mum. Honestly, I'm not even slightly hungry; I think maybe it's the painkillers. I'll probably have some cereal before bedtime." I lifted the lid that was covering the frying pan and wrinkled my nose. "Don't let me stop you, though; this looks delicious."

Josh laughed as he took the blackened mess from me and tipped it into the bin. "Perhaps cereal is a good idea, or maybe beans on toast."

I smiled gratefully at him and slipped away up to my room. I couldn't resist sitting at my desk and peering in the mirror, my hand clenched around my wrist where the amulet should have been. I sat there for ages, hoping that I would see some sort of movement, some indication that he was there, but there was nothing. "Callum?" I whispered forlornly. "Can you hear me? I can't tell if you're there or not, but I'm sure you must be nearby. I want to tell you that I'm going to find Catherine, and fight her if I need to. I *will* get the amulet back!"

A knock on my bedroom door made me jump. I hastily wiped my eyes as I answered. "Come in, Josh."

"It's not Josh, it's me. You said I could come over, remember? I need to talk to you." Grace's voice faltered as she took in the state of my face. I was glad that I was still wearing the long-sleeved shirt so she couldn't see the worst bruises. "Josh told me what's happened. He said it was that girl," she continued, trying not to stare. "The one from last night."

"Well, I didn't actually see her but witnesses saw a woman running off, and I can't see who else would do something like this."

"Alex, you have to go to the police, this has to stop! She's completely mad!"

I looked at Grace, my best friend in the world, and wondered what she would say, what she would do, if I were to tell her the truth. She would be sympathetic, of that I was sure, and supportive. But without the amulet as proof, I realised, she would also be very, very dubious. I had nothing with which I could convince her that I wasn't totally crazy.

"I can't go to the police, and I can't tell you why. It's far too . . . too. . ." I struggled for the right word. "Difficult. I need you to trust me on this." I looked up at her, hoping that she would believe me.

"Alex, I trust you completely, you know that, but I can't sit by and watch you get hurt. She could have killed you – she still could!"

"She has what she wanted." My voice was flat as I tried to keep the emotion down. I held out my empty wrist towards her.

"Your bracelet? What on earth would she want with that? I mean, I know it's beautiful, but why is it worth such violence?"

Grace's voice faded away and she stared at the floor for a moment, then she took a deep breath and looked up. "You have to tell me what's going on, Alex – about Catherine, and about Callum. That's why I wanted to talk to you tonight." She pulled a folded piece of paper from her bag and handed it to me. I took it, momentarily distracted from my problem. It was a page torn from a magazine and my heart sank as I smoothed out the final fold. The face I had told her was Callum's was staring out at me in glossy technicolour. The article alongside explained how the teenager from Leeds had got his first big modelling break. His name was Douglas Day.

I shut my eyes and massaged my temples. Could things get any worse? My traumatised brain was desperately trying to think of an excuse, something that Grace would believe, when she spoke again softly.

"Please don't lie to me again, Alex. Can't I help you?"

I crumpled. It was just too hard, too complicated to keep up the charade with Grace. "I do so want to tell you everything," I admitted, hiccuping between sobs, "but I don't think you're going to believe me and without the bracelet, I've got no proof."

"Try me," she urged, gently lifting my chin and making me look at her. "It's me, remember? You can tell me anything."

The thought of being able to explain, of not having to keep everything secret, was almost overwhelming. I suddenly realised quite how much I hated having to bottle it all up; I wanted her to know, and to understand, everything.

"I don't know where to start," I whispered, shoulders slumping.

Grace's voice became firm. "Well, let's try with Callum. This isn't him, is it?" She pointed to the piece of paper that was lying forgotten on my lap.

"No," I agreed. "It does look a bit like him, though."

"So there *is* a Callum?"

"Yes, definitely. I just can't show you a picture of him, and you were getting insistent, so I thought. . ." My voice petered out, ashamed.

"Why not? Why won't he have his picture taken? What's the matter with him?"

"Look, before I tell you, you must promise me something." I gazed at her through my tears.

"Anything. Just ask."

"You *have* to believe me. Everything I'm about to tell you is the truth, but a lot of it is – well, weird. And I can't prove any of it."

"Try me," she said, with an encouraging but nervous smile as she sat back on the futon. "Tell me everything."

"My bracelet – the one that's been stolen – isn't just a bracelet. It acts as a kind of key, it lets me— Oh, you're never going to believe me. It sounds so ridiculous!"

"Calm down. I promised, didn't I? Come on, just tell me."

I steeled myself with a deep breath. "Callum is a ghost. He drowned in the River Fleet ages ago."

Grace's mouth fell open and she looked at me incredulously for several long seconds. "You see, I said you wouldn't believe me," I muttered.

Finally she recovered herself. "Well, you can hardly blame me; it wasn't exactly what I thought you were going to say, but come on, tell me more. I want to understand." She was trying hard, I could see that, but the fact that her eyes kept darting away from mine gave her away. She thought I was mad.

"OK, look, I know it sounds crazy. It *is* crazy, in a way, and when I first discovered it, I thought I was losing my mind. But it's all for real." Grace's smile was politely encouraging. She was sitting back in her seat, struggling not to cross her arms. How could I convince her?

"Do you remember that trip to St Paul's, the one for the art club?"

"Yes," she said dubiously.

"Do you remember that I said I saw a ghost?"

"I do!" She sat forwards again, wanting to be convinced. "Was that Callum?"

"Yes, that was the first time I saw him, and St Paul's is the only place where I can see him properly."

"What happens the rest of the time?"

"I can see him in any mirror, and I can hear him when his amulet – or bracelet – is in the same space as mine. He has an identical one to the one I have, or rather *had*." My voice caught again as I thought about my loss. "Without the amulet he's . . . nowhere. I can't see him or speak with him."

"So what's Catherine's got to do with all this? Why has she stolen it? What does she know about Callum?"

Where to start? I shut my eyes briefly and tried to work out the best way to tell the story. "Callum isn't your average ghost," I began, trying not to notice the sceptical look that flashed across Grace's face before she composed herself again. I carried on quickly. "Everyone who drowns in the River Fleet gets thrown into some sort of purgatory. There are hundreds of them, and they all wear amulets they can't take off that make them do certain things. There is one amulet that, and I don't understand why, lives on our side, in the real world. Every so often it turns up in the River Thames."

"The bracelet that you dug out of the mud in Twickenham," Grace confirmed, nodding.

"Yes, and whoever finds it makes a connection with one of the Dirges, and that—"

"The what?"

"Oh, Dirges. That's what they call themselves. They live in a state of perpetual despair, so it seems apt."

Grace nodded again, and cupped her chin in her hands as

she rested her elbows on her knees. "OK. I didn't mean to interrupt. Sorry."

"No, it's OK. I know it's strange – more like a horror story, really." I paused for a second, shaking my head. "Where was I? Oh yes, when I picked up the amulet it made a connection with Callum. I had a strange vision that night, and I was going to tell you but you fell asleep. Then we went to St Paul's, and he was actually there! I don't know which of us was more surprised. Once he knew where to find me he would appear behind me in the mirror. The first time was a bit scary – actually it was a *lot* scary – and it took him a few days to work out how to talk to me, but then he did. We've been talking ever since, and we just fell in love." I paused, trying to contain my grief. Grace took my hand and squeezed it gently.

Looking at her gratefully, I carried on. "What I didn't know was that the Dirges can use my amulet to escape from their horrible lives. If someone on this side wears it, and then takes it off but keeps it near them, they can be found by a Dirge, attacked, and all of their memories stolen. And if that happens, you die and they use your memories to escape purgatory. We thought that meant they just died properly, but it turns out that they get the chance to come back to life. Catherine was a Dirge, and she stole all of my memories, nearly killing you in the process."

I could see Grace trying to make sense of all the information. "Is that what happened in Kew Gardens?" she asked, trying to keep the edge of accusation out of her voice.

"Uh-huh. It's a much longer story, but what's important is that Catherine stole all my memories and left me for dead. Callum was able to save me. He copied all my memories as she stole them and the second you put the amulet back on my wrist in the hospital, he was able to download them all back into me. It was a close call."

Grace was considering the carpet, her chin still in her hands. Swallowing nervously, I pressed on. "Catherine is now alive and is using all the memories she stole to do all the stuff with Geeky Graham and Abbi, clear out my bank account, everything. What I don't know is *why* she's doing it, why she hates me so much."

"So that weird accident was all because of her?"

I nodded. "She's determined to cause trouble."

"Have you got a picture of her? From the bank?"

"They were going to e-mail me a still from the video, but I don't know if they've done it yet."

"Can you look now?"

It seemed an odd request, but I quickly opened up my laptop and logged on to my e-mail account. I hadn't been on it all day, so there was a lot of junk, but in the middle was an e-mail from Oliver, the technical guy at the police station. Grace hovered behind me as I opened the attached image. He had captured the moment when Catherine looked up at the camera and gave that hideous smug smile. I heard a gasp from Grace.

"No, it can't be!" She started to pace up and down my small bedroom, shaking her head.

"What is it? Do you recognise her?"

"This really is all true? Everything you've been telling me? Dead people and reflections and stealing memories?"

"Every word, Grace. Have you seen Catherine before?"

The face that turned to me was stricken. "In Kew Gardens. I saw her just before I collapsed. I thought that it was a weird hallucination, so I didn't mention it to you. Are you really telling me that she was *dead* then?"

I nodded mutely.

"And now she's come back to life?" I nodded again.

Grace suddenly sat down on the futon with an uncharacteristic thump. "This is too much." She put her head in her hands.

"I know, I'm sorry, I've just dumped all this on you in one go, and it's a lot to take on board. I had weeks to get used to it. Why don't you just sit there for a minute and I'll make us a cup of tea, or something. For the shock." I was babbling a bit, it was the relief at having got all this stuff off my chest at last. I jumped to my feet, forgetting about my injuries. "Owwww!" Grace looked up in alarm, then her expression turned to one of concern.

"Don't move, Alex. You should keep still. I really need some air so I'll bring us some tea on the way back, OK?"

"OK. Just don't tell Josh anything, will you? He knows it was Catherine who attacked me, but not about the rest of it."

She snorted. "Well, it's hardly the kind of thing I'd suddenly drop into conversation, is it?"

"No, I suppose not." But I was talking to the closing door; Grace had already left the room.

I sat back in my chair and tried to ignore the thumping in my head. My hand moved to my empty wrist. "I gave away your secret, Callum, I hope you don't mind. I just can't do this alone any more; it's too hard."

When Grace reappeared, she was full of questions, so I spent the next hour telling her everything that had happened, with all the details. It was such a relief to be able to talk about it all with someone, and someone who, as far as I could tell, truly believed what I was saying. But it couldn't solve my biggest problem: how to find Catherine and get my amulet back. I also realised that I was physically drained. I was finding it harder and harder to think of the answers to all Grace's questions. Eventually I had to stop her.

"Grace, I'm so pleased to tell you all this at last. You're my best friend, and I've hated keeping secrets from you."

"I just wish I'd mentioned the hallucination sooner, then you wouldn't have had to do everything on your own for so long."

I smiled briefly. "The thing is, I'm exhausted, and I can't think straight. I'm going to have to rest now."

"Oh, Alex, I'm sorry! I've been asking so many questions. How are the bruises?"

"Well, just to add to the mess my face is in, I've got a lump the size of an egg above my ear and some spectacular marks down my arm." I pulled up my sleeve and Grace gave an audible gasp. The red welts had darkened, and there was a visible outline of the club head just below the shoulder.

"Alex, you really should go to the police. You were lucky she didn't kill you."

"I can't, Grace! What am I going to tell them? She knows so much about me that she'd just twist everything and I don't want to risk getting into any more trouble. No, I have to sort this out myself."

"Not completely by yourself, Alex. I'm here, and I'll do whatever I can."

"Are you sure you want to get involved? It's dangerous."

"You need help, and I'm your best friend. That's what best friends do."

"Thanks, Grace, I really, really appreciate it."

"I'm sorry, babe, I shouldn't have stayed so long, you must be in a lot of pain."

I squeezed her hand briefly. "It's been so good to talk to

you at last, but I do have a splitting headache, despite the pills, and I think I need to get to bed." I took a deep breath and looked directly at her. "Don't tell anyone about this, will you?" I gestured with my good arm towards the bruises. "I really don't want to have to explain myself to everyone."

She hesitated for just a fraction of a second before replying. "Sure, whatever you want. You're going to have to tell people something, though; you aren't going to be your usual gorgeous self overnight."

I swivelled around in my chair and looked at myself in the mirror. All the time I had been staring into it before I had been searching for Callum, so I hadn't taken too much notice of my face. The skin was scraped off my cheekbone, and despite my efforts to clean it earlier a few little bits of grit were still sticking to the torn skin. Nothing was bleeding heavily, but it was beginning to seep and my lip had a large scab on it. I picked up a tissue and pressed it gently to my face, gritting my teeth as I did so. When I peeled it off, I could see that a large bruise was forming lower down my cheek. Grace was right: I looked a mess, and I was going to continue to look a mess for a while.

"I look appalling! I'll have to say I'm sick tomorrow and give it time to calm down a bit." A large sigh escaped me before I could catch it, and Grace looked at me sympathetically.

"You're still going to need a cover story," she reminded me gently.

"I told the lady next door that I'd been pulled over by the puppy and got my hands too tangled up in the lead to be able to stop myself falling."

Grace considered that for a moment, pursing her lips and unconsciously highlighting her own perfect cheekbones.

"That'll probably do. You need to make sure that Josh knows the story, too. You don't want him telling your parents what really happened while they're still away. Can you imagine what they'd do?"

"No – well, what I mean is, yes, I can. It wouldn't be good. I'll make sure he keeps schtum."

"Good. OK, I'm going to go now. Call me when you feel up to it and I'll come round; you're going to need some lessons in camouflage make-up." She hugged me tightly, inadvertently squeezing my bruised arm and it took all my strength not to cry out in pain.

"Thanks for coming round, Grace," I finally managed to gasp. "And thank you for listening. I'll see you tomorrow."

I heard her talking briefly to Josh before the front door closed, and I sat back on my bed, my head pounding. Glancing at my watch I realised it was time to take another couple of the strong painkillers, but they still only dulled the pain a little. And that was only the physical pain; the pain and anger in my heart were going to be much harder to shift.

My miserable thoughts were suddenly disturbed by my phone erupting into life. I automatically checked the number before I answered, but it had been withheld. I hesitated for another ring, then pressed the green button.

"Hello?" I said firmly.

The now-familiar voice was crystal clear. "I just wanted to congratulate you on your very nifty manoeuvre this afternoon. I mean, really, you ought to be in intensive care right now."

"And you ought to be in a police cell, Catherine. For attempted murder."

"But there were no witnesses, sweetie. What a shame."

"I don't need witnesses. I have the evidence on my arm where you hit me."

"Do you really think that you're ever going to convince anybody that I was responsible? I don't exactly look like a murderer, do I?"

"Look, I've had enough of playing games. That amulet doesn't belong to you, it belongs to me, and I'm going to get it back."

"And just how are you going to manage that? You don't have any idea where I am. For all you know I could be at the other end of the country by now."

"You're not though, are you? How could you carry on making my life a misery if you were?"

Her tinkling laugh made the skin on the back of my neck crawl. "Oh, you have no idea, absolutely no idea, how much more miserable I can make you, wherever I am. With a bit of luck you'll soon be just as miserable as me."

But before I could ask her what she meant the phone went silent. My heart filled with dread at the warped things she might yet come up with to hurt me. And all the while I couldn't help imagining Callum trying to reason with her, his brow furrowed in a deep frown, his golden hair unruly, his soft lips pressed together in a hard, thin line.

I knew I shouldn't torture myself by thinking about Callum, that the important thing was to be concentrating on how to find Catherine, but I couldn't help myself. I sat at my desk and pulled the mirror towards me, searching every corner of it yet again for a glimpse of him. The ache I felt was gnawing deeper and deeper, and I kept thinking that my wrist was beginning to tingle. But every time I thought it might be OK, that he might have found a way around the problem, that he might be here with me, I realised that I was wrong. I was alone in my room, the silence deafening in my head. Defeated, I laid my head on my desk, trying not to dwell on all the happy conversations we had had in this spot.

Could he hear me, I wondered? Was he watching me right now? I had absolutely no way of knowing. A single tear escaped and ran down my face. I sat up hurriedly, cross with myself. Being maudlin wasn't going to get my amulet back. I needed to work out a plan for how I was going to track Catherine down, and once I found her, I was going to have to get the amulet off her, whatever the consequences. I had never fought anyone before, but I would fight tooth and nail to get back what was mine. I was going to make Catherine regret the day that she had taken my amulet from me.

Dreams

Something wasn't quite right. Richmond was sunny and warm, and everyone seemed to be smiling. I walked across the green, my loose skirt flowing in the breeze. As usual the green was dotted with people enjoying the weather – couples lying intertwined on the grass, mothers with toddlers racing around clutching ice creams, and teenagers gathering together in hordes. Every few minutes a plane roared overhead, but no one took much notice.

I had no plan about where I was going, no destination in mind, I was just walking. As I looked around me I saw a group of familiar faces on the other side of the green, so I veered in that direction. It was a group from my school and the boys' school next door. Someone had clearly been buying doughnuts; the wreckage of the box was on the grass in the middle of the group. As I got there I peered into it hopefully, but there were just a few sugar strands clinging to the edges. I sighed, and threw myself down on the ground with the others. The conversation was going on in a low hum, and I couldn't quite catch any of it, but I wasn't terribly worried. It was lovely lying in the sunshine.

I slowly became conscious that the conversation was changing. It had changed from the low, lazy, background noise to something more charged, as if people were suddenly anticipating something exciting happening. I rolled over and propped myself up on my elbows, looking at what had captured everyone's attention.

Two people were walking together over the grass towards us, but from this distance I couldn't identify them. The sun was behind them so they were in silhouette, but it didn't seem to stop anyone else recognising them. The hum of conversation became much more excited and every face was turned towards them. It was a tall man and a shorter, willowy girl. They didn't seem to be talking.

It wasn't until they were almost on top of us that my eyes were finally able to pick out the familiar features, and I felt my head snap up in shock. Callum was walking towards me, side by side with Catherine. I looked around wildly, but no one seemed to think anything odd was going on. Callum looked gorgeous, with his dark-blonde hair being gently ruffled by the breeze. His penetrating blue eyes fixed on mine. I tried to leap up, to greet him, to hold him tight, but I found my movements were suddenly slow and sluggish. The babble of excited talk finally broke through.

"Catherine! Over here!"

"Catherine, great to see you!"

I looked around wildly at my friends, who were all smiling at Catherine in welcome, gesturing to her to come and sit with them. No one seemed to be taking any notice of Callum. I turned back to look at him and saw his face was serious, stressed. He was staring at me intently, oblivious to everything else that was going on, as if he was willing me to do or say something, something that I didn't understand. I tried once more to get up and to go to him, but I couldn't seem to find the energy to move. The babble of noise around me increased again and I turned to watch Catherine being almost mobbed. They were all so pleased to see her!

I turned back to Callum again. He still hadn't taken his eyes off me, but now his look was urgent, almost pleading.

I tried to speak, to tell him how much I loved him, how

much I missed him already, but the words wouldn't come. I stared at him hopelessly, feeling the tears well up and roll down my cheeks. His mesmerising blue eyes with their flecks of gold flashed briefly in the sunshine, and his hand reached out towards me.

A voice echoed in my head. "Remember, Alex. You must try to remember. . ."

The alarm erupted next to my ear and I woke with a desperate sense of loss and longing, a sob rising in my throat. My face felt cold, and when I touched my cheek I was surprised to find it was damp; I had been crying in my sleep. The dream swirled around inside my head. Callum had been so close! I wished with all my heart that I could go to Richmond and find him walking over the green. If only my life was that simple. I tried to close my eyes and step back into the dream, to be somewhere close to him, but it was already too late. The outside world was pressing on my consciousness, forcing me to remember. The amulet was gone and my mission was to find it again.

As I tried to stretch I realised that I ached all over, and it was almost impossible to move. Even bits of me that I thought had been undamaged were hurting, and when I finally got out of bed and looked at myself in the bathroom mirror I could see bruises all down my side where I had hit the ground. There was no way I was going to make it into school. I rang the secretary's office and left a message, hoping that they wouldn't recognise the voice as being mine, and not my mum's.

I gathered my laptop, my painkillers and a mug of hot milk with honey and made for the sofa, preparing to set up camp for the day. I wasn't expecting Josh to appear much before lunchtime, so I had a few hours to try and fathom where Catherine might be and how I was going to force her to hand back the amulet. That was going to be the difficult bit. Locating her was just a logistical difficulty; persuading her to hand over her only form of defence was going to be much, much harder. I didn't want to resort to violence like she had, although a bit of me felt that it was the least she deserved, but I couldn't think of anything else that would give me leverage with her. I forced myself to stop worrying about that bit. Until I found her it was all academic anyway.

I settled back on the sofa and opened the Internet, waiting for inspiration. While I waited I checked the news, to see if anything exciting had happened in the rest of the world that I had missed. There was nothing that took my interest on the BBC website, so I surfed a bit wider, not really knowing what I was looking for. I was just desperate to keep busy, to not think of the gaping hole that I could feel inside me, but every time I glanced at my empty wrist the pain washed over me again. It hadn't even been twenty-four hours but I missed Callum acutely. Just knowing that I couldn't call him when I needed him, that he wasn't going to suddenly appear with a telltale tingle in my arm, was dreadful. And however hard I tried I couldn't shake off the sense of melancholy that had been with me since I woke up.

I was so wrapped up in my thoughts that I was startled by my mobile ringing, and even more surprised by the caller. "Hello, Ashley," I said, warily.

"I'm *so* not surprised that you're bunking off school today. You must be mortified that everyone has found out your little secret. And I have to say, it explains a lot!"

"What do you mean? What secret?" How could she possibly know anything? I knew that Grace wouldn't have said a word, especially not to her.

Ashley's laugh was brittle. "Have you not been looking at Facebook lately? The things you can learn!"

"Cut the crap, Ashley, and tell me what you're on about."

"It'll be my pleasure. We're all enchanted to learn you have an imaginary boyfriend, which is just *so* sweet, but also just a tiny bit disturbed, given your age." Her tone was hugely condescending.

"What are you talking about? What imaginary boyfriend?" I tried to keep my voice steady as my blood ran cold.

"Callum! Couldn't you have come up with a less ridiculous name?"

I couldn't believe it. I knew that Grace wouldn't have told anyone, so it had to be another of Catherine's cruel tricks. But I just didn't know what to say. If I told her he was real but living abroad I'd have the same problems I'd had with Grace, and I couldn't tell her the truth. I did the only thing possible: "I'm not going to discuss this with you, Ashley," I said and cut her off. Before she could call back to crow some more, I quickly dialled Grace's number, the only one I had committed to memory. She must have been in a class as it went straight to voicemail.

"Grace, it's me. Call me as soon as you can. Just had Ashley on the phone, loving telling me about Callum, my imaginary boyfriend. Do you know what's going on? Please, call soon!"

I slumped back on the cushions, exhausted and drained. I couldn't believe it. Catherine had found yet another way to hurt me, this time using my friends. And still I had no idea why she was doing all of this, and until I found her, I had no way of making her stop. I felt so impotent, so helpless. She could be absolutely anywhere. She had all my money, so she could travel. She probably couldn't leave the country as she wouldn't have a passport, but otherwise she could be on a train to any part of the country, well away from the Dirges and me. I could feel the self-pity creeping up on me again, imagining her face and how pleased she would be to see me lying on the sofa like an invalid.

It was that image that did it. I was doing *exactly* what Catherine wanted, wallowing in grief and misery. I sat up abruptly, wincing at the pain the sudden movement caused. There was no way she was going to win. No way. I was going to find her and I was going to get my amulet back, even if it meant me knocking her out to do it. I limped to the kitchen and threw away the remains of the hot milk. I needed strong coffee.

As I waited for the kettle to boil I decided that I had two distinct problems: finding out where she lived, and finding out what she wanted. She had clearly hated me from the minute that she came over; my troubles had started at exactly the same time that she had gone missing from the hospital. At the pub she had said that she wanted me to suffer, but had given me no idea why. I could only imagine that it was something in my past that she didn't like, some aspect of my life with Callum. Could she be jealous, I wondered. Perhaps she wanted to keep her brother to herself, or safe from the pain that falling for a non-Dirge would inevitably bring? But none of those options made sense, as she didn't seem to care about him at all.

I sighed. I was getting nowhere with motivation. Perhaps I would have more luck with location. I realised with a sinking feeling that I was going to have to log on to Facebook and see what rumours she had been spreading; there might be some clues to her location in the things she had said. I set up my laptop at the kitchen table, opened the French doors to bring in some fresh air, and took a deep breath as I started to scan my Web page. It was even worse than I had feared. There was a huge amount of chatter that morning, mostly among Ashley's little cohort of friends, all of it poking fun at me. I was surprised that so many of them had had the time to do it before school had started.

In the end I gave up reading it; a lot of it was unpleasant, and although there were some efforts by a number of my real friends to try and add a note of reason, they were being shouted down. Instead I focused on trying to find Catherine's comments and started scanning my friends' new contacts.

It was astonishing how many people we were now all connected to, most of whom we didn't really know at all. I didn't check Grace's profile; I didn't think Catherine would risk trying to get close to her. But she would enjoy getting close to Ashley, I knew. What better? Befriending someone who loathed me would suit Catherine down to the ground. I quickly pulled up Ashley's profile page and started looking through all her contacts. And there, halfway down the page, was a likely suspect. Catherine River – the irony of it made my mouth almost twitch in a smile – had started talking to her a few days ago. I opened Catherine's page – she hadn't bothered to hide her profile at all – and sat back in triumph. There was no picture, but the location given was Surrey, and all the activity on her brand-new account was in the last few days. And the further I dug back, I could see that she was the person who had first started the rumours about Callum.

Having got a name I was able to search a bit more thoroughly. I didn't think she would try and carry off multiple names; the risk of mucking it up was far too high. So I searched all the social websites to see what I could learn.

Catherine River had appeared out of nowhere a few days before. She knew which of my friends would accept any old invitation to connect and had targeted them first, and once she was in the circle she had made some chirpy, funny comments and gathered a load more people around her. Her story was that she had been in the area when she was little and had known a lot of the girls at infant school. She had recently moved back and was keen to reconnect with her old friends. She knew more than enough about the school to be convincing, even though none of them would have remembered her name. But what do you really remember in detail from when you were only seven? It was an inspired ploy. And as my friends had been told that they'd known her, Catherine had been welcomed with open arms. And once she had been accepted, she had started dropping her bombshells about my imaginary boyfriend. I couldn't begin to imagine what she might come up with next. I had to find her and stop her.

Her Facebook page said she was in Surrey, but that was bound to be a lie. The only thing I knew for sure was that Catherine knew what I knew. She had the same memories, the same knowledge as I did, so logic would dictate that she would be somewhere where I had been. She seemed to enjoy tormenting me, so that might keep her somewhere local, and if she had the amulet she didn't need protecting from the Dirges; she didn't need to be travelling away. The more I thought about it the more likely she was going to still be around the area somewhere.

I sat back from the table, sipping the coffee and starting to feel the sharp buzz it always gave me. Somewhere local, I reasoned, watching the dust motes float lazily in the sunshine, hoping for inspiration. As I let my thoughts skip randomly a fractured memory crept into the back of my mind. There was something vital, something I had missed, that was nagging at me. I tried to keep relaxed, to let it work its way into my consciousness. I could see Catherine in my mind's eye, her face carefully blank, but I couldn't tell where she was; I just knew it was somewhere really familiar. I sighed in frustration. Better to get on with something else then, and see if the thought sneaked back to me when I wasn't expecting it.

Unfortunately I quickly realised that I wasn't physically up to much that day. The longer I sat still, the worse the aches and pains became, but moving around to loosen up was unbelievably painful. I resigned myself to a day of research and of missing Callum before I went to tackle her. If I was going to have to fight, I was going to need to be able to move.

After a few hours on my laptop my energy began to fade. I wasn't sure what was in the painkillers, but I was feeling incredibly sleepy. All too soon I was back on the sofa and drifting off again.

I woke with a start after an hour or so, full of the same sense of gloom I'd had earlier. At least I hadn't been crying again, I consoled myself. The nagging thought was back though, that I was missing something vital, something really important. I sighed in frustration and thought about moving. I stretched carefully, checking my injuries. They didn't feel *quite* as bad as they had earlier, so I tried a little more, swinging my legs off the sofa and standing up slowly. As long as I moved my head gently, that wasn't too bad either. I decided it was time to take stock of the damage, and shuffled out to the hall where there was a full-length mirror.

I couldn't help the sharp intake of breath as I saw myself. My cheekbone had a dark-purple bloom that was studded with lines of scabs where the gravel had caught me. The edges were just beginning to turn a lovely shade of green. The lump on the other side of my head was still hidden by my hair, but I could feel it every time I opened my mouth. But worst of all was hidden under my T-shirt. I lifted the baggy sleeve and looked in horror at the imprint of the golf club, a hideous, livid, blue-ish colour. I shuddered at the thought that the blow had been intended for my head. She really had aimed to kill.

"Alex! Look at you! We *have* to report this to the police; you can see the golf club really clearly. If Mum and Dad see that. . ." Josh had crept down the stairs without me noticing, and had seen my arm. I hastily pulled the sleeve back down.

"Looks worse than it is, honestly," I smiled at him weakly. "And you promised not to tell them just yet."

"I know, but you can't let her get away with it!" He pulled me towards him in a protective but careful hug. "She has to be taught a lesson."

I patted his arm and drew away. "Thanks, Josh, for being so concerned, but I'll sort it out." I couldn't deal with sympathy. "She'll get what she deserves, I promise you," I added grimly.

"What are you going to do?"

"I'm still working on that," I admitted, "but she'll regret it."

"Well, you be careful. She clearly has no conscience at all. Do you know where to find her?"

"Not right now, but I'm pretty sure I'll be able to track her down." I could see the puzzled look on his face in the mirror as he stood behind me. The thought of Callum standing in exactly that position distracted me for a moment.

"How?" Josh prompted.

"Oh, well, she seems to know some friends from school, so I'm hoping to be able to lean on them for some information."

"I hope you're going to tell them all who did this to you, then she'll see who her friends really are."

"You know, that's not a bad idea," I said slowly. Maybe that was the leverage I could use. If she was keen to have some ready-made friends she would know and care that I could turn them against her in an instant. It all hinged on whether she did actually care though, but it was something. I began to feel a glimmer of hope. "She wouldn't like that at all. And these bruises should be nice and colourful tomorrow."

"That's an understatement," said Josh. "You'll look like a piece of bad modern art by then." He turned me around so that he could look directly at me. "Remember, whatever you do, be careful. Psychopath is too kind a word for this girl."

I shuddered a little as I nodded in agreement. He was right.

"OK, well, as long as that's all sorted, what are you making me for lunch?" His tone was deliberately jovial, trying to help me feel better.

"In your dreams! I'm an invalid. I can't possibly be expected to make a gourmet feast," I replied as lightly as I could manage, trying to match his mood.

"I suppose that means that it's beans on toast again, then," he agreed stoically, turning to the kitchen.

I decided to press home my advantage while I had one. "Perfect. Just bring mine through when it's ready. I'll be having a little lie down." I could see him hesitate in mid-stride, but I knew that he wasn't going to throw something at me, not this time. I even managed a small smile as I carefully made my way back to the comfort of the sofa.

During the afternoon I worried about how Grace was handling things. She had done really well the day before, but I was sure that she was going to have a million more questions.

I texted her to see when she would be free, and she was round almost immediately. I had forgotten that we had very few lessons on a Wednesday and that she would be able to get out early. Within about twenty minutes of getting my text she was knocking on the front door. I'd meant to put some make-up over the more livid of the bruises, but there was no time. She looked grim as she saw my face.

"You look even worse now; I'm not sure that cover stick will do much good," she said, putting her make-up back into her handbag. "It looks more like you need bandages and plasters."

She was still furious that Catherine had taken my bracelet, and annoyed that I had no intention of going to the police. "But she's stolen it from you, Alex. You just can't let her get away with it," she said, sitting on the edge of the sofa, her delicate frame tense. "I mean, you know it was her, why can't you shop her to the police? They'd never believe her if she told them the truth."

"But with the stuff she knows she could easily convince them that I was working with her. I mean, how else would she know all that personal information? And what if she runs off? If the police take her away? I'll never get the amulet back then."

"I suppose," she sighed. "It's just *so* wrong!"

"Tell me about it," I agreed. "She absolutely has to be stopped. So, has much stuff been going round school about me today?"

Grace looked glum. "It's not good. Ashley's really got it in for you, and is gleefully telling everyone who stands still long enough. All our friends are defending you like mad, of course, but we can't get away from the fact that you have been behaving a bit . . . oddly these past few weeks."

"I suppose that's all I can hope for, at least until I get back on my feet and can defend myself. But in the meantime, I need to find Catherine. That has to be my priority. If I can find Catherine I can get my amulet back."

"Well, I can help you with that. I'd like to give her a piece of my mind too." She paused for a second, waiting to get my full attention. "And I have a plan!" She was looking very pleased with herself.

"Really? What is it?"

"Well, she sent me a friend request yesterday. It was waiting for me when I got home and logged on."

"Did you accept it?"

"I wasn't going to at first, but then I wondered if it might be quite useful to have a little route in."

"So? What happened?"

"We ended up having quite a long chat online last night, her telling me where she remembered everyone from, and reminding me that she knows *lots* of details about my past. If I didn't know how she knew it all it would have been too much. Luckily she doesn't seem to have an 'off' button; with encouragement she just kept going."

"And? Where is she? Did you find out?"

"Ah, well, no. I did ask quite a few times but she's pretty slippery and managed to avoid answering. She did, however, agree to meet me in the pub tonight!"

"Really! Oh, Grace, that's brilliant! What're you going to do?"

"Obviously I'm not going on my own. That would be stupid, given what she's capable of. I thought I'd take Jack, if you think it would be OK."

"As long as you can avoid giving him too many details, that sounds like a great plan. Where shall I be?"

"Here, in bed, where you'll be safe. I'm not risking her seeing you. Jack and I can handle her."

"But I want to be there!" I complained.

"If she sees you, she'll be off like a whippet, so that wouldn't help. Anyway, the state you're in, you'd be a total liability. Honestly, Alex, you're moving around like an old woman."

I tested my arms again. She was right; I couldn't make any sudden movements. "OK," I agreed grudgingly. "But what are you going to say to her?"

"First of all we'll demand the amulet back, and then insist that she stops making your life a misery."

"And you expect her to do those things, just like that?" I didn't want to pour cold water on her plans, but it didn't seem that well thought-through.

"Well, she won't be able to hang on to the amulet, not with Jack menacing her." Grace pursed her lips as she considered the problem. "As for the rest of it, at least we can try and work out *why* she's doing all this stuff; that would be a step forwards." She paused for a moment, then said reflectively, "You know, it's almost as if, for whatever weird reason, she's trying to live your life. Your friends, your brother, your bracelet. If we don't stop her, what else of yours is she going to try and steal?"

That was a question I really didn't want to answer.

Thunderstorm

The wait that evening had been terrible; every time my phone buzzed it made me jump, but it wasn't until really late that Grace rang.

"Hi, Alex, sorry, I couldn't ring until after Jack had brought me home – I didn't want him overhearing."

"That's OK." I tried to hide my impatience. "So did she show up?"

"No, not a sniff of her." The disappointment washed over me as Grace continued. "We were there for ages and I kept a really close eye on the door in case she came and went without saying anything, but I didn't see her."

"Oh, well, I guess it was a long shot." I tried to keep my voice cheerful.

"It's infuriating! Jack was itching to get back your bracelet."

As she said the words I suddenly realised the danger I had put them both in, and felt myself go clammy. If Jack *had* got the amulet off her he would have been easy prey for Lucas, if he had been around. "Look, thanks for trying, Grace, but best to leave it now." She started to protest but I cut her off. "Catherine's dangerous, and so is the amulet. I can't risk you two getting hurt."

"Well, there's nothing else I can do at the moment anyway," Grace grumbled. "But I'm not letting her away with it, that's for sure!"

"Maybe you could try to find some more stuff out. She's all over Facebook. Maybe she let something drop to someone else?"

"I suppose. It just doesn't seem very . . . proactive."

"Please, Grace, it really is the best thing you can do at the moment. No one's going to talk to me, are they, not if they all think I'm deluded."

"OK, OK, I'll do that tomorrow, and text you as soon as I find out anything useful."

I switched off the phone and lay back on the pillow in relief. That could have gone so horribly wrong. I was going to have to continue investigating on my own.

The next day, Thursday, was the last full day of term, but as I still felt really stiff I made another call to the school office. I wasn't going to be able to avoid going in on the half-day on Friday as I had to empty my locker, but there was no pressing need to be in before that. I had more urgent things to do.

I spent several hours in the morning scouring the Internet and all Catherine's posts to my friends, trying to find out anything about her. I had no idea where she was living, except for the rather untrustworthy Facebook suggestion of Surrey, but that uncomfortable niggle in the back of my mind kept coming back to me. What had I missed? I decided to write down a list of all the places I had seen her or heard about her, to see what the common themes were. The first time was on the CCTV at the bank, next was in the pub, the golf course – where I didn't actually see her – then there was the plan to join everyone at the end-of-term party, and of course, seeing her on the green. . .

I jerked upright. I hadn't been to Richmond Green, not for weeks, but she had been there in my dream. The niggle at the back of my brain was suddenly bouncing around. Was that what Callum was trying to tell me? "Of course!" I suddenly exclaimed out loud, jumping out of my chair and instantly wincing with pain. Callum could haunt people's dreams; I remembered him asking me if I wanted him to go and annoy Rob that way. Callum had been trying to communicate with me every time I went to sleep. I hugged myself in excitement that he had been so close. I had just never told him that I rarely remembered any of my dreams in any detail.

"Callum? Are you there? I'm sorry it's taken me so long to work this out. You've been in my dreams, haven't you? You've been telling me where Catherine is, but I keep forgetting the important bits." I looked around, but of course could see nothing. "Thank you. I miss you so much. I hope you are listening. I love you, Callum, I'll work it out, I promise."

I sat back down and looked at my list. She had to be in Richmond. Almost everything related to Richmond in some way or another. I would start my search there, trawling through all the places that I – and therefore Catherine – knew. I sat back, pleased with myself. It wasn't much of a plan, but it was something, and it made me feel like I was doing my bit to get Callum back. I would check out the town from the station down to the river, scouting out my favourite coffee bars and the pubs.

I checked my watch; I had plenty of time to get ready and walk down to the station, and the train should get me into town just after lunchtime. Josh had gone out, so I wouldn't have to think of an excuse. But I needed not to be scaring people, and a quick glance in the mirror showed that my cheek was now going a lovely purple-green shade around the large scraped area. I looked awful, so I quickly started trying to follow Grace's instructions for covering it up. But it was hard to concentrate, sitting at my desk looking in the mirror, wondering if Callum was there. Was he trying to make contact with me again now, I wondered? At this very second was he there, positioning his amulet where mine ought to be?

"Don't worry, Callum," I said out loud. "I'm going to get it back. Later today we may be together again. And if I can't find her today, well, I'm going to keep on trying."

I could imagine his concerned look, and the image in my head was so clear I could almost see him in the mirror beside me, almost feel that delicate touch on my hair, my shoulder; the gentle whisper of his kiss. "I miss you so much, Callum," I whispered. "I'll be with you again soon, I promise. I just wish there was some way of knowing that you were listening." But all I could hear was silence.

During the walk down to the station I realised that I should have paid some attention to the weather forecast. It had turned from being pleasantly warm to unbelievably hot, so my long-sleeved top was really uncomfortable. I couldn't risk anyone seeing the state of my arm, but I could have chosen something a little lighter to wear. I was going to roast. I quickly got a bottle of water from the little shop before I got on to the train in the hope that it might help a little.

My nerves increased the closer to Richmond we got. I still wasn't entirely sure how I was going to tackle Catherine. The plan about exposing her to my friends would only work if she cared, and I was getting less and less confident that she would. Still, it was the best I had, and until I tried it, I would never know.

At Richmond I got off the train and made my way up the big staircase to the ticket hall. The heat was almost unbearable, and it was even worse outside in the sunshine. I quickly ran through in my head the various places and venues where I thought I would be most likely to find Catherine, and dived across the road into the shade. First stop was the Italian deli where Grace and I regularly got our sandwiches and cappuccinos, but a quick glance around showed me that Catherine wasn't there. I walked down the little lane full of jewellers' shops to get to the green, and for once wasn't tempted by the fancy chocolate shop as I went past. The green was like a dust bowl, with people scattered all around. I had a strange sense of déjà vu as I worked my way across, looking for any hint of her. It was tough not knowing what she might be wearing, because she didn't have my clothes or my taste. For all I knew she was a Goth at heart and would be sweltering in head-to-toe black.

I worked my way back again, but couldn't see her, so decided to make for the pubs near the river. I made a quick stop in the department store first, not least because I knew that it had efficient air conditioning, but also because I used to go to the café there a lot when I was younger. I trudged my way up the escalators to the top floor, and peered into the café. It wasn't that busy, and a figure at the far end caught my eye. It was a girl with her back to me, bending over a newspaper. She didn't seem to be troubling the coffee cup by her side. The hair looked the right sort of colour, but I couldn't tell from her back if she was wearing the amulet; both arms were tucked out of sight.

I made my way through the assault course of tables and chairs, keeping a wide berth. When I was level with her and about four tables away I sat down and picked up a menu. Pretending to consider it closely I peeped over the top of it to check her out. She was completely engrossed in her paper, head down low with the curtains of dark-blonde hair obscuring her face. Other than going over and sitting in front of her I didn't know what to do.

I looked around me for inspiration, over the tables that hadn't yet been cleared of lunchtime debris. At the next table there was a glass bottle near the far edge, and between it and me was a tray. I leaned over and gave the tray a quick nudge, pulling back immediately. The bottle wobbled for a moment, and I thought it was going to right itself, but finally it toppled off the edge of the table. The smashing noise cut through the quiet murmurs of conversation and every head automatically whipped around to see. Still camouflaged behind the menu I watched as the woman turned too.

It wasn't Catherine.

"Crap!" I muttered to myself as the staff started hurrying over. I shuffled to the far side of the table I was sitting at, as far away from the mess as possible, then stood up in a nonchalant manner. A girl in an apron gave me a look but I just shrugged and smiled. "I think you must have poltergeists," I said as I hurried past.

I slipped guiltily out of the store, enjoying the last of the cool air as the heat of the street hit me like a wave. Before I turned towards the river there was one more place to check: the little children's bookshop in The Lanes. It was a haven of peace, even keeping the toddlers quiet, and I knew that it was possible to browse there for hours. I was getting a bit old to be a regular customer, but I usually popped in if I was in town. I returned the smile of the guy behind the counter as I walked in, but tried to look as if I was in a hurry. He enjoyed a chat and today I really didn't want to get sucked into that.

A twenty-second tour proved that she wasn't there, and I was edging out when I got caught.

"Ah, good to see you. Looking for anything specific?" He was leaning on a marketing display for a new boys' adventure story and I thought for a moment that the whole lot was going to topple over. The cardboard was wobbling alarmingly.

"Thanks, but not today. I've just lost a friend of mine and I thought she may be in here." I carried on edging towards the door as I spoke. "No sign though. I'll see you soon!" I managed to get out of the door just in time. I heard a brief exclamation of horror and then the noise as the books and the display came crashing down.

I kept peering into the shops as I worked my way down to the river, but it was fruitless. Finally I ended up at the pub I had come to the other night with Grace. The big French windows out on to the terrace were open and the sounds of the river drifted up from below. The place was packed; it was an ideal venue for a hot summer day. I decided that I deserved a brief treat after all the searching, and went to the bar to order a cold drink.

Clutching my ginger beer I made a quick tour of the room, but yet again I was disappointed. My plan was failing spectacularly. There was no way I was going to be able to get the amulet back if I couldn't actually *find* Catherine.

For a change there was no one there I knew, which I guess shouldn't have been a surprise given that everyone else was in school. I found a small empty table and sat down, resting my feet for a while. As I sat there I became aware of my various aches and pains and remembered that it was time for another of my super-strength painkillers. I rummaged in my bag and then realised that I had left them on my desk. I was just going to have to manage without them. I dug a little deeper and found a couple of paracetamol, so I took them in the hope that they would take the edge off.

I didn't know where else to go; I had been sure that she would have been in one of those places. Had I been wrong? Had Callum actually been trying to tell me something else? I sat for about half an hour racking my brains and trying to figure out where else I should go, slowly sipping my drink and hoping that the painkillers would kick in. The pub was surprisingly full of people for a Thursday afternoon; it seemed as if plenty of office workers had abandoned their desks in the heat, and the terrace was the perfect venue to try and catch the breeze. I kept watching the people coming and going, but Catherine remained stubbornly absent.

Finally I gave in; she wasn't going to turn up. I could retrace my steps, or walk across the bridge and on towards Twickenham. That was a reasonable option, I realised, as it would take me past the White Swan pub, where I had found the amulet in the mud. It would also mean that I could walk along the towpath next to the river, and that was likely to be rather more pleasant than walking back through the hot and dusty town. I drained the last of the melted ice from my glass, and stood up, wincing at how stiff I had become. My hand automatically reached for my empty wrist. "I'm going to keep trying, Callum, I promise," I whispered under my breath.

As I had hoped, the towpath was much cooler than town. It was a long way round, walking by the river rather than by the road, but much nicer. This loop of the Thames was also fairly quiet, with the fields of Petersham on the far bank. It was almost like being in the country. I passed a few other walkers, but it was much less busy than it would be at the weekend. I was idly watching one woman with a pushchair who was coming towards me around the corner when she looked up at the sky and suddenly increased her pace; her head went down and the buggy started bouncing along over the gravel. I looked up to see what had caught her eye and realised that, behind me, a huge thundercloud was looming. As I watched, a jagged shard of lightning leapt across the sky, followed almost immediately by an ear-splitting crack of thunder. Even though I'd seen the lightning, the noise made me jump and I could hear the wail of the child in the pushchair fading into the distance.

The cloud was moving fast, and the oppressive heat and sunshine seemed suddenly intensified. It was a matter of minutes before the cloud rolled over, making the world darker and much, much cooler. There was another burst of lightning, close enough that I automatically looked around at the trees nearby, but down here by the river I was safe enough. The buildings at the top of Richmond Hill looked like they could be in trouble though. Finally big, fat drops of water started to fall, splatting on the gravel. I did a quick mental calculation of where I was; carry on or go back? As the rain started in earnest I realised that it made no difference; I was going to get soaked either way. I might as well enjoy it.

I stepped out along the towpath, now completely alone, enjoying the feeling of the water running over my face and cooling my aching arm. There was something very apt about the situation, and I let the rain wash away my worries for a while.

It was still pelting down as I got to the entrance to Marble Hill Park. There were old stone steps down to the edge of the river there, presumably the remnants of some long-gone jetty. I used to feed the ducks all the time when I was little. There were no ducks there today, though, it was too wet even for them. I smiled slightly at the thought, but was suddenly pulled up short by a chillingly familiar voice.

"Looking for me, are you?"

I whipped around; standing in the middle of the towpath behind me was Catherine. Rain had darkened her hair to a flat brunette colour, and water was dripping off the ends. She was dressed for cooler weather in a plain shirt and jeans, both of which were plastered to her. She held a large rock in one hand.

My heart sank. I knew that I wasn't up to brawling with her; I just wasn't fit enough. All my injuries were screaming out in protest as I automatically tensed, ready for whatever was coming next. I pushed the wet hair off my face and squared up to her, knowing that the worst thing you can do with a bully is to show fear. But she didn't back off, she just stood there, an evil smile on her face.

"You have something of mine, I believe." I decided I might as well get straight to the point.

Her smile was cruel. "Whatever makes you think I've kept that old tat?"

"Don't play games with me, Catherine. I know you have it, and I know why you wanted it."

"Hmm, it was such a shame about the golf course. If you hadn't moved when you did, you wouldn't be walking around here today, that's for sure."

"I'm tougher than you think," I said defiantly, sticking out my chin and feeling the rain run down my neck, trying to avoid looking at the rock.

"Pity." Her look was scathing.

I couldn't decide on my best approach. Appealing to her sense of friendship seemed quite laughable; she radiated scorn and loathing. I carefully and unobtrusively flexed my wrists, trying to gauge how they would stand up to a scrap. Pain shot up my arm. Not well then, I decided. But it was my only option for getting Callum back, and I would put money on the fact that he was here, watching us. If I could only get the amulet off her he would be able to disable her, I was sure. The thought that he was so close spurred me on.

"I don't want to hurt you, Catherine, but I will if I have to. Please give me back my amulet."

"You must be joking! You'll only get your little friend to steal from me again, and I'm not having that."

"Please don't blame Olivia. She was just worried about me; she wanted to keep me safe. I had no idea that she was even there, even less about what she was doing."

"I don't care about any of that. She did what she did, and I'm not going to forgive her for it. As I can't hurt her, you'll have to do instead." She paused, a nasty, scheming look on her face. "You and Olivia, two of my least favourite people; this way, I can kill two birds with one very literal stone." She casually tossed the rock from one hand to the other.

"But why? I don't understand. Why do you hate me so much?"

"Don't give me that!" she sneered. "You know perfectly well what you've done and why I hate you. I thought life as a Dirge was bad, but this," she waved her arm around, "this is just hell. A head full of *your* memories, you insufferable little brat, and knowing that all of it – everything – is your fault. Little Olivia has made sure I can't remember *why*, but I'm still absolutely sure that I hate you, and that you deserve everything that's coming to you."

As if to prove that point a huge bolt of lightning suddenly

split the sky above us and the immediate crack of thunder made my eardrums pop. Rain continued to pelt down, washing away any thin veneer of civilisation about her. She looked like a vulture, waiting to strike.

I had to try again. "If you don't give me back my amulet I won't give up, you know. I'll hunt you down and get it from you sooner or later. You look into my eyes and you'll see that I mean every word." I stared at her, refusing to blink until the driving rain made it impossible. She continued to stand there, rock in hand, a scathing look on her face. I tried to get my balance, weighing up how to block the rock when she threw it.

"Oh, don't be ridiculous," she said scornfully, spotting my movement. "There's no way I'm going to fight you with this. I have what I need and anyway, you're not worth the energy. The only reason I came here was to give you something."

That surprised me. "What?" I asked suspiciously. "If it's not the amulet, what else do you have that I want?"

A smug smile flashed across her face. "I thought you might like a few last words with your boyfriend."

"What do you mean?"

"As you might imagine, Callum is here. In fact, he's been bugging me ever since I got the amulet. He's even more irritating in my head than he was when we were in St Paul's."

Even though I had expected it, I was still surprised and spoke without thinking. "Callum's here? Now? Can I talk to him?"

"Do you think I'm stupid? I'm not going to hand the amulet over to you! I'm just prepared to pass on a few farewell messages, that's all." She hesitated for a minute, her eyes glazing for a fraction of a second. "He's quite cross. In fact, he's shouting so much I can't really make any of it out." The smug smile was back. "Perhaps it'll be easier to do it the other way around. What would you like to say to him?"

I couldn't resist. "Callum, I love you. I'll find a way, I promise!"

"Ah, how sweet. Did you get that?" She was looking across the river as she spoke. "What? No final words?" She turned back to me. "He's incandescent with rage. It's really rather funny."

A hollow dread started to creep through me. What was she planning to do? "Catherine, stop it! Look, give me back the amulet; Callum will be out of your head, and you can go and do whatever you want to do. I'm not going to press charges over the assault, and you already have my money. You can go wherever you want and I give you my word that none of the Dirges will bother you again." I looked at her flashing green eyes. "Start a new life somewhere else," I begged.

"You still don't get it, do you? I'm only here at all because of you, you little troublemaker. I didn't ask for this, and I don't want to be here. I hate this life, I hate having your memories, and I really, really hate you." Her voice was chillingly calm. She walked slowly down the steps towards the water until she was on the second-to-last step.

"But—"

"Don't bother," she shouted back up towards me over the noise of the pounding rain. "The only thing that's going to make this miserable existence any better is knowing that yours is even worse."

"I don't understand." As I spoke a huge flash of lightning lit us both up and the simultaneous roar of thunder made me flinch. Catherine just stood there, water running off her, a strange, hideous smile on her face.

"Say goodbye to Callum, loser!" she sneered, and with that she pulled back the sleeve of her shirt and ripped the amulet off her wrist. For a second I was rooted to the spot, then I leapt after her, seeing my chance to get it back. But before I had got down the first few steps Catherine swung the rock down from above her head, crushing the amulet against the stone step. Shards of blue flew in all directions, mingling with the rain.

"NOOOO!" I cried in horror. Before I could get to her she smashed the rock again into the mangled remains of the bracelet, laughing wildly. Then in a single, sweeping movement she scooped up the bent, disfigured silver and the last bits of the stone and hurled them far out into the Thames.

"No. . ." I moaned again, distraught, as my only link to Callum rained down in pieces into the grey water.

End of Term

Catherine left immediately afterwards, laughing at me sitting on the stone steps in the rain.

"Oh, get a life. That's what you just told me, remember? Now we're both free of him. You know, you're better off without him, the miserable swine," she cackled. "Don't ever come looking for me again, OK?"

I couldn't speak, I just sat, trying to memorise the patch of water where the remains of the amulet had fallen, but the driving rain made it impossible. I had thought things were bad before, but now, she was right, it was much, much worse.

I crawled over to the place where she had smashed the amulet. She had managed to pick up most of the bits with that one swipe of her hand, but a few tiny slivers still glittered in the puddles. Not wanting to believe, I picked up the largest piece I could find. The beautiful blue stone was utterly destroyed. This scrap had no glinting depths, just the deep-blue colour. The fire that had brought me Callum was gone. Clutching the tiny scrap tightly in my hand, I sat back on my heels and howled.

I wasn't sure how long I spent on the steps, the water running off me and the tears running from me. When I had lost Callum before, when I thought that he was playing games with me, I had been distraught. But that had been because I had lost my dream boyfriend and it had been my choice to break it off with him. This was different; this was a whole new world of pain, and I really didn't know how I was going to be able to survive it.

Eventually the rain stopped. I was lying on the steps, eyes on the river, trying to visualise the spot where the amulet disappeared. I still had the piece of the stone grasped tightly in my hand, a useless shard that would never again summon Callum to my side. I lifted my hand to look at it again, slowly uncurling my fingers. Something dark and sticky was running between those fingers, and I shook my hand in surprise. A fountain of blood traced an arc around me. Sitting up as quickly as I could, I saw that there was a deep puncture wound in my palm. I had been clutching the stone shard so tightly I hadn't realised it had pierced my skin. But the blue fragment had gone, washed away when I had shaken my hand. There was blood everywhere, and everything I touched made it worse, each drop falling into the puddles and growing alarmingly. It looked like a murder scene.

Numb, I tried to find a tissue to stem the flow, but I had nothing useful in my pockets. I sat, letting it drip into the river, waiting for it to stop. The clouds and the oppressive heat had gone, leaving a washed-out-looking sky but bright-green grass and trees. Sunlight sparkled off the drops of water on the leaves. I looked at them dispassionately. Would I ever care again? Finally the bleeding slowed, and I risked standing up. My aches and pains were irrelevant to me now that my heart was broken clean in two.

Soaked through and covered in bloodstains, I took the back route to the station in Twickenham, not wanting to walk past the police station. I walked on autopilot, not catching anyone's eye, just focusing on getting home. I didn't want to think beyond that. A couple of well-meaning people approached me, but one look at my dead eyes made them beat a hasty retreat. It seemed that I had spent hours by the river, so I had missed the afternoon rush hour. When I finally got to Shepperton I started the long walk home, trying not to think. I hadn't got far when a car pulled up next to me with a screech of brakes.

"Alex, for heaven's sake, where have you been? Everyone's been frantic." Grace's voice was full of concern, and her tone changed to horror as I turned to look at her. "What have you been doing? Are you OK?"

It was all too much. The emotion that I'd been holding in since I left Twickenham overwhelmed me and I crumpled into her arms.

She manoeuvred me efficiently into the front of her car, and I heard her on the phone as she walked round to the driver's side. "Josh, I've got her. Unharmed, I think, but not good. Shock, possibly. I'll talk to her and bring her back in a bit, OK? Let the others know, will you?"

I sat limply in the passenger seat, looking at my palm. It had started to bleed again. "Have you got a tissue?" I asked in a scratchy voice, holding it up towards her. Grace always had tissues, and plasters and everything you might need in an emergency. She gently held my hand while she wiped it clean, then pressed a clean wad into the wound.

"Hold that tightly for a minute. Let me see what else I've got," she instructed, and I obeyed mutely. I felt the astringent touch of an antiseptic wipe, and then she was prodding it all over. I couldn't face talking just yet, so I let her get on with it. She muttered quietly to herself as she worked. "Hmm, can't see anything in the wound, so should be OK to cover; deep, but not wide enough to need stitches. There's a plaster, nice and tight. Now, let's look at the rest of you. Messy. How did you get so much blood on yourself? I think I have . . . yes, just the thing." She ripped open a packet of wet wipes and started cleaning me up. I felt her hesitate as she wiped away the remaining make-up over my bruised face, but she didn't comment. I let her get on with it, lifting arms when instructed, turning to and fro. Finally she was done.

"There's not much I can do about your clothes, so thank goodness your parents aren't at home."

I nodded my head very slightly.

"Poor Josh has been frantic. He thought maybe you'd gone to school, so when the coach came without you on it he called me to check, and I told him that you hadn't been seen all day. Your phone has been unobtainable for hours."

I used my good hand to pull my phone out of my pocket and handed it to Grace.

"Well, I'm not surprised that this isn't working – it's full of water. Did you fall in the river or something?"

"Got caught in the rain," I said simply, unwilling to expand too much further.

"I know it chucked it down but you must have been out in it for hours to get this soaked." She looked at my jeans and my hair. "*Were* you out in it for hours?"

I nodded once.

"OK, babe, you are obviously not yourself, but it's all right, I'm here now." She slipped her arm around the back of my neck and gently pulled my head on to her shoulder. "Was it Catherine again?" she asked. I nodded slightly. "Don't worry, I'm here now," she repeated, gently rubbing my arm. "Tell me when you're ready." Hot tears fell on to her T-shirt as I let go.

We must have sat there for an hour, and at one point I was conscious that she was sending a text, but I couldn't bring myself to move. When I stopped sobbing, she offered me another wet wipe. "Here, run that over your face, it'll make you feel better." I sat up in my seat and did as instructed, and it did help a little.

"Thank you," I managed finally.

"No worries. Do you want to tell me what she did now. . .?" She tailed off, obviously not keen to start me off again.

"The amulet. She smashed the amulet. Now I'll never see Callum again," I whispered.

"Oh, Alex! How? What happened? Oh, poor baby, no wonder you're so upset."

"She found me on the riverbank, taunted me for a while and then smashed it with a big rock."

"Can't we get it fixed?"

"The stone was in tiny pieces, and she picked all of them up and threw them in the river."

"But why? Why would she do that?"

"She just kept going on about how much she hated me and how everything was my fault. I have no idea what she means. How can it be my fault? I've done nothing to her, nothing!" My voice was rising and I knew I was becoming hysterical.

"Shhh," Grace soothed. "Don't get upset, that's what she wants. We need to think our way out of this mess."

She was right. I needed to get a grip. "I'm sorry, it's just the thought of never. . ." The emotion overcame me again and I had to stop.

Grace nodded. "I understand." She carried on rubbing my arm and I tried hard to keep it all together. Finally she spoke again. "Look, everyone has been really worried; I need to get you home.

You could also do with getting out of those wet clothes. Are you going to be up to moving soon?"

I sat up straight and nodded. There was no avoiding the fact that I had to get on, but I really didn't want to go through it all again and again. "I don't really want to talk to anyone else," I pleaded.

"I understand. We do need to tell Josh something though; he's been beside himself with worry."

"I'm sorry, I didn't mean for everyone to get involved. It's not fair."

"That's what friends are for, Alex," she said, squeezing my good hand gently. "I'm sure Josh would understand too, if you told him."

I shook my head. "Don't be silly, he'll never believe it, any of it."

"All right, this is what we're going to do. We'll tell him that you had another run-in with Ashley over Rob. Josh will buy that, and he doesn't like Rob either, so that'll help. No one else needs to know anything."

My thoughts were too dulled with pain to bother wondering whether it was the right solution; it was easier to let Grace take charge. "That sounds all right, I suppose," and suddenly the contrast between her and Catherine became almost too much to bear. The tears started streaming again.

"Shush, shush. Don't upset yourself again." Grace passed me some more tissues. "Are you going to be OK to go now?"

For the first time I turned and looked her in the eyes. "Please, please don't say anything about C . . . C . . . Callum," I managed with a gulp.

She squeezed my hand. "I won't say a word, I promise." She

sat back in her chair and put her seat belt on. "Come on, belt up. Let's get you home."

The hours passed in a daze. Mostly people seemed to believe what they had been told. Josh was the most sceptical, especially since I had told him about Catherine, but he could see I was suffering and he kept quiet. The next day I went into school to empty my locker as it was the last day of term, but all the activity and celebrations went on around me without touching me at all. I felt as if my whole world was wrapped in cotton wool, every edge slightly dulled, every voice muted. Grace had persuaded Josh not to tell Mum and Dad anything. I didn't want them feeling worried about me and cutting short their break, and there was nothing they could do anyway. I had to work through this on my own.

There were two separate factions at school: one with me, the other with Ashley and her tales of imaginary boyfriends. They could all see that I was hurting, and my friends tried to rally around, but it was hard when I could give them no information. Ashley took that as a vindication of her story and got even louder in her crowing. I really ought to introduce her to Catherine, I thought at one point; they had a lot in common.

After school finished at midday, Grace and I filled her car with all our stuff and made our way home. I felt really guilty about keeping her from the traditional summer end-of-term celebration. Every year loads of our friends and classmates went straight to the Hampton open-air pool, and dozens of the boys from the next door school did the same. It was usually a great event.

"I really appreciate this, Grace," I said again, as we approached my house. "But are you sure that you don't just want to leave your stuff here and go back to the pool?"

"I don't want to leave you. You shouldn't be alone, not right now."

"Thanks, but honestly, I'm going to have to learn how to get on. He's not coming back." I tried very hard to keep my voice from cracking and I nearly managed it. "Why don't you go, and you can check on me when you come back for your stuff? Then I don't have to feel bad about destroying your social life." I paused for a second. "Is Jack going?"

"Yes, he's planning to. He won't mind if I'm not there, though; he'll understand."

"I'm sure there are plenty of others who won't mind if you're not there, either. Are you really going to risk letting all those girls see Jack half-naked and not be there to protect him?"

She pursed her lips, considering. "That's a good point, actually. I've been having a bit of trouble with Sasha – I think she might be planning to make a move on him."

"You really ought to go and keep an eye, then. Nowhere more public than the pool. . ."

She stopped the car smartly on the gravel drive outside my house. "Are you sure you don't mind?" she asked as we carried all my art folders and textbooks into the hall. "I mean, Jack won't do anything, I trust him completely."

"I know that, but do you trust Sasha?"

"Hmm, point taken. OK, I'll go. I'll be back about five. We can give some thought to what to do next then."

"Grace, the amulet is smashed, Catherine did what she wanted to do. There's nothing to give any thought to." My heart felt empty as I listened to my own words.

Grace was characteristically stoical about it. "You don't know that. It's a weird piece, you said so yourself. We're not

202

defeated yet." She smiled at me. "Don't get into any more trouble while I'm gone."

"I promise. Give Jack a kiss from me."

"I will, you can be sure of that. See you later." She gave me a quick hug. "Call me if you need me, remember."

I shut the door carefully behind her, heaving a sigh of relief. I loved Grace to bits, and knew that she would do anything for me, but I needed to be on my own. The strain of being with people had really taken it out of me and I sank exhausted on to the sofa. The house was cool after the heat and sunshine outside, and completely silent. At last I was somewhere where no one was going to ask me questions or look at me quizzically, or suggest that I go to the doctor or the police. I hoped that Josh would be staying out for a while longer, so I had a bit more time to myself.

I sat in the sitting room, looking out of the window and down the garden. The sunlight dappled the scruffy lawn and the birds were out in force, pecking away at my mum's strawberry plants. It was a perfect summer scene: tranquil, warm, and yet for me, absolutely wrong.

I tried to practice not thinking, to empty my mind, but Callum was always there. As I shut my eyes I could see his face, the line of his jaw, the worry in his eyes. I rubbed the plaster on my palm, and the pain as I pressed on the cut reminded me of the amulet. That was my last contact with the beautiful, mysterious stone that had changed my life, the last time I had seen its glittering blue depths. I wished that the cut would never heal; that the pain could be there as a constant, tangible reminder of what I had lost.

"Alex? Alex? Are you in here?" The voice reached down and pulled me up from the depths. I opened my eyes and saw that the garden was nearly lost in the gloom.

"Uh, yeah," I called back before Josh could panic.

"Oh, there you are, didn't see you hiding in the dark." The relief was evident in his voice.

"I've just been dozing, that's all. Didn't Grace fill you in?"

His shifty expression told me all I needed to know. Grace had come by late afternoon to collect her school gear with Jack in tow, and I had roused myself enough to make them coffee and listen to her gossip from the afternoon. I had excused myself from the party, which was going on into the evening, and finally they had left me to it. I was pretty sure that she was going to give an update on my status to Josh though, and I had been right.

"She might have called," he attempted in a nonchalant manner, but quickly abandoned it. "She's just worried about you, you know."

"I know, you're both being very kind. I just need a bit of time, that's all."

"Yeah, well, you know. . . If I can help. . ."

"Josh, I know you'd rather stick pins in your eyes than deal with a weeping girl, but I appreciate the offer, truly."

"Ah, maybe, yeah. . ." He suddenly leapt up. "Food, that's what I can do. I bet you haven't eaten, have you? You must eat."

"Mum would be pleased with you," I managed a half-smile. "I'm fine, I had a sandwich earlier," I lied. He'd never notice that nothing was gone from the fridge.

Josh sat back down again, looking serious. "The thing is, Alex, I'm supposed to be going to that festival tomorrow, and Mum and Dad won't be back until Sunday. Would you rather I stay home? I'm happy to do that if you need me here. We still have no idea where that weird woman has gone, and I'll be worried sick if you're here on your own."

"Don't be ridiculous, I'll be OK. I'm sure Grace would come running if I asked, and Jack. I'll be quite safe."

"It's just that, after the mugging as well, I can't help feeling that you might be in danger."

"She wanted my bracelet, and she got it. Why would she come back?"

"Are you sure that there's nothing else going on?" He grabbed my hands and waited until I looked at him.

"Positive. She got what she wanted. Now she's gone." I tried as hard as I could, but I couldn't stop the single tear that brimmed over my lashes and dropped fatly on my arm. Josh hugged me tight for a second.

"Well, let's sleep on it. I'll wake you first thing in the morning and we can decide if I'm going to go or not."

"Don't you dare!" I sniffed loudly. "I don't want to be woken up that early. If I'm left alone, with a bit of luck I'll sleep most of the day." I put as much emotion into the smile as I could find.

Josh came and checked on me in the morning, and I debated pretending to be asleep but then he would only have worried. Having reassured him again that I was quite capable of looking after myself he left, laden down with a rucksack and camping gear. My money was on him sleeping in the car, though. As I heard the tyres crunch down the gravel drive I carefully rolled over and considered the ceiling. I'd had another bad night, failing to translate the gnawing fatigue I felt into actual sleep. Lying in bed was an attractive option, hoping that at some point I would pass out, but it didn't seem very likely. I tried to think about something, anything, other than how much I missed Callum, but there were too many memories in the room. Defeated, I stumbled out of bed and into the shower.

The ache in my heart was joined by another feeling of emptiness as I made my way downstairs, and I realised that I was hungry. I couldn't actually remember the last time I had eaten, so I didn't want to overdo it. I threw a slice of bread into the toaster, and for a minute I was gripped with longing for my parents; usually on a Saturday morning there would be a freshly baked loaf in the machine, wafting fabulous smells through the house. It wasn't the same without them.

Josh had left me something too, a chunky old phone and a note.

Hi, I tried to fix your phone last night but it's completely knackered. Even the SIM card seems to have corroded – I hope you have a copy of your contacts! Anyhow, this old phone works and is now charged up. It's a bit basic and deeply uncool, but better than nothing. You'll need to give your mates the number. I've put my number in should you need me. Try not to get into any more trouble, J

For a big brother he was OK really, I thought, blinking back the tears as I put the note down, but they quickly evaporated as I picked up the phone. It was almost antique, and looked as if it could survive being run over by a bus.

The toast popped up, making me jump. It tasted like cardboard, but I kept nibbling away at it, hoping that it would take one of my pains away. I sat staring out into the garden as I ate, trying not to think, but the memories attacked me from all sides. I kept coming back to that very first moment when I saw him, when I was standing under the dome of St Paul's. He had looked so surprised that I was able to see him; I felt the edge of my mouth twitch a little as I remembered. They were weird, the rules of physics that seemed to bind the Dirges, all culminating at the top of the dome, where it seemed all bets were off.

The dome. My sleep-starved brain struggled for a moment; surely that was important?

Odd things happened at the top of the dome; before, when I had the amulet, I could touch and see and hear Callum when we were both on the Golden Gallery. That had been because Callum had passed some extra talents to me when he had returned my memories. What if those talents were still in me? What if Callum was waiting for me to work it out and meet him at the top of the dome?

I realised that I was sitting with my mouth hanging open, toast poised for another bite. I threw it down and stood up to go, then sat back down abruptly as the room started to spin. I put my head between my knees and counted to ten, kicking myself mentally. I had to eat something to get – and keep – my blood sugar up or I was never going to make it up the five hundred or so steps to the top of St Paul's. But the tiredness was gone, swept away like mist in a breeze, and the pain had receded. I had a plan.

Alone

I could barely contain my excitement as I made my way up to London. The journey seemed to take forever, and the train was full of shoppers and tourists. At Waterloo I had a quick debate with myself; the direct line to Bank didn't always operate at the weekend, I remembered, but the bus had been OK. I found my way through the station concourse to the right bus stop, dodging all the people standing aimlessly in huddles, watching the departure boards. I went past a doughnut stall as I headed for the steps and a girl in a stripy apron was giving away little tasters. Without thinking I took a piece, and was quickly reminded by my stomach just how hungry I really was. I had to double-back and buy a whole one, justifying it to myself as energy for the long climb ahead.

As I waited at the bus stop I found myself humming one of Callum's favourite songs, and I realised with a shock that I was almost happy. It seemed to have been such a long time since I first lost the amulet, but somehow I knew now that it was going to be OK; I would talk with Callum and he and Matthew would work out what I needed to do. They had had several days to come up with plans and options, and I was confident that they would have some. I couldn't quite work out what they could possibly be, but I decided not to let that worry me; I was just content being on my way to see him again.

I had hoped to be able to sit on the top deck of the bus

when it appeared so that I could see St Paul's as we approached, but the bus was packed and I ended up standing on the lower deck, squeezed in between a family of Japanese tourists and some teenagers in hoodies. One of the hoodies glanced at me then nudged his mate. They both smirked as they looked away, and I remembered that I hadn't bothered to cover up the bruise on my cheek before I left home. I tried to catch a glimpse of my reflection in the chrome surfaces around the bus, but couldn't really see how bad it was. My hand curled around the little travel mirror that was still in my pocket, but I didn't want to whip it out anywhere so crowded. I wondered briefly if I ought to stop and get some make-up to cover it before I saw Callum, but realised that he would have been watching me all this time anyway, so it wouldn't worry him.

Finally the bus lumbered up Ludgate Hill, and I fought my way off. The plaza in front of the cathedral was heaving with people, as were the steps up to the entrance. I smiled to myself as I thought of that day, not so long ago, when Callum had brought me here to meet with Matthew for the first time and I had seen the other Dirges, all clustered around in their long dark cloaks. I guessed some of them were there now, gathering happy memories from the unsuspecting tourists, or watching me. I wanted to acknowledge them in some way, but resisted the temptation and joined the queue to get inside.

As usual, the cathedral was a cool, calm oasis and seemed a million miles away from the activity outside. But I didn't linger to soak up the atmosphere, just made a beeline for the stairs. Climbing up was hard going, and I was almost grateful for the large number of tourists who made it impossible to go too fast. I was starting to feel the downside of not eating properly over the previous few days. So I plodded steadily upwards, and when I got to the Whispering Gallery I sat for a while, recovering my strength. I wondered which of the Dirges I was sitting next to, and hoped it was Olivia. It seemed so long since I had sat and talked with her on that very seat, before Lucas had taken his chance, but it had only been a week. I glanced around; no one was in earshot.

"Hi, Olivia, not sure if you're there as I can't see you any more, but just in case, I want to tell you that it's not your fault. You do know that, don't you?"

There was no responding tingle, but it had been a long shot so I wasn't too disappointed. Once my legs had stopped aching I made my way round to the far side of the gallery and up the relentless spiral stairway to the Stone Gallery. I stopped there too, but it was harder to find a free seat so I just sank down on to the stone floor and sat with my back against the wall, letting my breathing come back to normal. As usual though, my excitement was growing in leaps and bounds the higher up the building I climbed. I couldn't resist getting out the little mirror to check how bad my face looked, but also to have a surreptitious scout around for any hint of the Dirges. I couldn't see anything out of the ordinary, but I wasn't yet at the top, I reasoned. My face was a bit of shock to me, when I finally looked at it. The bruise had grown down my cheek from my cheekbone and was now a rainbow of different colours. It definitely looked like I had been fighting, so it was no wonder that the boys on the bus had laughed.

But Callum wouldn't care, I thought as I snapped the mirror shut and stood up, my heart already racing. I made for the familiar door and slipped through from the bright sunshine to the gloom inside. I kept a steady pace as I climbed, and was again helped by the pace of the other tourists. I was disappointed that the gallery was fully open, unlike during my previous visits, but perhaps I hadn't given Callum enough warning of my trip to do whatever it was he did to make sure it was closed. I shuddered as I passed the half-landing where Lucas and Callum had fought, wondering if he was still stalking me. When I reached the little room with the viewing panel down to the floor dozens of metres below, the line of people came to a complete halt, so while I caught my breath I fished out my phone earpiece, to be ready to talk to Callum unobtrusively as soon as I got outside.

One of the cathedral guides was stationed in the little room, and he was determined to keep us all in line and moving.

"No lingering up top today, please," he announced as he urged our line along and up the last flight of steps. "Keep it moving, then everyone gets to enjoy the view." But it was impossible to move; the line was completely stalled. I could see the old oak door to the outside but I was going to have to wait my turn. The old cast-iron staircase was incredibly narrow, just one person wide, so there was no way to jump the queue. It was lucky they had an "up" stairway and a separate "down" route, I thought, otherwise we would all have been stuck.

Finally, step by slow step, I made it towards the door. I could feel the fresh air on my face, and had to fight the urge to barge past as many people as I could to finally reach Callum. Eventually I stepped outside and grasped the rusty old railing with the peeling golden paint.

"Hi, Callum, I made it, top of the dome!" I announced joyfully into the mouthpiece. There was a strange silence. "Hi, Callum, are you there?" I found the mirror and scanned about, no longer caring what the other tourists thought. There was nothing unusual to be seen; no ghostly shadows, no strange tingling sensation. On a balcony packed full of people I was utterly alone.

I couldn't believe that, not yet. Maybe he was on the far side of the balcony. As I shuffled around with the people enjoying the view I tried to hold that thought, but the further round I went, the more futile I realised it was. "Callum?" I tried again as I stood on the spot where we had first touched, where I realised that I could actually see him and hold him and kiss him. But there was nothing. Tears ran unheeded down my cheeks as my calls became more desperate. I tried to linger, to see if there was any small area of the balcony where it might be different, but the press of people behind me made it impossible. It was as if I was in a nightmare conga line, being led where I had no wish to go.

As we shuffled towards the door to the stairway down I wriggled round to see if there was a way of staying up there, of going round again, but there was another cathedral guide stationed between the doors, next to a barrier that stopped people doing a full circuit. "Callum!" I cried again in anguish before I had to let go of the barrier and head back into the gloom. "Please, please let me know you're there!" I was sobbing out loud, and the guide looked at me in alarm.

"You all right there, missy?" he asked in a kindly but worried tone. "Do you need any help getting back down?"

I shook my head at him miserably, but couldn't speak. "Well, take care on the steps then," he said as he ushered me through the door, clearly relived to have got me away from the lethal drop on the other side of the railings. As the darkness enveloped me I felt as if my world would end. Stumbling down the steps through streams of tears, I finally found a place where I could sneak to one side and slump down on to the cold, hard metal staircase. I sank into the misery.

I opened my eyes when the person shaking my arm became too persistent to ignore. I tried to move away, but as I was wedged into a small space on one of the stairway landings there was nowhere much to go.

"Now then, missy," said a low voice. Was it the same guy who had talked to me at the top? At the top where there was no sign of Callum? The thought pierced my heart like a knife. I heard another voice in the background.

"Security? Yes, she seems to be conscious." There was a click and an indistinct crackling noise. "No, hold off on the ambulance for a minute, will you? We'll try and persuade her to walk down. I'll update you in five. Dome three out." There was a shuffling noise, then the same voice again, but louder. "Move along, please, folks, nothing to see here. Keep walking please." In the background I could hear the whispers of the people passing down the stairs. One voice was much more strident than the rest.

"Mummy, why is that lady sitting there like that? Is she sick?"

"Hush now, Julia, keep your voice down."

"But why is she sitting there? That's not allowed, and why is that man talking into that funny phone?"

"It's a walkie-talkie, darling. I expect she's just a little faint, but it's really not our business. Come on, look, you can see all the way down to the bottom of the inner dome over there." The voices faded as the clattering of feet on the iron stair continued.

The first man was shaking my arm again. "Come on, love, can you get to your feet? Are you frightened of heights? I know that it can get a bit scary in here. Much worse on the way down than on the way up. Is that the problem?"

It seemed easier to let him believe that that was the case, so I nodded briefly. The relief was evident in his voice; this was obviously something he had dealt with before.

"OK then, let's be getting you up on your feet. Reggie," he called to the older man. "We're going to make our way down. I'll go in front and you stay right behind her."

I let myself be helped up, then the two of them manhandled me down the stairs. I kept my mind as blank as possible, just thought about the next step, the next railing to hold, the next turn. I tried to tell them that I was OK when we got to the Stone Gallery level, but they seemed determined to escort me to the ground. Maybe they thought I was going to jump. For the first time I could see the appeal of that, the possibility of no future but no pain, but I carried on walking.

When we finally reached the huge checkerboard floor at ground level they still wouldn't let me go. One of the men led me to a line of chairs and insisted that I sat down, while the one with the walkie-talkie disappeared into the crowd. My companion tried a few conversational openers while we sat there, but I couldn't bring myself to chat. We sat in silence for a while, and I tried hard not to think about what might be going on around me, which Dirges might be watching and listening. There was no danger of any of them stealing anything from me today though.

Eventually the other guy came back, closely followed by an elderly woman in a cassock. The man sitting with me stood up with a relieved look on his face. "You'll be fine now, missy. Reverend Waters will make sure you're OK."

"I *am* OK," I protested, not wanting to get pressed into

conversation, but Reverend Waters put a surprisingly firm hand on my shoulder as I tried to get to my feet. She looked vaguely familiar and I realised with a jolt that she was the person who had been watching me in the Whispering Gallery the last time I had been in the cathedral, when I first met Olivia.

"Can you spare me a few minutes?" she asked gently, sitting down beside me. I shrugged and settled back in my chair.

"Thank you. I'm Reverend Waters, as you know. And you are. . .?"

"Alex," I mumbled, not keen to give her more than the basics.

"Nice to meet you, Alex. Now, my colleagues were very worried about you, and they thought that maybe you would like a little chat."

"It's very kind of them, but I've nothing I want to talk about."

She wasn't to be put off. "It's just that – well, they seemed to think it wasn't vertigo that upset you."

I shrugged again, hoping she would take the hint. "They thought that maybe you were going to hurt yourself, to jump maybe." She paused for a moment. "Is there something troubling you?"

I glanced at her face, so full of concern for a complete stranger, and for a split second I thought about telling her everything, just to get it off my chest. I even drew in a breath to start, but then realised that she would think I was crazy. Instead I pressed my lips firmly together and shook my head as a single tear traced its way down my salt-encrusted cheeks.

It looked like she realised that her opportunity to get the truth had passed. She sighed a little and took my hand, patting it gently. "You don't have to bottle it up, Alex, whatever it is. Sharing can be good."

"Th . . . thanks for the offer, Reverend, but there's nothing I want to say."

"I don't like letting you go like this. You've had some dark thoughts today, I'll warrant."

She didn't need to be a clairvoyant to guess that; just looking at the state of me it was clear that I wasn't having a good day. "I'll be fine," I protested. "Just a bit of an upset, that's all." I wiped my fingers over my cheeks, hoping to catch that last tear and make myself look a little less frazzled.

"If you say so, dear." She patted my hand again, and then reached inside the voluminous cassock. She pulled out a little white card. "Here, take my number. If you want to talk, at any time, please don't hesitate to call."

I took the card and pretended to read it closely, although I could see nothing through the film of tears. It was rude to refuse it, but I could stick it in a bin as soon as I got outside. "Thank you," I said with as much sincerity as I could muster. "I promise I'll think about it." I smiled as much as I could manage, which was little more than a twitch of the lips, then got to my feet. She also stood.

"I'll walk you to the door," she announced, falling into step with me as I started to move down the long nave to the exits. The place was still packed with people, and the usual quiet was turning into more of a hum of conversation. As we walked I was suddenly overwhelmed by the smell of sausages. Beneath my feet was a brass-coloured grating, below which I could see the Cathedral Café. The smell made me feel quite sick, so I increased my speed as much as was possible, given the crowds. Reverend Waters kept pace effortlessly despite her age. Finally I made it to the exit turnstile.

"Thank you again for your offer," I said, finally looking her in the eyes. I was was struck by the understanding in them.

"Anytime, Alex, I mean it. And please keep the card – you might find you need it."

I nodded briefly, unable to drag myself away from her gaze.

"Remember that there are a lot of unhappy souls here, Alex. Keep the faith." With one last squeeze of my hand she was gone, lost in the crowds of people.

What did she mean by that? I turned the phrase over in my mind as I walked back out into the frenetic activity and heat outside the cathedral. I held the card in my hand and as I passed the first bin I reached out to drop it inside. But something made me hesitate. I had the unsettling feeling that the Reverend Waters knew something I didn't. I slid the little white card into the back pocket of my jeans and started the long walk back to Waterloo.

Beesley

I let myself go numb as I started the long trip home. I didn't want to think about the fact that my plan had failed; that I hadn't been able to see Callum after all. Having given myself some hope I now felt even worse. I walked down Ludgate Hill and was about to cross the road to walk up Fleet Street on the other side when I realised where I was. Right under my feet, somewhere underneath the pavement or the tarmac, was the River Fleet.

There *was* a way to be with Callum; I just had to be brave enough to take it.

Unconsciously I started walking down towards the river, to Blackfriars Bridge. It was a busy road, packed full of cars and taxis, and a nightmare to cross. As I got closer to the bridge I could see the entrance to the underpass that also took you to the station and the Tube. Almost on autopilot I walked down the slope, looking for directions to the right exit. Callum had told me that the water from the Fleet poured into the Thames underneath the bridge, so I followed the signs to the Embankment.

The world around me was muffled somehow, detached from what I was doing. The people's voices were thick, and I couldn't decipher any words. I just kept moving, one foot in front of the other, with no plan except to get to my destination. The underpass was a warren of tunnels with about eight different exits, and as I selected the one I wanted I became aware of a strange beating noise in front of me. When I turned the last corner I was almost bowled over by the noise; a group of buskers were playing enthusiastically further along the corridor. The noise was deafening, and the music appalling. There was an accordion player who seemed to be bashing out some sort of polka, a guy with a trumpet whose ear-splitting contribution was entirely different, and two others beating old tin cans. They all smiled at me hopefully, but I shoved my hands in my pockets and kept my head down as I hurried by. The noise followed me like a wave, and it wasn't until I was actually out on the riverbank that I could even hear myself think.

The footpath beside the river was unexpectedly wide where it went under the bridge, and it was very dark after the bright sunshine. There was no one around and I waited for a few moments while my eyes adjusted to the light. I peered over the metal handrail, trying to see exactly where the water of the Fleet emerged, but I couldn't be sure, not from directly above. I looked around and saw that the staircase up to the bridge might give a slightly better view as it was suspended over the river. But it was about thirty paces away, so it wouldn't be great. It was also back out in the sunshine.

I walked over and got out as far from the bank as I could, then tried to peer around the stairs to see. The gloom was even more difficult to interpret from there, so I shielded my eyes from the sun and waited to see if details would emerge. Finally I was able to pick out a slightly darker patch on the brick wall of the bank; underneath the patch the wall was streaked with green algae, and next to it was a rusty old ladder. There didn't seem to be much water coming out of it at all. I had been expecting a swirling torrent, but this was no more than a dribble.

Once I had gone back round under the bridge and peered

over the railings again, I was able to pick out the ladder, and for a moment I debated jumping over and climbing down, but it was obvious that there wasn't enough water to drown in. If I was to jump in there all I would do was drown in the muddy Thames.

I slumped down on the railing, defeated; I didn't even have the option of becoming a Dirge. Callum was as lost to me as ever. This time the tears didn't come though; none were left. I felt like an empty shell. The rest of my life stretched ahead of me, and all of it would be without him.

It was a slow journey as I walked listlessly from the station back home. I shut the door behind me with relief, knowing that Mum and Dad wouldn't be back until the following afternoon, and Josh was away, so I wouldn't have to make conversation or think of any excuses for not eating. I could just sit. I went to the bathroom to wash my face and jumped when there was a loud knocking at the front door.

I groaned to myself. It was bound to be Grace, and, much as I loved her, I just wanted to be alone. I didn't want to talk about Catherine, or to have to try to talk about Callum without sobbing. I was desperately trying to think of an excuse so that I could stay on my own as I opened the door, and was very surprised to see Lynda.

"Hi, Alex, this is good of you. Yet again it really helps me out! Are you sure that it's going to be OK?" She spoke quickly as Beesley shot past me and tried to slip his lead. She hauled him back.

"I'm sorry? I don't quite. . ."

"Josh said that you'd be happy to give Beesley his evening walk. He mentioned it when I saw him this morning."

She hesitated, seeing the look on my face. "He didn't tell you, did he?"

I shook my head briefly, automatically reaching for the lead as the puppy had wound himself around my legs in his excitement.

"Look, don't worry, if it's not convenient I can easily do it myself."

I looked down at Beesley; his chocolate-brown eyes were wide and he was jumping up and down, trying to lick me. With my legs tied together with the lead it was all I could do to keep my balance. There was nothing but joy in the little dog; everything was perfect for him. It wouldn't do me any harm to spend some time with him.

"No, it's fine. Josh didn't tell me but I'd love to take Beesley out."

"As long as you're positive. Don't let him pull you over this time either. You don't want a matching one of those." She pointed at my cheek as she spoke.

For a fraction of a second I had no idea what she was on about, then I remembered I'd told her that Beesley had pulled me over when I'd been attacked on the golf course. "He won't get me again, Lynda, you can be sure of that. Here, hang on to this for a minute while I get my keys." I unwound myself and handed the lead back to her, then quickly got my keys and phone from my bag. Within minutes I was being dragged down the road, watching Beesley's tail wag faster than I would have believed was possible.

We went to the field next to the playground as I didn't fancy the golf course again. After a couple of circuits he was nowhere near worn out, but I was exhausted, so I sat on one of the benches and let him run around on a long lead. He kept dashing off, then reaching the end of the lead and pulling up short. He didn't seem to learn, but it clearly didn't bother him either. He could just make it to the shallows of the little river, and after one quick paddle he returned with a soggy ball and dropped it at my feet. He looked up at me expectantly, his pink tongue flapping.

"OK, you daft dog," I murmured, throwing the ball just far enough that he would be able to reach it, and he shot off. He was tireless, and as long as I kept throwing the ball carefully I could give him all the exercise he needed without leaving my seat. It was quite therapeutic, but it wasn't enough to actually make me cheerful. I couldn't help thinking about the last time I was in the meadow, with Callum and Olivia, and the tears were suddenly back. I wrapped my arms tight around my knees to make myself as small as possible and to stop from howling out loud, and found myself rocking as I wept. Beesley was oblivious to it all, running for his ball.

The tugging on his lead suddenly stopped, and I heard him bark excitedly. I ignored him for a moment, too wrapped up in my misery to care, but his eager barking was persistent. I peered over my knees to see what his problem was.

The little puppy was standing by the riverbank, and the sun was catching the swirling clouds of insects in the evening with a golden shimmer. He was jumping up and down, eyes fixed on something I couldn't see from that distance.

"Beesley, leave the midges alone, you'll never catch them," I called, sniffing loudly. I reached in my pocket for a tissue, but could only find a very soggy one. I should have known better than to leave the house without at least a handful of new ones. I wiped my eyes with the back of my hand and tried to compose myself, watching the strange antics of the dog. Josh had been right; getting out with Beesley was a good idea.

The ball was now lying ignored at Beesley's feet, and he was looking upwards, his tail wagging furiously. As I watched he walked towards me, looking up and to the side as he came. I found myself leaning forwards, curious to see what had caught his attention. Every so often he jumped up, always to the same side. He was about ten paces away when it struck me; he was walking with someone next to him, but it was someone that only he could see, someone he knew and liked.

I slowly got to my feet, hardly daring for it to be true. I couldn't bear another disappointment today.

"Callum?" I whispered. "Is that you?"

The little dog stopped just in front of me, a soppy look on his face as he sat in response to a command I couldn't see or hear. I reached out, feeling only empty air.

"Are you really there this time? I can't feel you." The feeling of loss and helplessness threatened to overwhelm me again, and I sank back down. "Please, please let me know you are there."

Beesley suddenly started to bark enthusiastically. "Is that really you? Oh, Callum, I thought I'd lost you for ever." Beesley's gaze shifted slowly towards me, and he looked exactly as if he was staring at my ear. He then put his head on my knee next to the wrist that still showed the marks where the amulet had been wrenched off.

"I know that you're there. I can almost feel you, almost believe that you are stroking my hair, kissing my neck. . ." I automatically lifted my hand to stroke his face, a gesture so familiar, so right, but nothing was there. No hint of resistance, no gossamer touch, nothing. "Callum. . ." I whispered, struggling to contain the tears. My excitement was quickly overtaken by a feeling of huge frustration. To think that he *could* be there, but to have no sensible means of communicating was simply awful. Beesley continued to sit there, his eyes flicking between me and the shadow only he could see.

"Is . . . is there a way to fix this, do you think?" I asked eventually, hoping that Beesley might give me a clue. But he just sat there, apparently staring at me with the same soppy look on his face, his tail whisking up the dust. I watched him intently but nothing happened. "What can I do, Callum? Help me!"

Beesley got up and walked around in a small circle before sitting down again. "Was that some sort of sign?" I cried. "A clue? Does that mean we can fix things?"

Beesley suddenly put his head on one side and gave one of his ears a thorough scratching with his back paw. He shook his head a little, as if he were slightly surprised, yawned hugely and lay down with his head on his front paws. "No, Beesley, it's not time to stop playing just yet." I tried to cajole him into action, scratching his head and tickling him under his chin, but he was having none of it. He shut his eyes and within seconds he had started to snore.

"Crap!" I exclaimed, slapping my palm against the seat in frustration. But it was frustration edged with excitement. For the first time in days I knew, *really* knew, that Callum was by my side. There was something to fight for, some reason to keep going. I was not going to let Catherine win. "Callum, it's brilliant to know that you are still there, even if we can't yet talk. But I'm not going to give up. I'll . . . I'll, I don't know, borrow him again tomorrow and work out a way to get him to help. I could maybe make that work, you never know. It's just so good to know that you're with me, that I haven't lost you forever." There was no responding twitch from the dog; he was sound asleep. I gathered him up in my arms and walked home, feeling a small spark of hope grow as I went. He *had* been there, I was sure of it.

Lynda was rather surprised when I handed back a sleeping puppy. "Gosh, Alex, what have you done to him? I've not seen him this exhausted before."

"I just took him for a walk down by the playground. We found a ball and I was throwing it for him. He seemed to enjoy it."

"Ooh yes, he does like a bit of fetch. Daft dog!" She rubbed his ears and he grunted contentedly.

"So, term has ended, and I have plenty of free time," I said as casually as possible. "Would you like me to walk him again for you tomorrow?"

"Thank you so much for the offer, but we're both off to my parents' place for a few days in the morning. I'm not sure how well he's going to deal with the long car journey though."

"I'm sure he'll be fine," I smiled at her, fighting back the disappointment. "It'll wait until you get back. We had a good time today, didn't we, Beesley?" His tail twitched as I said his name but his eyes stayed shut. My canine Dirge detector had had enough for the day.

Back at home the house seemed less gloomy somehow, and I realised that I was actually hungry. I smiled to myself; Callum was still there for me. All I had to do was work out a way to communicate with him using the dog. Perhaps I could get Callum to make Beesley bark to command: one bark for yes, two for no, that sort of thing. What I had to do was to work out lots of Yes/ No questions for him. I grabbed a piece of paper and a pen as I worked in the kitchen, throwing together a simple pasta dish. I tried to write down exactly what I could ask, to give me a bit of an idea about where to start, but it was fiendishly difficult. I decided that the best thing I could do was revisit all the places I had been with Callum, to see if questions came to me. And while I was out and about he might be able to hijack a different dog of course. It didn't have to be Beesley.

Pleased with my plan I had a long, hot soak in the bath, then settled down to watch a movie. It was just getting interesting when the house phone rang.

"Hi, Alex, it's me. Is your mobile still out of action? You need to get another one."

"Hi, Grace, how's it going?"

"You sound much more cheerful than I was expecting. That's good."

"I *am* more cheerful. I had a pretty dreadful morning, but this afternoon I think I saw Callum – well, nearly saw him anyway."

"Oh, wow, Alex! How did that happen?" She couldn't keep the confusion out of her tone, and I realised that I was never going to be able to explain about the dog over the phone.

"It's a bit complicated, but I was down by the little river in the field, with next door's dog and I'm sure Callum was there because dogs can see them, the Dirges that is. . ." I realised quite how ridiculous all of that sounded and ground to a halt. There was a brief silence as Grace struggled to find something to say. "Look, I know it sounds mad. It is mad, but I'm sure that I saw what I saw, and it has cheered me up."

"Then that's good enough for me, honestly," Grace said in a rush. "Now, what time do you want me round?"

"Umm, have I forgotten something? I wasn't expecting you round this evening."

"It's Saturday night and I don't like to think of you sitting in all alone. I promised Josh I would look after you while he was away tonight, so I'm coming over."

"Thanks for the offer, but I've just had a bath and set up a film, then I'm going to get to bed early. I've not been sleeping well."

"Are you sure? I've ditched Jack for the evening and I can be there in five minutes." She sounded as if she didn't quite believe me.

"Honestly, Grace, I'm fine on my own. There's no danger any more, go and give Jack a nice surprise by turning up at the cricket party."

"You're a disappointment to me, Alex; you were my cast-iron alibi for not going to the excruciatingly dull cricket presentation and disco," she scolded in a mock stern voice. "*Please* can I come? I'll bring popcorn and I can sit very quietly on the edge of the sofa while we watch the dodgy film. How about it?"

My resistance crumbled. It would be nice to sit and watch the film with someone. "OK," I agreed, knowing that I had been masterfully manoeuvred to exactly where she wanted me. "But no difficult questions, I'm not up to it. Promise?"

"I promise. See you in a few minutes. I'll bring my pyjamas too, just in case I decide to stay over." She clicked off the phone before I had a chance to protest.

I yawned as I reset the film back to the beginning and waited for her to arrive, and I realised that I was happy for her to come and take over for a brief while, to keep me safe. Because whatever I said, I really didn't know if Catherine was finished with me, and if she wasn't, what her warped mind would come up with next.

Doubt

Grace left me to have a long lie-in the next day. It was Sunday, and we had the house to ourselves until my parents got back. I had slept well and for the first time in days felt refreshed when I woke up. Downstairs I could smell the comforting aroma of toast and hear the faint sound of the radio. She was making herself at home. I looked at the ceiling as I worked on my plan; I decided to search some of the places I had been with Callum, and see if his presence was any stronger there. It didn't seem likely though, not if I couldn't get any sense of him at all at the top of the dome. But the alternative – doing nothing – wasn't an attractive one either. I levered myself out of bed, wincing as my aching body protested, and made my way downstairs.

"Morning, Grace," I said as perkily as I could manage. "You look like you've been up for hours."

"Well, I didn't wake that early, but you were sound asleep so I thought I'd leave you in peace. You don't have any plans for today, do you?"

"No, only cleaning up the place and slapping on camouflage make up before my parents turn up."

"Good point," she said, eyeing the kitchen, which still showed evidence of some of Josh's more experimental efforts. "Well, at least I can give you a hand with all this."

"Really, you don't have to, I'm quite capable."

"If you say so." Grace raised an eyebrow as I reached for the toast and winced. "Look, I can stick around for a bit, till I need to go and get some stuff done at home." She peered more closely at my face. "And nothing's going to cover that up; it needs days yet."

"I know you're going out later, but can you be here when Mum and Dad get back? You can stop them questioning me half to death." I gingerly touched the healing scabs on my cheek; my skin felt like a cheese grater.

"Sure, just let me know when you think they'll arrive and I'll pop back. But your Beesley story is pretty watertight. Just don't let them see your arm."

Over several coffees and numerous pieces of toast we polished my story, then finally conversation turned to Catherine. It was such a relief to be able to talk with someone who knew, and who understood.

"So do you think she's gone?" Grace asked me as we started trying to load everything into the dishwasher.

"I don't know. She has what she wanted – first the amulet and then the ability to make my life dreadful. But she really, really loathes me."

"That's so odd, given that it was technically you who made it possible for her to come back to life. You think she'd be a bit more grateful!"

"You would, wouldn't you? It doesn't seem to have worked that way for her though." I paused, remembering the night in the alley behind the pub. "She kept telling me that she knew it was all my fault, but unfortunately the details of why it was my fault got wiped when Olivia stole that memory from her." I realised as Grace's perfect eyebrow shot up that I hadn't actually told her about Olivia and the stealing of individual memories. "It's a long and complicated addition to an already unbelievable story, I promise you. Just accept that it happened," I pleaded.

"Fine, OK, carry on."

"So, she was massively cross about whatever it was that I'm supposed to have done, and the fact that she no longer remembered it did absolutely nothing to help. She was livid." I rammed the shelf of the dishwasher back into place, making all the cups rattle. "I mean, what is it that's my fault? Why am I responsible? It doesn't make sense."

"Maybe it's something to do with the amulet. It's obviously a powerful source of something. Maybe when you put it on something happened to her."

"I guess that could be it," I agreed dubiously, considering the empty space on my wrist. The amulet *was* powerful, that was true. A small idea started to circle my brain, and I wondered just how powerful it could be.

"Hey, dozy, are you going to switch that machine on?" Grace's question cut across my thoughts.

"Oh, sorry, yes. I just can't help remembering, you know?"

"Hey now, don't you start getting all emotional again." She caught me by both hands and pulled me around to face her. "I thought I'd been doing a pretty good job so far, and I don't want to have to leave just as you are slipping back into your deep gloom."

I was about to deny it when the phone rang. It was Mum, sounding more flustered than I could ever remember hearing her.

"Oh, Alex, thank goodness you're home. I couldn't get you on your mobile. We've had a terrible morning, and I need your help."

"Whatever's happened? Are you both OK?" It wasn't like

Mum to be in a panic and I found my fists were clenched, palms already damp.

"We're both fine, love – I didn't mean to worry you. We've been robbed though. At the airport. Someone took the bag with the passports."

"What! How on earth did they manage that?" Dad was famously paranoid about keeping the passport wallet safe.

"Oh, it's a long story, but it's broadly my fault. I didn't keep a close enough eye on the bag when I was standing in a queue talking to someone."

"Oh, bad luck." Dad would be furious, I thought. "What do you need me to do?"

"Can one of you please stick around the house today? I'm sorry if that mucks up your plans, but I'm not sure what documents the embassy will need faxing over in order to issue us with temporary passports." She sounded tired and harassed.

"Of course, I'll do it; Josh has gone to that music festival. I've got no specific plans for today anyhow."

"I'm sorry, love, I'd forgotten you'd be on your own this weekend. When's he due back?"

"Um, tomorrow I think. I don't remember, but I can text him and find out."

"Well, I'm not sure quite how long it's going to be before we can get on a plane. Everything seems to be shut here today, and no one is ever much in a rush about anything. It could be a couple of days. I really don't like the fact that you're on your own."

"Honestly Mum, I'll be fine. Term's ended, so I don't have to get anywhere in particular, and Grace has been staying over. If you need me though, call the home number, not my mobile.

I, er. . . well, I dropped it in some water and it's not working any more."

"Oh, Alex, you should be more careful! That was an expensive phone."

"I know, Mum, I'm sorry. Anyway, for now, until I can get it fixed, I'm using the spare one. Have you got the number for that?"

"I'm not sure. Will you text it to me? I guess that explains why I couldn't reach you earlier."

"Sorry, I should have told you. I didn't mean to worry you."

"Well, it did seem odd. You're usually welded to that phone. Look, I have to go; Dad's trying to talk to the police at the moment, and with his grasp of Italian and their grasp of English, it's not going well."

"Oh, poor Dad," I sympathised, knowing how much he hated trying to deal with officials. "Why don't you remind me where all the documents are, then I can have them ready for you when you ring and tell me what to do with them?"

She gave me detailed instructions on where to dig in the office, which was just as well as it was packed to the ceiling with books, files and old post. Finding anything in there was a bit of an adventure.

Once she rang off Grace made a move to go. "Look, I'm sorry, I'm going to have to go now, but we'll talk later, yes? This afternoon I should have a bit of time to check through the conversations on Facebook, and see if Catherine has given away any clues about where she might be, not that we have any real reason to find her now."

"That would be great. Thanks for all your help."

I shut the door behind her with mixed feelings. It had been great to have a conversation about Callum with someone, but once

I was on my own I didn't have to keep up the pretence about being OK. It also meant that I had some time to consider something that had occurred to me earlier. Grace had made some mention about the amulet being powerful, and I had started to think about just *how* powerful it might actually be. Every time someone found it and released a Dirge from their purgatory, the amulet managed to find its way back to the river, but no one had explained to me how that worked. Sometimes I guessed that it put people into the state of mind that they just threw it back into the Thames in despair: I had nearly done that at Hampton Court when Catherine had convinced me that Callum didn't love me. And when I had found it, it was tied to a large rock that someone must have thrown in.

But over the years, surely someone would have tried to smash it? What if one of its powers was to regenerate itself in the river, ready for the next victim? The more I thought about it, the more feasible it seemed to be. Not feasible enough to share with Grace though; this idea I was going to have to explore on my own.

I started to mull over the implications as I searched the office, but soon found that I had to keep my mind on the one task. The piles of paperwork were huge, and although there were files for things, they were mostly full and the overflow was stacked up in random places. Eventually I found what Mum needed, and the old envelopes stuffed with ageing certificates proved quite distracting for a while.

It was a while before Mum rang back to get the information, by which time I had abandoned any thoughts of doing anything practical or useful for the day. But it had given me time to think; about the amulet, and about Callum.

My main difficulty was actually trying to work out just

what I felt: on the one hand I was distraught because Callum was as good as dead to me with the amulet smashed; on the other I was positive that I had sensed him in the park with Beesley, so I knew that he was still there somewhere. So should I grieve or not?

My head was beginning to spin, going round and round the problems. I was grateful that Mum and Dad were going to be away for a while yet though, so I didn't have to explain myself to them. I pulled up the sleeve of my T-shirt to see how the bruise was looking and quickly rolled it back down again. It was still very clearly a golf club head. I was going to have to keep that hidden for at least another forty-eight hours. After that I might get away with it.

I sighed, and went to make myself a cup of coffee. The kitchen was warm, so I opened up the French windows and took my drink out on to the terrace. As usual the birds were attacking the nut feeder, flitting to and fro from the nearby tree, the young fledglings trying hard to stay on but regularly falling off. It would be so much easier if Callum could influence the garden birds, not just a dog who didn't belong to me. I watched them carefully as they fed, but there was no pattern in their movement, nothing that would make me think that he was around. And the more I watched, the more I wondered if I had imagined it with Beesley; had I been so desperate to hear from Callum that I had put my own warped interpretation on a perfectly innocent situation?

No, he was around, I was sure of it, I had to put those sorts of thoughts behind me and cling to the hope that he was there, that there was a way for us to be together again. The amulet *had* to be able to regenerate. I realised that my hands were clenched into tight fists and I forced myself to relax. It would be OK, I was *not* going to give up: the alternative was unbearable.

Dad rang as I was contemplating my evening, with news that they were going to have to spend an extra couple of days in Italy but were hoping to get on a flight on Wednesday. He was also worried that I was sitting in the house all alone.

"Why don't you get Grace to stay over again? You could watch a gruesome chick-flick, or whatever they're called."

"Dad, I'm fine, I don't need a babysitter."

"I'm not suggesting you do," he said, surprised. "Whatever gave you that idea? I thought it might be fun, that's all. You seem to like those terrible films."

"Well, I suppose that's true," I admitted grudgingly. "But she's out tonight. I'll try someone else, Dad, if you really want me to."

"Good girl. It would be nice to think that you were being entertained this evening, not just sitting there all alone."

"There are some distinct benefits to being here all on my own for a change," I mumbled to myself after I said my goodbyes. But only a few minutes after I had put the phone down on Dad, it rang again.

"Hi, Grace, what a coincidence! Has my dad just called you?"

Grace laughed. "What are you on about? I don't generally chat with your dad. Why would he ring me?"

"Oh, as he and Mum aren't going to be back from Italy for a few days, he thought I should get you over again tonight."

"Well, given your ability to annoy complete strangers, I agree with him. I could come back later if you want me to? It would be pretty late though, and I have to be back home first thing."

"Don't worry, it's fine. Your mum will go mad if you're late setting out for your gran's house. Catherine has what she wanted

235

– the amulet is gone. What would be the point in her persecuting me any further?"

"Well, I suppose," Grace said cautiously. "There's nothing at all from her on the Web. She hasn't posted anything about anyone, so I don't have any leads as yet. I'll keep going though. Maybe she's gone."

"Maybe she has. Look, I'm going to be in the house all night. I can lock up now if it'll make you feel any better. And Josh comes home tomorrow. What more harm can come to me here?"

"I suppose you're right. But if you want anything, just call me or Jack, OK? We're here to help."

"I know, Grace, and I really appreciate it. I'll talk to you tomorrow."

The next morning I woke with a start, as if a noise somewhere in the house had disturbed me. I listened hard but there were just the usual creaks and groans of an old building. I had a strange feeling that I had been dreaming about something familiar, but as usual I could remember none of the details. Some people seemed to be able to recall their dreams in fantastic detail, but I never did. I just knew that Callum had been there, telling me what to do, what my next move should be, but I couldn't remember any of it. I turned over and punched the pillow in frustration.

"I'm sorry, Callum. However hard I try the dreams are not working. I still don't know what you are trying to tell me. We are going to have to work out another way of talking."

I sat up in bed considering my day and realised that what I had said wasn't entirely true. I had remembered about Richmond Green. Perhaps if I let my thoughts wander then eventually my subconscious would let something useful and relevant through again.

The day was bright and clear, so I decided to retrace some of the walks I had done with Callum just in case something useful struck me. I threw a bottle of water into my bag and set out, remembering to set the house alarm before I left. If Catherine was going to come back, I didn't want to make things easy for her.

The long walk down to Walton Bridge was uneventful. The swans at the sanctuary took no notice of me at all, much to my disappointment. Callum obviously wasn't with me on my walk, but I carried on, hopeful that at some point, something would become clear. The Thames was looking very still as I started to walk along the path, and the birds were quiet; it was almost as if the entire place was waiting for something. I walked as quickly as I could to the little glade on Sunbury Lock Island, which I always thought of as our special place, but when I got there it was just an empty patch of grass. There was no evidence of Callum, and absolutely no clues about what I should be doing. I sank down on the grass, defeated.

I sat there for ages, looking at the river and hoping that something – anything – would show me that he was around, but nothing changed. The river continued to slide gently past on the long journey that would take it through Twickenham and Richmond, and finally into central London and the shadow of St Paul's. My thoughts went back to that first day, the day everything changed, when I found the amulet in the mud. I remembered the hissing swan and the feeling of the wire biting into my fingers as I tried to break it off, and that first glimpse of the sparkling stone as it saw daylight for the first time in . . . who knows how long. I could imagine Veronica tormenting the poor man to the point when he took off the amulet and sank it into the river, tied to that big rock, and then let her take his memories. And I remembered the moment when I had nearly thrown it back too. Callum had been there then, and his voice had stopped me, but I bet Catherine had been close by, waiting to pounce. I shuddered again at how close I had come to losing everything.

I glanced at the empty patch of pale skin on my wrist, and longed to have the amulet, to be lifting it out of the sand again. As I pictured the little beach I realised that I had to go, I had to return to where I had found it. Maybe there I would find the answers I needed.

I had missed the train, so I unlocked the garage and dusted off Josh's bicycle. He had stopped using it the minute he had passed his driving test, but it all seemed to still be in reasonable working order. I gathered a few essential supplies and set off for Twickenham.

Given how unfit I was I made reasonable time, and was at the White Swan within an hour. I chained the bike up against a railing, making sure that I had put the wire through all the bits that someone could steal, then made my way round to the front of the pub. The water level in the river was falling so the terrace was in no danger of flooding. About half the tables were taken, and there was a low hum of conversation. I had a quick look at all the tables, but there was no one there I recognised.

Up in the bar it was dark and gloomy after the sunshine outside, and the barman looked as if he would much rather have been anywhere else. He served me a glass of lemonade without trying to draw me into conversation, and I was quickly back outside where I could keep my sunglasses over my bruises. I picked my way through the tables until I came to the only free one overlooking the little beach. The water wasn't quite low enough yet to see where I had uncovered the amulet so I sipped my drink and let my mind wander. This had to be an important place, I reasoned. Everything that I had had to do with the amulet had started right here.

This had been the place where I had first seen the strange movement in the stone, and where I had been when Callum had first seen my image. Despite everything that had happened, all the pain, all the heartache, I wouldn't want to change the past. Given the choice again to forget, to not pull the bracelet from the mud, I wouldn't take it. I knew that I would rather have loved Callum and lost him, than never to have felt his love.

I couldn't help sighing, encircling the wrist where the amulet had been, tracing the tan line with my finger. Even that was fading away; within a week it would be gone forever too, I realised. I wished I knew what I was supposed to do! But even as I had that thought the fear gripped me again. Did I really see Callum or had I only seen what I had so desperately wanted to see? Was all of this a wild goose chase? Did I really believe that the amulet could regenerate? It had been smashed into a thousand tiny pieces, the metal twisted and torn, the delicate plaits ruined. That fabulous, shattered stone. . . I looked at my palm where I still had a grubby plaster covering the wound. Slowly I peeled it off. The line on my palm was red and angry, but it was on its way to being healed. Would I, in time, heal too? I slowly rubbed it, the part of me that had had the last contact with the amulet's heart, and stared into the water with all its secrets. I desperately hoped that we would find a way to communicate, but if it didn't happen, well, at least I *had* loved him. I also knew that I should move on, put all this behind me and find someone new, someone nicer than Rob, someone *normal*.

No, I decided, I wasn't going to heal, and I wasn't going to settle for someone normal. I was going to *fight*. I wanted Callum too much to give him up. I needed to think, to discover what he had been trying to tell me, to remember what else might be in my elusive dreams. I had to find a clue, to discover if I should start digging, or trawling the Thames, or what.

Digging. That word triggered a memory; perhaps that was what Callum had been trying to tell me? Maybe I needed to start digging again. Maybe the amulet was already back in the sand, waiting to be rediscovered.

I had been so engrossed in my thoughts I hadn't noticed that someone had slipped into the seat opposite me, and the voice made me jump.

"What's so interesting about the muddy old water then, Alex?" Rob's voice was as sarcastic as ever.

"I don't remember inviting you to sit down." I sat up straight and looked him in the eye, trying to appear unflustered.

"I couldn't resist when I saw you here. Back to the scene of the crime, eh?"

"As usual, Rob, I don't know what you're talking about."

"I think you do. In fact, I *know* you do." The irritatingly smug smile was playing around his lips. I couldn't remember what it was about Rob that I had found attractive. The more I looked at him now, the more he reminded me of a weasel.

"Well, you're going to be disappointed." I shrugged and looked away, back towards the water. I desperately wished Callum was with me. I couldn't fathom what Rob wanted, but I bet that it wouldn't be anything that would benefit anyone but him.

He was clearly keen to draw me into conversation. "I've

been talking to your friend, Catherine. I didn't realise that the two of you were so close."

"What do you mean?"

"Well, you take that bracelet back off Grace, and then give it to Catherine. That's not very nice for poor old loyal Grace, is it? She must have been gutted."

"What bracelet?" I replied sullenly. I didn't want to be drawn into a conversation about the amulet, especially not with Rob.

"Oh, don't play games with me. The one you've been so protective about. The one you clearly still wish you were wearing because you keep rubbing your wrist where it used to be." That was a bit observant for him, I thought, and I resisted the temptation to put my hands under the table. "She must be such a good friend," he continued in his sneering tone.

I sidestepped his question, trying to change the topic. "So when did you see Catherine? I thought she'd left town."

"No, not yet. We had a drink yesterday."

Everything stopped.

If he had seen the amulet yesterday, Catherine couldn't have smashed it.

I realised that I was staring at him with my mouth open and shut it with a quick snap. "Yesterday?" It was all I could do to stop my voice from quivering. "Did she have the bracelet on then?"

"Uh-huh," he grunted, taking a long swig of his pint. I didn't see how it could be possible, I had watched her smash it with my own eyes, I had seen the pieces. My fingers instinctively rubbed the scar on my palm as I replayed the scene in my head. She had ripped a bracelet off her arm, that was true, but given the distance between us and the pounding rain, I hadn't got a really clear look at it. I had seen what she had told me I was seeing. The pieces clicked into place: the blue shard that had cut me had seemed more like glass than the complex layered facets of the amulet's stone. I had assumed that was because the life had gone from it, but it was because it really *was* only glass!

Catherine had tricked me to stop me searching for her and the amulet. She must have known that I would never give up, never rest until I got it safely back. She had smashed a fake bracelet. This way she got the amulet's protection and at the same time got me out of her hair. It was inspired.

All of this had flashed through my mind in a fraction of a second. I smiled tightly at Rob.

"So did you finally get to have a good look at it?"

"I've seen what I needed to see." He smiled enigmatically.

Catherine still had the amulet, that was what Callum had been trying to tell me. I was so excited it was all I could do to stay in my chair. Callum wasn't lost to me for ever. I tried hard to stop myself from laughing with delight. That was the answer I had been searching for. I was going to see Callum again! I beamed at Rob, and he sat back in his chair, startled.

"You're positive it was the same bracelet, though? My bracelet?" I needed to be sure.

"Uh-huh," he grunted again. "It looks valuable too. I'm surprised you gave it up."

"Let's say Catherine was very persuasive." I lifted my hair and took off my sunglasses for a minute so he could see the full extent of bruises, expecting him to be shocked, but he just raised his eyebrows.

"Quite the little minx, isn't she?"

"You know, Rob, it would be really helpful if you happened to know where she might be now. I've got something for her."

He gave me a knowing smile and took another long swallow of his drink.

"Come on, what do you care about Catherine?" I continued. I could almost hear his brain whirring and I wondered what it was that he was plotting. He wasn't generally that sophisticated.

"I don't know where she is right now, but I do know where she'll be tomorrow."

I sat up straighter in my seat.

"Where? What's she going to do?"

"As you said, she's going away. She seems pretty fed up with everybody here."

"Where's she going?" I repeated the question, trying not to be tetchy. "Did she say?"

"West Country, I think. Was it Newquay? I can't really remember. She told me that she has a train ticket for tomorrow morning."

My heart sank. I needed to find her before she disappeared. If she left the area it would be next to impossible to find her again, and I had to get the amulet back. I tried to keep calm, to not appear too overexcited.

I took a sip of my drink while I considered Rob. "You two seem to have been getting on very well. It's a shame for you that she's leaving."

"Well, she and I do have a certain . . . understanding, that's true."

"Don't you fancy your chances then, Rob? She is gorgeous. And with her winning personality, she's just your type."

"Oh, I'm in there, I know that. Just not sure I fancy all the baggage she carries around with her," he said, with more than a hint of arrogance.

"Really? What baggage is that?"

He shot me a knowing look. "Don't give me that, Alex. You know all about Catherine and her weird ways."

"What exactly do you mean?"

"She's got some very strange ideas, and a certain unconventional way of solving problems, wouldn't you agree?" He gestured towards my cheek.

I was with him on that. "She's not going to be on my Christmas card list, that's for sure. So, um. . ." I hesitated, trying desperately hard to work out a way of getting him to tell me what he knew. "Couldn't you just put her weirdness to one side, especially as you have an 'understanding'?"

"Well, I did think about it, and I have to admit, we've spent some time together." The smug smile was back.

"So, you must be meeting up later then, given it's her last night in the area? A bit of a farewell drink while you help her to pack her bags?"

He gave a hollow laugh. "Not my idea of a fun night, that's for sure."

"Really? Why ever not? Has she turned you down?"

"No! As if!"

"I see. She's too much even for you to handle, is she?" I smiled sweetly at him as I said it.

"I just don't fancy carting myself all the way over to North Sheen, that's—" He stopped suddenly and looked flustered. I raised an eyebrow at him.

"Where was that, Rob? North Sheen? Is that where she lives? Is that where she'll be getting the train in the morning?"

He looked trapped. "What are you talking about? I never said that!"

I smiled to myself. Rob had given away what I needed to know.

He was silent for a moment, swirling the remains of his pint around in his glass. Finally he looked at me. "You think you're so clever, Alex, but you're the one with the mashed-up face."

He drained the last of his drink and put the glass carefully down in the middle of the table.

"It's been good to see you. I'm glad we've been able to have this last drink. No hard feelings, eh?"

"For what? No hard feelings for what?"

"Oh, you know, everything." He stood up and I felt suddenly cold in his shadow. "See you around."

I watched him go with mixed emotions: some annoyance and frustration but mostly exultation. Catherine had tricked me. Somewhere, not that far from here, the amulet was waiting for me. And with the amulet, Callum.

Tactical Error

I knew what I had to do the next morning. I couldn't risk missing Catherine. Once she got on the train and into London the amulet would be lost to me as effectively as when I thought it had been smashed. I couldn't sleep, trying to remember the details of what I had seen that day in the rain. It had been so murky I guessed that it wouldn't have been so hard for her to pass off a fake amulet as the real thing. And of course, once I thought it was destroyed, I wouldn't be troubling her again. Olivia had been right: Catherine was downright evil.

I scoured the train timetable and got myself out of the house really early. Josh had come home late the night before but I had managed to avoid too much in the way of conversation and sneaked off to bed. The festival had clearly been a good one; he looked exhausted and was sound asleep in the morning when I put my head round his bedroom door. I left him a note and walked quickly to the train.

Even at six in the morning the carriage was full of commuters off to their offices. All looked equally miserable and no one said a word. I fought against the tide to get off the train at North Sheen and considered my options. I was lucky that it was that particular station. There was only one way in and out, over a narrow footbridge and on to a single central platform. I set myself up so that I could watch the people coming over the bridge before they would notice I was there, with my hair tucked into the hoodie I was wearing as a feeble disguise.

After several hours and an interminable number of trains coming and going, the glint of sunlight on someone's hair caught my attention. The familiar dark gold made my heart leap for a moment as the head bobbed along the footbridge. I slunk back into my hoodie as she turned to come down the steps towards the platform.

It was Catherine, swathed in huge dark glasses and carrying a small wheelie bag. It obviously wasn't heavy as she was having no trouble carrying it down the long flight of steps, and she looked poised and elegant as she wheeled it along the ramp towards the ticket office.

The second she was out of sight behind the little building, I ran to the bench seat on the platform, pulling out my paper. I slumped down low and held the paper up as high as I dared without looking like a bad detective. I could see her out of the corner of my eye as she walked past the ticket window and on to the platform. She looked up at the departure boards and then at her watch. I couldn't see the amulet and I had to try really hard to resist the temptation to leap up and wrestle her to the ground. I was going to follow her until we were somewhere slightly more private, then demand it back. I knew that I wasn't physically strong, but I also knew that her passion and need were going to be no match for mine. I could win, and when I looked her in the eye she would be able to tell that she had no chance. I just needed to be away from too many witnesses, so I clenched my fists in my pockets and waited.

She took me by surprise when she got on to the train heading away from London, and then I almost missed her getting off at Richmond. I saw the oversized glasses before I realised it was her, and hurriedly stepped off the train. She was standing on the platform looking at a pocket timetable. I dodged the people walking down the platform and nipped behind the old ticket inspector's booth. I could peer through the grubby glass without too much danger of being spotted.

Two trains went past and she didn't move, and I was beginning to think that I had been rumbled, that she was playing with me, but then the fast train pulled in. With limited stops to Reading and a change there to the main West Country line, it was a fast option for getting to Cornwall without going through London. Catherine boarded the train and I got on a couple of carriages down from her. I kept a lookout that she didn't get off again, but she disappeared down inside the carriage.

It was time to decide what to do. The train didn't stop for a while so I had her captive, but then once I had the amulet off her, I had nowhere to go either. But it was too late to worry about that. I had about twenty minutes before the first stop. I walked through the next two carriages, surprised at how few people were actually travelling. At the door of the one where I thought she was I stopped and pulled down my hood as far as I could. I couldn't see her through the little window. Ready to fight to get my amulet back, I opened the carriage door.

It was eerily quiet. There didn't seem to be anyone in there at all, no one making phone calls, no mothers with toddlers, no businessmen folding their newspapers noisily. I sat down in the first set of seats and leaned my head towards the window. From that angle I could see down the long line of seats but there were no shoulders or elbows in view. I got up silently and moved to the other side of the train, and peered down the line there. About halfway down I could see an arm clad in black, the elbow resting on the window sill. Suddenly she moved, leaning her head against her hand, looking straight towards me.

I shot back upright, hoping that she hadn't seen me. This was my chance. This was my last opportunity to get Callum back. I wasn't going to waste it.

I took several deep breaths as I considered my totally unsophisticated plan. Utter determination was my solitary tactic. I decided not to creep down the carriage, but stood tall, head covered by the hood, sunglasses in place. I wiped my sweaty palms down my jeans, and curled my fists ready to fight. Moving swiftly down the carriage, within seconds I was standing facing Catherine, boxing her in.

"The game's up, Catherine. Hand it over."

She ignored me completely, looking out of the window as a dreary industrial estate slid past.

"Don't play games with me. I know you still have the amulet, that you tricked me last week. Now, I've asked nicely. If you don't give it to me, I'm going straight to the guard to call the police. You tried to kill me, and there are witnesses to both that and you stealing from the bank. No one is going to believe a word you say. I'll just tell them that I was a victim of identity theft, and you'll spend years in a prison so horrible it will make life as a Dirge seem quite pleasant."

I paused in my tirade, hoping that she would look at me, but she continued staring out of the window. "Give me back my amulet!" I stood in front of her, instinctively balancing on the balls of my feet, my fists tight.

Still nothing. It was a brilliant tactic on her part, and hugely infuriating. I steadied myself, trying to remain in control; losing it wasn't going to help. But I could almost feel the tingle in my wrist – Callum was so close! All I had to do was get the amulet off her and he and I would be together again. I thrust my hand towards her. "Now," I said in a low voice, hoping to sound quiet and menacing. Finally she moved, turning her huge sunglasses towards me.

"I don't think so." Her voice was dead, completely stripped of emotion.

"What makes you think you have the right to keep it, Catherine? It's mine and you know it," I hissed, still struggling to stay calm. She shrugged and returned to looking out of the window, hands resting in her lap.

I couldn't resist, and grabbed for her wrists. But there was no fight in her; she offered no resistance as I shoved her sleeves up to her elbows. She wasn't wearing the amulet. Holding both her arms tight I leaned in close. "Where. Is. My. Amulet?" I hissed at her.

She turned to look at me and the sudden closeness of our faces made me back up. Behind those huge glasses it was really hard to gauge her mood. I let go of her arm and pulled the glasses from her face, determined to look her in the eyes.

She considered me contemptuously. "It's gone. I don't have it any more, OK?"

I sat back on the seat opposite in shock. "But. . . but who. . .?"

"Oh, pull yourself together, you pathetic creature. Does it really matter?"

"What! Of course it matters!" The anger was slowly overcoming the shock. "I'm going to get it back – it's mine."

"Well, good luck with that." She smiled icily, leaning

forwards and snatching her sunglasses back from my numb grasp. She slipped back behind her impenetrable mask.

"Who was it? Who's got my amulet?"

She ignored me, looking back out of the window at the passing scenery. I felt like shaking her. The disappointment at losing Callum again, just when I thought he was so close, was almost unbearable. "Why do you care now? Why not tell me?"

"Actually, I just don't like you. Isn't that enough?"

I was speechless again, this time with the injustice of it. Without me she would still be a Dirge, stuck in a miserable existence. She turned the great, fly-like lenses towards me, and a small smile started to play around her mouth.

"You know, I can't decide which would be more enjoyable actually; telling you now and watching you suffer, or making you wait and find out tomorrow."

"I don't understand. What do you mean, tomorrow?"

Catherine looked at her watch and then gazed at me coolly. "I might as well get to see it. I do like watching your agonies. You're so *obvious* in your emotions." The sarcasm dripped from her tone.

A feeling of dread started to creep across me. What now? I took a deep breath. "Come on then, get it over with."

"Well, it's all your fault anyway. Without you telling him all that stuff he would never have worked it out."

"Told who what? Come on!"

"Can't you guess? Who dislikes you almost as much as I do? Any ideas?"

I frowned, trying to work out what she was getting at. "No, not with you."

"You are *so* dim," she muttered under her breath. "Rob. That's who hates you. I'm so glad to see that you took the bait. I didn't

251

think that he could drop the hint subtly enough, but he assured me he'd got you hooked. The boy's gone up in my estimation."

"What are you talking about?" I gasped.

She shook her head in disbelief. "Getting you on to this train. It was much easier than we expected."

I stared at her open-mouthed, realising that I'd been completely outmanoeuvred.

"You and Rob?" A hollow pit had opened up in the bottom of my stomach. "What does Rob have to do with it?"

"Listen, you stupid girl. *He knows what the amulet is*, what it does."

"How can he possibly know that? I didn't tell him."

"Ah, but you *did* tell him, just not directly."

I resisted the urge to slap her. "How many times do I have to tell you? I told no one, least of all that self-centred idiot!"

"Let me take you back, back to that day in Kew Gardens when you so willingly gave up everything for me. I believe that you lost something."

The penny finally dropped. "The memory card? Rob found the memory card?"

She nodded, smugly. "As I said, all your own fault."

My mind whirled, and various things suddenly became clear. That was why Rob had the passworded files about me on his computer that had upset Ashley so much, why he was suddenly interested in talking to me again, and why he wanted to see the amulet more closely. "Is that what you meant about it being my fault? When we were talking at the pub?" One perfect eyebrow rose briefly from behind the glasses in response. "But I thought that you had lost that memory, that Olivia had taken it from you?"

"Oh no, I'm perfectly clear on this. It's definitely your fault."

"So what did Olivia take? The memory of how the Dirges could escape? Was that it?"

Catherine didn't answer, just continued to regard me silently. I knew she was trying to irritate me, and I also knew that I couldn't afford to get distracted. Finding the amulet was my priority.

"What on earth does he want with the amulet? I mean, talking to Dirges is hardly Rob's sort of thing."

"He doesn't intend to keep it. He's smarter than he looks, that boy."

"What's he going to do with it?" I asked, puzzled.

This time Catherine laughed out loud, startling me. "He has a beautifully malicious streak along with his greed. He's going to sell it to the papers. In fact, he's organised a bidding war."

"But why would they be so interested?"

"You know," she said reflectively, "that's what I'm going to miss about you; you are so trusting, so . . . naive." She made it sound like some sort of disease.

"Get to the point," I said tersely.

"I suppose I might as well amuse myself. The train isn't stopping anytime soon, so you have nowhere else to go." She gave me one of her thin, evil smiles. "Let's go back to the beginning; what does the amulet let you do?"

She was deliberately winding me up, her voice hugely patronising. I took a deep breath and willed myself to stay calm. "It allows me to talk to Callum."

"Exactly. And who else?"

"The other Dirges, of course."

"Excellent!" Her voice was dripping with sarcasm. "And for

a bonus point can you tell me what you have to do to qualify to be a Dirge?"

"You have to drown in the River Fleet," I hissed through gritted teeth.

"Give that girl the prize! That's right, *drown*; that would be the key word. The amulet allows us to talk to people who have drowned – Who. Are. Dead!" She punctuated each word individually, but I still wasn't sure what she was getting at.

"So, what's your point?"

"Let's think about that for a moment, shall we?" she continued in the same patronising tone. "Who else has something that allows you to talk to dead people? That could be tested by scientists?" She paused and took off her sunglasses. "Definitive proof of life after death? It's dynamite, and Rob knows it."

I felt my mouth drop open in horror: she was right. If Rob told the papers then the world of the Dirges would be turned upside down. People would pay small fortunes to gawp at them, and the scientists would have a field day. The amulet would become so important, so valuable, that my chances of ever getting to use it to speak to Callum would be effectively zero. And as soon as the Dirges started draining the memories of the people who had taken it off, killing them in order to escape, all hell would break loose. It would be impossible to ever get the amulet back, and Callum would still be comprehensively lost to me.

"I have to stop him," I muttered, getting to my feet. "He has to be made to understand."

"Oh, it's far too late for that. That's the delicious irony of you chasing me all this way on the non-stop train. That's why we made sure you followed me, to get you well out of the way. He's on his way to the publicist right now." She laughed again. "You've already missed him. By the time you get into London the amulet will be *way* out of your reach!"

"You're joking; you must be." I could feel the tears starting to come again and fought them back, but what she said rang true. I couldn't believe that I had fallen for Rob's trick.

"No, sweetie. Time to say bye-bye, I think. Such a shame that Callum will always be just too far away for you to be able to reach him. I'm sure the publicist will have a field day with his chiselled good looks too. He'll become quite the ghostly pin-up."

It was such a hideous prospect, and so inevitable too. "Catherine, help me. Please. You can't want to see that happen to them all. They were your friends, your family. Just tell me where Rob's going and I can stop him."

"What makes you think I know where he's going?"

"If you've been so clever making plans with Rob to trick me, you must know."

She shrugged and looked away, and I knew that she knew she had made a tactical error. I pressed on. "Come on, he was bound to be bragging about how clever he was to have worked it all out. I'm surprised that you didn't want to benefit more from that. Why are you running away now?" She put her glasses back on as I spoke, hiding her face, and turned to look out of the window. It all suddenly became clear to me.

"Did you do a deal with him?" I asked incredulously. Catherine continued to ignore me. "You did, didn't you? What is it, you get a cut of the cash in exchange for leaving you out of the story? Ongoing anonymity for the only undead person on the planet? Frankly I'm amazed that you care."

"Well, that shows just how stupid you are then," she spat

back, unable to maintain her silence. "I'm not doing this for free, and anyway, I'm not the only 'undead person', as you put it."

"What do you mean?" Catherine suddenly looked shifty. "Come on," I pressed. "Who are you talking about? Is it Veronica? Is she still here too?"

Catherine turned as far as possible towards the window but stayed silent. I realised that, for the first time, I had the upper hand. I decided to go for it. "So under the circumstances you'll want me to stay quiet too, I presume?"

I paused for a second, enjoying her discomfort. Catherine shifted even further in her seat, trying to turn her back to me. "OK, this is the deal. I won't tell either, but only if you tell me where Rob is going."

She turned and shot me a look of pure venom. "You'll never get there now anyway, so actually it doesn't matter. He had an appointment this morning, with the guy who does the publicity for all the celebrities – Steve Scales. Or with his people, anyway. He was childishly excited about it."

"You mean the one who deals with the reality TV contestants?"

"Yeah, him. He'll get Rob some good coverage." Infuriatingly she was right; the guy was good at his job.

"Do you know where his office is?"

"If you think I'm going to tell you anything else then you are very much mistaken. I've already told you more than you deserve. Now, go away. I don't want to have anything else to do with you ever again."

"Suits me, and if I find that you have been messing about in my life again, there'll be trouble."

"Oh, I'm so scared," she bit back sarcastically as I turned to leave. I ignored her and started to walk down the carriage to find the guard. I heard her voice call after me. "I look forward to reading all about you both in the papers. It couldn't have happened to a more deserving couple."

I slammed the carriage door behind me as I left.

Station

My mind was racing as I walked down the train looking for the guard. I had to get there before Rob talked to the publicity people about the amulet. If someone else got to see the Dirges it was all over, I would never get the amulet back. It would be too valuable, too exciting for them to give up. But the other, bigger, problem was the danger. If he made a good connection with them, Rob could end up summoning the wrong ones when he started showing the amulet off. That had the potential to be suicidal. I shuddered at the memory of watching Grace being attacked by Catherine and I couldn't wish that fate on anyone. But to be able to stop Rob I first had to find out where he was and get there as fast as possible. I pulled the huge phone out of my pocket and started trying to work out how I was going to persuade him. I was pretty sure he wouldn't take the slightest bit of notice about what I was saying, but he had to be warned of the danger; I had to try. I unlocked the keypad and groaned out loud: the only number in there was Josh's. I had no idea what Rob's was. I was just going to have to chase after him.

I finally found the guard sitting in his little cubicle in the middle of the train. I took off my glasses and tried to look as miserable as possible, letting myself well up again. I knocked gingerly on the window.

He slid the door open. "Yes?" he asked in a bored voice.

"I'm really sorry," I said in a voice suddenly more full of tears than I had intended. "I think I've got on the wrong train. I need to be in London." I offered him my ticket. He looked faintly horrified at being confronted by a potentially hysterical teenager. "All right, love, calm down. I'm sure we can work it out. Now. . ." He pursed his lips and picked up a well-thumbed thick directory off a shelf. "Let's check your connections."

He quickly worked out that my best option was to continue to Reading and then get the non-stop express directly into Paddington. From there I could get the Tube wherever I wanted. He sold me an extension to my ticket and closed his door again with a distinct air of relief.

The next thing was how to find out where to go. There was no browser facility on my mobile, so I couldn't do it that way, and waiting to get to an Internet café in London was just going to slow me down. I needed someone to help me. Luckily I had one number memorised.

"Grace, hi, sorry, look I need a favour, really quickly."

"Alex, calm down. What's the matter? Are you OK?"

"Not really. Catherine tricked me. She didn't destroy the amulet but she doesn't have it any more, either."

"What! Where is it then? What's she done with it?"

"I haven't got time to explain, I'm sorry. I'm on a train, and I need an address in London. Can you look it up for me?"

"Of course, hang on a sec while I log on." There was a pause and I could hear her long fingernails tapping on the keyboard. "Right," she said finally. "Google is ready and waiting. What do you need to know?"

"The office of that publicity guy, Steve Scales; the one who does all the reality TV people."

"Really? OK, if you say so."

"I need the address, and the quickest way to get there from Paddington."

"Paddington," she said evenly. "You know, you have a lot of explaining to do."

"I know, and I'm sorry, but there's just no time. Now, have you got it?"

"Hang on. . ." Grace was muttering away to herself and tapping on the keyboard as we finally pulled into Reading station. I hurried off the train to check which platform I needed for the express. Further along I could see Catherine stepping casually down to the platform, her almost empty suitcase in her hand. I took a wide route so that I didn't have to go too close to her, grateful that I was never going to have to speak to her again.

I ran up the stairs and looked at all the departure boards. My train would be arriving in just a few minutes, so I didn't have time to lose. I hurried down on to the right platform and positioned myself where the front of the train was going to stop. Across the tracks I could see Catherine on the westbound platform, studiously ignoring me.

Grace was still muttering to herself on the other end of the phone. "They don't want you to find them easily, you know. Won't the phone number be enough?"

"No, Rob is taking the amulet there to show them what it does. I *have* to stop him."

"What! Rob? How on earth did he get involved in all this?" Grace's voice shot up about three octaves. "The little—"

"Grace!" I interrupted her. "Please, calm down. Just find me the address."

"OK, OK. I'm just going to try somewhere else on the

site." At that point there was a deafening announcement about the imminent arrival of my train. "I'm not going to ask about that either," she said in a resigned voice. "Not yet anyway. Don't you think that's good of me?"

"You are, as usual, the most loyal and best friend a girl could have, and I do appreciate it."

"Alex!" The voice calling from across the tracks surprised me. I looked over to the other platform. Catherine was waving at me. "I forgot to ask," she shouted. "That memory, the one Olivia stole – did you find anything out from that?"

"Are you trying to be funny?" I shouted back. "Olivia has nearly been broken by your warped mind."

"Really? The thing is, it seems I wrote it all down, just in case." She reached into her pocket and pulled out a folded piece of paper. "I wrote *everything* down. I know exactly how to rescue my dear brother and his friends, but you will never find out!"

"What?" I shouted. "What do you mean?" The last words were drowned out by the express thundering into the station, and Catherine disappeared behind the blur of metal and windows. As soon as the train screeched to a halt I wrenched open the nearest door and ran across the carriage to peer at the opposite platform. It was impossible to see, so I dragged down the really stiff window and stuck out my head, scanning the platform. Catherine was nonchalantly walking up the platform away from me. I wasn't going to be able to run up the train to get closer to her, there were too many people getting on. "Catherine!" I bellowed at the top of my voice, causing every other person on the platform to turn and stare. "If you know that you have to tell me! Don't be so cruel!"

She stopped and turned, and the smug smile was back on her face. Slowly she waved. "Goodbye, Alex."

"Wha—" My shout was cut off by an ear-splitting horn, blaring right behind me. I pulled my head back inside the window a fraction of a second before the West Country train thundered in beside me. Shaken, I lost sight of Catherine as it rumbled to a halt between us. I jumped back from the door to see if I could run down the carriage and catch up with her, but I was suddenly conscious of everything outside slowly starting to move. As the train picked up speed I slumped back against the wall, beaten. Whatever it was she was taunting me with, I wasn't going to find out any more now.

"Damn it!" I muttered to myself, and was then conscious of a distant voice calling.

"Alex? Are you there? What on earth is going on?"

I looked around wildly, hoping for a fraction of a second that somehow Callum was back, then realised that I was still clutching my phone. I lifted it to my ear. "Sorry, Grace, that was Catherine, but she's gone now."

The anxiety was evident in her voice. "Alex Walker, this isn't funny any more. You have to tell me what's going on."

"I know, and I'm sorry, really I am. I will tell you just as soon as I get back, I promise."

"Are you safe? You're not doing anything dangerous, are you?"

"I'm fine, honestly. I just need to get to that address before Rob does."

"Wait a sec. I stopped searching while all the noise was going on. Now . . . got it! I don't suppose you have a pen?" she asked in her best withering tone.

"Umm, no, you're right. Nothing useful like that at all."

"I'll text it all to you, OK? To this new number?"

"Brilliant, yes, to this number. My old phone is completely dead. Thanks a million, Grace. I'll call you later and give you all the details, I promise."

"You'd better. In the meantime just keep safe, all right?"

"Yeah, I'll try. Thanks again. Bye." I snapped off the phone and within minutes there was the beep of an incoming text. I took a quick look. She had given me the full address and the nearest Tube station. One problem solved, then, but a much bigger one looming.

I couldn't stay still enough to sit in a seat crammed in next to someone else, so I stood by the doors and watched the London skyline approaching from the unfamiliar angle. I wondered where Rob was, how far he had got on his journey to the publicist. I felt quite sick at the thought that at that precise moment he might be handing over my precious amulet to some stranger, someone who would only use it to make money. I couldn't believe that someone I knew, and had once trusted, could be so mercenary. I still had no idea about how I was going to persuade him to hand it back, I just hoped that something good would come to me.

I didn't dare let myself think about the other things that Catherine had said. One problem at a time, that was all I could deal with. I would get the amulet back and then worry about her and her strange comments.

Surprisingly quickly the train was pulling into Paddington station, and I was on the platform looking wildly around for the entrance to the Tube. There were huge numbers of people milling aimlessly about and I had to resist the urge to knock them out of the way as I tried to run to the escalators. It was equally busy down in the ticket hall, with hordes of tourists consulting maps and peering at the self-service machines.

I rummaged around in my bag and pulled out my Travelcard, scanning around for directions to the right line. I needed the Bakerloo line to take me down to Piccadilly Circus. I finally spotted the sign over the heads in the crowd, and darted towards the escalators. Luckily everyone else was in a hurry too so I was able to run down to the platform.

It was warm down in the Underground, and stuffy, and it was a relief when the train finally thundered towards us, pushing a welcome blast of air up the tunnel towards the platform. The carriage was packed, but I was too nervous to sit anyway, so I hung on to one of the poles near the door, checking out how many stops I had to wait. Five stops before the one I wanted. Five interminable waits while the people shuffled off the train and another crowd forced their way on. I hung on tight to my pole, not wanting to get pushed back down away from the door. The last stop at Oxford Circus seemed to take for ever, as all the people getting on were carrying huge carrier bags full of shopping.

I checked my watch for the hundredth time, wishing I knew what time Rob's appointment was. I clenched my hands and realised that they were damp with sweat. I wiped them down my trousers again, taking a couple of deep breaths. Finally the train set off and I positioned myself next to the door so I could get off as quickly as possible. As we sped into Piccadilly Circus station I could see that the platform was packed with people. The door seemed to take an age to open but finally I was free, dashing up the platform towards the exit. I ran as fast as I could, dodging around people dragging wheelie suitcases and shopping, apologising over my shoulder when I knocked into others. The tunnels to the exit were like a maze, but finally I was running up the last escalator and through the ticket barrier.

I ran up the stairs of the nearest street exit without thinking, blinking as I emerged into the bright sunlight, then stopped abruptly as I realised that I didn't know where I was going. Looking around I could see the huge advertising boards of Piccadilly Circus, flashing their messages, the statue of Eros, surrounded by people taking photos, and as I turned further, I saw that there were six different roads I could choose. I had no idea which was the one I wanted.

I was about to run back down into the station where I was sure that there would be a map when I caught a glimpse of someone coming up out of another exit. There was something familiar about his arrogant swagger that made me take a second look and hesitate, mid-turn. The sunlight had caught the bright shock of his blond hair – Rob. I couldn't believe my luck; I was in time, he hadn't handed the amulet over. All I had to do was follow him and stop him.

But he was on the far side of the junction; I had about three roads to cross to get to him before he disappeared again into London's crowds. I hesitated for a brief second. The quickest way was probably to go back into the Underground and out of the exit he had just used. But that meant that I would lose sight of him, and I really didn't want to do that. I scanned the various queues of traffic and decided to run for it. Dodging between taxis and white vans, I ran across the bottom of Regent Street, then straight across the next little road, putting out my hand to stop an oncoming car. The driver hooted crossly at me as he screeched to a halt, but luckily there was so much noise going on that the sound didn't cause Rob to turn. He was striding purposefully up a wide road, and I glanced at the building on the corner to see which street it was: Shaftesbury Avenue. That was where I was supposed to be heading; he was definitely still on his way to the agency.

He was about fifty metres ahead of me, on the other side of the road, a small briefcase in his hand. I quickly pulled my hood up over my own blonde hair, shoving my hands deep into my pockets. After a couple of minutes he slowed down and pulled a piece of paper out of the side pocket of the case. He studied it for a second, then looked across at my side of the road. I had managed to close some of the gap between us, so I turned to look in the shop window next to where I was standing. I watched in the reflection as he crossed to my side and turned up a narrow street, then I broke into a run as he disappeared out of sight. Even though I knew the address of where he was going, I didn't want to lose him.

It was darker in the little side street, and much quieter, but he was too far ahead for me to be able to tackle him. And I still had no clear idea about what it was I was going to say to him. Fighting was out of the question, and he obviously had no moral conscience to appeal to. The only thing I could think of was to accuse him of stealing, and to do that I needed to be nearer to some other people, people who might intervene on my behalf. I fell back slightly, keen that he didn't spot me too soon, but kept a careful eye on the road names in case we reached our destination. We passed dozens of restaurants, and the wonderful smells wafting out of the kitchens made me realise that I hadn't eaten for hours, but I knew I was still far too nervous to be hungry. There would be time for that later though, after I had been reunited with Callum. I just hoped that he was here, that somehow he had been able to follow me.

Eventually the tiny streets of Soho opened out into a leafy

square that was surrounded by tall, modern buildings. I glanced quickly at the text message Grace had sent me earlier: the building I wanted was in the far corner.

Rob was peering at his sheet of paper again, then he set out round the left-hand side of the square. I saw my chance, and ran at full pelt around the other side, keeping behind the vans and taxis as much as I could. I wanted to be at the door as he arrived. I slowed to a fast walk as I neared the building, checking over my shoulder that he was still coming. He was too engrossed in his plans to notice anyone else, and by the time he approached the front door, I was leaning nonchalantly against a post box, the only feature on the wide pavement.

As I watched, he examined the paper one last time, then folded it and put it back in his jeans pocket. He looked towards the building, which was a sleek, modern design made entirely of mirrored glass. But Rob wasn't admiring the architecture, he was admiring himself. He was looking at his reflection, running his fingers through his hair to maintain its carefully tousled appearance, brushing something off the shoulder of his expensive casual shirt. I wasn't going to get a better chance.

Mirrors

"Hi, Rob, fancy seeing you here," I said as I pushed myself off the post box and sauntered casually towards him. For a second he lost his composure completely, his jaw dropping.

"Er. . . umm . . . Alex. What are you doing in Soho?" he asked eventually.

"Oh, I think you know that."

"Not sure I do," he answered, obviously playing for time.

"You have something that belongs to me, and I'd like it back." I stood facing him, arms folded, trying desperately hard to keep my nerves under control. I couldn't afford for him to think that he could frighten me into submission. His eyes kept darting over my shoulder towards the door of the building where he clearly thought that he would be safe. He tried the denial route again.

"No, really. I have no idea what you're talking about."

"Don't give me that. Do you think I'm stupid? You know *exactly* what I'm talking about."

As I watched, his eyes narrowed. He was recovering from the surprise and moving swiftly on to the offensive. "Are you stalking me, Alex? I mean, I know you've had some issues, but really, do you have to follow me to London?"

I gave him a withering look. "I have much better things to do with my time, thank you, than follow you around all day. Just give me back my bracelet!"

He ignored me and carried on. "Because, you know, stalkers, they're dangerous. I'm sure that the police would be interested in having a little chat with you. You've become quite familiar with them over the last few weeks, haven't you?"

"I'd love it if you called the police, and you could then explain to them what you're doing with stolen property."

Finally he laughed. "The thing is, Alex, it was no longer yours, was it? You gave it to Catherine."

"You know full well that Catherine stole it from me!"

"I know nothing of the sort. She said that you gave it to her because the two of you are friends. What could be more straightforward than that? It's great that the two of you are so close." I could see the sarcastic smile on his face, and I took a step closer, clenching my fists.

"So close, in fact, that Catherine told me all about your little money-making scheme."

His smile faltered for a second but he quickly regained his composure. "As I believe I said yesterday, we have an understanding."

"Once you get in there and start talking," I jabbed towards the shiny building with my finger, "don't you think they'll want to know how you came to have the amulet?"

"Once they see what it does, they won't care. They'll be falling over each other to get the best price for the story, and I'll be rich."

"Is that what this is all about, being rich? You're prepared to ruin my life and those of countless others just because you want to cash in on your fifteen minutes of fame? You're pathetic! And don't forget, I've still got proof of Catherine's methods of persuasion." I lifted up my sleeve to show him the bruises on my arm.

He raised his eyebrows at the multicoloured marks. "And

I thought it was just your face. She really went to town, didn't she? But you won't shop either of us, I'm sure." He smiled at me slyly. "I mean, we can do a deal here; come to some sort of mutually beneficial arrangement."

"I don't think so," I huffed, crossing my arms.

"Are you absolutely sure? Don't you want to talk to Callum again? Isn't that what this is all about, for you to be together again?" He used his hands to put inverted commas around "together", infuriating me even more.

"So you'll give it back then?"

"Don't be ridiculous! I can just see a way to get what everyone wants, that's all. You keep quiet, and I'll ensure that you and Callum get some amulet time. Under careful supervision, of course. I know I can't trust you that much. Then Catherine and I get to split the money. Everyone is happy!"

"That's not what I want. Give me back my amulet now, or I'll have you arrested for theft."

"Now, that wouldn't be a good idea. Let me explain the deal in a little more detail. If you cause trouble – *any* trouble – I'll make sure that you never get to see Callum again. Everyone else will; we can really go to town on finding out all about him, his family, his real girlfriend, however old she is now. Then I'll give the papers your video diaries, all that angst and sobbing will fill pages for the tabloids. You'll have people bugging you about it for years, but all the time he'll be just out of your reach." He paused, and gave a brief leer. "They could even have you and his old girlfriend slugging it out."

I felt a wave of horror shimmer through me. Rob had inadvertently stumbled over the one thing that would make me hesitate. Callum had been very clear on that point: knowing his past, who he was, what had happened to his parents, would make his daily existence unbearable. I couldn't let that happen, but I couldn't let Rob know that either. I glared up at him from under my hood. "If I agree – *if* . . ." I emphasised, looking at the sudden smile on his face, "what else is in it for you? It can't just be to keep me quiet."

"Well, the truth is," he started to look shifty again, "the video diaries are good, but if you're there, willing to answer questions about how things work, well. . . Catherine won't even consider talking to anyone, but if you answer the journalists' questions, we'll get so much more money."

Money. That was what it was all about: pure greed. At least I knew what I was dealing with.

"OK, if – *if* – I join you, how do you plan to do things? What do they know already?"

He could barely contain his excitement. "I've talked to them, but not shown them anything yet; that's what today is about." He glanced at his briefcase.

"What are you planning to show them?"

"The video, and then I'll get them to see one of the Dirges. They said that if I could prove it, I could pretty much name my price."

I tried to keep my voice steady. "Have you been communicating with *them?*"

"I tried it last night after Catherine gave me the amulet. I didn't even have to say anything – this bloke just skulked up behind me in the mirror. Made me jump, I can tell you!"

"Was it just the one of them?"

"Yeah. You know," he dropped his voice and looked around furtively, "it's a bit freaky. I'm surprised that you didn't chuck it back in the river as soon as you saw them. At least I knew what was coming. You must have been scared half to death, with weird cloaked people looming up behind you!"

"It was a bit of a shock," I agreed.

"He didn't seem to be very friendly, either. He didn't say anything, just glared at me a bit. I guess I'm not his favourite person, so I'm kind of relieved that he's stuck on the other side of the mirror." He took another quick glance in the building's shiny surface. "But it *is* creepy, thinking that he could be here, right next to me at any point. In fact, it's bloody weird!"

I shoved my hands deep in the pockets of my hoodie to keep them from shaking. "Is there anyone here now? Is he watching us?" My heart was leaping in my chest to think that at that very moment, Callum could be by my side.

Rob scanned around. "No one around at the moment. You know, I'll be glad to prove my point and get rid of this thing."

"So you're wearing the amulet?"

"Yeah," he admitted, in a slightly embarrassed tone. "It's a bit girly, so I had to wear long sleeves. Didn't want to be seen wearing it really."

"And you didn't have a conversation with Callum?" I asked as casually as I could manage.

"No, I just checked out that he was there, that this wasn't all some weird hoax. Luckily he disappeared pretty quickly, and he's not been back. Catherine says that he should come if I call, as long as I don't annoy them by taking the amulet off."

"Catherine told you that?" I struggled to hide my surprise before realising that if Callum disabled Rob somehow, she wasn't going to get her cut of the cash. That was bound to be her motivation, not concern for Rob's welfare.

Rob had stopped listening to me anyway and was expanding on his clever plan. "The guys here, they'll be able to work out who he is, when he died, everything. My idea is, we get the dead guys to talk to us in return for information about who they really are. They don't know that, do they? We can drip-feed them information in return for their cooperation. I mean, they're bound to want to know."

I saw my chance. "Why don't you let me have a word with them first? They like me, I'm sure I can get them on board."

Rob's laugh was harsh and callous. "Do you think I'm stupid? I'm not handing this over to you! You'd never give it back." His left hand automatically circled his right wrist. Now I knew where it was, so I had one last try.

"I didn't expect you to do that," I said, shrugging as if I didn't care. "But the thing is, Rob, we could do with one of them being around when we talk to the publicist, don't you think? It'll be a bit embarrassing if you get the PR team excited and no one appears. If you let me see it – not wear it, obviously," I added as he put up his hand to protest. "If you let me see it, I can tell if any of them are around; if someone is nearby. If not, you can line one of them up. How does that sound?"

I could almost hear his brain ticking over.

"How do you do that, then? Tell if they are around?"

"Just practice," I said as casually as I could manage. "It sort of blinks sometimes, in the right light, when someone is there. Haven't you noticed?" I couldn't believe he was buying all this. Or that he had accepted my sudden agreement to join forces with him. His greed was clouding his judgement.

"I've not noticed anything like that at all."

"You're probably not tuned in enough yet. Thinking about

it, it took me a few days. Do you want me to check now? If someone is around we might not have to wait for too long." I shrugged as non-committally as I could manage. How could Rob not hear my pounding heart? He needed distracting. "Never mind, I'm sure Steve and his colleagues will wait. So, did they say exactly how much money?"

The word money galvanised him back into action. "I guess you could have a quick look, but I'm not handing it over, is that clear?"

"Perfectly clear," I said, as soothingly as possible. "Show me your wrist." I leaned towards him, hands carefully in my pockets. Rob took a quick, furtive look around us, as if to check that we weren't about to reveal ourselves to a mugger, then slowly began to unbutton his shirt cuff. I couldn't help holding my breath.

Slowly, slowly, he pulled back his sleeve and there, nestling on his wrist, was my amulet, perfect and whole; the deep blue and green stone flashing in the sunlight, the intricate silverwork gleaming against Rob's pale skin. I had forgotten just how beautiful it really was, and before I realised I was going to do it I let out a sob, which I hastily changed to a cough. Yet again Callum was so close I could almost feel him.

"Come on then," Rob said impatiently. "Can you see anything or not?"

I frowned as I peered at it from a distance, my hands still firmly in my pockets. "I can't tell. Turn it this way a bit." He did as I asked, angling the stone towards the light. "Ahh, left a bit, no, stop there, over a little. Oh, never mind! I'm sure it'll be OK."

"What? Can't you see anything? Come on, try again!"

"It'd be much easier if I could see it more clearly. Can I come a bit closer?" I was careful not to move until he nodded, warily.

"I'm watching you, so no funny business, right?" he said in a snide voice, with his free hand covering the amulet completely as I came within reach.

I stepped back, hands up in the air. "It's up to you, Rob. It's your party."

It was his turn to frown. "OK, OK, calm down. Come on." He gestured me forward again.

"Look, why don't you keep your hand on the band while I check it out? Then I can't possibly do anything you don't want me to." I could see him trying to find the flaw in that argument, but finally he gave in, and holding on tightly to one side of the amulet, he held his wrist out towards me.

My mind was racing, but I had to stay calm. I was just so close, so close to everything I wanted. Tears pricked my eyes and I blinked quickly to get rid of them. I examined the stone from about an arm's length, making more non-committal noises. "It's really not clear. Can I just move your arm slightly?" I put my hand up but made no move towards him until he nodded.

My hand closed around his wrist just above the amulet, and I realised as I gripped him just how clammy my palms were. It was too late to do anything about it; I could only hope that he didn't notice. I continued to move his wrist in strange directions as if searching in the hidden depths of the stone, making quiet umm-ing and err-ing noises. Then, when he too was concentrating hard I shouted, "Yes, look!"

He jumped, instinctively jerking his arm inwards, pulling my hand down towards the amulet as he did so. I was ready, and in that swift movement I managed to wedge my finger under the silver band. "Callum! Help! It's me – come quickly!" I was shouting loudly now, hanging on to Rob's wrist, unable to keep the longing from my voice. "Cal—" Rob pushed me away viciously, breaking my grip on his wrist before I could finish saying his name again. My contact with the amulet was broken. I stumbled as I tried to move my legs quickly enough, and found myself sprawled on the floor.

"What are you doing?" he hissed. "I can't believe that you thought I would fall for that. The deal's off!" His eyes narrowed as he flashed a cruel smile at me. "We get to keep all the money then. Don't say I didn't offer. Kiss goodbye to your last chance to speak to your boyfriend!" He leered at me maliciously as I sat in a heap on the pavement, then looked over my head towards the door of the building. He couldn't help himself, automatically preening and straightening his shirt in the mirrored wall, a self-satisfied look on his face.

And then, as I watched, his whole demeanour changed. His mouth fell open in horror, his eyes fixed on something I couldn't see. His arrogant swagger changed almost imperceptibly into one of fear as he took a hesitant step backwards, his hands up in front of his chest as if he was trying to protect himself. My plan had worked: Callum had arrived and was giving Rob the fright he deserved.

"Get back! Leave me alone! I know you can't hurt me – GET BACK!" His voice rose to a squeal and his arms started to flail around, beating at the empty air next to him. "Don't you dare, I won't . . . I won't . . . I . . ." His head was shaking hard, and then his hands clamped over his ears. I could see that his eyes were screwed tightly shut. "Stop it, stop it, STOP IT!" he yelled, staggering around the pavement. A small crowd of people had gathered, and I could see two of them debating whether to intervene. I could remember only too well the unbearable noise that Lucas had made in my head; I guessed that Callum was doing something similar to Rob.

Rob was stumbling in circles now, head down, hands still wedged over his ears. "Ha! I can make you stop, you freak!" he bellowed, making the crowd take a step backwards. "You're not so clever! *Get out of my head!*" With that he tore the amulet from his wrist and hurled it to the ground, sinking to his knees in relief.

I darted across the pavement and grabbed the amulet, my euphoria growing with the thought of what I would see in the glass when I put it on. I slipped it back on to my wrist, feeling complete for the first time since it was stolen. I could feel the power of the amulet course through me; it felt as if I were clamping a living, pulsing thing around my wrist. Feeling inexplicably stronger I glanced quickly towards the windows, desperate to see Callum again. Directly in front of Rob was a tall Dirge, and I started to smile as he threw back his hood. But the smile was quickly wiped from my lips as I recognised the face behind the cruel sneer. It had all gone horribly wrong. Lucas was poised to strike; this time his plan had worked beautifully. Rob was about to lose his mind.

"*Callum!*" I bellowed at the top of my voice, oblivious to all the people milling on the pavement. Rob was kneeling a couple of metres away, breathing heavily, now completely oblivious to the danger. Lucas was standing by him, his hand reaching out towards Rob's blond head. I shouted again. "Rob! Look out!" But there was nothing he could look out for, no form of defence he could use. I remembered Callum's words about the amulet with perfect clarity: "*While you wear it, it will protect you from us, but being close and not touching it . . . well, we know where to find you, and you have no protection. That's how whole minds are stolen.*"

I also knew that Rob would resist, would fight, which was

the worst thing he could do. I was suddenly consumed with rage. However mean and misguided Rob was, he didn't deserve this; he didn't deserve to die. Somehow I had to stop it.

The anger, frustration and general injustice were growing inside me, and I felt a strange coiling sensation as if a snake was winding itself around my wrist. The amulet knew it was home, I realised, and a wave of soothing calm settled over me: I had the amulet, I was in charge, and I was going to stop this.

"Lucas!" I shouted, hoping that I could distract him. He turned to look at me in the mirrored windows, a humourless leer on his thin lips, his long greasy black hair emphasising the pallor of his face. "I'm warning you, don't do this!"

I looked at Rob. He was sitting back on his heels, eyes closed, head bent back at an uncomfortable-looking angle. His arms were straight out beside him, fingers scuffing the ground. He was twitching like an animal in a macabre experiment. There was no time to lose. I leapt in between them without thinking, forcing Lucas to take a couple of steps backwards in surprise. But it was no good; he started to advance again, to go straight through me to get to Rob. I racked my brain for something, *anything*, with which I could threaten him. But it was no use, I felt so helpless, and so furious that he was about to kill Rob. A wave of anger rolled over me and I stared up at Lucas's cruel face. "Leave him alone!"

Without thinking I thrust my amulet into his and pushed hard with my mind, willing some of the energy from my amulet into his. I had no idea what would happen, it just seemed like the right thing to do. My amulet flared briefly, like a fire had suddenly been lit underneath the stone, and Lucas howled. The noise was like a wounded animal, and he glared at me, making a vicious snarling noise. Behind me Rob fell in slow motion into a heap on the ground. I pushed again, harder this time, and the effect was electrifying. The fire in my amulet seemed to pour out over Lucas's wrist, and suddenly his hand was outlined in a golden glitter, like a hundred tiny sparklers. The sparks started to move up his arm, accelerating as they went, and within seconds he was a mass of glittering lights. He held up his arms in front of his face in horror, the place where his mouth should have been opening and closing, and he took a couple of steps backwards. He gave a final, hideous roar, and the sparks fell to the pavement, leaving a momentary impression of where he had been.

I leapt back in surprise as the sparks formed a strange puddle on the pavement, not wanting my feet to touch it. As I watched in the window the sparkling mass seemed to roll and move towards the nearby rainwater drain. Within seconds it had gone, lost beneath the road.

It was suddenly eerily silent.

I looked down at my amulet, and the remains of that strange glow were still there, but fading fast. In the mirrored window I could only see the crowd; there was no sign of Callum. But something was still there; I could see in the reflection the pile of heavy fabric next to my feet. All that was left of Lucas was his cloak. Whatever I had done, however I had done it, it hadn't been enough: I had failed. Lucas had drained Rob of everything and gone.

Rob was lying motionless on the ground, and the crowd of curious onlookers started to re-form. I quickly checked him for vital signs; he was breathing but unconscious. Reaching for my mobile I called for an ambulance, shouting for someone in the crowd to get some water from one of the nearby offices. He looked utterly defenceless and years younger. All I could do was put him in the recovery position and wait for the paramedics to arrive. After all that effort I hadn't been able to save him; Lucas had won. No one had been able to copy Rob's mind the way that Callum had done for me. Rob was about to die.

Decision

Within minutes the ambulance arrived and the paramedics started to work on Rob, moving me gently to one side. I was completely distraught; not only was Rob as good as dead, but there was still no sign of Callum. I tried to focus on what the paramedics were saying, but all the while I was searching in reflective surfaces for the smallest glimpse of his face.

"What happened here, miss? What caused his collapse?"

"I . . . I really don't know. We were arguing, and suddenly he clutched his head and started screaming. Then he keeled over." It didn't matter that I was lying; if they knew what had actually happened it wouldn't have made any difference to their treatment of him as there was nothing that could be done. Rob's brain was fried. Lucas had gathered everything from him despite my best efforts to stop him. I couldn't stop the tears from streaming down my face, overwhelmed by the events of the day.

"What's his name? Any medical history that we should know about?" I watched as one of them put a breathing mask over Rob's face, checking him for a pulse, looking for any sign of life. The other one was waiting for the answers to his questions.

"Umm, Rob. Robert Underwood. I don't know about his medical history, but he's always seemed pretty healthy," I mumbled.

"And his relationship to you?"

"I'm just a friend, that's all. A friend." I could barely make myself understood through the sobbing.

"Address?" he asked gently.

"Somewhere in Hampton. I know how to get there, but I don't know the full address, I'm sorry." I looked at him bleakly. "Can you help him?"

"It's OK, we'll get him straight to the hospital. They'll work out what needs to be done."

"Can I come with you? I don't want to leave him."

"Of course. It's always best to have someone there who knows a patient."

"OK, Clive, I've got him stabilised. Let's get him on board," called the other one. "There may be some ID on him in here, with a bit of luck." He handed Clive the wallet from Rob's back pocket.

"Look," said Clive as he moved towards the ambulance. "Why don't you have a quick flick through this stuff as we drive, see if you can find something with his address on it?" He handed the wallet and briefcase to me, and I took them reluctantly. I was pretty sure Rob wouldn't want me rifling through his things.

They loaded him into the ambulance and Clive jumped into the driver's seat. I was sitting in the back with Rob and the other guy when the sirens started, making me jump. Rob lay there, looking as if he was already dead, and I turned his wallet over in my hands. What was I going to tell his mum? The tears started streaming again, and the paramedic silently handed me a box of tissues.

"So, got an address yet?" he asked, nodding towards the wallet as he adjusted Rob's drip.

"Umm, no, not yet," I sniffed. "I'll check now."

Inside the wallet were the usual bits of paper and junk,

old tickets for gigs, scraps with phone numbers on, and nestled at the bottom, nice and safe, a memory card. *My* memory card. My eyebrows shot up in surprise, but I quickly tried to cover it up. When the paramedic wasn't looking I slipped the card out of the wallet and into my palm. Within seconds it was securely in my back pocket. I could make sure it was destroyed before it caused any more trouble.

I finally found something with Rob's address and handed it to the paramedic, who noted down some of the details on a form he was filling in. Rob continued to lie there, motionless, while we sped through the streets of London. I could hear the sirens wailing as we approached junctions, but it still seemed to take forever, and I was thrown from side to side as the ambulance cornered violently around the traffic.

Numbly, I looked at the amulet, now back securely on my wrist. How long had I been wishing for this? To get it back, safe and sound? And now I had it, but Rob was as good as dead and Callum was nowhere to be found. I couldn't work out how it had all gone so horribly wrong. The amulet looked as harmless as ever, the blue and green of the stone occasionally flashing when the light caught the hidden red and gold flecks that were buried deep inside. I found that I was rubbing the stone compulsively, feeling again the delicate silver ropes that somehow secured the stone within its cage. But still nothing strange moved in its depths, and no tingle appeared in my wrist, and the tears ran unchecked again down my cheeks.

At the hospital Rob was whisked away into the depths of the A&E, and I was shown into a small family room. It was mercifully empty, so there was no need to pretend any more. I made sure that the door was securely closed before trying again.

"Callum! Please, let me know that you're OK. I'm here and I need you. Please come."

I waited, but nothing happened, and the creeping despair that had become so familiar over the last week started to claim me again. He wasn't there, and I couldn't fathom out why. Nothing could hold him against his will, he seemed to be able to hear me wherever he was, and he could run much, much faster than any mere human. So why wasn't he with me? The more I thought about it, the more my mind kept circling back to a nagging fear: that whatever I had done with my amulet to stop Lucas hadn't only affected him. What if the energy I had produced had got them all, sent them all in sparkling streams down the nearest drain? I looked at the seemingly harmless bracelet. Something subtle had changed; I could practically feel the power in it. The more I thought about it the sicker I felt. What *had* I done?

I was working my way through the box of tissues on the little table when the door opened and a nurse came in.

"Are you with Robert Underwood?" she asked in a kindly tone. I nodded bleakly. "Are you family or friend? We need to contact his next of kin."

"I'm just a friend. I lost my phone and don't even have his mobile number." I sniffed unintelligibly at her before pulling myself together. His parents needed to be here now. "Could you look in his phone for his parents' numbers? I'm sure he has them listed."

The nurse looked at me sympathetically, patting my arm. "We'll be doing that next. I just wanted to check that you weren't family before we started. Is that his wallet?" She pointed at Rob's belongings, which I had carried in from the ambulance. I nodded briefly and she picked up the phone. "You stay in here and I'll let you know just as soon as he regains consciousness." Her shoes squeaked on the floor as she left the little room, carefully closing the door behind her.

I slumped back in my chair, drained, wondering what on earth I was going to tell his parents when they turned up. Had they seen the files on his computer? Had he told them what he was doing? Somehow I thought it was unlikely but I couldn't be sure. My problems could be a long way from over, but they were nothing compared to what Rob was facing. Sighing, I looked at the briefcase lying on the little table in front of me. It was no more than a computer bag really. A laptop bag.

I sat bolt upright, appalled at what I was thinking, but I knew that I had to do it. Taking a deep breath I pulled the case towards me and unzipped it. Inside was Rob's laptop, and on it would be the copies of the memory card files that Ashley had seen. I could feel my heartbeat racing as I lifted out the computer and pressed the on button. Quickly scanning the hard drive I discovered the videos and heaved a great sigh of relief as I deleted the entire directory. Shutting it all back down as fast as I could, I slipped it back in the case. All evidence of the existence of Dirges was gone.

Suddenly exhausted, I stood up and moved stiffly over to the small water cooler in the corner of the room, favouring my bad arm. The water was icy, and for a second I pressed the plastic cup against my forehead before draining the whole thing in one go. I could feel the cold water hit my empty stomach, and it made me shiver briefly as I refilled it.

"Alex?" The voice was hesitant, but joyful. "Alex, are you OK?"

The cup fell from my fingers unnoticed, drenching my feet. "Callum? Is that really you? Are you here?"

"I'm here, I'm right here. You're all right, I can't believe it."

I could barely make my voice work, the tears were coming so fast, but this time they were tears of relief, of joy, of release. "Yes, I'm fine, just fine." I grabbed a tissue from the table and blew my nose noisily. "Sorry. I can't believe that you're back – what's been going on?"

"I'm sure that this has been the worst – the absolute worst – day of either of my lives," he said with considerable feeling.

"I need to see you; let me sit down." I couldn't believe it was actually him. I wanted to see his eyes, feel his touch to believe that one part of the nightmare was over. I pulled the little mirror out of my pocket, and found the wires for the headphones, hurriedly tucking them into place. "Where have you been? I've been calling you for ages. It's all gone horribly wrong." My voice caught as the tears overwhelmed me again.

"Don't cry, Alex, please." Callum's voice was equally strained, and I finally found him perfectly reflected in the mirror. His beautiful, familiar face was etched with pain, his eyes dark, the wayward hair sticking up in all directions. He manoeuvred himself into position looking over my shoulder, his free arm wrapped tightly around me in the mirror. At long last I could feel the whisper of his touch, and everything became too much for me. Tears streamed down my face and my shoulders heaved. He let me cry, murmuring gently to me and stroking my hair.

When the emotion finally subsided I straightened up and mumbled an apology. "I'm sorry, Callum, I didn't mean to do that; it's just been so awful." I reached up to stroke his face, catching the hint of his skin as my fingers skimmed the air around him. "What happened?"

"I was going to ask you the same thing. I've not had time to talk to any of the others yet."

"What do you already know? I mean, have you been around at all?" I pulled yet another tissue from the box and dabbed at my eyes, noticing briefly that the make-up covering my bruises had yet again been washed away.

Callum briefly pinched his fingers to the bridge of his nose. "I've been with you for almost every minute, Alex. Every minute I could manage of every day, until today. It's been complete torture."

"So you were there at the pub yesterday? You heard what Rob said about Catherine?"

"Yes, and I had a decision to make." The pain was evident in his voice. "I made the wrong one."

I looked at him quizzically.

"Rob told you that she was going to Cornwall," Callum continued. "I saw you at the station first thing this morning and realised what you were going to do. I didn't want you to be fighting Catherine in Cornwall without me being nearby, but I knew it would take a while to get there, so I set off straightaway." He gave me his familiar rueful look. "I'm fast, but I'm not Superman. I realised that I wasn't going to be able to make it all the way there, so I waited at Swindon where I knew the trains would stop, just to check. I hoped that maybe I would find a way to talk to you when I saw you, give you a bit of encouragement, you know." His arm was back around me, holding me as if he would never let me go. "But it was Catherine I found, and I saw she had an aura, and a really miserable one at that. She clearly didn't have the amulet with her either; I would have been able to sense it. I thought you'd won, that you'd already fought her and got it back."

"I wish I had," I said in a small voice. "She did a deal with Rob and gave him the amulet last night. She must have realised that Cornwall was far enough away to be safe from you all."

"I'm not surprised she wanted to get rid of the amulet, and the difficulty will have been to do it safely. I tried to make her life as miserable as possible while she was wearing it, but she's already phenomenally depressed, so it was quite a challenge."

"So how did you find me? What did you do?"

The pain crossed his face again. "I was on my way back already, running as fast as I could, when I heard a call. I couldn't quite work it out, because there seemed to be two voices, but one of them seemed to be you. I was so pleased; I thought it meant that you had the amulet back." He paused for a moment, his free hand dropping down towards my amulet. "I guess I wasn't the only one who heard the call."

"No," I shuddered, remembering.

"Who was it? Who connected with him?"

"Lucas. He—"

"Lucas!" exploded Callum. "I might have known it was his fault." His eyebrows knitted together in a huge frown. "Wait till I get my hands on him. . ."

"But you can't; he's gone."

His beautiful face was a picture of horror. "So that means Rob's actually. . ." He didn't finish, but he didn't need to. I nodded mutely.

"They said they would come and get me when he regained consciousness. I'm not expecting them back."

"He will have resisted." Callum's lips were pressed together in a tight line as he thought about what had happened.

"Yes, he did. It was horrible, and there was nothing I could do." My voice caught but I took a deep breath and carried on. "I did try, but Lucas got what he wanted and now he's gone."

"So what exactly happened to Lucas at the end?" he finally asked.

"I don't know. One minute he was standing over Rob and I couldn't bear it." My voice was catching again but I had to carry on. "I tried to get between them, to stop him being able to get to Rob, but it didn't work. All of a sudden Lucas was covered in this sort of glitter. After that he disappeared and the glitter formed a small puddle, which ran into the drain." I paused, watching it all again in my mind's eye.

"That sounds odd," said Callum, frowning. "I mean, that's not what happened to Catherine. She exploded – the sparks went everywhere."

"So what did I do to him?"

"I don't know – maybe he's gone or maybe you did nothing."

"Maybe I've made him even more cross," I wondered out loud. It didn't add up though. From what I had seen I couldn't imagine Lucas coming back.

"Well, we'll know tonight, when or if he comes back to St Paul's. I'll be waiting for him." Callum looked murderous.

I sighed. "It's all such a mess. Rob was greedy, callous and spiteful, but he didn't deserve this. No one does."

Callum was looking really confused. "I know he was an opportunist lech, but that's quite a harsh description. What else did he do to you?"

"Oh, you have no idea. He had my amulet, and he had the memory card, so he was going to expose you all to the papers."

The confusion still hadn't left Callum's features. "Memory card? Am I missing something?"

"Ah, yes, well – I didn't mention that, did I? No." I rubbed my free hand over my temples, trying to dislodge the headache that was forming again. "The thing was, when I took the amulet off before, when Catherine made me think that you no longer loved me, I couldn't bear the thought that every single record of you was about to go from my memory. So, as a sort of back-up, I made a video of me telling your story." He raised an eyebrow at me but said nothing. "I recorded everything, finding the amulet, how we first met, what you told me about your world. Everything. I put a password on it and put it in the envelope with the amulet, which I gave to Grace." I paused for a minute, remembering with awful clarity seeing the card on the ground in front of me as Catherine got to work, and shuddered again. "It fell out, and Rob must have picked it up while he was waiting for the ambulance. It wouldn't have taken him long to break the password. Once he had all that info, all he needed was the amulet and he was on his way to being a rich celebrity." I couldn't keep the bitter twist out of my voice, despite what happened to Rob afterwards.

"So what was he going to do with it all? How does that make him rich?"

"He told a publicist he had proof of life after death. He wanted to bribe you all with information about yourselves so that you would reveal yourselves to people over here."

Callum's hand was clenched in a tight fist. "I wish I *had* got here in time. I'd have made him realise that he was messing with something that was none of his business, believe me." He radiated fury.

"I know, I couldn't believe it either." I hesitated a moment before continuing. "He doesn't deserve this though."

"No, I guess not," Callum said tightly, and I wasn't at all sure he meant it.

We sat in silence for a while, wrapped as closely together as we could manage, waiting for news, but, as I expected, nothing happened. The nurses came and checked on me from time to time, but they had no information about any change in Rob's condition. I was desperate to leave, to go somewhere where I could be alone with Callum, but I knew that I had to wait and see his parents.

Soon enough they arrived, and after a brief visit to his bedside, they were ushered into the little room with me. I really didn't know what to say; I couldn't be sure that he hadn't told them any of his plans, and I absolutely didn't know what they might find later on, when they were tidying things up. I swallowed hard at the thought. Later – that meant when Rob was dead, when he finally succumbed to the creeping fog. I could still remember the malevolence lurking in that fog, and I hoped for his sake that his end would be quick. None of us could help him.

Rob's mother was surprisingly upbeat; the doctors clearly hadn't got to the stage of declaring him brain dead just yet. She was worried, but her optimistic nature didn't let her consider any option other than total recovery. I tried hard not to bring her down as she questioned me about what had happened. It seemed that Rob hadn't told them what he was doing, but there was a trail of evidence that was difficult to explain away. The most difficult was what we were both doing in that square in Soho, and she kept coming back to that. I continued with my story of coincidence, that I had just bumped into him there and moments later he had keeled over, hoping that the repetition would make them believe it. It slowly seemed to be working with his mum, but his dad was less easily fooled.

"What I don't understand," he suddenly interjected after sitting in near silence for twenty minutes, "is why he was heading for that building in the first place. And your story," he looked at me with piercing eyes, "is plainly nonsense."

I didn't know what to say, and sat there with my mouth open, panicking, while Rob's mum looked in confusion between the two of us. "What do you mean?" she asked finally when I remained silent.

"I mean," said her husband, with considerable feeling, "that Rob had no business with those publicity people, or at least as far as I know he didn't. So he must have been going there with you." He jabbed his finger angrily at me. "I don't buy this coincidence rubbish. What are you up to, and why did you need to involve our Robert?"

My blood ran cold. I had no idea what I could tell him. I knew that if I started to lie I was just going to end up in more and more trouble. Rob was going to die, so there would be the police, investigations, endless questions. I couldn't possibly sustain a lie through all that. I was going to have to tell him the truth, or at least something close to it. I could feel my eyes brimming over again.

"Tell him Rob didn't want to tell anyone, including you, that it was his secret." Callum's voice was calm and soothing. "Then at least we buy some time."

It was a sensible idea. I nodded imperceptibly, tears marking fresh tracks down my battered face.

"It was Rob's idea, honestly. He wouldn't give me the details, but he had an idea that he thought would make him a celebrity." I lifted my eyes from the floor and looked directly at his dad. "He told me not to tell anyone, *anyone* at all, that he was even thinking about it. You're just going to have to ask him when he comes round."

Mr Underwood looked furious, straining on the edge of his seat as if he were about to leap towards me.

"Leave the poor girl alone; she's as upset as we are," interrupted Rob's mum, leaning over and patting me on the knee. "As she said, we'll just ask Robert when we can." She smiled brightly, almost as if she believed what she was saying.

I couldn't quite return the smile.

The three of us sat there in near silence for the next hour. Callum left to go and do a quick bit of gathering, promising that he would be back in an instant if I called. I knew it was pointless my waiting, but it seemed callous to leave Rob's mum. His dad continued scowling at me, sitting back in his plastic-covered chair, arms folded across his pot belly. I glanced at him surreptitiously from time to time; this was what Rob was going to look like when he got to middle age, I realised with a shock. Arrogant and angry and running to seed. Then I remembered that he was never going to make it that far and felt hugely guilty for the thought.

Finally I could take it no longer, and excused myself to go to the bathroom. I stood in the long corridor in the glare of the overhead fluorescents and tried to decide what to do. It was strangely silent but I started to walk up the corridor in the direction that the last nurse had come from. Turning a corner I was faced with a long line of windowed cubicles, most of which had curtains drawn on the inside, but some of which had open doors. Looking purposeful I walked up the line, taking a quick glance into each one that was open. As I went past one cubicle, a man in a white coat and a stethoscope came out hurriedly, looking at his pager as he walked. I nodded at him in greeting and he nodded back, seemingly convinced that I had a reason to be there. I checked through the open door but Rob wasn't in that one either.

As I walked down towards the final set of doors I could hear the monotonous beeping of a heart monitor, and I was suddenly gripped with fear. I put my head around the door and peered inside. Rob was lying on the high treatment trolley, which had its sides up to stop him falling off. He was hooked up to several machines but seemed to be breathing on his own. I stepped into the room and realised that there was a nurse writing something in a file that was resting on the cupboard at the side. She smiled as she recognised me.

"I'm sorry," I blustered quickly. "I was trying to find the loo and I saw Rob. How is he doing?"

She smiled encouragingly. "I don't think it'll be too long now. There's nothing physically wrong with him that we can find. I was just about to come and get you all actually; he might wake up quicker if you talk to him."

"Oh, right, that's good then, isn't it?" I stood there, uncertain of what to do next. The nurse was obviously used to dealing with relatives, and came over to the door and took me by the arm. She led me gently to Rob's bedside.

"You make a start, and I'll go and get his parents, OK?" She nodded at me, and I nodded carefully back. "I won't be a minute. There's no need to panic."

"OK, it's fine, really." I stood up straighter and smiled at her, putting my hand on the chrome bar at the side of the bed. The second she was out of the door I leaned over Rob. If there was nothing I could do to save him, the least I could do was to comfort him and tell him what to do, however much I disliked him. But I had to be quick.

"Rob, it's Alex. I know you can hear me, and I know that you have no idea of who you are or who I am for that matter. I'm really, really sorry about what happened, that I couldn't stop it. But it has happened, and I want to try and make it easier for you now. There's no way back."

I bit back the catch in my voice. How could I possibly tell him that he was dying? Wouldn't it be kinder not to know, to just drift off into the apparently welcoming fog? But I couldn't get him to go before his mum saw him; that would be too, too cruel.

"Rob, it's not yet time, but when you feel ready, go to the fog; that will be the best, believe me. But your mum is just coming now, though. Wait for her, please."

I reached over the railing and picked up his lifeless hand, remembering all too well what it felt like to be on the other side. It was all such a mess. I lifted his hand up towards my lips, holding it tightly in both my hands and kissed it briefly. "Bye, Rob, I have to go now. Remember, go to the fog. Take care." I pressed it against my cheek before laying it gently back down again. I was done. I turned away, too spent to cry any more.

"Alex?" asked an unexpected voice. "What are you wittering on about? What fog? And where the hell am I?"

I spun round. Rob was sitting up, rubbing his wrist and looking at me with a puzzled expression.

Questions

I looked at him, stunned. Rob was shaking his head and rubbing his eyes as if he had just woken from a long sleep.

"What's going on, Alex? Where am I?" He stopped briefly and peered at me closely. "What's happened to your face?"

I could feel myself starting to hyperventilate. This wasn't possible; he should be dead, or nearly dead, not sitting up and talking. "Rob?" I finally found my voice. "Rob – you're OK!" I couldn't help myself, and grabbed his hands. "You're not dead!"

"Huh, no, obviously," he said in a slightly bemused voice. "Where am I?" he repeated, looking around the treatment room. "What are you doing here? And what was all that stuff about fog?"

My mind was racing. Whatever Lucas had done hadn't killed him. "Look, Rob, you're in hospital. The doctors will tell you everything, but you've been unconscious for a while. What do you remember?"

"I remember everything, I think," he said with a frown. "I'm not sure why you're here though, pleasant as it is." He gave me a brief smile.

"So what exactly is the last thing you do remember?"

He lay back on his pillows for a moment and considered the ceiling. "It's all pretty clear really. I was on my way to, oh, what was it?" He paused for a second and my heart almost stopped. Then the frown cleared from his face. "Yes! That was it. I was on my way to the pub in Richmond. We're going to see the new James Bond film tonight with the others." He glanced quickly towards his wrist where his watch would be, but the nurses had taken it off. "Have we missed it? What's the time?"

I realised that my fingernails were digging into my palms and that I had been holding my breath. I slowly exhaled. "I'm afraid it's a bit later than that. We went to the cinema weeks ago."

"We did? Are you sure?"

"Absolutely sure. It's July now, term has ended."

He suddenly sat bolt upright. "No! How did that happen? Why don't I remember?"

"I'm not sure. Maybe the doctors will know, but you sort of collapsed, and you've been unconscious for the last four or five hours. That's all I can tell you."

"And it's now July, right?"

I nodded in response, gripping the bars of his bed tightly. I couldn't quite believe any of it. I had watched Lucas drain him and go, so why wasn't he dead?

"Freaky." Rob lay back down again. "Really freaky. . ." I could see him thinking and he turned to look at me, a question in his eyes. "So if we went to the cinema weeks ago, but you are with me here now, does that mean that we. . .?" He left the question hanging, but his smile was turning into more of a leer.

"No, Rob. We didn't," I said firmly.

"Are you sure? I distinctly remember that I was going to give it a go." The leer was in full evidence now.

"Actually, we had one date and decided that it wasn't going to work."

"Really? That's a shame." His hand found mine. "You don't

fancy giving it another chance then, do you? Just to help my recuperation, obviously."

"It's a tempting thought, Rob, but no. We decided that what we both wanted were two very different things."

"Oh, well, maybe later." He looked so smug and sure of himself, and yet again I wondered what it was I had ever seen in him. "So I've been unconscious for four hours but forgotten what? Four weeks?"

"More like five or six, I guess." I needed to check quickly, as voices were now approaching down the corridor. "So while you were unconscious, did you dream at all?"

"Nah. I was on the way to the pub, then suddenly I was waking up here, listening to you talk drivel. What was it you were saying again?"

I laughed as convincingly as I could manage. "It *was* just drivel. The nurse said to talk to you as it would help bring you back round. I think I was explaining about some school trip or other. I forget now." As I said it Rob's parents came through the door, his mum with a huge smile on her face, his dad still looking suspiciously at me.

"You still here?" he scowled. I backed away from the bed, seeing my opportunity to escape before the discussions about what had been going on started.

"I'm just leaving, Mr Underwood. Bye, Rob, glad to see you back in the land of the living."

"Oh, OK, Alex. See you soon. Steady on, Mum, what do you think you're doing?" The last part was muffled as Mrs Underwood wrapped him in a huge bear hug. I hurriedly made for the door.

Outside, the streets were packed with people. It was rush hour again. I had no idea where I was, having arrived in the back of an ambulance, but I knew someone who could help. With a feeling of huge contentment I looked at the bracelet on my wrist, seeing the flecks of gold glinting in the afternoon sun. I pulled out my earphones as I started to walk. "Callum, everything is OK. Come and find me when you can. I'm walking down. . ." I paused as I came to a junction and read the sign. "Tottenham Court Road. Come and find me soon."

Callum arrived within minutes, and quickly directed me to a quiet square where we could sit and talk unobtrusively. Despite being exhausted I was bouncing with excitement. I could barely sit still as I set myself up on a bench in a corner, the mirror propped up on the armrest, luxuriating in the fact that Callum was back. He was right behind me, obviously confused about my behaviour.

"Are you OK, Alex?" he asked gently. "Was the end . . . bad?"

"It wasn't bad at all – Rob's absolutely fine!"

"What? What do you mean?"

"I mean that he woke up and had a conversation with me! He's OK."

"I thought you said that Lucas had drained him, that he had got enough and disappeared like Catherine?"

"Well, he certainly disappeared, but he definitely only got a few of Rob's memories. He seems to have forgotten just the last month or so. Perhaps for Lucas that was enough," I added wonderingly. Having watched him dissolve into that puddle of glittering sparks I was pretty sure he wasn't coming back. But the most exciting question was where he had gone, and what was it that I had done that had changed things?

Callum was clearly about to start asking me more questions so I stopped him. I didn't want to start discussing theories until I had a few more answers, and there was no point getting him excited until I knew for sure if Lucas was going back to St Paul's, until I understood. "Enough about Rob; I don't care about him right now, I just want to enjoy being here with you." He looked at me with such tenderness that I thought my heart would burst with love. He was back in my arms and for now, all was well.

"What I don't understand," Callum asked eventually, "is why I couldn't get through to you in your dreams. I seem to manage it with all sorts of other people, but every opportunity with you failed."

"I rarely remember my dreams, but I suppose I never had a reason to tell you that. I remembered the one about Richmond that first night, but after that, nothing. I kept waking up feeling like I was missing some vital clue though. Was that you?"

"I guess. I kept trying, just in case, because it made me feel closer to you." The arm around me tightened, and I could feel the gossamer touch of it against my shoulder.

"When did you realise that Catherine had stolen the amulet?"

"It was really weird. I was coming towards your house with Olivia. She was still feeling miserable about mucking things up, but excited about seeing the dog again, when suddenly everything around me seemed to shift."

"What do you mean?"

"It was as if someone had put a slightly different colour filter over my world, but with no way of seeing what it had been like before. Everything just changed. Olivia didn't notice anything but I was worried, so I got her to run faster. I had a good fix on the amulet, it was near your house so I wasn't too worried, then it suddenly started to move quickly and I knew you had got on a train or in a car or something, and I lost track of you. Olivia and I stopped, wondering what to do next. I knew you had been planning to take the dog for a walk, but obviously your plans had changed and I had no way of working out what they were.

"Olivia and I went back to St Paul's, and I waited around, not really knowing what to do. I just had this awful feeling that something wasn't quite right. You didn't call, so I didn't know where to go. Eventually I couldn't stand it any more and went to your house, hoping that you'd be back before I had to return to London for the night. I didn't want to be spying on you, but I went to your room to try and find out where you might have gone. And there you were, battered and beaten, with no amulet and an awful, dreadful aura. I... I..."

"I know," I said quickly, as his eyes shut tightly for a moment. "I remember sitting there that night hoping that you were watching me but with no way of knowing. I'm glad that you *were* actually there." I reached behind me to stroke his face, ignoring the puzzled look of a woman in a suit who was passing by. "When did you realise it was Catherine who had taken it?"

"There weren't that many possible suspects really. It would have been a huge coincidence for someone else to have mugged you. I could hardly bear to leave you, not when you were in such a bad way, but I knew that I had to find her. I ran back towards Twickenham, trying to retune in to the amulet. Once I knew why it had changed, that someone else was wearing it, it was a bit easier. I found her in Richmond and gave her a very unpleasant shock." His face was grim.

"What did you do?"

"I can be pretty loud too, especially when I sneak up on someone." His stony features twitched into something that wasn't quite a grin. "She embarrassed herself pretty spectacularly in that pub, I can tell you."

"Good, she deserved it."

"She deserved rather more than that, but unfortunately she was able to resist me very well." He paused for a moment, reliving the evening. "I had to go back to St Paul's then, but first thing in the morning I came back out to you, hoping that you would still be asleep. I thought I had managed to get into your dream, but I couldn't be sure, and it was so frustrating to see you there and not be able to communicate with you at all. Once I realised that you weren't going to school I shot off to do my gathering, then came back to spend the rest of the day with you. I couldn't believe the bruises you had. I could kill her!"

I remembered I had been looking at my injuries in the big hall mirror when Josh had spotted them too. "It was luck that she missed my head," I said with feeling, "otherwise it would have been me in the hospital again."

"Don't even say that!" Callum shuddered at the idea. "At least you had Josh there, and Grace, keeping you safe." He paused for a moment and smiled. "So you told Grace about me?"

I nodded. "I had to speak with someone; I was going mad trying to deal with everything alone. I hope you don't mind."

"Why would I mind? I was just hugely impressed that you got her to believe what you were saying when you had absolutely no proof."

"It was such a relief." It was my turn to smile. "She's very keen to meet you, you know. She would have been here helping me but for some long-standing visit to her grandparents. Instead she's been feeding me information when I needed it. Luckily for me she really doesn't like Catherine."

"I'm glad you had some help. I knew Catherine wasn't a nice person, but I had never thought that she was downright evil, and with murderous tendencies too."

"She and Rob actually made quite a good couple, I think. Wicked, the pair of them." I shook my head, trying to dislodge the thought. "So were you following me all the time after that?"

"Yes, I stayed with you as you walked around Richmond. I knew she was following you, I could sense the amulet, but I couldn't find a way to get your attention, and then, when she confronted you on the towpath, well. . ." He paused for a moment and took a deep breath. "When she told you I was incandescent with rage she wasn't even close."

"That was an awful moment, just awful," I agreed, thinking back to that rainy day when I thought that all hope was lost. I couldn't help reaching for the amulet to check that it was still safe on my wrist.

"I made her life hell after that, believe me."

"What I don't understand is why she had such a vendetta against me. I mean, she had all my memories, so thanks to me she got a real life back. What was it that ticked her off so badly?"

"I wish I knew. While she was wearing the amulet I kept a careful eye on her, but she never seemed cheerful about anything. Of course, it would have been easier to be sure if I had actually been able to see her aura. She does seem massively depressed."

"She said something odd to me on the train; that everything was my fault, that I was the one who let Rob know everything and set all this in motion. But I don't understand why that would make her hate me so. It doesn't make any sense."

Callum frowned. "Perhaps she meant that you shouldn't have found the amulet?"

"No, it has to have something to do with the memory that Olivia took. Has Olivia been able to give you any clues about it yet?"

Callum shook his head silently.

"Can't she even give you the flavour of it?"

"No, she's too scarred by it, whatever it is."

"Poor kid! I keep forgetting that it's different to when Catherine took all my memories and you took the copy to save my life."

"That's not gathering, it's totally wiping clean, and is completely different. When everything streams out, the good and the bad, it comes complete. It surprised me a bit, I can tell you." He paused for a second and held me tighter. "That's what made it possible for me to keep your memory of our island." He kissed the top of my ear and smiled at me, remembering.

I smiled back; he had needed just one really good memory to stay sane, so he had swapped his memory of that encounter for mine. So now we both knew exactly how we felt about each other, and no one would ever be able to convince us otherwise again.

I suddenly felt guilty for letting my thoughts get so sidetracked; we had some problems to sort out. "So, what does Olivia say that the general feeling is for that memory? Does that help us at all?"

"I can't ask her to even try; she's really struggling now. Whatever that memory was, whatever Catherine had locked up in her warped brain, it was pure poison. And of course Olivia feels really responsible for all the mess."

"But she mustn't! It really wasn't her fault, any of it. Will you let me talk to her?"

"She's not really up to talking to anyone at the moment.

Now I know you are safe I can try to help her properly, so maybe in time we'll find out."

My heart went out to her, and I wished there was something, anything, I could do to make her young life better. "Give her my love when you see her, won't you? Tell her that Beesley will be back soon and I'll be able to take him for some more walks."

Callum smiled weakly. "I'll tell her, I'm sure it will help."

Both of us fell silent for a moment, lost in our own thoughts. I couldn't fathom what it was I had seemingly done to upset Catherine, and that was all tied up now with Olivia. I felt torn: the largest part of me was swamped with relief that Callum was back by my side, and that the threats we had been facing had been, for the most part, dealt with. But part of me was horrified by what was happening to Olivia. She was just a child and didn't deserve any of this. My thoughts kept returning to what Catherine had crowed about at the station. She had said that Olivia had stolen the memory of how the Dirges could escape, and woven through all of that was why Catherine loathed me. Something in that, some detail she couldn't see or understand had almost unhinged Olivia's mind. Was it the hatred that had scarred Olivia?

I needed to know the facts, and then I might be able to help her. If I couldn't get the information from Olivia the only way to help would be to find Catherine again. I shuddered at the thought.

A sudden breeze brought me back to the present and the London square I was sitting in. I felt like I had been existing in a box, away from everything else; but of course it was all still there. London was passing by, everyone making their way home, and I suddenly became reconnected with it all. Looking around the park I could see a cloud of little lights; all the office workers with their happy, going-home auras. The yellow lights bounced and leapt above their heads, and I was overwhelmed with relief that they were back.

I sat back, exhausted. "I love you, Callum, and I really want to stay here with you, but I'm whacked and I need my painkillers. Can you come home with me? There's still loads more I need to try and understand: why isn't Rob dead? What happened this time that was different to last time?"

His face was a picture of concern. "Of course. I'll come with you to the station, and then go and find Matthew. He might have some answers, and I can come back later."

"If I have a decent night's sleep, perhaps I can try to come back up here tomorrow, and meet you at the dome?"

In the mirror his arm tightened around me again. "I can't think of anything better. Come on then, let's get you home."

I realised as I sat on the train that what I had told Callum had been more accurate than I realised: I was completely and utterly exhausted. I had been running on nothing but emotion and adrenalin for days, and now it was all spent. I wanted to curl up into a small ball and sleep for a month. Luckily the train terminated at my stop, so I didn't have to worry about dropping off on the journey. At one point though I was woken up by an unsubtle dig in the ribs, and I found that I had been snoozing on the shoulder of the cross-looking commuter sitting next to me. I apologised and twisted slightly in my seat so that my head was leaning against the window. I couldn't help smiling slightly to myself as I glimpsed the auras of the people on the passing platforms. It was strangely comforting, this weird talent that I shared with Callum, and I let my eyelids droop again as my thoughts became less focused.

I was woken abruptly by the strident ringtone of a mobile,

and it took me a few moments to realise it was mine. The clunky old phone had a really cheesy ring, and I looked apologetically at the commuters as I finally manoeuvred it out of my back pocket. This time the name registered on the display.

"Hi, Josh, what's up?"

"Thought you might like an early warning that the parents are back," he told me in a very quiet voice.

"Oh, right, thanks. What's the mood like?"

His voice dropped even lower. "Mixed, I'd say. I've warned them about your face, but they'll go ballistic if they see your arm. Where are you?"

"On the train. I'll be home in about half an hour, I guess."

"How are the bruises looking?"

"I haven't checked recently."

"Well, make sure they're covered up."

"Good point." I paused for a second. "Thanks, Josh, I appreciate the heads-up."

"No worries. Is everything else OK now? You've been gone all day."

"Yeah, it's all sorted out. It took a while, but it's done."

"Good. I'll see you later. Bye."

I peered at the unfamiliar phone to work out how to cut the call, then put it back in my pocket. The little mirror was in there too, so I quickly glanced around the train but no one seemed to be watching. I had spent ages looking in the mirror earlier but I'd been focusing only on Callum and had taken absolutely no notice of what I actually looked like. It had been over a week since Catherine had hit me, but the bruises and scuff marks on my face were still bad. They were mostly green, which gave me rather an unpleasant complexion, but finally most of the scabs had gone. My arm still showed the obvious imprint of the club though. I sighed quietly. Josh was right; Mum would go up the wall if she saw it and realised that I had been keeping quiet about it. Luckily my sleeves were long enough to cover it completely.

As the train pulled into the station I rummaged through my bag to see if I had any cover stick but drew a blank. Luckily my face could still be explained by the story about Beesley, so I was just going to have to wing it. I threw my bag over my shoulder and started the long walk home.

Hope

Callum was there when I woke in the morning, holding me close while I slept away the day.

"I can't believe that she did this to you," he breathed, kissing the angry welts on my arm.

I snuggled down in his embrace, feeling the gentle touch of his fingers tracing a path down from my shoulder. "I don't want to spend a second more thinking about her. She's gone, and good riddance to her. It's time to worry about us now."

He sat back a little. "What are we worrying about this time then?"

"Nothing, silly. It's just a phrase. We have nothing to worry about except for being trapped in different dimensions, which is just a wee bit irritating, that's all."

"Well, you seem to be feeling a bit better today," he laughed, resuming the stroking.

"I'm actually not so stiff, and I guess I had a decent night where my dreams weren't being invaded, either," I said, stretching carefully so as to not move the amulet.

"You know, that's a good point. I wonder if it has that effect on everyone."

"How many people do you visit in their sleep then? Are you a regular visitor to many heads?"

"No, not really. I have one particular victim though, and he seems particularly susceptible. Much better than you, anyway." He was looking hugely smug as he told me.

"Go on then, who is it?"

"John Reilly."

"And who might he be then?"

"He, my love," said Callum, his voice muffled as he kissed my neck, "is the head of maintenance at St Paul's. He's woken up really worried about the Golden Gallery this morning, and will be insisting that it's kept closed."

"You little marvel!" I beamed at him. "I've been wondering how you did that."

"So you probably ought to get out of bed and into London so that we can make the most of it."

"Too right. I don't want to be missing an opportunity like that. Give me ten minutes and I'll be ready for breakfast." I thought back to the conversations I had had the night before. "Umm, are my parents around?"

"No, they've both gone into work, and Josh is still asleep. They have left a note though, on the blackboard."

"I bet they have," I muttered under my breath. They hadn't been too happy when I had turned up last night with no good explanation of why I had been so difficult to contact over the last few days. "I guess it tells me that I'm grounded or something similar?"

"Close. Not those exact words but I think they expect you to be around. Did they see this?" He pointed towards my shoulder.

"No, they didn't! If they had they would have been furious, and I would have spent another night talking to the police. I'm going to be wearing long sleeves for at least another week, I reckon." I paused as Callum's mesmerising blue eyes found mine and I momentarily lost all coherent thought. "Now, scoot; I need to get showered and dressed. I'll be down in ten minutes." I glimpsed the remnants of the bruises on my cheek in the mirror. "Make that twenty. I'm going to have to make some running repairs."

On the hour-long train ride from Shepperton to Waterloo I could sit back and relax, at long last able to spend some time thinking about everything. The three problems I needed to solve plaited themselves together inside my head. I knew that, somehow, they were interlinked. I just didn't know how. What did Catherine know that had so devastated Olivia; why was Rob still alive; and where had Lucas gone? As usual my gaze returned to the amulet. The answers were in there; I just had to find a way of getting them out.

I was suddenly disturbed by the hideous ring of my ancient phone. Not being able to identify the caller before I picked it up was really beginning to annoy me, and I vowed yet again to spend some time re-entering all my friends' numbers.

"Hello?" I asked warily, just in case it was Mum.

"Ah, my protector! And how are you this morning, then?"

"I'm sorry? Who is this?" I asked, confused.

"It's Rob, you daft bird. Whose life you apparently saved yesterday. Glad I mean so much to you!" There was a distinct teasing note in his tone. I was so surprised I didn't think about the effect of my response.

"Oh, hi, Rob, I was just thinking about you." I tried to bite back the words immediately but they were already out there.

"Excellent, excellent. You have great taste in thoughts. Now, I need to thank you properly. Where are you?"

"Umm, actually, Rob, I'm on a train, and I'm kind of busy."

"Well, just tell me where you're going and I'll be there to meet you. I've been discharged from hospital, and I've got something special planned." There wasn't a hint of a question in his voice. In his world I was about to do exactly as he asked.

"Look, Rob," I said as gently as I could, "do you not remember what I told you yesterday? We are not going out together, and neither of us wants to go out with the other. We tried it and decided against it."

"You're just saying that, Alex, I know you are." The arrogance of his assumption was breathtaking.

"I'm not! We absolutely don't want to, you've just forgotten."

"No, you're teasing me, I can tell!"

I was beginning to lose patience with him.

"I'm going to say this just the once, do you understand, then I'm going to put the phone down. We *are* not going out, we *will* not be going out, and I will *not* be meeting you anywhere. Am I making myself absolutely clear?"

"So is that a no, then? To meeting up today?"

"Goodbye, Rob." I clicked off the phone and glared at a woman across the carriage who had been listening.

I looked out of the window and my irritation with Rob evaporated; central London was coming into view and within the hour I would be with Callum.

I had a straightforward trip over to St Paul's, and Callum met me at the Tube station. Both of us were in a more reflective mood than usual, and there was no inane chatter or gossip about the people we were passing. We were both focused on getting up to the Golden Gallery.

"Did it work?" I asked as we rounded the corner and the full spectacle of the cathedral came into view.

"I'm sorry?" replied Callum, puzzled at my sudden question.

"The gallery. Is it shut today? Did the poor man's nightmare do the trick?"

"Oh, that, yes, yes, it's shut again. You should have no problems. Do you want me to come up the stairs with you?"

"Actually, no, I'd rather you didn't. Gasping and wheezing is not a good look. Go and wait for me at the top."

I worked my way through the queues, past the ticket collector and into the vast, cool interior. As usual the little yellow lights were flicking on all over the place as people were overawed by the sheer scale and majesty of the place. Callum kissed me as I got to the bottom of the long spiral staircase. "Take your time, don't rush. We have all day if we want."

"OK, I'll see you in a bit." I started to make my way up the stairs, and was soon not thinking about anything other than the pain in my legs and how dizzy I was getting walking in circles. At the Whispering Gallery I stopped, conscious as ever of the misty cloaked figures. This close to the top of the dome I could see all the Dirges without the mirror, but they were still semi-transparent. As I watched I could see them wafting out of my way, and I realised there was something else I needed to do. "Olivia?" I called gently. "Are you around? There's something I want to tell you."

I scanned the circle of insubstantial figures sitting around the gallery, and slowly one got to her feet. I waited while she gently glided through all the tourists and stood in front of me.

"Olivia?"

The slight figure nodded and gently pushed back her hood. I gasped in horror. Her face was a mask of misery.

"Oh, Olivia, please, please don't be upset. None of it was your fault, truly!"

Her hooded brown eyes couldn't meet mine, and I wished that there was some way I could reach out and comfort her properly. "Sit down, please; sit with me for a moment and let's talk."

I sat down on the long stone bench that circled the gallery, for once oblivious to the spectacular view of the cathedral floor. Slowly Olivia lowered herself into the seat next to me, her hands still folded under her cloak. I put my arm out towards her, amulet glinting in the bright lights. I resisted the temptation to try and get her to hurry; it was like coaxing a frightened kitten to come out from under the sofa. Finally her thin, delicate hand appeared and she slid her amulet into place with mine. The tingle told me when the connection had finally been made.

"Hi, it's really good to see you, really good." I paused for a moment but she said nothing. "Do you know, Beesley has been begging me to get you out on our next walk. Every time he sees me he walks around behind me to see where you are. I might be able to borrow him tomorrow; would you like to come over?"

There was still no response but I noticed a small movement in the semi-transparent mist. I wished I could get my mirror out to see her properly, but it seemed better somehow to try and have a conversation sat together like friends. I turned towards her and realised that the movement was tears, tears falling unheeded from her cheeks and on to her lap where they made no impression on the strange cloak.

"Please don't cry," I whispered as someone walked past. "She's gone now, and Rob can't remember anything, so no harm has been done." I mentally crossed my fingers, hoping that I wasn't lying. I had no idea what Catherine was up to, but I wasn't going to tell Olivia that.

The pale face finally turned towards me, the haunted look etched deep, and I realised just how much harm really had been done. "She was pure, pure evil," she said eventually. "I got what I deserved taking something from her head."

"I'm going to try to help you, to figure out what it was that's done this to you, I promise. Until then, can you just bury it?"

"I can't make it go away." Her voice was suddenly like a child's, and it tore my heart to remember that that was exactly what she was – a child. Her tears continued to fall.

"Well, maybe we can crowd it out with something happier. Do you think that might work?"

There was silence, and then she slowly shook her head. "It's too awful."

"Callum told me that you can't get any of the details, that you don't know what it was that she was thinking."

"No, I just know it was dreadful, terrible, but I didn't see the actual memory." I cursed Catherine silently; what was it about saving the Dirges that could be so toxic? It would be so much easier if we could just lift the knowledge out of Olivia's head.

"Well, if you don't have to live with the actual thought, I'm sure we can do something about the feeling. A feeling is just that – a mood, nothing more. Callum and I can help you to feel something else." I paused for a moment, but that clearly wasn't helping. I tried another tack. "I'm thinking of seeing if I can get the job as Beesley's daytime walker during the holidays. So that would mean walking him every lunchtime and seeing how much we could teach him. Of course, it'll be quite difficult for me on my own, but if there were two of us, well, that would make things so much easier."

I paused again and let that sink in.

"Every day?" asked a small voice.

"Every day when I can borrow the dog. What do you say?"

"Can . . . can we start tomorrow?"

"I'm sure I can arrange it, as long as he's back." I sneaked another look at her, watching her make that constantly moving chain link with her thumbs and index fingers. It was all still a bit indistinct, but I was sure I saw a tiny spark of hope in her eyes. "I'll talk to you later, Olivia, but we'll make it better, I promise. I have to go now, Callum's going to be waiting for me at the top."

She nodded briefly and shrugged back inside the hood of her cloak. I gave one last attempted squeeze of her arm and stood up, ready at last for Callum. As I scanned the gallery over towards the door to the next set of stairs I could see his familiar figure. Even here he was more substantial to me than his fellow Dirges, and I was thankful yet again for the deep connection our two amulets had, which made this strange magic work. As I reached him he quickly slid his amulet into position.

"I was wondering where you had got to so I came back down. I caught the end of your conversation; that was a very nice thing to do for Olivia."

I made a non-committal grunting noise as a large tourist squeezed past me. "I know, you can't talk right now. I'll see you up there." I smiled at his ghostly-looking face, in front of me but still obviously not solid. Then the tingle shifted and he was gone.

Seeing Olivia only strengthened my resolve. Catherine said that she knew how to help all the Dirges to escape, and if that was true, then I had to find her, to find a way to help Olivia out of her misery. Leaving her like that was just too cruel. Finding Catherine was going to be a challenge, but with Grace to help me I reckoned I could do it. I smiled grimly to myself as I started up the next spiral staircase. There was no point in mentioning it to them until I was sure, but it looked like there was a chance. I just had to keep Olivia going until I could sort it out.

I didn't rush all the way to the top. Wearing myself out wasn't a smart thing to do, so I took it steadily, jumping the barrier at the Stone Gallery to get to the last set of stairs. As usual, no one seemed to notice.

On the way up I tried not to think of my last visit, when I had been helped back down by the staff. I never wanted to feel that crashing misery again, and although I knew Callum was up there ahead of me, I realised that I would never be able to walk up those stairs again without worrying that he would be gone. As I reached the little round room with the viewing panel to the floor I called his name softly. For the first time I saw him appear, gliding through the door at the top of the final steps, a concerned look on his face. The novelty of seeing him really walk towards me made me smile. This close to the top he was very nearly solid-looking; there was just a hint around the edges that gave away the fact that he wasn't quite like me.

"Alex? Are you OK?"

"I'm fine, I just wanted to walk up the last bit with you. Is that OK?"

He smiled and put out his hand. "It would be my pleasure. Shall we?"

As we walked up the last few steps, him leading, his hand got more and more solid, until as we reached the door it was no different to my own.

This time the embrace we shared wasn't one of passion but one of relief, relief that we were both safe, and both back in each other's arms. He felt so strong and capable, and as his arms finally locked around me I felt an overwhelming sense of completeness. I buried my face in his chest, holding him tight. Callum held me close too, understanding that nothing needed to be said, just stroking the length of my hair with a firm hand and resting his chin on the top of my head. I could feel his heart beating under my bruised cheek.

Finally I felt able to speak. "I'm sorry, Callum," I sniffed. "It's been so long – it's just so good, so perfect, to hold you again."

"I know," he agreed, still holding me close to his chest. "That last visit was unbelievably painful."

I pulled back a little in surprise and looked at him. "You were here?"

"For every minute of it. I knew you would be suffering, but to see it, to see such pain. . ." His voice caught on the last word, and I could see the tears welling in his eyes. He held me even closer.

"I hoped you were here. I tried to talk to you, but without the amulet it was a waste of time. And all the people . . . I don't even really want to think about it."

"I know. It doesn't matter now. Catherine's gone, and Rob, well, how is he now?"

"He's forgotten everything from almost exactly the time I found the amulet. He even still thinks he fancies me, which is rather creepy. I've had to be pretty direct with him to get him to go away."

"Do let me know if you need any help on that score. I'd be more than happy to give him a hard time." I glanced at Callum's face, and the emotion in his eyes had been replaced by anger. His lips were pressed together in a thin line.

"Thanks for the offer, but I can handle Rob. What's the news on Lucas, though?" I had deliberately not asked earlier as I wanted to be in his arms when I heard.

"We've had no sign of him. We really can't ignore the compulsion to come here every night and he wasn't here yesterday, so he must have gone."

"I guess the question is where. . ." I tried to sound as nonchalant as possible.

"Actually, I don't care. He's gone, I've got you back, Catherine has run away and we have the whole summer holidays ahead of us." The thought of Catherine still made me shiver, but I pushed it to one side as Callum kissed the top of my head and tenderly stroked down my arms, careful to avoid my bruises. "I think it's time for us to concentrate on us for a while, don't you?" He slowly ran his hands back up again and cupped my face gently. His lips found mine, and I was suddenly dizzy with desire, catching my hands in his hair to pull him even closer to me.

As we sat together ignoring the view, concentrating only on each other, I realised that the interwoven problems in my head had straightened themselves out. I hugged my secret tightly to me. It would be wrong to give Callum hope until I had checked everything, but all I had to do was to find out what had happened to Lucas, to make sure that he had made it into the Thames alive. Because if he had, if my intervention had caused that, then I didn't need to find Catherine. I didn't need the secret of how to let the Dirges escape or what she had done to Olivia. I had the power to save them myself. I glanced down at the amulet, quiet and peaceful with no sign of the strange fire that had appeared at my command the day before. It was mine to control now. I nestled into Callum's firm embrace and sighed contentedly.

Hearing my sigh, he lifted my chin and gave me a look of such love and tenderness that I thought my heart would burst. As I gazed into his mesmerising eyes I knew I had to try, and I couldn't help smiling at the thought. One day soon I would bring him over to me, and we would be together forever.

Epilogue

The three men and one woman were hunched over the table, deep in concentration. The noise of the traffic on Waterloo Bridge didn't disturb them, even though the water was rising and the floating building was over halfway up its stanchions. They all watched as the oldest, the guy with the most pips on his shoulder, slowly picked up a small cup and threw its contents across the table.

"And that's a six!" he exclaimed with glee as the small dice rolled to a stop.

"You're so jammy, Pete," sighed John as Pete picked up the little silver dog and tapped it across the board, deftly missing John's hotel-laden Mayfair and Park Lane and stopping on the big square marked Go.

"That's two hundred pounds to me, I believe, banker." Yvonne shot him an exasperated look as she handed over the well-worn paper note. He slid the end of it under the Monopoly board in front him, where it joined a couple of ones and a five.

"You are the luckiest player I know, Pete. You should have been out hours ago." She turned to the others. "You guys want to carry on? See if we can bankrupt him eventually?"

Dave pushed back his chair and got up, stretching his arms above his head where they brushed the ceiling of the little recreation room. "I could do with a bit of air. I'm just going to check the boats." As he walked towards the open doorway a low wailing noise filled the room. As if pulled by strings the other three leapt to their feet, all thoughts of the game forgotten. John ran to the computer as the others ran to the nearest boat, collecting their bright-orange life jackets from the rack by the door as they went.

The boat was fully prepped and ready to go. Pete leapt on board and fired up the powerful engines. It was a small, agile inflatable boat that used water jets instead of propellers and was perfect for negotiating the Thames. Yvonne and Dave held it tight against the jetty while they waited for John to give them the details of the shout.

"It's a close one," he called as he came out of the communications room. "Man in the water just under Blackfriars Bridge, north side. Still moving. I'll get the ambulance boys over."

"OK, we're on our way." Pete turned to the crew. "Let's go." Dave and Yvonne dropped the thick ropes as the boat leapt underneath them, arcing away from the jetty and out into the main channel of the Thames. Blackfriars Bridge was the next one along, just a few minutes away, so they were confident that they would get to the casualty in time. It was easy to see where they had to go; there were people leaning over the edge of the Embankment and shouting, pointing at the water. A lifebelt was bobbing around nearby.

They swiftly pulled up alongside the lifebelt, scanning around in the water for the man in trouble. "He's here," called Yvonne, pointing towards what looked like a pile of rags being tossed around in the water by the wake. Pete deftly manoeuvred the boat alongside. Yvonne was leaning out, ready to grab the man, prepared to jump in the water herself if necessary. His head was just above the surface but he wasn't making any noise.

"Another metre, that's it!" she called to Pete as he negotiated the draw of the tide. Luckily they weren't fighting a huge undertow, but he didn't want to get too close to the huge pillars rising out of the water that supported the train tracks overhead.

Dave and Yvonne got the man around to the back of the boat and hauled him aboard. The action of pulling him up and over the edge pumped a huge spume of water from his mouth. "OK!" shouted Dave. "We've got him aboard, let's get him back to the station as quickly as possible. He's going to need the ambulance."

Pete swung the boat in a wide arc, blue lights flashing to warn the other river traffic that he was coming through. He shot past the Thames Clipper, which was coming in to dock at the Blackfriars Millennium Pier, and within minutes was back at the station. On the front deck Dave and Yvonne were working on the guy, trying to save another life. They got a lot of practice: from their little floating building by the bridge they ran the busiest lifeboat station in the whole country, attending more shouts than any other. The Thames was a dangerous place. As Pete pulled the boat up alongside the landing platform John was there, ready to tie it up.

"Ambulance is on its way, but there's heavy traffic. They reckon their ETA is about seven minutes. Can you keep him going that long?"

Yvonne didn't even look up; as a trained paramedic she was used to this. Their boat was so fast that they often got called out to accidents near the river, not just ones on the water; last year she even got to deliver a baby. She and Dave were confident that this shout would be another success as the guy couldn't have been in the water for more than a few minutes before he was spotted, and he looked young and fit. She was pumping his chest, hoping to get as much of the deadly water in his lungs out as quickly as possible.

Dave was preparing the airway, ready to start the mouth-to-mouth resuscitation. They worked well as a team and were proud of their record in saving lives.

But this victim wasn't doing so well. Despite their efforts there was no responding gasp of breath, no racking cough as he tried to dislodge the murky water in his chest. No words were exchanged; they kept on going, knowing that people could recover even if they looked long past hope. After another minute Yvonne looked up.

"I've lost the pulse – we're going to have to shock him. Are you ready?"

"Here," said Dave, lifting up the hand-held pads that were connected to the portable defibrillator. Yvonne took hold of the man's shirt and ripped hard. She was strong, and the buttons didn't resist for long.

"Whoa!" she exclaimed, looking at his chest. "Have you ever seen that before?" Across his body were deep black lines, radiating outwards from his left shoulder and tracing a strange irregular spider's-web pattern across his chest.

"That's weird. Clear!" called Dave as he pressed the pads on either side of the man's heart. He pushed the button by his thumb and the man's back arched slightly before slapping back on the damp deck with a hollow thump. Yvonne picked up his hand to check his pulse and his sleeve fell back, revealing a blackened circle around his wrist. Abandoning that as a possible pulse point she leaned back over, pressing her fingers into the corner of his jaw again, and was delighted to see that his eyes were open.

"Hey, good to see you. Stay with us, OK? The ambulance will be here any minute."

The man's dark eyes swivelled towards her voice. He blinked

once but then his gaze turned glassy. "Dave, we're losing him," she shouted. "Shock him again."

They continued to work on the man until the ambulance arrived, but it was clear that it was no use: he was gone. Yvonne sat back on her heels, wondering what she could have done differently, what else might have helped. The ambulance team also did their best, removing his shirt completely to set up a drip, but it was too late. She looked at the tattoo on his weirdly marked arm. Poor Emily was going to get some very bad news later.

The ambulance team called a time of death and Yvonne started to clear up all the debris from around the body. Finally the driver brought down the trolley from the back of the ambulance and Dave and John hefted the man up on to it. "Sorry, Tommo," she said to the driver. "Couldn't save this one. Don't know why though. I don't think he was in the water that long."

Tommo started to unfold a thick red blanket but hesitated as he looked at the body laid out on the trolley, the dark lines even more obvious against the greying skin. "You wouldn't have been able to save this guy, I guarantee it."

"Why do you say that?"

"You might have fished him out of the water but I don't think he drowned." He pointed to the strange markings all over the body. "He's got massive electrical burns, the kind you usually only get from lightning. You had any storms here today?" Yvonne shook her head. "I didn't think so. There is one way to get burns like this, but it's not common. Someone has been torturing him. Somebody wanted this guy dead, and they succeeded."

Yvonne shuddered. "Poor guy. What a horrible way to go." She gently lifted up the blackened arm that was hanging off the side of the trolley and laid it across his chest before Tommo drew the blanket up over his face. She realised as she stood back that his arm had felt unusually warm.

In the dark under the blanket, the strange burn around the dead man's wrist suddenly reignited, the fire flashing around the black marks that criss-crossed his body. Within moments, while the lifeboat and ambulance crews watched in horror, Lucas's body was reduced to a smoking pile of ash.

About S. C. Ransom

Sue Ransom, the author of *Small Blue Thing* is a senior head-hunter, but on the way to work and in the evenings she's a writer: she wrote *Small Blue Thing*, her debut novel, as a birthday present for her daughter, and she composed it mostly on her BlackBerry. Serendipity led her to Nosy Crow, and she's now busy finishing the third book in the trilogy. She lives with her husband and two teenage children in Surrey.

Acknowledgements

Writing a second book has been a much less lonely journey than the first: I have been surrounded by people who are hugely encouraging and supportive, especially all the people at Nosy Crow. Kirsty has done sterling work helping me to whip the manuscript into shape, Camilla has been fabulous with her input to lyrics, Imogen magically gets things done, and Kate remains an inspiration. Thank you all.

I must also thank all the friends who donated their names, especially those in L4L – you know who you are! Finally I want to thank my family for their ongoing support, even when they haven't seen me for days. I know Dad would have been very proud.

The story concludes in

Scattering
Like Light

Read on to find out what happens next...

ℰAirport

I could feel the sweat prickle on my forehead as the man in uniform glared at me. "Just go back through and put all your jewellery in there, please, Miss," he repeated, nodding towards the small plastic tray. "All of it, like it says on the instructions," he emphasised, seeing my hand hesitate over my wrist.

"I ... I ... I just need a minute," I stuttered. "Callum!" I hissed under my breath. "I need you now, *quickly!*"

"Come on, please. You're holding up the line." The security guard was getting annoyed. Ahead I could see my parents, picking up their belongings from the other side of the X-ray machine. They hadn't noticed that I'd stopped. I couldn't believe that I hadn't thought this through, that I hadn't realised that the amulet would set off the alarm on the metal detector. Where *was* Callum?

The security guard picked up the tray and thrust it towards me. I couldn't help looking around me, knowing full well that I wouldn't be able to see Callum, but searching for inspiration to explain my odd behaviour. I was clammy with fear. "Callum!" I hissed again, as loudly as I dared.

"What's the hold up here?" An officious-looking man in a suit was pressing up behind me, desperate to get through and on to his flight. I looked wildly between the two angry men, and swallowed hard.

"There's something not right here. I'm calling the police," announced the guard, taking in my obvious discomfort. He pressed a red button on the side of the metal detector. Within seconds, armed policemen converged on the spot, their guns conspicuously at the ready.

"Really, there's no need for that," I said as calmly as I could. "It's just that my bracelet is very tight, and it hurts to take it off, that's all." I smiled at him as sweetly as I could, trying not to look at the machine guns. They hadn't pointed them at me yet, and I really wanted to avoid that happening. On the other side of the detector my parents had noticed the commotion and were heading back towards me.

"Can't you just examine it where it is?" I asked, trying not to sound too desperate, hoping that I could avoid a confrontation between Mum and the guard.

"That's not possible. All jewellery has to be removed so you can go through the scanner without setting it off."

"Alex? What's going on?" called my mum. "What's happening?" she asked the guard pointedly. "Why won't you let my daughter through?"

"Stand back, please," said one of the policemen, stepping in front of her.

"Look, I'm just taking it off now, OK? Then I'll come through the machine." I put my finger under the bracelet and eased it off my wrist, making sure that I kept my finger inside for as long as possible. "Come on, Callum, get here now!" I muttered. I was just about to drop the amulet into the tray when there was a welcome tingle in my hand and a familiar voice in my head. "Go, I've got everything covered here. You'll be fine."

Heaving a sigh of relief I slipped the amulet into the little tray along with my watch and necklace. "OK, shall I come through now?" I asked the guard. His colleague at the X-ray machine picked up the tray and lifted the amulet out with the end of a pen. Trying not to look at what they were doing, I took a tentative step towards the metal detector. "Is it OK to go ahead?" I asked, catching the eye of one of the policemen, not daring to take another step until he had finally nodded. Mum had wisely kept silent as soon as she had seen the guns, but one glimpse of her tight-lipped ashen face told me that she wasn't finished.

I stepped carefully through the threshold of the detector, which remained mercifully silent. They weren't done with me, though. A female guard stepped forward and gave me a thorough pat-down, and all the while I was trying not to look at what the guys by the machine were doing with the amulet. Finally the guard declared me safe, and I turned towards the conveyor-belt to retrieve my belongings. Dad had picked up most of the stuff, but the guard holding my amulet was clearly waiting for me.

"This yours?" he asked, dropping the amulet from his pen into a separate tray.

"Yes," I nodded. "Can I have it back, please?"

"It's been randomly selected for further testing," he announced, sounding bored.

I tried not to panic as I thought about what Callum was having to do to keep me safe, and how much longer he could keep it up. Desperately trying to keep my fear contained, I smiled at the guard. "Oh, I see. What does that mean?"

I was trying to talk to him as luggage from the people behind me started to pour through the X-Ray machine and down the conveyor-belt. The man in the suit brushed me aside impatiently so that he could retrieve his laptop case, and I could feel him radiating disapproval.

The guard continued in his bored tone. "It's got to be tested for traces of explosives." He placed a small cloth in some special tongs and started to wipe the bracelet with it, being careful not to actually touch it himself. I bit my lip.

"What are they doing now, Alex? What's the hold-up?" Mum was at my side, bristling with indignation.

"They seem to think that my bracelet might be dangerous, that's all," I answered as calmly as I could, wondering if at any second Callum might lose the fight that was no doubt raging around us. If he was beaten I would be as good as dead within moments.

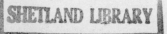